Two sought-after sisters, a slew of suitors—and a vow to hold out for true love. How many proposals will it take to get to "I do"—especially when the stakes are high . . .

There have been six suitors so far, all vying for the attention—and generous dowry—of the beautiful, elusive Eleanor Sutherland. What does this woman really want? Who has what it takes to melt the heart of the so-called Lady Ice? These are the questions Camden West keeps asking himself. But rather than wait for answers, Cam takes matters into his own hands . . . for he has a secret weapon.

Cam knows that Ellie's sister, Charlotte, harbors a scandalous secret—one that could bring ruin to the Sutherland name. If Ellie marries him, Cam promises to keep mum. But is she willing to sacrifice her own happiness for her sister's reputation?

To Ellie's surprise, it becomes clear that Cam doesn't need her money, nor is he interested in her status. Soon, what begins as a sham engagement transforms into something deeper, and more passionate, than Ellie could have imagined. Is it possible that all Cam truly wanted was her? And is that reason enough to say yes—or is handsome Cam hiding something else? Even for a lady in love, only the truth will do . . .

Lady Eleanor's Seventh Suitor

The Sutherland Sisters

Anna Bradley

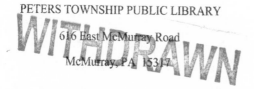

LYRICAL PRESS
Kensington Publishing Corp.
www.kensingtonbooks.com

First Electronic Edition: September 2017
eISBN-13: 978-1-5161-0516-8
eISBN-10: 1-5161-0516-8

First Print Edition: September 2017
ISBN-13: 978-1-5161-0517-5
ISBN-10: 1-5161-0517-6

Printed in the United States of America

Dedicated to my twelve-year-old niece, the original Amelia.

Acknowledgments

My deepest thanks to my agent, Marlene Stringer; my editor, John Scognamiglio; and the talented, creative team at Kensington.

Chapter One

London, 1815

Lady Eleanor Sutherland clutched her fan and studied the young lord before her, a polite smile frozen on her face, her heart sinking into her slippers.

Lord Tidmarsh had placed a wager on her in the betting book at White's.

Ellie didn't want to believe it of him, but she'd seen this performance—the shifty eyes and twitchy fingers, the sheen of nervous sweat on his upper lip, the hint of a smirk on his lower one—too many times to deny the truth. Yes, his lordship was definitely in the throes of a violent, and feigned, passion.

She knew a sham suitor when she saw one. Lord Tidmarsh was her third this season.

Several weeks ago she'd rejected her fifth marriage offer—one offer too many, she now realized, for the gentlemen of the *ton* to overlook. Since then it had become quite the fashionable game for them to attempt to pry some sign of affection from her. They teased for dances, begged for smiles. A few of the bolder ones had even written sonnets to her sparkling dark eyes. *My heart flies, my soul cries*, and so forth.

It was enough to make one shudder for the fate of the rhyming couplet. Alas, whoever had said a single sonnet could drive love entirely away had the right of it. It wasn't a romantic sentiment, perhaps, but true for all that.

The same could be said of wagers.

Ellie had her own page in the betting book at White's. A smile from her would earn her swain a sovereign, a walk on the terrace was worth five guineas, and as for the higher denominations . . . well, perhaps the less said about *that* the better, though she did wonder what value they'd placed on her virtue.

As for her love . . .

It must be worthless indeed, for not one of the gentlemen seemed at all interested in securing it.

"Won't you favor me with a smile, my lady?" Lord Tidmarsh dragged a gloved hand across his damp forehead. "You know I exist only for your smiles."

Poor Lord Tidmarsh might be able to produce a bit of perspiration, but she couldn't see any other signs of impending manhood. Not a single whisker shaded his smooth upper lip. She'd have settled for the merest hint of fuzz, even—anything to indicate a hair had tried to hatch there.

"Will you consent to one more dance this evening? *Please*, Lady Eleanor."

She sighed. It had come to this, then. She'd be compelled to rebuff a mere lad this time. The *ton* already called her Lady Frost behind her back, and once she sent young Lord Tidmarsh on his way, she was sure to be saddled with a far worse nickname.

Icy Ellie, perhaps, or the Artic Queen?

But the sooner she put an end to this scene, the better. "I beg you'll excuse me, my lord. I've already danced twice with you this evening. If we dance together again, the *ton* will gossip, and—"

"Would that be so terrible?" He arranged his lips into a perfect schoolboy pout.

She pasted a smile onto her face. "Now, Lord Tidmarsh, you know very well a third dance will encourage Lady Foster's guests to assume we have an understanding. We wouldn't want that, would we?"

"But we *could* have an understanding, even now. It's the very thing I want." He pressed her fingers against his bony chest, his face twisted with a passable imitation of passionate despair.

Eleanor tried to withdraw her hand, but he hung on with such determination her arm began to slip out of her glove. Well, how absurd. She *would* have her hand back, even if it meant he ended with her limp glove clutched to his chest.

"I'll run mad if you refuse me, Lady Eleanor. Indeed I will!"

Eleanor's cheeks heated with embarrassment. Must all of her pretend suitors fall into wild hysterics? Next he'd fall to his knees, beat his chest, and tear his hair out from the roots.

Another tragic hero, right here in the middle of the Foster's ballroom.

She supposed it *was* more amusing if he fell into fits. Whichever lord had sent him to torment her would want to see the thing done with a dramatic flourish. No doubt Lord Ponsonby, Mr. Fitzwilliam, or another of her rejected suitors was watching the entire performance from a shadowy corner of the ballroom.

Eleanor straightened her spine. Well, there was no help for it. Lady Frost would have to make an appearance. A pang of guilt pierced her chest for Lord Tidmarsh's tender young heart, but if he had any true affection for her, it was a flimsy thing, at best.

She fixed him with a steady gaze, and after a moment his blue eyes darted guiltily away. Ah. Just as she'd thought. A dare, or a wager. "I must insist you release me."

He clutched at her fingers. "But Lady Eleanor, I swear—"

"At once, my lord."

He studied her for a moment, no doubt hunting for some tenderness in her eyes, some hint of breathlessness, some softening of her lips.

Eleanor gazed back at him, her face expressionless.

He dropped her hand and stepped back. "Very well. I wish you a pleasant evening, madam."

It was far more likely he wished her to the devil, just like the rest of them, but it wouldn't do to say so. "How kind you are, my lord."

He folded his lanky frame into a stiff bow, turned on his heel, and disappeared into the crowd. Eleanor watched him go, her chin raised as she fought the urge to let her shoulders slump in defeat.

Just as she'd suspected. Flimsy.

* * * * *

Camden West stood off to the side of the ballroom, half-obscured behind a white marble pillar. Lady Foster had a fondness for pillars, it seemed— pillars, and wide gilt mirrors. Every turn brought him face to face with his own reflection: severe black evening dress, stark white cravat, tight mouth. Damn unsettling, but like the rest of the *ton*, Lady Foster must want to see an endless echo of herself in every shiny surface.

But the pillars suited Cam. He preferred to remain unobserved tonight, which was difficult to do when one was the tallest gentleman in the room. Of course, his height did offer certain advantages. If he were a few inches shorter, he'd have spent all evening craning his neck to see around the crowds of gentlemen swarming Lady Eleanor Sutherland, like bees buzzing around their queen. As it was, he had a perfect view of the little drama unfolding about twelves paces to his left. The adolescent lord who'd cornered her didn't look to be an especially sharp specimen, but he was sharp enough to have found a way to separate Lady Eleanor from the rest of the swarm.

That young lordling—what the devil was his name again? Cam had been introduced to him. He had a vague memory of watery blue eyes, but he couldn't remember the boy's name. No matter. The lad's time would be better spent attempting to grow some chest hair rather than buzzing around a bee of Lady Eleanor's majesty.

Her sting was legendary.

Cam couldn't hear a word they said, but he didn't need to, for this was a pantomime worthy of the Parisian stage.

The besotted swain grasped the lady's hand and pressed it dramatically to his breast.

The lady remained unmoved.

The swain pleaded, cajoled, looked tragic, and finally, in desperation, hurled his throbbing heart at the feet of his cruel mistress. The lady, her face composed, dark eyes unblinking, brought one dainty foot down and crushed that tender organ under her heel, then kicked it back in his general direction with a careless flick of her satin-covered toe.

Cam suppressed an urge to laugh. Or applaud. He'd gladly pay a crown to see that performance again.

What did that make, then? Three seasons, five offers, five refusals, and now this poor devil, who hadn't even made it as far as Lady Eleanor's brother. Impressive, how she'd dispensed with him before he had a chance to come to the point. Lord Carlisle was said to be fond of his sisters, and he must be. Fond enough to permit Lady Eleanor to reject suitor after suitor.

Reason enough to bypass the earl altogether.

How fortunate for Cam that Lady Eleanor thought herself too good for every gentleman in London, and how lucky none of these fine lords had the remotest inkling how to handle a woman like her.

Cam didn't have that problem. Handled she would be, and soon.

Poor lord whatever-the-devil-his-name-was slunk off into the crowded ballroom. He looked like a puppy who'd taken an unexpected and vicious kick to the ribs. Lady Eleanor looked as if she found the whole thing tedious, as if she made it a habit to kick a puppy every day.

Lady Frost. Cam smiled. Oh, yes. She was every inch the proper aristocratic lady.

She'd do. She'd do quite nicely.

Lady Eleanor flapped her fan in front of her face, no doubt to cool the flush of irritation from her cheeks. Cam's lips twisted in a cynical smile. It must exhaust the poor lady to be the object of such constant adoration. Did she encourage them, and then refuse them? He thought it likely. What were the chances five suitors could have been so mistaken about her affections?

He waited, watching her from behind his pillar. She wouldn't take much time to fume. No more than a few minutes, and then she'd remember.

Her hand dropped to her side and she looked around, and a slight frown creased that smooth, white brow. She grasped a fold of her silk gown, rose to her tiptoes, and moved her gaze over the crowd, searching.

Ah. There. Cam knew it the moment she spotted her sister in the sea of whirling couples. He followed her gaze to the other side of the ballroom, though he knew what he'd find before he saw them.

Lady Charlotte Sutherland, the younger of the two Sutherland sisters, rumored to be a bit on the wild side. Indeed, from what Cam had heard, Lady Charlotte had driven the *ton* right out of countenance this season. If she placed another toe over the line of propriety, she'd suffer dire social consequences.

Charlotte Sutherland was dancing with Cam's cousin, Julian West. Handsome, charming, irresistible Julian. Damn shame he was such a rake. With every turn of the dance Julian drew closer to the open French doors leading onto the terrace and the dark garden beyond, his quarry caught in his arms.

Such a scenario was a bit worrying for the young lady. Someone could get hurt. Or ruined.

Lady Eleanor must have thought so too, for she hurried past Cam in a cloud of wine-colored skirts and a faint scent of black currants, her gaze fixed on the opposite side of the ballroom.

Cam slid out from behind his pillar and started after her.

What a pity she wouldn't reach her sister in time.

* * * * *

"You are presumptuousness itself, sir."

Julian gazed down into a pair mischievous dark eyes and couldn't resist the smile that curved his lips. Lady Charlotte might speak in a scolding tone, but her eyes gave her away, for nothing but invitation shone in those wicked depths.

Good Lord. Her eyes were sin itself. How had she managed to escape ruination for this long, with eyes like that?

Julian pressed his palm against her waist and maneuvered her a few steps closer to the terrace doors. "Presumptuous? I don't know what you mean. You look flushed, Lady Charlotte. Too much dancing, perhaps? A breath of fresh air will restore you."

A tiny smiled played about her lips. "Oh, indeed. How solicitous of you, Mr. West. I do beg your pardon, for I was sure you thought only of your own needs when you began to move me toward the doors."

Julian's smile widened. Clever. No doubt that was how she'd avoided seduction so far—that cleverness. Not one gentleman in ten would expect it of her, for they'd be too taken with her eyes and mouth to notice her tongue, except for the most carnal of purposes.

He didn't flatter himself he was the one in ten who *would* notice, but then this wasn't one of his usual seductions. Under normal circumstances he'd have his mouth over hers by now, but Lady Charlotte wasn't a courtesan, and she wasn't his mistress. She was an innocent, and Julian drew the line at debauching dewy-eyed maidens. He'd give her a chaste kiss or two, and keep her out of the ballroom long enough for her absence to be noticed, but this was hardly a scandalous seduction.

He eased her through the doors and out onto the terrace. "I promise you, my lady, I have no needs beyond assuring myself of your comfort."

She slid her arm away from his, strolled to the edge of the terrace, and leaned back against the low stone wall separating it from the garden beyond. "No proper young lady could be comfortable near a dark garden with a man of your reputation, sir. I hope you don't mean to imply I'm not a proper young lady?"

Julian's lips curved into a grin. How delightful to find a wit to match that wicked red mouth of hers. He followed her across the terrace, stopping only when he was so close the deep violet silk of her skirts brushed against his black breeches.

He bent his head toward her so the other couples on the terrace couldn't overhear them. "I meant to imply no such thing, and yet I do wonder whether a proper young lady should be as accomplished a flirt as you appear to be."

She didn't draw away from him, but instead gave him a teasing half-smile. "Perhaps not, and yet my skills at flirtation are wasted on you, for you need no encouragement whatever from me. I might flirt with you or not, and you'll still attempt to lure me into the garden either way, won't you?"

Julian stared at her. Jesus, but she was tempting—so much so he began to imagine they stood on the edge of the Garden of Eden. He'd expected a dim-witted debutante, not Eve herself. Cam should have warned him.

"I begin to think it's *you* who lure *me*, Lady Charlotte."

He'd expected to be the serpent in this scenario, but it seemed more than one ardent gentleman had tried to lure the delectable Lady Charlotte into a dark garden. He wasn't the first serpent she'd encountered, or the most cunning. She knew what he was about. She was merely toying with him now, and delighting in doing so.

A gentle breeze wafted over them, lifting the loose locks of hair away from her neck. The cool draught blew under Julian's coat, but it did nothing to cool the heat of his skin.

She gave a low, throaty laugh. "I, lure you? Yes, I suppose it would be more convenient for you to believe so. No need for an attack of conscience, in that case."

"Ah, my lady." Julian caught a lock of her dark hair between his fingers. "What makes you think I have a conscience?"

That surprised a genuine laugh out of her. "No conscience, Mr. West? My, such refreshing honesty. I confess I've never heard the like of it before, not from any gentleman, but especially not from one intent on a solitary stroll in a dark garden with an innocent young lady. I believe you do have a conscience, after all."

Julian felt the first frisson of regret shoot down his spine, but he ignored it. She was lovely and intriguing, but it was too late to change his mind. Cam would be halfway across the ballroom by now.

"I have no fear of my conscience, Lady Charlotte, for I've done nothing I need reproach myself for."

His tone, his casual smile, the self-deprecating lift of one shoulder—all perfect. He waited, his breath held.

Her thick, dark eyelashes brushed against her cheekbones as she let her eyes fall shut. When she opened them again, she looked straight at him. "No. You've no need to reproach yourself. Yet."

* * * * *

Charlotte waited for her words to sink in, for understanding to cross his smooth, handsome face, for his lips to part in anticipation. Then she brushed past him, stepped off the edge of the terrace, and strolled into the dark garden beyond.

She didn't look back to see if he followed her. He would. They always did.

Such pretty lips he had—full, with just the slightest hint of a pout, almost like a woman's, though there wasn't anything else the least bit feminine about him. It wasn't his lips that decided her, though. She did want to taste them, but his honesty was more seductive even than his handsome face. So sudden and unexpected. More than one gentleman had tried to tempt her into an indiscretion, but she couldn't recall any who'd admitted to it before. How refreshing, not to be treated as if she were a complete fool.

Of course, the pretty lips didn't hurt.

A few kisses, nothing more, then she'd send him on his way and return to the ballroom before the next dance began. Eleanor wouldn't have to know. She wouldn't be gone long enough to be missed.

Charlotte skirted around the edge of a tree at the far end of the garden. The light from the terrace didn't reach this far, and the low-lying branches would shield them from any curious eyes that might chance to glance their way.

She felt more than heard him come up behind her. "Just as I thought. It's you who have lured me."

She gave him her profile, but didn't turn around. "Lure is such a wicked word. Are you here against your will, Mr. West?"

He gave a soft, amused laugh. "Oh, no. Quite the contrary, as I think you know."

His lips were right at her ear—she felt his breath stir the tendrils of hair at her temple, felt the heat of his body against her back. He'd take her shoulders in his hands now, turn her to face him, and kiss her.

Charlotte waited, trembling, but he didn't touch her. She could hear him behind her, his breath working in and out of his chest, ragged. He was close, so close, his lips nearly touching her neck, and yet he hesitated for so long every inch of her body drew taut, waiting for his touch. Longing for it. She imagined she felt it every moment, and yet it didn't come. He simply stood behind her, a starving man with a feast spread before him, unsure where to begin, but savoring the moment before the first taste touches his lips.

Charlotte moaned aloud when it came at last, so light, his fingers in the loose waves of hair at her nape, brushing them aside to clear a path for his lips, open and soft against the tender skin of her neck.

Dear God. Her eyes slid closed.

"Never tasted anything so sweet." His whisper was hoarse, stunned.

He fumbled with the buttons at the back of her gown, his fingers shaking as he slipped them loose, one by one, then spread the silk open to bare her shoulders. He teased his hot, wet mouth over her flesh, and Charlotte caught her lower lip between her teeth to keep from whimpering.

Just a few more innocent kisses. That was all, and then she'd return to the ballroom, find Eleanor . . .

He spread the fabric wider to nip at her shoulder blades, then knelt to touch his tongue to the arch of her back before trailing the damp heat of his mouth up her spine until he stood upright behind her again. "Lean back against me. *Yes.* Like that." He wrapped his other arm around her waist and splayed a hand low across her belly.

She hadn't known it could feel this way, hadn't realized—

"It's all right, sweetheart." His mouth brushed her ear. "Wrap your arms around me."

No. No, she couldn't let herself touch him . . .

But her arms rose, and her fingers slid into the soft waves of hair at the back of his neck. He pressed his mouth to the inside of her arm, and a soft puff of warm breath touched her damp skin. A ragged groan rose from his chest at her touch, and she felt it everywhere, deep in the darkest recesses of her body.

His mouth found her neck, and she felt his lips curl upward against her skin.

He's smiling.

Charlotte let her head fall back against his shoulder, and knew she was lost.

Chapter Two

Blast it. Dash it. Confound it, and d—

Eleanor caught herself before any truly wicked curses could escape. There was no need to be unladylike, even if it was only in her head.

No need *yet*.

Charlotte couldn't have gotten far. Eleanor had seen her just there not even a minute ago, on the other side of the ballroom. She made her way toward the terrace doors, doing her best not to look hurried or anxious, but before long her feet fell into the same frantic rhythm as her heart. A few ladies called out greetings as she flew past, a few gentleman bowed, but Eleanor merely nodded at them.

She came to a breathless halt on the other side of the ballroom.

Blast it. Dash it. Confound it. She may as well have saved herself the effort. Charlotte had disappeared, and it didn't take a fortune-teller to see the only place she could have gone was into the dark garden beyond the terrace.

Eleanor scanned the ballroom, but Charlotte's dance partner, Julian West had also disappeared, no doubt into the garden, panting after Charlotte.

Very well, then. The situation now called for curses, and why should the ladies be denied the truly wicked ones?

*Damn it, devil take it, a*nd bloody hell.

This was all Lord Tidmarsh's fault. If he hadn't tried to tease her into a third dance, she'd have had her eye back on Charlotte before her sister finished dancing with the Marquess of Hadley.

Lord Tidmarsh, Julian West—why did it seem whenever trouble was afoot, some gentleman or other was always at the root of it?

Either some gentleman, or Charlotte, devil take her. What in the name of heaven had come over her this season? She disappeared into dark gardens with dubious gentlemen as often as Eleanor rejected offers of marriage.

If Charlotte must have a stroll through the garden, why couldn't she have taken Hadley? But no, nothing would do for Charlotte but a stroll with Julian West, a rake of the first order, and worse, a handsome and charming one. Charlotte thought herself sophisticated, but she hadn't any idea the sort of tricks such a man might pull from his sleeve.

Or his breeches, for that matter.

Eleanor might be a little fuzzy on the details regarding a gentleman's breeches, but she knew enough to know a young lady didn't disappear into a garden with a man like Julian West if she didn't care to see him pull out something he oughtn't.

She and Charlotte had become quite the notorious pair this season, and the *ton* hadn't failed to take notice of it. Eleanor's dismissal of Lord Tidmarsh wouldn't help her cause, but Charlotte in particular couldn't afford any more questionable behavior.

Julian West was questionable, even if he kept his breeches fastened.

Damnation. There was no help for it. She'd have to go after Charlotte. Again.

Eleanor stepped out onto the terrace and took a quick measure of the situation. A few couples wandered about, but she didn't overhear any eager whispers, and none of the ladies had fallen into a shocked swoon. Charlotte *had* wandered off into the garden with Mr. West, but no one seemed to have taken notice of it yet. If Ellie could just find them, she could drag Charlotte back inside before anyone did notice.

All might still be well.

She hurried across the terrace, but froze before she could step into the garden. She spun around, one foot hovering over the damp grass, the hair on her neck prickling with awareness, certain she'd find curious eyes following her every move.

Nonsense. No one had even noticed her. What was it they said about suspicion haunting a guilty mind? But, dash it, why should *she* be haunted? She'd done nothing wrong. Charlotte was the guilty one—Charlotte, and that blasted Julian West.

She entered the garden and melted into the gloomy shadows. Between Lord Tidmarsh's unwelcome declarations and Charlotte's disappearance, Eleanor had had quite enough of this ball, and she wouldn't attend another without reinforcements. She couldn't be expected to fend off suitors and guard Charlotte's virtue at the same time, especially when Charlotte herself was so determined to discard it.

Goodness, it was dark. Far too dark for any proper young lady. Eleanor picked her way along, pieces of wet grass clinging to her hems. She peered over a low shrub and darted around a tree or two, expecting any moment to see a guilty couple spring apart, but the garden appeared to be deserted. Not even a giggle or a breathless sigh interrupted the silence.

Where in the world was Charlotte? How would she ever find her sister in this gloom without an obliging sigh or giggle to guide her?

Unless . . . Eleanor paused for a moment, listening. Was that a soft shuffle behind her? It sounded like the tread of booted feet on damp grass, but the moment she stopped, the sound ceased. She turned to look behind her, but all she could see were dense pools of darkness.

Oh, for God's sake. She'd be better off returning to the ballroom. Perhaps Charlotte had come to her senses and returned by now, as well? Yes, yes, of course she had. Charlotte had grown rather reckless over the past few weeks, but even she knew better than to vanish in the middle of a ball with all the *ton* gawking at her behind their fans.

Eleanor took one determined step back in the direction of the ballroom, but stopped again before she could take a second one. When had Charlotte ever let *knowing better* stop her from doing precisely as she wished?

Damn it, devil take it, and bloody—slam!

She stumbled backward, stunned. What in the world did the Foster's mean by planting a tree in the middle of a garden path? For pity's sake, she might have knocked herself unconscious—

"I beg your pardon." Two enormous hands came down on her shoulders to steady her. "Are you injured?"

Eleanor gaped at the row of buttons in front of her. A tree with an embroidered silk waistcoat? No, no. That couldn't be right. Perhaps she was injured, after all. Had she concussed herself?

She shook her head to clear the dizziness. A silk waistcoat . . . trees didn't wear silk waistcoats, but gentlemen did. Gentlemen like Julian West. But if he was here, where was Charlotte? Had she come to her senses and returned to the ballroom, or had Julian West hidden her in the garden somewhere?

"What have you done with my sister, you scoundrel?"

There was a surprised silence, then a low laugh. "Have you misplaced her, Lady Eleanor? That's unfortunate, but perhaps we'll find her in the shrubbery."

Eleanor squinted into the darkness, her belly fluttering with sudden nerves. She recognized that voice, and it wasn't Julian West's.

It was his cousin, Camden West.

Damnation. Of all the gentlemen a lady might stumble upon in a dark garden, Camden West would be her last choice.

They'd been introduced at a ball at the start of the season, shortly after he returned to London from a prolonged stay in India. Once they'd met, his gaze seemed to follow her everywhere, fixed on her with an intensity that made her whole body quiver with . . .

Anticipation?

At first, perhaps. Until she realized she was quivering for the wrong reasons.

When he looked at her with that glittering green gaze, it wasn't admiration she saw in his eyes, but something else. She couldn't quite put her finger on it, but it was a bit sinister, as if he was contemplating how quickly he could devour her, then spit her bones into a pile at his feet.

He was as handsome as sin, but that look in his eyes . . .

In the end, she'd discouraged his attentions. If he'd been disappointed by her curt rejection, he'd still behaved like a gentleman. She'd caught him watching her a few times since then, but he hadn't spoken another word to her.

Until now. "I'm no scoundrel—at least, not in this instance—but I'll grant you a dark garden can hide a multitude of sins."

"Sins and sinners both, Mr. West. If you're not a scoundrel, then why should you be skulking about a dark garden?"

"Ah, but I might ask you the same question, my lady. Perhaps you're the scoundrel."

She shrugged. "Perhaps I am. It can't be safe for you to linger in a dark garden with me then, can it? You should return to the ballroom while you still have the chance."

He chuckled, and moved a step closer. "You're eager to be rid of me. I wonder why?"

Because you're too tall, for one.

Eleanor craned her neck back another notch to see his tight jaw and strong chin above the folds of his cravat, a pair of unsmiling lips above the chin. She folded her arms over her chest, irritated with him. How dare he loom over her in such a rude manner? It was unfair, somehow, that he should tower over everyone else.

Before she could succumb to a dizzying fit of vertigo, he spoke again. "Did something in particular tempt you out into the garden tonight? A liaison, perhaps?"

"Oh, dear. Have you wandered outside hoping for a scandal?" She gave an exaggerated sigh. "I'm afraid I'll have to disappoint you, unless taking the fresh air is a sin."

"If it's only fresh air you want, then why leave the terrace?" He shook his head, his hard green eyes narrowed on her face. "No, I don't think that's why you're out here, Lady Eleanor."

His bow was proper and his address correct, but his voice was cold and detached. Eleanor swallowed against the dread rising in her throat. Camden West had followed her out here, and now he was looking at her as if she were a garden slug he'd like to crush under his boot heel.

"You may think what you like, Mr. West, but it hardly matters, does it? It's not proper for me to be alone in a dark garden with you, so I'll take my leave." She dipped into a shallow curtsy. "Enjoy your solitude, sir." She turned and began to walk back toward the terrace, but she had to force herself to take slow, measured steps when everything about this situation urged her to run.

She didn't get far.

"If your sister were as concerned with propriety as you are, neither of us need be out here at all."

Eleanor froze, then turned slowly around, her back rigid. Oh, no.

His teeth flashed white in the darkness, and when he spoke again, his voice was an amused drawl. "Don't tell me you'll return to the ballroom before you've found her?"

She fixed him with the same bland expression she used on gentlemen who proposed marriage to her. "What do you know about my sister, Mr. West?"

He shrugged, as if it didn't matter one way or another to him. "I know she disappeared into the garden fifteen minutes ago. I assume you've come out to find her and return her to the ballroom before she's missed, and her reputation is ruined."

Eleanor fought to keep her face blank as panic and fury surged in her breast. This awful man, with his cold voice and perfect cravat—he knew everything, and now she found herself in a damnable predicament. She hated to return to the ballroom without Charlotte, but what was to stop Mr. West from following her through the garden? It was bad enough he knew about the indiscretion, but it would be much worse if he saw it with his own eyes.

She gave him a thin smile. "So you've wandered off into the garden tonight to retrieve your cousin before *he's* missed, and *his* reputation is ruined. Oh, but wait, how foolish of me. His reputation as a wicked rake can only be enhanced by a dalliance in a dark garden with an innocent young lady, can't it? It's only my sister who need worry about discovery."

If he heard the suppressed fury in her voice, he took no notice of it. The bland expression on his face never altered. "Yes, that's generally how it works, but I'd just as soon find my cousin all the same. Shall we search together?"

Eleanor restrained an unladylike snort. She had no intention of joining forces with him in this, or anything else. No, the best she could do now was try to make sure Camden West couldn't provide the gossips with an eyewitness account of her sister's indiscretion. "They'll be back in the ballroom by now, so if you'll just be kind enough to escort me—"

The moon moved from behind a cloud at that moment, and there, not twenty paces away, under an enormous tree with wide-reaching branches, a flutter of violet silk caught the light.

Eleanor tried to school the sudden knowledge from her expression, but Camden West was cleverer than she'd hoped, damn him, for he turned at once to follow her gaze. The silk skirts fluttered obligingly for him, billowing in the breeze.

"Ah. I believe we've found the sinners."

Eleanor didn't answer, but gathered her skirts in her hands, and without another word shot past him at a run. If she could reach Charlotte before he did, she had a chance to at least minimize the damage. She caught a glimpse of his dumbfounded expression as she scurried past, aware his slack-jawed astonishment was the only pleasure she'd get from this evening.

Her delight was short-lived. He didn't chase after her, but he didn't need to, for he easily matched her wild sprint with his long-legged strides. By the time she reached the tree he was right behind her, and he didn't even have the courtesy to be winded.

"Charlotte?" Eleanor scooted under the branches and dodged around the thick trunk, elbows out and skirts held wide, doing everything she could to block Camden West's view. "It's no use pretending you aren't there, Charlotte. I saw your gown. Come out at once, or—Charlotte!"

Eleanor clutched the neck of her gown in nerveless fingers, all the blood rushing from her head at once. She swayed back against Camden West, who pressed his palm into her lower back to steady her, a gesture that would have infuriated her under any other circumstances.

As it was, she forgot all about Camden West. She forgot Lord Tidmarsh, the garden, and the Foster's ball entirely. *Dear God.* She'd reconciled herself to a shock, but *this?* This went well beyond a stolen kiss or two.

Hairpins, hooks, buttons, and, Eleanor suspected, closing her eyes in despair, the tapes on Charlotte's drawers had all fallen victim to Julian West's seeking fingers. Her sister's elegant chignon lay in ruins across her bare shoulders, and her bodice sagged around her waist and neck, leaving plenty of room for his hand to slip into her chemise to caress her breast. He clutched a fistful of violet silk in his other hand, raising Charlotte's skirts so high Eleanor caught a glimpse of her sister's lace-trimmed garters.

And Charlotte . . .

As much as Eleanor wanted to blame this entire episode on Julian West, she couldn't deny her innocent sister was . . . well, rather an enthusiastic participant in her own disgrace. She was on her tiptoes, her fingers tugging at his hair to bring his mouth closer to hers, and unless Julian West had torn a button off his own waistcoat . . .

"Charlotte! Step away from him at once!"

But neither Charlotte nor her seducer appeared to hear her, or to notice they had an audience, for they kept on with their debauchery as if Eleanor and Camden West were invisible. Eleanor struggled to pull some air into her lungs so she could shriek, but despite her gasps, they refused to fill, and she could do nothing but stand, horrified, as that dreadful rake debauched her younger sister.

Eleanor was about to leap upon Julian West and wrestle him to the ground when she heard a sound behind her—a discreet cough, or a muffled laugh? She clenched her fists until she drew a drop of blood from her palm. Did Camden West think a quiet cough enough to pry his cousin from her sister, then? He certainly didn't look as if he were about to step forward and separate them.

Or perhaps he found the whole thing amusing?

Rage took hold of Eleanor then, and she scrambled forward and grabbed her sister around the waist. She hadn't any idea where she got the strength, but she succeeded in dragging Charlotte backward, out of Julian West's embrace, and then she threw herself in front of her sister so she stood between them.

Just let Julian West try to touch *her* breast, or pull up *her* skirts. He'd come away with fewer fingers, the rogue.

"Not. One. Step." She spat the words and held a hand out in front of her, glaring at him.

Camden West moved to his cousin's side and waved a careless hand in Charlotte's direction. "I can assure you my cousin won't stir from this spot. See to your sister, Lady Eleanor."

Eleanor stared at him. *Bored.* Camden West sounded bored, as if his cousin's ruination of an innocent young woman was all part of a pleasant evening's entertainment. Her fingers curled into claws. *Villain.* Oh, how she'd love to scratch his eyes from his face.

But she couldn't. Not only couldn't she do him a physical injury, she'd also have to find a way to swallow her rage and treat both men with some modicum of civility, for Charlotte's reputation was theirs to ruin, should they choose to do so. Bitterness flooded the back of her throat, choking her. She wanted to rage at the unfairness of it, and yet it was no use. There was only one thing she could do.

See to her sister, just as Camden West told her to.

She turned on Charlotte then, her earlier anger swelling in her breast. Eleanor opened her mouth to deliver the furious scold Charlotte deserved, but as soon as she saw her sister's face, she closed it.

Charlotte stood unmoving and silent, her face drained of blood.

Eleanor instinctively reached for her hand. "Charlotte? My dear . . ."

Charlotte's hand was ice cold, trembling. A wave of dread swept over Eleanor. She'd expected defiance, or perhaps careless dismissal, not this look of lost, numb shock.

She took Charlotte by the shoulders and turned her around. "Here now, it's all right. I'll just button you up, shall I? I'm afraid your pins are gone for good, but I can secure your hair with a few of my own."

Eleanor patted and fussed and soothed until she'd pulled Charlotte together as best she could. By the time she finished Charlotte had regained some of her color, but she looked to be on the verge of tears. "Eleanor, I . . . I beg your pardon. I never meant . . . I . . . I didn't think it would go so far—"

"Hush." Eleanor laid a hand against Charlotte's cheek. "Never mind. We'll talk about it later."

There was no way they could reenter the ballroom. Charlotte was decently covered, but by no means presentable, and she'd been gone for far too long. Her absence would have been noticed by now. No doubt the whispers had already started.

No, it wouldn't do. She'd have to leave Charlotte here, alone in the dark garden while she went to call for their carriage, and then they'd have to find a way to slip from the garden to the carriage without going through the ballroom.

"Shall I fetch your carriage, Lady Eleanor?"

Camden West again, all smooth solicitousness now. The perfect gentleman. Eleanor, provoked to the last degree, opened her mouth to tell him to go to the devil, but she didn't get a chance.

"There's a gate at the far end of the garden that leads directly into the mews behind the house," he added. "Your driver can meet you there. There's no need for you to return to the ballroom."

Eleanor swept her gaze over one West, then the other, and prayed her scornful look conveyed how contemptible she found them both. Oh, to be a gentleman, skilled at the sword, or accurate with a pistol! But no, a stony expression and a few tepid curses was the best a lady could do.

Julian West avoided her eyes, but oddly, despite his actions tonight, it wasn't *that* Mr. West who'd earned all of Eleanor's animosity.

Camden West merely looked at her, waiting, one eyebrow raised in polite enquiry.

It was that one.

She dropped into an extravagant curtsey. "How *excessively* helpful of you, Mr. West. How can we ever thank you for your kind assistance?"

"It's my pleasure, my lady." He bowed again, all polite attention, as if he'd just put his name on her dance card, and Eleanor clenched her teeth against what she suspected was intentional mockery.

As it turned out, neither Eleanor nor Charlotte thanked either of the Wests. Julian West waited in the garden with the ladies in some twisted parody of a polite escort while his cousin went off to call the Sutherland carriage. Not a word passed between the three of them while they waited, and neither lady deigned to speak to Camden West when he returned to direct them to the carriage.

The sound of the horses' hooves ringing against the cobblestones had faded away before either gentleman spoke, but at last Julian stirred. "That was badly done, Cam."

Cam didn't argue, but the hard expression on his face didn't soften. "Badly or not, it's done."

Julian shook his head. "I don't like it."

Cam smiled without humor. "You looked as though you liked it well enough. Christ, Jules, I never asked you to tear the chit's clothes off."

Julian winced and ran a hand through his hair, then turned away without answering.

Cam relented and put a hand on his cousin's shoulder. "There's no other way. Think of Amelia." His voice gentled as he said the name.

Julian sighed and turned back to face his cousin. "I always do, cuz. I always do."

Chapter Three

"What a shame you had to leave the ball early last night." Lady Catherine shook out the wool blanket at the end of the chaise and draped it across her knees. "I do hope Charlotte hasn't caught my cold. She hasn't been downstairs at all today."

No, she hadn't, but she couldn't hide forever. One way or another, Eleanor would have the explanation Charlotte refused to give her last night, even if she had to scale the roof and go through Charlotte's bedroom window to get it.

She rose and crossed the room to tuck the blanket around her mother's legs. "Are you chilled, mama?"

"No, no, I'm well enough, only tired of being cooped up with this cold, and so sorry to miss the Foster's ball last night."

Eleanor stifled a sigh. Her mother couldn't be as sorry as she was, and that was to say nothing of Charlotte, who'd looked sorry indeed on the carriage ride home from the ball. Her sister would never have escaped to the garden at all last night under their mother's watchful eye, but as it was, Lady Catherine felt too ill to attend the ball, and their brothers Alec and Robyn had gone to Kent this week to see to some flooding at Bellwood, the family's country estate.

Eleanor and Charlotte had been obliged to content themselves with Lady Archer's chaperone. Poor Lady Archer had a fondness for wagering, however, and she'd disappeared into the card room the minute they arrived.

*A wretched thing, wagering. No good ev*er comes of it.

"Did Charlotte dance with Lord Hadley last night?"

"Yes. Twice." Such a perfect gentleman, Hadley. If only Charlotte would marry him.

"And you, dear? Did Lord Tidmarsh ask you to dance?"

Ask? It wasn't *quite* the right word. Begged? Yes. Pouted like a child who'd been denied a sweet when she refused? Yes. Stormed off in a temper when he lost his wager? Yes, that too. "He did. We danced twice together."

Her mother gave her a tentative smile. "He intends to offer for you. Soon, I think."

Eleanor returned her mother's smile, but shook her head. "He's too young to marry."

Too young, and too flimsy.

"He's three-and-twenty." Lady Catherine frowned. "Many gentlemen marry at his age."

Chronology, alas, had little to do with maturity. Lord Tidmarsh had no business marrying until he knew better than to wager on a lady's affections.

Perhaps some facial hair would help, as well.

"Why, he never once let you out of his sight at the Chester's rout last week," her mother added. "He followed you about all night."

He had. His attentions had become so tedious she'd spend the last hour of the evening hiding in the lady's retiring room.

"He seemed so determined, Eleanor."

Oh, he was determined, all right. Determined to win his wager.

Eleanor crossed the room to ring the bell for tea. "Indeed, mama, you're mistaken."

She was wicked to tell such lies to her mother, but people often *were* wicked, weren't they? She thought of the cold, dismissive look Camden West had given Charlotte last night, his bored tone when he'd told Eleanor to look after her sister.

Some were much wickeder than others.

Her mother was still puzzling over Lord Tidmarsh. "I can't account for his not making an offer—"

A quiet knock on the door interrupted the discussion, much to Eleanor's relief. "Yes?"

Rylands, their butler, entered the room. "Excuse me, my lady. There's a gentleman below requesting a visit with Lady Eleanor."

A gentleman? Oh, good lord. Hadn't she made herself clear to Lord Tidmarsh last night? He'd scurried away in a perfect sulk, and she'd thought the matter rather tidily concluded, but perhaps that was too much to hope for.

Her mother let out an irritable sigh. "We said no visitors today, Rylands."

"Yes, my lady. I beg your pardon. This gentleman is quite insistent, I'm afraid. He demands to speak to Lady Eleanor at once."

Drat. It did sound like Lord Tidmarsh, deep in the throes of another imaginary passion. Good Lord, her head ached. "Who is it, Rylands?"

Rylands sniffed. "I've never seen him before, my lady. Mr. Camden West."

Oh, no. Eleanor's heart leapt into her throat. "Camden West?"

No sooner did the devil cross one's mind than he showed up at one's door, and here was proof of it. Why, she'd rather face a dozen tragic Lord Tidmarshes than spend another moment in Camden West's company.

Eleanor's mother turned to her. "Who is Camden West? I don't recognize that name."

"You remember Julian West, I think? This other Mr. West is his cousin. He called our carriage for us last night when Charlotte was taken ill. I'm sure he's only here to enquire after her health."

"How kind."

Eleanor stretched her lips into what she hoped was an agreeable smile. "Yes, isn't it? That's the very word that came into my head when I met him—kind." *The worst kind of devil, that is.* "Very well, Rylands. I'll be down at once."

But Eleanor dragged her feet every step of the way to the drawing room. What could Camden West mean by coming here? He wasn't here to inquire after Charlotte. He hadn't batted an eye when they found her sister half naked in the Foster's garden, and Eleanor doubted he'd developed a conscience since then.

So what in the blazes did he want?

A shiver of dread raced down her spine. Did he plan to expose Charlotte? Tell the *ton* the whole sordid tale? As far as anyone knew, Charlotte had been taken ill last night, and they'd left the ball early. No one had any proof to contradict that story.

No one except Julian and Camden West.

Eleanor made her way downstairs, paused in the hallway outside the drawing room, drew in a deep breath, then swept inside and closed the door behind her. "Mr. West. What a pleasant surprise." *As pleasant as a sliver in one's thumb.* "To what do I owe the—"

He stood with his back to the door, facing the fireplace, but at the sound of her voice he turned, and just like that, Eleanor's thoughts scattered like an overturned tray of hairpins.

Goodness, he was handsome. It was his eyes—they were a remarkable shade of green, rather dark, like moss. She'd never seen eyes quite that color before, and he had a headful of thick, chestnut-colored hair, streaked with gold from the sun.

Eleanor bit her lip. He appeared remarkably . . . sturdy. His shoulders were half the length of the mantle, for pity's sake, and he wasn't thin or gangly like so many men of such imposing height. Perhaps he padded his coats? Yes, that must be it. The chest and the arms, anyway.

Eleanor's gaze dropped to his tight, buff-colored breeches. He must pad those, as well.

Her face heated. *My. That is a great deal* of padding.

"You're kind to see me, Lady Eleanor."

He bowed politely, but Eleanor didn't miss the hard glint in his eyes, and it snapped her back to herself as if cold water had been thrown in her face. It mattered not one whit what he looked like. Lions were handsome, too, but they could still claw your belly open and feast on your entrails.

Camden West was a villain, and anyway, it likely took him hours in front of the glass to coax those silky waves of hair to fall across his forehead in such a fetching, boyish manner.

"Mr. West. Why do I feel certain this isn't a social call?" She may as well get right to the heart of the matter. The sooner he told her what he wanted, the sooner she could be rid of him.

His green eyes narrowed at her frankness, then crinkled at the corners in what could have been appreciation.

Eleanor hoped it was a digestive complaint. She didn't need or want Camden West's admiration.

"Perhaps I've come to inquire after your sister's health?"

She considered him for a moment, then shook her head. "No. I think not. But since you make the pretense of concern, I can tell you she's more upset than I've ever seen her, and she hasn't left her bedchamber all day. A tidy night's work for your cousin. I do hope he's pleased with himself."

"He isn't, though I doubt you'll believe that. But I didn't come to discuss my cousin, or to inquire after your sister."

"Indeed? Then I fail to see why you've come at all."

He studied her face for a moment, then let out a low laugh. "The gossips didn't exaggerate about you."

Her eyebrows rose. She could just imagine what he'd heard about her. "Gossips always exaggerate. Do you make it a habit to listen to them, Mr. West? How disappointing."

"I'm distressed to have disappointed you, my lady, but gossip occasionally proves a useful source of information."

"Certainly, if you're not troubled by a small thing like the truth. A gentlemen never listens to gossip."

He shrugged. "I'm not a gentleman, Lady Eleanor. By the time we finish our conversation, I'm sure you'll agree that's true."

"I agree even now."

He smiled. "Just as I'd heard. Cold."

Eleanor cleared the sudden lump from her throat. She knew the gentlemen thought her cold—they'd dubbed her Lady Frost, after all. Still, to know it was one thing. To hear it from a pair of full, handsome lips quite another.

But she didn't have any use for his lips, full or otherwise, and she'd do well to remember it. "Not cold enough, for you're still here."

The handsome lips parted on a laugh. "You do have a certain frigid charm. I'll give you that."

She bit back a sharp retort. It would only encourage him, and she'd rather he make whatever demand he intended to make so she could refuse, and be rid of him. She didn't care for this conversation, or the cat-in-the-cream smile on his face.

"Why are you here, Mr. West? You haven't come to enquire after my sister, and you haven't come to offer an apology for your reprehensible behavior. So, what do you want?"

There. She couldn't be any plainer than that.

"I want a number of things from you, Lady Eleanor, but let's start with the easiest, shall we? I want you to call me Camden. It won't do for you to call me Mr. West once we're married."

Eleanor stared at him.

Married. But . . . that word didn't make sense. Not in the context in which he'd used it. Her brain groped blindly for another meaning, but none came.

Married? No, surely not.

"Married," she repeated.

"Married. Yes, that's right, my lady." He sounded as if he were encouraging a dim-witted child to work out her sums. "You may call me Mr. West in company, but I prefer you call me Camden when we're being, ah . . . private."

Private? No. That word didn't make sense, either. "Private," she repeated, aware she sounded like a trained parrot.

He was mad, of course. It was the only explanation. Utterly mad. She'd no more marry him than she would the devil himself.

Though if they did marry, they'd have lovely children. Tall, with green eyes.

A hysterical laugh escaped her at the thought. Perhaps she was the one who'd gone mad.

He wasn't amused. "I'm serious, Lady Eleanor. It would be too bad if Lady Charlotte's indiscretion became fodder for vicious gossip. From what I understand, it would take far less than a scandalous seduction for the *ton* to turn their backs on her once and for all."

Eleanor's brain ground back into motion with a vengeance. "Are you threatening me, sir?"

He draped his arm over the mantle. "Yes. I believe I am."

Her entire body went rigid. Marry him? Impossible. One didn't marry a man like Camden West, or any of the gentlemen like him who ran amok in London. If a lady wasn't careful about whom she chose, she could find herself married to a man like her father.

Lady Catherine's marriage to Hart Sutherland had been nothing short of disastrous. He'd been a cruel husband, and a cruel father. He'd been a cruel man, period, and his wife and children had felt only relief when he died three years ago.

No, one married a man like her brothers—a kind man, an honorable man. A man who loved her, and whom she loved. Oh, she knew love matches among aristocrats were rare, and she also knew the odds of her making such a match faded with every suit she rejected. Things couldn't be much worse, in fact. She was twenty-one and in her third season, she had her own section in the betting book at White's, and every gentleman in London was mocking her.

And yet despite all this, Ellie still held onto the promise of love, clutched at it with both hands. She deserved love—real, transformative love—and she wouldn't let anyone steal it from her.

To marry a man like Camden West . . .

No. It would mean years of misery. Decades. "Do I understand you, Mr. West? You seem to be saying if I don't agree to marry you, you'll ruin my sister."

He gave her a cordial smile, as if they were discussing the chances of rain this afternoon. "You understand me perfectly, my lady."

Good Lord, the man truly *was* mad. Why, her brother was liable to flay his skin from his body when he heard about this. "My brother. Lord Carlisle. You haven't—"

"Asked him for your hand? No. I have a suspicion he'd refuse me. I see no reason to get Lord Carlisle involved. I'm sure you'll come to the sensible decision on your own."

Refuse him? Both her brothers would rain hell's fury down upon Camden West's head.

Eleanor drew herself up, but even at her full height she just reached his shoulder. "I'm afraid I don't agree. My brothers will take it quite ill indeed to find you and your cousin have seduced one of their sisters so you could force the other into a sham marriage."

Mr. West released a heavy sigh, and shook his head as if he were disappointed with her. "Do you suppose one of them will take it ill enough to challenge me to a duel? Your younger brother, Mr. Robert Sutherland nearly lost his life in a duel last year, from what I understand. He's just married, I believe? And Lord Carlisle—didn't Lady Carlisle just bear him an heir? The child can't be more than a few months old. Tell me, Lady Eleanor, does your brother prefer swords or pistols? Either would suit me. I'm an expert with both."

Eleanor's hands turned to ice as he spoke. There was no question Alec would issue a challenge, and Robyn was no better. He'd gone mad when he found out about the wagers at White's. It had taken every one of her persuasive skills to dissuade him from calling out half the ton.

If one of her brothers should be injured in a duel, or worse . . .

No. To even think it was unbearable. Robyn's duel last year had sent her mother into a collapse, not to mention what it had done to Lily, who was now Robyn's wife. Then there was Alec, husband to Lily's sister Delia, and doting father of the Sutherland heir, also named Alec, Ellie's six-month-old nephew.

She raised her chin. Camden West might deserve to be run through with a sword, shot in the forehead, or both, but she wouldn't put her family through such misery. She'd just have to drag herself out of this quagmire, and Charlotte along with her.

There would be no duel, and no marriage. Not to Lord Tidmarsh, and not to any of the other swains who trailed after her at balls and routs, trying to convince her of their devotion while they panted after her dowry.

As for Mr. West . . .

She studied him. Such a handsome man—perhaps the handsomest man she'd ever seen— but under his striking looks lurked a terrible darkness. To be married to this man, completely in his power . . .

Eleanor shuddered. Such a man must be cold down to his very marrow.

"Does your silence mean you accept my suit?"

Mistake number one, Mr. West. When a lady is silent, it rarely indicates agreement.

She gave him a tight smile. "I'd like to ask a few questions first, please, with your permission."

"Of course, my lady. You'll find I'm a generous husband."

She gritted her teeth. "Why me?"

He bowed, and gave her a charming smile. "You don't give yourself due credit with that question, Lady Eleanor. Your beauty alone—"

"Please, Mr. West." She held out a hand to stop him. "I'm well aware you have no romantic interest in me. You're not proposing a love match, and you insult me when you pretend otherwise. So, I repeat my question. Why me? Is it my dowry? It's a generous one, I'll admit. It's tempted many gentlemen before you."

He appeared surprised for a moment, but the look was there and then gone. "I don't care about your money. Keep your dowry in your name, or use it as pin money. Whatever you like."

Keep her dowry? *What nonsense.* Did he think her a half-wit? He'd strip her of every shilling before the champagne had gone flat at the wedding breakfast.

"I see you doubt me, but I assure you I have no interest in your fortune. Perhaps you've heard of the ship, the *Amelia*? She's mine. I own her, as well as a dozen or so others."

Eleanor's eyes widened. She'd heard of the *Amelia*, yes. The *ton* considered anything to do with trade beneath their notice, but all of London knew of the *Amelia*. The ship had attained mythical status among the laboring classes because of the enormous fortune she'd made her owner, and even the *ton* couldn't ignore that kind of money.

That explained why he'd been invited to the Foster's ball. She'd known he was wealthy, but his fortune exceeded even hers. Indeed, it made the fortunes of half the aristocracy in England look like a paltry pile of coins.

If this wasn't about money, what the devil did he want her for? "Is it my social connections you want, then?"

The Carlisle earldom was an ancient and well-regarded one, and the Sutherlands were a large, tight-knit, handsome family. Their fortune was substantial, and despite the whispers about Charlotte, and Eleanor's growing list of rejected suitors, they wielded considerable social influence.

But Camden West, with his devastating green eyes and piles of money could wed whomever he liked, and have a grateful wife in the bargain.

He shrugged. "In a manner of speaking, yes."

Hope flared in her breast at this admission. "But there are several other young ladies in London with fortune and family equal to mine. Why force me into marriage when you could have one of them for the asking?"

His face closed. "I don't want them. I want you."

Eleanor's jaw clenched. No, he didn't. He didn't want her any more than any of the others did, but he wanted something, and she wouldn't rest until she found out what it was. "But why? Why me?"

"My reasons are my own. Will you accept my suit, or shall I enter a bet about Lady Charlotte into the book at White's?"

Eleanor looked into his face, tight and hard as a fist, and realized he was deadly serious about this. For his own twisted reasons, he wanted to marry *her*, and if she refused, he'd ruin Charlotte.

Time. She needed time to come up with a scheme.

"Don't you think my brothers will find it suspicious if I announce I'm marrying a gentleman I met only last night? My mother will find it so, I assure you, and don't suppose Charlotte won't ask questions."

He gave her an impatient look. "What do you want, then? You wish me to court you?"

"Oh, I think we've put aside my wishes at this point, Mr. West, but if you want your nefarious plot to work, a courtship is in order, yes."

Perhaps he was lying about her dowry, or perhaps he wanted to win the one woman in London who'd evaded all the others. She could believe it of him—a man of obscure origins who'd achieved such success, and amassed such a fortune. Camden West liked to *win*. He may not have a title, but he was as callous as any aristocrat. Marriage was simply another challenge, another game to him.

A game, with my hand as the prize.

"Two weeks," he said. "You will accept every invitation I extend to you during that time. Rides in the park, escorts to balls—whatever I wish. A whirlwind love affair. Aren't you pleased with the romance of it, Lady Eleanor? It's what every young lady dreams of."

I'm not every young lady.

He hadn't any idea who she was, and his ignorance would cost him.

"At the end of two weeks' time, we'll announce our betrothal."

"Or else? You sound like a villain, Mr. West. I can almost imagine I've stumbled into a drama at Drury Lane. Or is this a farce?"

"A comedy, my lady. Do you recall how those typically end?"

She gave him a cold smile. "Let me see if I remember my Shakespeare. Ah, yes. Weddings."

He returned her smile with an even colder one of his own. "Very good, Lady Eleanor. Now, if you'll excuse me, I have other business to attend to today."

"Extort a lady into marriage, and now it's off to Tattersall's?"

"No." He raised a mocking eyebrow. "I went to Tattersall's first."

"Wise of you." Eleanor managed a sweet smile through clenched teeth. "Wives are easily had in London, but one can't say the same of excellent horseflesh."

"You'll soon find, Lady Eleanor, I insist on only the finest pedigrees in both my horses and my wives." His icy green eyes swept over her. "There's a great deal to be said for superior breeding stock."

Eleanor managed another tight smile. "Indeed."

He bowed. "I'll return this afternoon to take you riding in Hyde Park."

He wasn't going to waste any time, then. Well, neither would she. "I do hope you don't plan to abscond to Gretna Green with me under pretense of a jaunt around The Ring."

She followed him into the entryway, where he collected his coat and hat from Rylands. "Two weeks, Lady Eleanor."

After he was gone, Eleanor stood still for a long moment, hiding her shaking hands in her skirts, and staring at the place where he'd stood.

Two weeks. Two weeks to beat the devil at his own game.

Chapter Four

"What did Lady Frost say to your marriage proposal? I'll wager she had a footman throw you onto your arse in the street."

Cam tossed aside a sheaf of unanswered letters, leaned back in his chair and smirked at Julian, who'd fallen into a full sprawl on one of the leather chairs in front of Cam's desk. "You'd lose that wager."

"Indeed? Don't tell me she accepted you. She didn't look like the meek and biddable type to me. More like this type." Julian picked up a letter opener, idly tested the point with a fingertip, and then drew it across this throat.

Cam laughed. "If she'd had a letter opener to hand, she might well have taken a chunk of my flesh."

She'd never let her temper overcome her, but Cam had seen how furious she was. It seemed no one ever made Lady Eleanor Sutherland do anything she didn't wish to do. She was a typical *ton* female in that regard.

In most regards.

He rose, crossed to the sideboard and poured two whiskeys. He handed one to Julian, then reseated himself behind his desk. "She didn't *not* accept me, and she agreed to go riding with me this afternoon in Hyde Park."

Julian balanced one booted foot over the other knee. "She agreed? Or you bullied and threatened her until she understood she hadn't any choice, and gave in? Be honest, Cam."

Cam shrugged. "What difference does it make? The result is the same."

"On the surface, yes. But I'd keep an eye on the blades once you're wed, or you may wake one morning to find one at your neck." Julian ran a thumb over the point of the letter opener again. "Lady Eleanor would make a fetching widow, and a wealthy one."

"Anticipating my demise, cousin? You forget the lady must be a wife before she can become a widow."

"Details. Besides, to hear you tell it, a ride in the park is a mere step removed from a betrothal." Julian tossed the letter opener onto the desk. "A jaunt today, a marriage tomorrow. Isn't that what they say?"

"I've no idea what they say, but for Lady Eleanor a jaunt around the park will lead to a marriage soon enough. I've given her two weeks."

Julian raised an eyebrow at this. "What, a two week grace period? You didn't say anything about that before."

Cam turned his whiskey glass between his fingers. No, he hadn't, because he was done being gracious or merciful to Eleanor Sutherland. When he first returned to London he'd tried to court her in the honorable way, but she'd rebuffed him, much as she had every other suitor.

This wasn't a courtship anymore. It was conquest and surrender.

As irksome as he found the delay, the lady had a point, and her sister's reputation would be as much at risk two weeks hence as it was now.

"Lady Eleanor pointed out she couldn't simply announce an engagement to me without any warning—her family wouldn't like it, and I'd rather not attract unwanted attention from those hot-headed brothers of her. Besides," he added, with an innocent look, "I couldn't refuse the lady's one request. I'm a gentleman, after all."

Julian choked on the sip of whiskey he'd taken. "Yes, of course. Once we put aside the blackmail, extortion and threats, there's nothing left but gentlemanliness at its finest."

Cam took a sip of his own whiskey and eyed his cousin over the edge of his glass. Another attempt to make him feel guilty? It wouldn't work. He had a conscience much like any other man, but not when it came to the Sutherlands.

"How did you find our Lady Frost, then?" Julian asked. "Does she live up to her reputation? I hear she's clever."

Cam leaned back in his chair, considering. "She has a sharp tongue. I suppose some might mistake it for cleverness."

"Not you, of course."

Cam waved a dismissive hand at his cousin. "I'd sooner call it arrogance. No doubt her wit and accomplishments have been exaggerated. Gentlemen tend to lose their heads over extraordinarily beautiful women."

"Ah, so you noticed the extraordinary beauty, did you? I thought you might have overlooked it."

"I don't care for her sort of female, but I'm not blind, cousin."

Eleanor Sutherland had the kind of beauty men crawled across deserts on their bellies to possess. The huge dark eyes and regal cheekbones, set off by that red, wickedly full, pixie of a mouth? He didn't care for brunettes, and he didn't care for Eleanor Sutherland, but even he hadn't been unmoved by the sight of that mouth, and more so when it delivered a sarcastic comment or set down. The lady had spirit, if not true wit, and he did appreciate a challenge.

He'd enjoy bedding her, at least until he wearied of her sharp tongue. Once the inevitable tedium set in, she could do as she wished, and he'd go about his business much as he had before he married.

Julian snorted. "Never mind blind, Cam. A man would have to be dead to overlook Lady Eleanor's beauty. I was about to check your pulse this minute if you didn't acknowledge it."

"It's strange, though . . ." Cam frowned as he remembered something she'd said that surprised him.

"What is?"

"She talked about the gentlemen being enamored of her dowry, as if she believes all those swains sniffing after her only want her fortune." Cam shook his head. "She didn't seem to think any of them might want her."

"That is strange. In my experience, most ladies tend to overestimate their charms, not otherwise. Unless her dowry is large enough to drown England in gold sovereigns, I believe the lady is mistaken. It would explain her coldness, though."

"What do you mean?" Cam tossed back the rest of his whiskey. "Why would it?"

"It's obvious, Cam. If she thinks her suitors are only after her dowry, it's no wonder she's cold to them, is it?"

"I suppose so." Or perhaps she wished to be known as the most unattainable lady in London, or some other foolish thing. It didn't matter. He didn't choose to delve into the reasons Lady Eleanor might feel as she did. Cold or warm, clever or featherbrained, dark-haired or fair—she was a Sutherland. For his purposes, that was good enough.

Julian wasn't willing to let the matter drop, however. "Did *you* find her cold?"

"Let's just say I should have brought a greatcoat into the drawing room with me when I spoke with her. By the time I took my leave, the windows had iced over."

Julian laughed. "I hope you weren't foolish enough to expect a warm welcome from her. Threats and blackmail do tend to cool a lady's ardor."

Cam only grunted in reply. His cousin was showing a disturbing inclination to champion Lady Eleanor. There was no point in arguing with him, for it would only make him more insistent. Julian could behave with stunning perversity on occasion. Before long he'd have Eleanor Sutherland as some poor victimized maiden, and Cam as Lucifer himself.

Julian stared down at the last swallow of amber liquid in his glass. "I don't suppose you happened to see Lady Charlotte while you were there?"

Cam raised an eyebrow. "Christ, Julian, that's the third time you've mentioned Lady Charlotte since last night. Don't tell me you've let that chit crawl under your skin."

"Unlike you, Cam, I *do* have a conscience."

Cam gave his cousin a sour look. "Yours is a recent affliction, I think. You've pawed through dozens of bodices without suffering any ill effects."

"Bodices of actresses, yes, and opera singers. Those are a different matter altogether. I wasn't the first to get a handful of those ladies' charms, and I won't be the last. But Charlotte Sutherland is—"

"A flirt, if the gossip can be trusted."

"A flirt, Cam. Not a whore."

"Still—"

Julian's foot dropped from his knee to the floor with a heavy thump. "Bloody hell, Cam. Just answer the question, will you? Did you, or did you not see Lady Charlotte this afternoon?"

Cam jerked back in surprise at his cousin's harsh tone. "Very well. No, I did not. Lady Eleanor said—"

He stopped. Did Julian need to know Lady Eleanor had said her sister hadn't left her bedchamber all day? One never knew when his cousin would be taken with some wild notion or other. He might visit Lady Charlotte to beg her pardon for his behavior. It wouldn't do for Julian to complicate things now—not when Cam had Eleanor Sutherland where he wanted her.

Conquest, then surrender.

No, the sooner Charlotte Sutherland's part in this scheme was forgotten, the better. She'd served her purpose. He had no further use for her now, and he'd rather Julian didn't, either.

"Lady Eleanor said she was out."

Julian finished off his whiskey and dropped the empty glass onto Cam's desk with a crack. "No lasting ill effects from last night, then?"

Cam avoided his cousin's eyes. "Not that I'm aware of, no."

Oddly, this seemed to anger Julian rather than reassure him. "I congratulate you then, Cam. It's all fallen into place just as you said it would. You'll have your Sutherland bride. Not just any bride either, but a rich and beautiful one, and despite your reprehensible methods, neither Lady Eleanor nor her sister will end up the worse for it. At least," he added, "that's what you tell yourself."

Cam jerked up straight in his chair. Damn it, he would not feel guilty about this. Julian knew better than anyone he hadn't any choice. "Neither of them *will* end up the worse for it. Charlotte Sutherland's reputation will remain intact, and she'll go on to marry some wealthy, titled lordling, with no harm done."

But this only made Julian angrier. "Will she? But what of Eleanor Sutherland? Won't she be harmed? She's to be forced into a marriage she doesn't want to satisfy some twisted need for revenge on your part—"

"Not *revenge*." Cam kept his voice calm with an effort. "Justice. I only want what's owed to me, and what's owed to Amelia."

Julian shook his head. "There's only one problem with that logic, Cam. It's not Eleanor Sutherland who owes you. Either of you."

Cam jerked to his feet and strode to the window. She didn't owe him, no, and yet she'd pay nonetheless, because someone had to, and she was one of only two people left in the Sutherland family who could. Perhaps it wasn't fair, but then life rarely was. Amelia would find that out soon enough. Why shouldn't Eleanor Sutherland find it out as well?

"She'd be forced into a marriage one way or another, likely to a man who wouldn't give her any of the freedoms I will." Cam didn't look at Julian. "She'll get everything from a marriage to me she could reasonably expect to get from marriage to an aristocrat."

"Not everything. You don't love her."

Cam swung around to face his cousin. *Love her?* He didn't even like her. "No. I don't love her, but she's a daughter of the *ton*, Julian. She doesn't expect love from marriage. She expects to be taken care of. She will be, and handsomely at that."

Julian's expression darkened. "You call *her* cold? You turn everything into a business transaction, Cam, even marriage."

Cam held onto his temper by a thread. "Marriage *is* a business transaction, Julian, and Lady Eleanor knows it as well as I do. Why do you think I'll succeed in securing her when all those fine lords have failed? No false protestations of romantic love will move the lady, but force will, just as it does in business."

"What about *real* protestations of love? Did you ever consider you're stealing those from her?"

It's not more than what was stolen from Amelia and me.

Cam didn't bother to say the words aloud, however. He and Julian had had this same argument time and time again, always without a resolution. "I will never love her, it's true, but I will treat her with respect. I'll be kind to her. Kinder than many husbands are to their wives."

Julian raised his eyebrows, then cleared his throat.

Cam stiffened. He knew what was coming. Julian was about to say something he didn't want to hear, but hear it he would. He and Julian had been inseparable since Cam was nine years old, and Julian had earned the right to have his say.

"You're not her equal socially, Cam. You're rich, yes—richer than any man should be—but you're still in trade. She's a lady, the daughter of an earl. Even with your money, her friends will see this marriage as beneath her."

Bitterness welled in Cam's throat at Julian's words. Cam's father had been landed gentry, and his mother the only child of a respectable country solicitor. His family was genteel, but he couldn't claim an equal social footing with Lady Eleanor.

"That's the price she'll pay for being a Sutherland." Cam's voice was frigid. "She can't have everything, any more than the rest of us can. Do you think Amelia will have everything she deserves, Jules?"

He didn't give a bloody damn if the *ton* shunned Lady Eleanor after their marriage. It was fitting she should experience some of the shame he'd felt as a young boy, a shame that was still part of him even now, like a broken bone that hadn't healed properly.

Perhaps Julian was right—perhaps he did want revenge. The dark thing that clawed at his heart whenever he thought about the Sutherlands didn't feel like justice. He could admit the possibility to himself, but he'd never confess it to Julian, who'd batter relentlessly if he saw the tiniest chink in Cam's armor.

He changed the subject instead. "Where's Amelia now?"

Julian didn't answer for a moment, then he sighed, and Cam knew the argument was over. For now.

"My mother took her to Gunter's for an ice."

Cam's spirits lifted. Since he'd returned to London, he'd invited his Aunt Mary numerous times to come stay in Bedford Square to see Amelia, but she'd declined every invitation. "My aunt is in London, then?"

Julian rubbed a hand over the back of his neck. "Yes, and no. She's come to London, but she's staying with Mrs. Drumwhistle in Leicester Square."

Cam's heart sank. "Ah. Well, at least she's here."

"It's not her choice to stay away, Cam. You know that."

"I know. No doubt your father refuses to allow her to spend a night under my roof."

His dear Uncle Reginald hadn't spoken more than ten words to him since Cam returned to London and informed him he'd be moving into the Bedford Square townhouse.

He did own it, after all.

The townhouse became available while Cam was still in India—some young earl or other lost his family's fortune at dice and cards and was obliged to sell it to pay his debts. Julian discovered the house, and he'd written to Cam, who'd leapt at the chance to buy it. Julian arranged the purchase for him, and Cam agreed to allow his uncle and aunt to use the house while he remained in India.

Now he was back, but his uncle hadn't welcomed him with open arms.

"Your father still hasn't reconciled himself to my return, then?"

Julian snorted. "No, not yet. Give him time. Another ten years or so, perhaps."

"If he hasn't made peace with my existence these first twenty-nine years of my life, I doubt another ten will help."

It was most inconvenient for his uncle Cam had managed to survive his travels, and then he'd had the nerve to return not only sound in mind and body, but disgustingly wealthy, as well. He'd upset all his uncle's plans, and Uncle Reggie had responded like any rabid animal backed into a corner—with teeth bared, snarling curses and threats.

Except Uncle Reggie hadn't threatened Cam.

He'd threatened Amelia.

It could be an empty threat. His uncle stood to lose a great deal if he angered Cam, but Cam wasn't willing to take any chances with Amelia's future. If the truth were to come out, his sister would need protection. Cam intended to secure it for her, and soon—no matter what it took.

If Amelia was out of time, then so was Eleanor Sutherland.

"Amelia doesn't have ten years." Cam's voice was quiet. "You know that, Jules."

Julian flushed a dull red. He didn't have any illusions about his father. "He thinks he's doing what he must to hold onto Lindenhurst."

Lindenhurst. Cam both loved the place and hated it at once. Sometimes he thought the beautiful memories of his childhood home haunted him even more than the heartbreaking ones. He ran a frustrated hand through his hair. "I've told him time and again I don't want Lindenhurst. As long as your mother chooses to live there, it's hers."

Cam didn't forget debts, either those owed to him, or those he owed to others, and he owed his aunt a debt of gratitude. Aunt Mary had taken Amelia in less than a week after she was born, leaving Cam free to go off to seek his fortune in India. It was the only time he'd ever seen his meek aunt defy his uncle, but Mary had fallen in love with the child, and had refused to be parted from her. Mary was the closest thing to a mother Amelia had ever known, and she'd done a wonderful job with her. His sister had become everything Cam hoped she would—lovely and quick-witted, a child who smiled often, and laughed easily.

Cam was in India for eleven years. The time he'd been away hadn't felt long to him—not until he returned and found not an infant, but his eleven-year-old sister, her angel's face so like his mother's. He realized eleven years might not be a long time in his head, but it was a lifetime in his heart. *Amelia's e*ntire lifetime.

But he'd written his sister every day, and his aunt read Amelia his letters, even when Amelia was too young to understand them. To Amelia, it was as if he'd always been there, and Cam had his Aunt Mary to thank for that.

"She looks just like your mother," Julian said, with that uncanny ability he had of reading Cam's mind. "The fair hair, and the shape of her nose and mouth—"

"Not her eyes, though." Cam's voice was hoarse.

Julian didn't try to deny it. He couldn't. "Shall we ride over to Berkley Square and meet them? You can buy Amelia another ice and ruin her appetite for dinner. It will drive my mother mad."

Cam took a deep breath to work the pang from his chest, then smiled at his cousin. "Let's take the carriage. I'll go straight from Gunter's to collect Lady Eleanor for our drive."

Julian's smile dimmed. "It's not too late to put a stop to this, Cam."

Cam's jaw went hard. "But it is too late, cousin. Eleven years too late."

Chapter Five

Camden West arrived at the Sutherland townhouse just as the long-case clock on the first floor landing struck five.

Eleanor swept down the stairs at precisely one minute after five, wearing a demure blue carriage dress that flattered her trim waist. "Good afternoon, Mr. West. My, you're prompt."

She'd hadn't chosen the dress to entice Mr. West—she'd chosen it because the matching hat was so large it looked like a ship heaving into port. If Mr. West wished to see her face, he'd have to tread water to get under the brim.

Clever idea, accessories that both flattered and disguised a lady at once.

He bowed. "I said five o'clock. You'll find, Lady Eleanor, once I've decided on a course of action, I pursue it through to the end, no matter what."

Eleanor hovered two steps above the bottom of the staircase. A warning, already? For goodness' sake, they hadn't even left the entryway yet. "What a fascinating personal philosophy, Mr. West, but a simple, 'Yes, I *am* prompt,' would have been sufficient."

He stiffened. "I think it best we understand each other from the start."

Eleanor raised an eyebrow. She understood him already, far better than he suspected she did. "All right, then. What would you have me understand from that speech, Mr. West?"

He observed her through narrowed eyes. "That I pay close attention to details, my lady."

"Do you, indeed? How reassuring." She took care to sound bored, but Eleanor ducked back under her hat to hide her uneasiness. There was no denying Mr. West was wilier than her previous suitors. He'd skirted the problem of Alec rather neatly, and she and Charlotte had fallen right into the trap he and his loathsome cousin had set at the Foster's ball.

Then again, anyone could stumble into a trap they didn't know was there. He'd have a much harder time of it when he tried to stuff and mount his trophy.

He might be clever, but her task was a simple one—discover what he wanted, and make it difficult for him to get it. And after all, his motives were transparent enough. He wanted her because she'd eluded everyone else. No doubt he expected to find a shallow, pliable female—one he could easily manipulate. He didn't seem to understand she'd become rather an expert at dodging unwanted suitors over the past two seasons. He'd give up soon enough when he found she wouldn't be led meekly down the aisle. No, she'd kick and scream the entire way, and by the end of it, Mr. West would be relieved to be rid of her.

After all, stubbornness was *such* an unbecoming trait in a woman, particularly a wife.

He held out his arm. "Shall we go?"

She frowned at him. "Why no, of course not. You can't imagine I'll ride in the park with you without a chaperone, can you?"

"A chaperone? That's not necessary, Lady Eleanor—"

"But of course it is, Mr. West. My goodness. I wouldn't *dream* of venturing out the door with a gentleman without a proper chaperone." She gave him a sweet smile. "Now, wherever has Tilly got to? Can you fetch her please, Rylands? Mr. West is anxious to be off."

Rylands bowed and disappeared down the hallway.

"Tilly, is it?" The faintest hint of a smile touched one corner of his mouth.

Eleanor's own smile wavered. If he was furious about her trick, he showed no sign of it. He even looked amused, in a tolerant sort of way, as if she were a child who'd hid in plain sight during a game of hide and seek.

Well, no matter. He wouldn't be quite so amused when he met Tilly.

They heard her before they saw her—a heavy thud, the tread measured and slow but determined, every other step punctuated by an irritated grunt. Tilly, the dear, had a habit of muttering what sounded like dark curses and magical incantations as she walked.

Eleanor glanced over at Mr. West. He shifted from foot to foot, his gaze fixed on the hallway from whence these ominous noises originated. She could have clapped her hands with glee. If the sound of Tilly's approach gave him pause, she couldn't wait to see what happened when he saw her.

For her part, Eleanor adored Tilly. The whole family did. She'd been their nursemaid for years, but despite their affection for her, there was no denying Tilly was a cross old thing—

Ah! Here she was. The dragon had emerged from her lair. With steel gray hair pulled tight under a prim, white lace cap, a stiff, gray wool gown, rounded shoulders that ended in startlingly large, meaty hands, and grey eyes set deep into a rough, ruddy face, Tilly looked like a steel trap right before it snapped closed on one's leg. In other words, she was the perfect chaperone.

The heart of a lamb beat under that frightening exterior, but Camden West didn't know that, and Eleanor could swear she heard a faint, distressed sound escape him when he got his first look at Tilly. Was it a gasp? Or a whimper?

Oh, please let it have been a whimper.

Tilly lumbered to a halt in front of Eleanor. "That him, then?" She jerked her chin in Mr. West's direction.

Tilly never stood much on ceremony.

"Yes." Eleanor had to concentrate to keep the delight out of her voice. "Tilly, this is Mr. West. He's kindly offered to take us for a drive in the park today."

Tilly surveyed Camden West as if he were a rodent she'd just smacked with her broom. "A drive, is it? Well then, Mr. West. Take care that's all you're offering."

Eleanor tried to dive back under her hat in time, but she was sure Mr. West saw her bite her lip to keep from laughing aloud.

As far as Tilly was concerned, every gentleman was a notorious rake, and every outing a potential seduction. Tilly was a staunch defender of maidenly virtue, and her stratagems were as complex and precise as a military campaign. No gentleman would successfully storm a lady's fortress on Tilly's watch.

But despite Tilly's glower, Camden West looked rather pleased with himself. "But Miss, ah . . . Tilly? Surely Lady Eleanor has told you we're betrothed?"

Eleanor's mouth dropped open in horror. *Oh, dear God.* If Tilly told her mother such a tale, Lady Catherine would take it straight to Alec, and then she'd have the hounds of hell nipping at her heels, indeed. "What nonsense, Mr. West! We're nothing of the sort—"

"Lady Eleanor." Tilly planted her massive hands on her hips and turned a stern grey eye upon Ellie. "You're not playing games with this gentleman, are you?"

So he was a *gentleman* now, was he? Just a moment ago Tilly had been scowling at him as if he were no better than a marauding pirate. "Games?" Eleanor widened her eyes. "Why no, Tilly. Of course not."

She glared at Mr. West, who gave her the most maddening smirk before he turned an angelic smile on Tilly. "After you, Miss Tilly. My carriage is right outside."

Eleanor stared at him. Why, in the name of all that was fair, should a scoundrel like Camden West have such a charming, boyish smile? Even Tilly blinked for a moment before she gave them each a suspicious glare, and stalked out the door.

Eleanor turned a baleful eye upon Camden West. "Just the drive this afternoon, if you please, Mr. West. We won't have time for the marriage today."

With those crushing words she attempted to sweep past him, but he stopped her with a hand on her arm. "Your scheme won't work, Lady Eleanor."

Eleanor flicked a piece of lint from her sleeve. "Nonsense. You can't know that. You've only seen the start of my scheme."

It *would* work. It had to. Her chance at love—her very freedom—rested on the success of this scheme. She'd do whatever it took to hold onto it, even if she had to make herself very disagreeable, indeed. She'd earned the nickname Lady Frost with no effort at all on her part, and by the time she finished with Mr. West, she'd have a worse one.

She quite liked "The Terror of London." Perhaps that would catch on.

He pulled her closer. "You don't deny it, then?"

Eleanor's eye widened. Dear God, if she weren't wearing such an enormous hat, she'd be able to feel his breath against her neck. An involuntary shiver skidded down her spine. Goodness—did he have to put his lips right next to her ear to speak to her? "I deny nothing, Mr. West. I also admit nothing."

To her surprise, he chuckled. "You won't capitulate easily, I see."

Eleanor's brows drew together. Why should he sound so pleased about it? What was wrong with the man?

"Let me be understood right now, my lady. You can drag a chaperone everywhere with you for the next two weeks, and we'll still be betrothed at the end of them."

Her smile returned. Did he think Tilly comprised the whole of her scheme, then? As clever as he was, it seemed Mr. West would make the same mistake all her suitors had made. He'd underestimate her. "Certainly, sir."

His fingers tightened on her upper arm. "I didn't agree to these two weeks so you could find a way to squirm out of our bargain."

"No? Well then, it seems you've made a tactical error already, Mr. West, for you *did* agree to them."

He didn't reply, but looked at her for a moment with . . .

God in heaven, it looked like *interest*. His grip loosened, but before he released her, he teased his fingertips down her arm.

Eleanor's breath caught. Had he just . . . caressed her? She gaped at him, but he only raised an eyebrow at her with a hint of lazy amusement, his eyes gleaming.

He did have lovely green eyes, and such long lashes—

For pity's sake, not this again.

Eleanor wrenched her gaze from his and attempted to collect her scattered wits. No doubt Mr. West was accustomed to manipulating ladies who were befuddled by his good looks, but she didn't lose her wits over any gentleman, and especially not this one.

"I suppose you could always change your mind about the two weeks now. Tell me, Mr. West. Are you the sort of man who goes back on his word? Are you a gentleman, or a scoundrel?"

To her surprise he hesitated, as if to give her question serious consideration, then, "I'm both."

Eleanor stared at him for a moment, then retreated back under her hat to consider this alarming response. *Both?* Nonsense. One was either the villain or the hero. Never both at once.

He took her arm again and tucked it into the crook of his elbow. "There isn't much difference between the two, in any case. Between gentlemen and scoundrels, that is. I'm sure we can agree on that."

No, they could not, but if he believed they'd agree on anything, she was making a muck of this. Was it possible he *appreciated* a sharp tongue? He'd be the first of her suitors who ever had. The others hadn't paid much attention to anything she said, clever or otherwise.

"One point of agreement?" She peeked out from under her hat brim to gauge his reaction. "Not enough to build a marriage upon, is it?"

He shrugged. "It shouldn't be, but more than one marriage has been built on far less."

Oh, this was splendid. Not only did the infuriating man appear to agree with her, but now he'd made *her* agree with *him*. That was far too much agreement for two people who'd never marry.

It hadn't occurred to her he'd *want* a clever wife, but then all the gentlemen who'd courted her were aristocrats whose days were taken up with dressing and visiting, afternoons at their clubs, and evening entertainments. Mr. West didn't spend his time lounging at White's, drinking whiskey and wagering on young ladies' marriage prospects. He was a businessman, and a successful one. A clever, determined wife with the right social connections could be invaluable to him. She could open doors he'd never get a foot in otherwise.

Well, that put her scheme in an entirely new light, didn't it? If he wanted a clever wife, she was about to become startlingly dim-witted.

"I await your pleasure, Lady Eleanor."

She took his arm and let him lead her outside, where a barouche sat at the curb, the soft top down, despite the indifferent weather. Eleanor bit her lip. He did pay attention to details then, just as he'd said. With the top down, everyone on the fashionable promenade would see her in his company, and the gossip would start before they'd even made it once around The Ring.

Mr. West signaled to the driver to ascend the box, then held out his hand to her. "Lady Eleanor?"

She gave him the tips of her gloved fingers and tried not to notice the way they disappeared into his hand. His palm was so large it swallowed hers, and he'd swallow the rest of her if she couldn't find a way out of this mess.

She was about to spring into the barouche and take the place next to Tilly when a glance at the seating arrangements made her change her mind, and she took the opposite seat instead.

Mr. West swung up after her and settled himself in the seat beside her. She jerked back like a scalded cat when his knee brushed against hers, but he didn't appear to notice.

"Are you quite comfortable, Miss Tilly?" he asked.

Tilly gave him a non-committal grunt in reply.

Eleanor, lost in her own thoughts, ignored them both.

". . . spend much time driving in the park?"

Goodness, his legs were long, and his thighs were . . . muscular. They took up an awful lot of room in the carriage. She hadn't realized she'd be able to feel the heat of his thigh next to her own. She hadn't wanted to sit next to him, but if she seated herself to his right, her hat blocked his view of her face, which made it much harder for him to carry on a conversation with her.

It gave her time to think.

". . . perhaps some better weather before the season is over."

Was it too late to persuade him she was addle-pated? She'd been so shocked this morning she hadn't said anything coherent at all to him, so perhaps it was still possible—

"Do you prefer to drive in The Ring, or walk around the Serpentine?"

Blast it. How had she so misjudged him? Her schemes were generally quite effective; her siblings had thoughtfully provided scrapes and scandals enough for her to hone her skills in that quarter, but here she'd made a tactical error, and right at the outset, too.

"Lady Eleanor, Mr. West is speaking to you."

She'd made a mess of this, and now so she'd have to backtrack, and pray he didn't notice. It wasn't ideal, but perhaps all was not lost. He wanted to marry her, yes, but he didn't seem to like her much, and unless she was mistaken, he also didn't have any use for the *ton*. If he already thought her frivolous and spoiled, surely it wouldn't take much effort on her part to encourage him she was a peahen, as well.

Well, it would have to do, wouldn't it? She'd simply present him with what he expected to see, and hope for the best. Perhaps he wouldn't think to question it.

"Can you hear me, Lady Eleanor?"

Eleanor jumped. "My goodness, Mr. West! Why are you shouting in my ear?"

He gave her an exasperated look. "I beg your pardon, my lady, but I feared you'd fallen into some kind of a fit."

"Fit? Why, how ridiculous. As you can see, I'm perfectly well."

Tilly grunted again. "Mr. West asked you a question, my lady."

Eleanor hesitated. Did she dare?

Foolish question. She did dare, because she hadn't any other choice, unless she wanted to find herself married to Camden West.

And that was no choice at all.

She let her jaw go slack, opened her eyes wide, and turned this blank expression upon Camden West. "Question? What kind of question?"

He drew in a long, slow, patient breath. "Shall I repeat it for you, Lady Eleanor?"

Eleanor furrowed her brow, as if her answer required the utmost concentration, then turned to him with a vapid smile. "Oh, how kind. I wish you would."

"Would you prefer to drive around The Ring, or take a walk along the Serpentine?"

"Oh!" Eleanor clapped her hands together in glee. "I do so love a drive!"

He startled, then frowned down at her. "Of course. A drive it is."

She tilted her head to the side, as if disappointed, and sighed. "Oh, but I do so love a walk, as well."

Too much? If the change were too abrupt, he'd think her mad.

Then again . . .

Madness. Yes, that might work, too. No gentleman wanted insanity in the family line. She'd keep it in mind in case the mind-numbing foolishness didn't work.

"Why don't we see which you prefer when we arrive?" His tone was polite, but his hands, which rested on his knees, closed into fists.

Not too much, then. She bit her lip to hold back a sigh. It was silly of her to be disappointed. Mr. West was giving her just the reaction she wanted, and yet . . .

She'd expected more of him. As observant as he was, shouldn't he be able to see through such a ruse? How disheartening that even the cleverest of gentlemen should be so willing to believe a lady is a featherbrain.

She pushed the thought aside. This was what she wanted—for him to find her silly and tedious. "What a wonderful idea! How clever you are, Mr. West." She laid a hand on his arm and gave him a dazzling, vacant smile.

A featherbrain, and a flirt.

It was a delicate maneuver, flirting with Mr. West, but there was nothing in the world more tedious than excessive adoration. One need look no further than poor Lord Tidmarsh for proof of that. As handsome and wealthy as Mr. West was, the ladies likely did fawn over him, so he might find it more tedious than most.

He looked down at her hand, which lingered on his arm a touch longer than was proper, then into her face. She gazed back at him, careful to keep her expression worshipful.

He shifted back in his seat, as if he wished to get away from her. "Yes. Clever. Thank you, Lady Eleanor."

After a moment, Eleanor removed her hand and ducked back under her hat, but not before she got a glimpse of his face. Oh, dear—he did look annoyed, as if nothing irritated him more than a scatterbrained woman.

What a shame, for she felt an alarming case of scattered brains coming on. Like seeds on the wind, they'd scatter all over London.

Chapter Six

Whoever had said ignorance was bliss was an infamous liar.

Eleanor cocked her head to the left, then to the right, but it was no use. Try as she might, she couldn't think of one insipid comment to make about the painting. After three days of pretending to be a half-wit, her brain had at last rebelled. It refused to produce a single inane observation.

Ignorance, as it happened, was dreadfully hard work.

Camden West studied her, waiting for her to say something about Benjamin West's painting *Cupid* Stung by a Bee.

But she had nothing to say. Her fountain of foolishness had run dry.

Blast it. She'd been looking forward to the Royal Academy's exhibit. She'd planned to view the selection of paintings and drawings at her leisure, but now her visit was spoiled by Camden West, who'd insisted on escorting her here today.

Three days. Three endless days, during which time he'd called on her three times, taken her on three afternoon drives in Hyde Park during the fashionable hour, escorted her to Lady Davenport's musical evening, and monopolized her dance card at Lord and Lady Henslow's masque ball. All of London was gossiping about them, and her mother had given her a speculative look at breakfast this morning.

Three days, and he'd not yet tired of his pursuit. She couldn't account for it. She'd been so staggeringly silly she could hardly stand *herself* anymore. Since their arrival at the Royal Academy she'd confused a Raeburn portrait with one of Mr. Wilkie's landscapes, and referred to Mr. Beechey's portrait of the Duke of Cambridge as "lopsided."

Camden West hadn't so much as twitched an eye.

"Well? What do you think of the painting, Lady Eleanor?"

Ellie bit her lip with annoyance. How condescending he sounded! No doubt he was smirking at her, his full, handsome lips lifted at the corners.

She stole a glance at him out of the corner of her eye. *Infuriating man.* He *was* smirking. Oh, how she'd love to put him in his place. She longed to say that though she preferred Reynolds' work to West's, she thought West's portrayal of Venus, with her cold, detached profile, was a fine example of the Neo-classical school.

"The poor child," she said instead. "He's rather pretty, isn't he? Whatever is the matter with him?"

"He's been stung by a bee. If you look here, my lady," he pointed to the brass plaque displayed underneath the painting, "you'll see the work is titled *Cupid S*tung by a Bee."

Eleanor hadn't thought it possible for him to become *more* condescending, but she hadn't given him enough credit. She gritted her teeth to bite back a sharp retort, and squinted at the plaque. "Ah, so it does. But I don't see a bee in this painting. Where do you suppose the bee is?"

He made a noise that sounded like a hastily smothered snort.

"I believe we're meant to imagine the bee has come and gone already. See how Venus is holding Cupid's hand? It looks as if she's inspecting the sting."

"Venus?" Eleanor moved so close to the painting her nose nearly brushed the canvas. "Where?"

Mr. West cleared his throat. "Cupid's mother, Lady Eleanor. Venus. Perhaps if you back up a bit you'll gain a better understanding of the composition in its entirety."

"Who, the half-dressed lady reclining on the couch?" Eleanor sniffed. "She looks like a scold."

He appeared not to know what to say to this, and Eleanor felt a surge of hope. Surely speechlessness was a good sign? "Mr. Thompson's Eurydice is in questionable taste," she said, determined to press her advantage. "Her pose is vulgar, and I don't think the infernal regions an appropriate subject for ladies. Don't you agree, Mr. West?"

Mr. West did not appear to agree. In fact, if she could judge from the irritated flush on his cheeks, he wished someone would drag *her* to the infernal regions, right along with Eurydice.

Ah, wonderful—a crack in his façade. "As for William Westall's view of Richmond—"

"Denny! Over here!"

Eleanor didn't recognize the high-pitched voice, or the name Denny, and she wouldn't have paid the shout any mind at all, except Mr. West's gaze jerked from her face over her shoulder and fixed there with such an odd expression, such a surprising combination of exasperation and affection, Eleanor turned at once to locate the source of the voice.

Julian West was walking toward them from the other end of the hall. He held a fair-haired young girl, who looked to be no more than eleven or twelve years old, by the hand. "Ah, here you are, Cam. Amelia wouldn't rest until we found you. Good afternoon, Lady Eleanor," he added, with a polite bow.

Eleanor gave him a nod, her face as stiff and cold as Venus's. He might act the gentleman if he pleased, but she hadn't forgotten his infamous behavior toward her sister. Charlotte still hadn't told her the whole story, but she knew enough.

Julian West was as guilty as the bee that stung Cupid.

She half-turned away from him to indicate her displeasure, but she couldn't resist a peek at him from the corner of her eye, just to see if he . . .

Yes, blast it. Unbearably handsome, much as his cousin was. Tall, with dark, tousled hair and a wide, infectious smile. Goodness. She didn't approve of Charlotte's behavior in the least, but even Eleanor could understand how a man such as this could tempt a lady into an indiscretion.

She swept a resentful gaze over Camden and Julian West. How maddening the two of them should look so absurdly handsome standing there together, as if they were a painting themselves, rendered in vibrant colors and loving detail by a besotted artist's brush. Zeus and Apollo, perhaps?

Eleanor curled her lip. *Zeus and Apollo, indeed.* More like Lucifer and his mirror image.

"Uncle Julian said we might see the pictures today, Denny."

Eleanor peered down at the girl, who appeared to be speaking to Camden West.

Denny?

Mr. West held out his hand to her. "It's odd, Julian, but I don't recall you saying you intended to visit the Royal Academy's exhibition today. Whatever could have tempted you here, I wonder?"

Julian shrugged. "Nothing less than a love of art, cousin, and a concern for Amelia's classical education."

The girl, Amelia, took Mr. West's hand. In her other hand she held an artist's box. She looked up at Eleanor with a shy smile, then turned her attention back to Camden West. "I've brought my box with me. Mightn't I stay, and copy some pictures?"

Amelia looked from one adult to the next, her dark eyes pleading, and Eleanor had the strangest urge to sink to her knees, take the child in her arms and reassure her that yes, of course she might stay. She hadn't the vaguest notion who this child might be, but she pled so prettily, and she was so positively cherubic, with her cloud of blonde hair and her dark, intelligent eyes.

Eleanor couldn't imagine how anyone could refuse her anything.

Except perhaps Camden West, who, like Lucifer, must hate cherubs, and would no doubt send this one back from where she'd come—

"Well, I suppose we can't send you away without a sketch or two." He ruffled her hair. "Can we, minx?"

Eleanor gaped at him, dumbfounded. He'd sounded almost . . . human. No, more than that. Worse than that. His soft, teasing voice made her skin prickle with awareness, as if someone had slipped a finger inside her gown to stroke her neck.

He looked as if he couldn't bear to disappoint the child, either. He chucked her under the chin, then placed a gentle hand on her head and turned her toward Eleanor. "Since you will stay, Amelia, you must make your curtsy to Lady Eleanor Sutherland. My lady, this is my sister, Miss Amelia West."

His sister? How odd. Lucifer didn't have a sister, did he?

She hadn't any time to sort it out, however, for Amelia West sank into a dainty curtsy before her. "How do you do, Lady Eleanor?"

For the first time since Mr. West arrived in Mayfair to collect her this morning, the steel stiffening Eleanor's spine began to melt. She held out her hand to the little girl. "I'm pleased to make your acquaintance, Miss West."

Amelia wrapped her small fingers around Eleanor's. "Are you a real lady?"

"Amelia," Julian West began, but Eleanor shook her head at him. She leaned down so she could look into the child's face. "Yes. My father was an earl."

Amelia hesitated for a moment, then said in a rush, "What does it feel like, to be a real lady?"

"Hmmm." Eleanor closed her eyes and kept her face grave as she pretended to give this question the utmost consideration. After a moment she opened them. "I think," she said, smiling at Amelia, "it feels quite the same as not being one."

Amelia's eyes opened wide in surprise, then she laughed. "How silly. It doesn't really!"

Eleanor, charmed by the girl's reaction, couldn't help but return the laugh. "Oh, yes. Really."

Her smile faded, however, as soon as she straightened and caught the look of pleased surprise on Camden West's face. Eleanor's heart lurched in her chest. She'd forgotten herself for a moment, and she couldn't afford to do so again. She'd managed to annoy him with her chatter today, and she didn't intend to lose the ground she'd gained.

Mr. West offered his arm. "Shall we go view Mr. Lawrence's work? His portrait of the Duke of York is said to be a good likeness."

Eleanor took the proffered arm with an inward sigh. Thomas Lawrence was one of her favorite painters, and she'd particularly wanted to see his portraits, but now instead of rational artistic observations, she'd be compelled to feign ignorance. Whatever would she find say about the Duke of York's portrait? Perhaps she could pretend to mistake him for Prinny . . .

A small hand cupped her elbow. Startled, Eleanor looked down to find Amelia grinning up at her. "Is Mr. Lawrence a fine artist, Lady Eleanor?"

Eleanor gave Camden West a sidelong glance. "He's said to be by those who know such things, yes."

"Oh." Amelia nodded, but before Eleanor could congratulate herself on her vague answer, the child spoke again. "Do *you* think he's a fine artist?"

Eleanor looked down into Amelia's trusting face. *For pity's sake.* Was she to be made to lie to this sweet child now? Or, worse, fill her head with ridiculous untruths about Mr. Lawrence's paintings? She hated to mislead a young artist, yet at the same time she was aware of Mr. West to her left, listening to her every word.

She pressed her lips together. *Very well.* She'd find a way to get rid of Camden West for long enough to give Amelia an abbreviated lesson on Thomas Lawrence. "Shall we see what we think when we view his paintings?"

Amelia, satisfied with this answer, nodded and walked along at Eleanor's side. When they arrived at the part of the exhibit featuring Mr. Lawrence's work, Eleanor kept hold of Amelia, but released Mr. West's arm. "There's the Duke." She nodded at the Duke of York's portrait. "I believe you wished to see it?"

Mr. West raised an eyebrow. "You don't wish to see it?"

"I *did* see it. It's just there."

Before he could reply, she turned back to Amelia. "Shall we go to the other end of the hall to see the portrait of Lady Leicester? Look, Mr. Lawrence has painted her as Hope, and her gown is a lovely shade of russet."

She led the child down to the other end of the hall, careful to natter on about the gown until she was out of earshot of both Mr. Wests, who stayed where they were to admire the Duke.

"You know, Miss West," she said, as soon as they were alone, "now we've had a chance to see his work, I believe I do think Mr. Lawrence a very fine artist. Do you like this picture of Lady Leicester?"

Amelia gazed at the painting for a moment. "Yes. Her face is peaceful, and she looks as if she's floating, rather like an angel."

"She does, indeed. Now, won't you open your box and see if you can sketch Lady Leicester's likeness from her portrait? Mr. Lawrence learned to paint by copying other artist's portraits when he was young, too."

"He did?" Amelia looked impressed with this information. She opened her box and pulled out a sketching pencil and some blank sheets of paper.

Eleanor nodded. "Oh, yes. He practiced and practiced, and when he was a young man he painted a portrait of Queen Charlotte, and it was such a true likeness he became quite famous for it, and now he's considered one of England's finest Romantic painters. Do you know what it means to be a Romantic painter?"

Amelia turned back to Lady Leicester. "Well, the word romantic has to do with love, but with painting it doesn't mean the same thing, does it?"

"Not quite, no. It means an artist like Mr. Lawrence is skilled at expressing emotion through his paintings. What kind of feeling do you get when you look at the portrait of Lady Leicester?"

Amelia cocked her head to the side and considered the painting. "Not a happy one, exactly, but something like it. Perhaps it's more like the feeling I get right before I fall asleep."

"Yes, I know just what you mean. My, you're clever. It feels peaceful, doesn't it? The way the light shines on the white part of her dress makes me feel as if I would have sweet dreams once I did fall asleep. Do you think you can copy it?"

"I'm not sure, but I'd like to try." Amelia made some tentative lines on her sketchpad while Eleanor watched over her shoulder, flushed with success. Oh, she didn't expect a child to be able to sketch Lady Leicester with much accuracy, but an aspiring artist had to start somewhere. An interest in art was a good place to begin, and she could see by the intent look on Amelia's face she was interested.

She leaned over Amelia's shoulder and traced a line on the sketchpad with her finger. "Is this her hand, holding the branch?"

"Yes. Does it look right, do you think? Perhaps it needs to be a bit longer." Amelia looked over her shoulder at Eleanor, then they both looked up at Lady Leicester.

Eleanor smiled. "It looks perfect."

* * * * *

"Well, how do you and Lady Frost get on?" Julian abandoned his study of Lawrence's Duke of York to sweep a critical eye over Cam. "I don't see any gaping wounds, so she hasn't resorted to the letter opener yet."

Cam glanced toward Amelia and Lady Eleanor, drew in a long, deep breath, held it for a moment, and then let it out in a pained sigh. "No, but at this point I'd prefer a stabbing. At least it would be quick."

Julian chuckled. "Means to kill you slowly, does she?"

"Slowly and tortuously, with ceaseless, inane chatter."

"Oh, come now, it can't be that bad."

"Is that so? Why don't you go find out for yourself? At one point I think my ears began to bleed."

Julian didn't look in the least sympathetic. "You know I'd love nothing more than to assist you, cousin, but the lady won't speak to me. You saw the welcome she gave me when Amelia and I arrived. I almost mistook her for a piece of sculpture, she was so cold and stiff."

"She has the wit of a piece of sculpture," Cam muttered. "I thought she had a least a passable intelligence, but I was wrong."

He hadn't expected a great deal of wit from a spoiled *ton* belle, but he'd begun to wonder how Lady Eleanor managed to get her slippers on the correct feet.

"I can't understand why she's accounted so clever." Julian glanced toward the other end of the hallway, where Lady Eleanor was bent over Amelia's shoulder, watching her sketch. "She looks animated enough now."

Cam gave an indifferent shrug. "She must be blathering on about Lady Leicester's gown. She's done nothing but babble incoherently about the paintings, but she did manage to go on at tedious length about the trim on some lady's bonnet."

He followed Julian's gaze without interest and saw Lady Eleanor standing in front of Lady Leicester's portrait with Amelia. He swept a disparaging eye over her, and as quickly dismissed her to return to his study of the Duke.

"Quite animated, in fact," Julian said in a surprised tone.

"She's only going on about—" Cam began, turning to glance at her again, but he fell silent, watching her. Something about her expression, the liveliness in her face, caught his attention.

Julian was right. She did look animated. Her cheeks were flushed, and even from this distance he could see her eyes were bright and alert. She leaned over Amelia's shoulder to point to something on the page, then they both looked up at the painting of Lady Leicester. Cam couldn't hear what she said, but he could see by the movement of her lips her words were rapid and earnest. Amelia nodded, as if in understanding.

Cam's eyes narrowed to slits. It didn't look as if they were talking about Lady Leicester's gown. He abandoned his study of the Duke of York and started toward them. "They look as thick as two pickpockets. What the devil do you suppose they're discussing?"

Julian didn't move. "Lady Charlotte."

Cam turned back to him impatiently. "Lady Charlotte? Why would Lady Eleanor discuss her sister with Amelia?"

Julian seemed to be rooted to the floor, but he jerked his chin toward the other end of the hall. "No. Lady Charlotte is here."

Cam looked over his shoulder. By God, she was, and Lady Carlisle with her. "Come on, then." He tugged on Julian in an attempt to break the hold the floor seemed to have on his cousin's feet.

"Lady Charlotte," Cam said with a polite bow as he joined them.

She ignored him entirely. At first he thought she intended to give him the cut direct, but then he realized she was so focused on Julian, who stood beside him, she hadn't even noticed he was there.

"Lady Charlotte," Julian murmured, a trifle hoarsely.

His tone and his bow were as polite as Cam's, but Lady Charlotte must have heard the husky note in his voice, for she turned scarlet, her expression both defiant and mortified at once.

Lady Eleanor rushed forward and hastened to smooth over the moment. "Ah, this is my sister-in-law, Lady Carlisle. This," she added, with a touch to Amelia's shoulder, "is Miss Amelia West. I believe you know Mr. Julian West, Lady Carlisle. This gentleman is his cousin, Mr. Camden West."

Lady Carlisle couldn't help but notice Lady Eleanor's cool tone when she introduced him, but she was far too well bred to reveal any surprise. "How do you do?" She curtsied to the gentlemen, then held out her hand to Amelia. "It's a particular pleasure to meet such an enthusiastic young artist, Miss West."

Amelia curtsied. "Thank you, Lady Carlisle. Lady Eleanor has been telling me all about Mr. L—"

"You must promise to show me your sketch next time we meet, Amelia," Lady Eleanor interrupted, with an anxious glance at Cam. "Especially her gown."

"Next time we meet?" Cam asked. "Are you leaving?"

She nodded. "I thought to save you the trouble of escorting me home. I'm already fatigued, and you've hardly had a look at the paintings yet. I'll only slow you down, and my sisters are just leaving."

Cam frowned. For a half-wit, she was quick to take advantage of an escape route. He couldn't protest without appearing rude, however. "Very well. I'll see you this afternoon at five, for our drive."

Her mouth tightened, as if she'd tasted something sour. "Our drive. Of course. Lovely." She gave Amelia one last smile, and then, before he could say another word, she walked away.

High-handed chit.

Cam turned to say as much to Julian, but closed his mouth without bothering when he saw his cousin gawking after Lady Charlotte, like a famished dog denied a juicy bit of meat.

Cam turned to Amelia with a sigh instead. "Well, minx, what did you think of Lady Eleanor?"

Amelia dimpled. "Oh, I like her very much. She's clever, especially about art. She knows a lot about Mr. Lawrence's paintings."

Cam stared at his sister. *Clever? Knows about paintings?* Perhaps Amelia had misunderstood. "I—what? What does she know?"

"Oh, all kinds of things, but she mostly told me about Mr. Lawrence, and why he's considered a Romantic."

Julian, who'd snapped out of his trance, asked, "You mean she said he was a Romantic painter?"

Amelia nodded. "Yes, that's it. She said it means he's talented at expressing emotions in his paintings. He painted Queen Charlotte, you know. Lady Eleanor said if I want to learn I should copy the great paintings, like Mr. Lawrence did when he was a child, and—what's so funny, Uncle Julian?"

Julian made a series of choking noises, but he couldn't quite smother his glee. "Well, well, not so dim-witted after all, is she?"

Cam glared at the archway through which Lady Eleanor had disappeared moments before, and his hands curled into fists.

*No. Not so dim-wit*ted, after all.

Chapter Seven

"Have you made up your mind yet, my lady?"

Cam arrived on Lady Eleanor's doorstep promptly at five o'clock, bowed, and escorted her with polite attention to the carriage. To all outward appearances, their drive began much as every other afternoon drive they'd taken over the past three days.

But it wasn't. Not this time. This time, he was ready for her.

"The Ring?" he asked, as they entered Hyde Park. "Or a stroll around the Serpentine?"

Lady Eleanor tapped her gloved fingertips anxiously against her lips. "Oh, dear. I'm just not sure."

Cam smothered a snort. "Take your time, my lady."

She turned wide, troubled eyes on him, as if he'd asked her to explain a complicated mathematical theory instead of whether they should turn left or right. Her performance was spot on. If the carriage hadn't been in motion, he might have risen to his feet to give her a standing ovation.

The empty smile was inspired. She was good enough to tread the boards alongside Mrs. Siddons. Sooner or later, though, she'd discover her theatrical talents were wasted on him, and she'd move on to her next scheme. That there *would* be a next scheme went without saying. A gambling addiction, perhaps? Madness in the family?

He should be furious at her antics, outraged by her charade. He should launch oranges at the stage, hiss, whistle and brawl drunkenly like the rest of the spectators in the pit. Instead, he was looking forward to her next act with painful anticipation. When she realized she played to an empty theater and gave up her game, some small part of him would be disappointed.

After their illuminating visit to the Royal Academy, he'd spent the entire afternoon closeted in his study, determined to strip away Lady Eleanor's disguises until he'd bared her to the skin. He peeled each layer, one by one—her gestures, her expressions, her conversation. He studied them, played them over and over in his mind until at last he arrived at one inescapable conclusion.

She'd whittled, carved and honed her natural intelligence to an extraordinarily fine, sharp point, and she wielded it like a rapier. She was clever, yes—intriguingly so, and not only because he'd been fooled by her charade. No, what stunned him was how well she'd read him, as if he were a character in a play she knew by heart. She'd cast him as the villain, and memorized all his lines before he even realized he was on the stage at all. She saw at once he thought her a vain, silly, feeble-witted belle, and she presented him with exactly that.

It shouldn't have worked. Now he looked back on it, he couldn't understand how he'd ever believed her a half-wit. From the start, he'd seen evidence to the contrary, but he'd dismissed it with a snap of his fingers the minute she offered another version of herself.

An easier version. A more believable one. The version of her he expected to see.

Well, now he wanted to see past it, straight to the raw, tender skin underneath, and he would. This very afternoon. "Have you made a decision yet, my lady? The Ring, or the Serpentine?"

She darted a look around them as if trying to decide, but Cam suspected she was looking for the least crowded part of the park. The *ton* was gossiping about them, and she wouldn't want to feed their speculation by being seen in public with him again.

"The Ring!" she announced, then smiled proudly at him.

Cam tried for an indulgent look, and an air of congratulations. "Very good, my lady."

They hadn't gone more than ten paces before she began to fret and wring her hands, however.

"Is something amiss, Lady Eleanor?"

"No. That is, yes. I fear I've made a mistake, Mr. West. I believe I'd prefer a stroll, after all."

The dark eyes seemed about to fill, and her lower lip trembled. *Good Lord.* Was it possible she could squeeze out an actual tear? "I beg you not to distress yourself. It's no trouble to turn the carriage around."

She slid him a coquettish glance and fluttered her long, dark eyelashes. "Oh, would you? How kind you are, sir."

Cam let his gaze drift from her eyes to her plump, red mouth. Perhaps he should try and convince her he detested flirtatious, forward ladies—the kind of lady who let a gentleman kiss more than her hand, or who sat on his lap during a drive through Hyde Park . . .

His body snapped to such sudden, aching awareness at the thought he was forced to abandon it at once, or else be obliged to cover his lap with the edges of his coat for the rest of the afternoon. Instead he lifted her gloved hand and gave it a reassuring pat, which would have been innocent enough if he hadn't also stroked a thumb across her palm. "Not at all, my lady."

Her dark eyes flashed, but she recovered at once and managed to disguise her reaction with a simper.

Tilly, however, wasn't so forgiving. "Keep your hands to yourself if you don't mind, Mr. West."

Cam turned to her in surprise. He was so distracted by Lady Eleanor, he'd forgotten Tilly was there. The woman hadn't said more than two words since they left, but now he found her eyes narrowed on him, as if she thought he'd try to ravish Lady Eleanor right here in the carriage. The thought may have crossed his mind, but he wouldn't even get his lips on the lady's gloved hand with Tilly's beady gray eyes on him.

"Ah. Here we are." The driver brought the carriage to a halt on the drive. Cam alighted and held out a hand to assist Lady Eleanor, who couldn't quite disguise her hesitation at touching him. He hid a smile, helped her down and offered his hand to Tilly, who eyed it with a pinched expression, then clambered down without his assistance.

He tucked Lady Eleanor's hand into his elbow and started to walk, leaving Tilly to stalk after them. Unless he was mistaken, they'd out-distance the older woman before they reached the bend in the river.

"Tell me, Lady Eleanor, do you often walk in Hyde Park?"

She gave him a bright, meaningless smile. "Oh, yes. There always seems to be some gentleman or other about who wants to escort me."

Fascinating, the way every word she spoke now seemed heavy with hidden meaning. She meant for him to realize she was surrounded by gentlemen who wished to court her, and she regarded him as no more significant than any of the others.

She'd soon find out otherwise. "Do you wish to walk with them?"

She hesitated, then shrugged, as if the thought had never occurred to her. "They wish to walk with me, and I have no objection to it. Oh, look at the ducks! Aren't they precious?"

"Perfectly so, yes." Cam didn't spare the ducks a glance. "What do you do, Lady Eleanor, when you're not accommodating the wishes of all these gentlemen you mention?"

"*Do?*" Her mouth fell open a little at the idea she might do anything at all once the gentlemen in question had disappeared.

Cam glanced at her mouth again and his breath came shorter, as if a fist were squeezing his lungs. Did she believe her half-open mouth would persuade him of her witlessness? All it did was make him think of her tongue. *Damnation.* This had been easier when she bored him into unconsciousness.

He cleared his throat. "I suppose you must spend time with your nephew?"

"Yes, I do. He's precious."

Cam drew in a deep breath and tilted his head back to gaze at the tree branches above them. They hadn't yet walked ten paces, and already this felt like the longest walk he'd ever taken. "What sorts of things do you do with your nephew, then?"

"Oh, I play with him. He has the sweetest little toy boat, you know. It's . . ." She paused, as if she couldn't quite figure out what it was.

"Precious?"

"Yes!" She beamed at him. "Just so."

Good Lord. She was far too good at this. He knew she was performing, yet even so his brain was turning into pudding. "It must be gratifying for a family like the Sutherlands for Lord Carlisle's wife to have so quickly produced an heir."

She paused just long enough for Cam to grow wild with impatience to hear how she'd manage to answer such a pointed question with a few bland words.

"Gratifying?" she asked, with the air of one who wasn't sure of the meaning.

He almost smiled. She was determined not to reveal a thing.

He wanted to reveal *her.* Explore her every word, every thought, every maddening half-smile. He wanted to bare her from her hairpins down to her slippers, slowly, until she stood exposed before him.

Metaphorically, that is.

For now.

"Yes, my lady. Gratifying. Satisfying. Surely you know what it feels like to be satisfied?"

He shouldn't have said it. One didn't speak of satisfaction to a lady, especially not in such a low, suggestive voice, but he couldn't help himself.

He burned with curiosity to see what she'd do now. Would she acknowledge the innuendo? Or better yet, return it? Take it into that saucy mouth of hers, turn it over on her tongue—

Her steps faltered. Cam's lower belly surged with anticipation.

"I think you must refer to that feeling," she whispered, "that feeling a lady has when she, well, when she . . ."

"Yes?" Cam asked, surprised at how hoarse he'd grown.

"She finds a particularly flattering bonnet?"

She didn't say another word or make a noise of any kind, but her entire body vibrated with suppressed laughter.

The breath he'd been holding left him in a heated rush. *Damn her.* She'd held him right on the edge just now, and had delighted in hurling him to the ground. Risky, to toy with a man's lustful urges, but if he didn't want a knife in his back from Tilly—who no doubt hid one under those folds of gray wool—he'd have to ignore it.

He glanced back to find the servant had fallen far enough behind she couldn't overhear their conversation. That was the best he could hope for today, but tomorrow he'd take care to get Lady Eleanor to himself.

"I can't comment on the heights of ecstasy a lady might reach in relation to her bonnet." At least *he* could enjoy the innuendo, even if she refused to. "But I imagine Lord Carlisle's satisfaction with his son must be comparable."

She gave him a puzzled look. "But my brother doesn't wear bonnets, Mr. West. At least, not that I know of."

Cam stifled a laugh. Oh, she was enjoying herself. "No, I imagine not, but you see, my lady, one thing hasn't anything to do with the other."

Her brow furrowed. "It hasn't?"

"No. I mean to observe for a family like the Sutherlands, a family with such an ancient and respected title, it must be comforting to know the family is secure. Not just for Lord Carlisle, but for all of you. I believe you're a close family?"

If they weren't, she wouldn't be playing these games with him to secure her sister's future.

"Oh, yes, very close. My sister is not two years younger than I am, and Lady Carlisle and I are of an age."

Cam sighed, amazed he'd managed to lead her this far in the conversation, as skilled as she was at making sure it went nowhere. "Ah, yes, but I don't refer to your ages, my lady. I mean "close" in the emotional sense, not the chronological one."

She blinked at him. "Oh. Well, that too, then."

He pressed on valiantly. "I only mean to say that as you all *are* so close, Lord Carlisle's happiness must be your own."

"Happiness? Yes. We're all very much concerned with each other's happiness."

Her tone didn't change—it remained vague and pleasant—yet Cam sensed a subtle shift in her, undetectable for one who wasn't attuned to every nuance of her conversation.

But he was. He'd underestimated her once, and he wouldn't do it again. She didn't seem to realize it, or detect any shift in his attitude toward her, but she had his full, undivided attention now.

Lady Eleanor had just delivered a warning—an oblique one, yes, but a warning nonetheless.

"With each other's happiness, and with the security of the family, just as you said earlier, Mr. West."

Well. Not so oblique, after all.

Trifle with one Sutherland, and you trifle with us all.

She hadn't broken character to do it, but it was a near thing, which meant she'd felt it necessary he understand . . . what? The depths of her loyalty to her sister? Cam already understood that kind of loyalty. In Lady Eleanor's case he depended on it, for that loyalty would be her downfall in her dealings with him.

He understood it, and he wouldn't hesitate to exploit it.

And now it was time he delivered a message of his own. "Anyone who knows the Sutherlands, either personally or by reputation, knows that, my lady."

She gave a bright, tinkling laugh. "Indeed? How would they?"

Cam paused to choose his words. "Because, my dear Lady Eleanor, if your brother weren't concerned for your happiness, he would have forced you to accept one of the five suitors who've asked for your hand since you made your debut."

I know all about you.

A slight tightening of her fingers on his arm indicated she'd understood his warning, but otherwise she remained calm, controlled. "My. You *do* listen to gossip."

"Perhaps gossip exaggerates in your case? Or have you really declined five suitors?"

"Hmmm." She tapped her fingers one by one against his arm, as if counting them off. "It's so difficult to recall, you see. There was one, two . . . oh, bother! Shall we just say five, and allow the gossip to be correct? It usually is in these cases."

It would be so simple to dismiss this speech as nothing more than a stream of nonsense from a frivolous belle, but Cam heard the scorn underlying the carelessness—scorn for the *ton's* vicious gossip, and for him, for listening to it.

He couldn't help but admire such a brilliantly played game, but her intelligence made no difference at all in his plans, any more than her stupidity would have, had it been real. "Do you count Lord Tidmarsh among the five? I don't believe he got as far an actual offer, so perhaps not."

She sighed. "Poor Lord Tidmarsh. He didn't seem to understand in the least what he'd got himself into." She tapped her finger against her bottom lip regretfully, but Cam knew her words for what they were.

Another warning.

"If you mean he was surprised to find his heart crushed under your slipper and handed back to him at the end of the quadrille, then I'd have to agree with you. What can have made him believe your affections were engaged? Him, or any of your five suitors?"

She stilled. The expression on her face didn't change, but Cam sensed a sudden anger spark to life under her cool facade. Ah. He'd struck a nerve. Justified or not, the *ton* thought Lady Eleanor a tease. She knew it, and she resented it.

She waved a careless hand in the air. "Oh well, as to that, Mr. West, I suppose I *must* have encouraged Lord Tidmarsh, and all my suitors, without realizing I did so. It's excessively mortifying."

She'd gone breathless partway through this speech. Not from mortification, as she'd have him believe, but from anger. "It's just the gentlemen are so impressive, you see, and so worthy of my regard. I suppose they believed my affections were engaged when they weren't, and so my brother was compelled to refuse his permission on my account."

"How unfortunate." He lapsed back into silence.

Was it possible she hadn't encouraged any of her five suitors, but their arrogance had led them to pursue her? He could believe it of Lord Tidmarsh, but what of the others, the gentlemen who'd made her legitimate offers of marriage? Mr. Fitzsimmons? Hadn't Lord Ponsonby also made her an offer?

Five suitors, all mistaken in her affections? Unlikely.

"Your brother obliged you each time. You're fortunate, Lady Eleanor, that Lord Carlisle is so concerned with your happiness."

For the first time that day, she looked him straight in the eye. "Perhaps my brother wishes to ensure I won't marry beneath myself, Mr. West."

Cam stiffened. Ah, there it was—that Sutherland arrogance. In this, at least, she fulfilled his expectations. "There are many, many ways a woman can marry beneath herself, Lady Eleanor."

"Yes. There are." Her voice was flat. "We've come a long way, sir, much farther than I intended. I'm sure Tilly is fatigued. Tilly?" She dropped his arm and turned toward her servant, who'd now fallen some distance behind. "We'll return to the carriage now."

Tilly turned and began to walk back in the direction from which they'd come. Lady Eleanor followed after her without a backward glance at Cam.

That was it, then. He wouldn't get any more out of her today, except perhaps another observation on the preciousness of the ducks. He caught up to her to escort her back to the carriage, but didn't attempt to take her arm again.

He'd pushed Lady Eleanor as far as she would go this afternoon, but tomorrow, well . . .

That was another thing entirely.

Chapter Eight

"Lady Abernathy's roses are lovely, aren't they?" Ellie laid a hand on Charlotte's wrist. "See? Just there. She's famous for the yellow ones."

Charlotte turned obediently in the direction Eleanor indicated, but her expression remained absent. "Hmmm. Yes. Lovely."

"She grows nettles, as well. Did you know? Perhaps you'd care to take a stroll with me among the nettles, Charlotte?"

"A stroll? Yes. That would be lovely."

Eleanor gave her skirts an irritated jerk and the pile of daisies in her lap spilled to the ground. "Lady Abernathy keeps the poisonous plants well hidden, of course—behind the roses, in the shady area just by the terrace steps. But then you've heard the tales about how she poisoned Lord Abernathy, I'm sure."

"Shady area?" Charlotte murmured. "What a lovely place for plants."

"One day he had the headache, and the next, just like *that* . . ." Eleanor snapped her fingers next to Charlotte's ear. "Dead."

Charlotte nodded, but she didn't look up from the rose she held on her lap. She'd torn the petals off, one by one. "Yes. Dead. That would be—"

"If you say *lovely* again, Charlotte, I vow I'll stick a thorn in you."

Charlotte looked up at last with a surprised expression. "How cross you are, Eleanor."

"You haven't listened to one word I've said since we sat down. I wasn't at all cross until I realized I was talking to myself." A lie, of course—she'd been cross before she lifted her head from the pillow this morning.

Usually she loved Lady Abernathy's annual garden breakfast. The garden club matrons brought their daughters, and it was a tradition for the ladies to help the younger girls string daisy chains. Eleanor looked forward to it every year, but this morning she'd almost asked to be excused. Her mother was a founding member of the Society for the Relief of London's Poor & Indigent, however, and the garden party and breakfast was their grandest charity event of the year. Eleanor couldn't hurt her mother's feelings by begging off today.

Besides, what was her alternative? Another drive through Hyde Park with Mr. West? She had no doubt he'd force his company on her again today if he found her at home, and she still hadn't recovered from yesterday's fiasco.

She'd promised to make herself available to him for two weeks as part of their agreement, but she'd rushed out of the townhouse this morning as if it were on fire.

Agreement be damned, and honor right along with it. Why should she be the only one who had any? She never promised to sit at home and breathlessly await his every whim. Anyway, there wasn't a thing he could he do about it, unless he wished to chase all over London searching for her.

"I'm sorry," Charlotte muttered. "I have the headache, I suppose."

They were sitting outdoors on a blanket spread in a corner of Lady Abernathy's wide green lawn. The society ladies were gathered under a white tent to the west side of the grounds, ready to greet the guests as they arrived. The ladies were all atwitter, for there was to be a guest of honor this year. At the last minute someone had donated a large sum of money to the charity, and she was to be introduced this morning as a principal patron.

Charlotte plucked another rose from the enormous pile at their feet and began to rip it to shreds. Eleanor grabbed it by the tip of the stem and slid it from Charlotte's grasp, careful not to prick her.

"We're meant to be stripping the *thorns* from the roses, Charlotte, not the petals. Here. Shred this instead." She handed her sister a long piece of grass from a clump the gardeners had overlooked. "No need to spoil the roses."

Charlotte took the grass with a sigh and laid it in her lap. "I feel out of sorts."

Eleanor hesitated. Every time she brought up the Foster's ball, Charlotte retreated behind a stony wall of silence. Eleanor hadn't pressed her, because she was afraid if she did Charlotte would demand to know why Ellie was spending so much time with Camden West.

Eleanor had no intention of explaining herself. She'd make *that* problem disappear before Charlotte or anyone else figured out what was going on.

They'd spent the past few days circling each other warily, like two dogs deciding whether to sniff or attack. But here at last was an opening, and Eleanor was determined to plunge ahead before it slammed shut again.

"You've been out of sorts since the Foster's ball. You spent all day in your bedchamber again yesterday, didn't you?"

"Yes." Charlotte spread her skirts over her legs and surveyed the ruined remains of her flowers. "I'm . . . ashamed of myself, Eleanor."

Eleanor dropped the rose she'd rescued into her lap. Charlotte had always pushed against boundaries. Even as a child she'd been the first to disobey their father's commands, but—

"I suppose you're ashamed of me, as well," Charlotte added, her tone resentful.

"Ashamed? No. That's not so, Charlotte."

She'd never been ashamed of her sister, and she wasn't now, but at the same time she'd never understood her, either. Charlotte found Eleanor equally inscrutable, and they'd clashed more than once over the years, especially when they were children. As adults, they'd settled into a more predictable pattern.

Eleanor lectured, and Charlotte ignored her.

She didn't scold Charlotte for pushing the boundaries—a lady had no choice *but* to push, unless she was satisfied to spend her days shopping and gossiping while her husband whiled away his days at White's and his nights bedding his mistress.

No, she scolded Charlotte for pushing so recklessly. One didn't take the stage and shout at the other performers. One jerked the strings from behind the curtain, not in front of it.

They didn't agree on their methods, but Eleanor had never known her sister to be ashamed of her behavior. Until now.

An icy sliver of fear lodged in Eleanor's breast. "Is this about Julian West?"

Charlotte refused to meet Eleanor's eyes. "I thought I could manage it—manage *him*. Once we got out to the garden I knew I'd made a mistake, but it was too late by then—"

Charlotte's eyes filled with tears.

Eleanor stared at her sister, horrified. "Hush. You're all right now, dear. Did he frighten you? Hurt you?"

She was going to kill Julian West.

Charlotte shook her head. "He didn't hurt me, no, but I've never felt so vulnerable in my life, and that part *did* frighten me. It felt like . . . drowning. Have you ever felt that way before?"

Vulnerable? The very word made the hair on Eleanor's neck rise. "I never have, but it sounds awful."

Charlotte shivered. "It was awful and wonderful all at once, and so dreadfully confusing."

Eleanor took Charlotte's hand in hers. "I'm sorry for it, but it's over now. I do hope you can put it behind you, but if not, well, we can always poison Julian West with one of Lady Abernathy's deadly plants."

As long as we save enough poison for his cousin.

Charlotte laughed and squeezed her fingers, and Eleanor breathed a silent sigh of relief. This was the sister she recognized. Charlotte hadn't yet encountered a situation she couldn't dismiss with a laugh.

"What nonsense, Eleanor. You know Lady Abernathy hasn't any . . ."

Charlotte fell abruptly silent. Color surged into her face, and her fingers went slack around Eleanor's hand.

"Charlotte? Whatever is the matter? Are you ill?"

Charlotte didn't answer, just stared over Eleanor's shoulder.

Eleanor was sitting with her back to the terrace, so she craned her neck around to see behind her. Quite a few guests had arrived and were wandering around the tables, admiring the baskets of flowers, but Eleanor didn't see anything shocking, so what—

Just then their mother turned and spotted them on the other side of the lawn. She took a few steps toward them, smiled, and beckoned for them to join her.

That's when Eleanor saw him.

Camden West stood behind her mother, his face turned in Eleanor's direction. Julian West was at his side, holding Amelia by the hand.

"Ouch!" Eleanor looked down to find a thorn lodged in her thumb. She'd snapped the stem of the rose in half. She dug the thorn out with her teeth and stuck her thumb in her mouth to catch the tiny drop of blood welling at the tip.

Oh, no. What the *devil* was he doing at Lady Abernathy's garden party, and with his rake of a cousin, no less? How had he known she was here? Had he had her followed? She didn't doubt it. There seemed to be no depths to which Mr. West wouldn't sink. "I won't leave you alone with him. I swear it."

Charlotte rose to her feet and tugged Eleanor up beside her. "I know. I'll be all right, Eleanor." Her voice shook a bit, but she lifted her chin in the air with some of her old bravado.

Eleanor wasn't sure *she* would be all right, but at the moment she hadn't any choice, for their mother was waving them over.

Very well. She'd obey her mother and be polite, but she'd go in search of poisonous plants at the first opportunity.

A lady never knew when she might need a little poison.

"There you are, my dears," their mother said, as Eleanor and Charlotte joined her. She turned to address Camden West. "My daughter Eleanor tells me she and Charlotte had the pleasure of making your acquaintance at the Foster's ball last week, Mr. West. I believe you called the carriage for them when Charlotte was taken ill?"

He bowed. "Yes, my lady. We were fortunate to be of service that evening."

Eleanor looked into his green eyes, narrow and cold, like a serpent's eyes, or two slivers of mossy ice.

Don't flinch. He'll strike if you do.

She held his gaze as she dipped into a shallow curtsy, then gave a defiant little toss of her head. "Mr. West, and Mr. West. What a . . . pleasure to see you both again."

Julian West, who seemed unable to tear his gaze from Charlotte, stepped forward and bowed. "How do you do, Lady Charlotte?"

Eleanor stared at him, surprised. He addressed her sister in a soft, gentle tone, not at all the arrogant, satisfied one she'd expect a rake to use with his latest conquest. Camden West had said his cousin wasn't proud of his behavior that night. Eleanor hadn't believed him, but perhaps it was true. Julian West did look more like a besotted schoolboy than a hardened rogue at the moment.

Charlotte curtsied. "Good afternoon, Mr. West."

Eleanor examined her sister. Charlotte's voice was composed, but her cheeks were flushed.

"I'm relieved to see you've recovered from your indisposition at the Foster's ball," Julian West murmured.

Eleanor and Charlotte glanced at each other. He sounded sincere, even a touch regretful, but then perhaps he was just an accomplished liar.

Like his cousin.

"Mr. West, that is, *this* Mr. West," their mother said with a laugh, indicating Camden West, "is the society's newest patron. He's made a large donation to our cause. How can we ever show our appreciation for your generosity, Mr. West?"

Camden West raised an eyebrow at Eleanor. The subtle smirk on his lips said more clearly than words what he wanted in return for his generosity.

Eleanor managed a bland smile, but underneath it she seethed. Why, the man was incorrigible. Did he truly imagine she'd capitulate because he'd donated to the society?

Before anyone else could notice Mr. West's smirk, he hid it under a gracious smile. "No thanks are necessary, my lady. Just knowing I've helped London's poor is thanks enough."

Eleanor's lip curled. *Good Lord.* Such touching modesty, delivered with such polished charm. Well, liars did tend to be accomplished performers.

Her mother nodded, then looked down at Amelia with a smile. "Who is this?"

Camden West laid a hand on the child's shoulder. "This young lady is my sister, Amelia West. Amelia, this is Lady Carlisle. You already know Lady Eleanor and Lady Charlotte."

Eleanor shook her head. It still seemed wrong, somehow, that he should have a sister at all. Or a mother or father, come to that. Surely he'd sprung fully formed from Satan's skull?

Still, Amelia was the one thing Eleanor admired about Camden West, and it wasn't the child's fault her brother was more devil than gentleman. She held out her hand to the little girl, her face relaxing into her first genuine smile all day. "Good afternoon, Amelia. I'm pleased to see you again. Have you finished your sketch of Lady Leicester?"

"Not yet, my lady, but I will. I started a new sketch, instead."

"Ah well, you must follow where inspiration leads you. Now, I don't suppose you like flowers, do you?"

Amelia giggled. "Oh yes, I do, especially daisies."

"Do you indeed?" Eleanor pretended to be surprised. "That is good news, for we've a great many flowers here. But you don't like cakes, do you? I'm afraid you must not, and it's too bad, for we've as many cakes as we do flowers, and someone must eat them."

Amelia opened her eyes wide at the thought of so many uneaten cakes. "But I do—I do like them!"

"Do you mean to say," Eleanor asked, raising her eyebrows at the child. "You like to eat flowers? Or cakes?"

Amelia went off into another fit of giggles at this. "How silly. Cakes, of course."

"How fortunate. I've been quite worried about those cakes. Thank goodness you're here."

"Before we descend on the cakes," Lady Catherine said, "We'd like to formally introduce you to the society, Mr. West, and thank you properly. Perhaps you'd care to make a speech? Almost everyone is here now."

Eleanor tried not to roll her eyes. For pity's sake. Not a speech.

He held up his hands with a modest laugh. "No, no speech if you please, my lady. I prefer to be a silent patron, if it's all the same to you. What I would enjoy is a chance to see Lady Abernathy's flowers. Perhaps Lady Eleanor will be kind enough to show them to me?"

Eleanor's mother smiled at her. "I'm sure she'd be delighted."

Eleanor pressed her lips together. Oh my, yes—as delighted as any young lady thrown into a serpent's path would be. "Oh, what terrible luck. I'd so love to show you the garden, Mr. West, but I'm afraid I'm engaged to help the children with the daisy chains."

"Never mind that, Eleanor," her mother said. "Charlotte can help the children."

Julian West intervened then. "Amelia and I would be pleased to help Lady Charlotte. Would you like to make a daisy chain, minx?"

Amelia hopped up and down with excitement, her sunny curls bouncing against her shoulders. "Yes, please. May I, Denny?" She turned her wide, dark eyes on Camden West.

He grinned at her obvious excitement. "Do you know how to make a daisy chain?"

"No, but Lady Charlotte will show me. Won't you?" Amelia turned her absurdly appealing eyes on Charlotte.

Charlotte gave Eleanor a helpless shrug, then smiled down at Amelia. "Of course. Have you ever made a daisy chain before?" She took the child by the hand to lead her across the lawn.

"Mind you don't forget the cakes, Amelia," Eleanor called after them.

Amelia turned back to give her a cheerful little wave, but Eleanor's heart sank as she watched Charlotte walk off to the far end of the garden to spend an entire afternoon with Julian West. Nothing untoward could happen on Lady Abernathy's lawn with a hundred or so society members milling about, but that didn't change the fact that they'd been outmaneuvered by the Wests.

Again. At this rate she'd find herself married within a month.

With a reluctant sigh she turned to face the artic green eyes of her furious would-be-betrothed, but to her surprise, he regarded her now with an odd, speculative expression, not the cold anger she'd expected.

Oh, no. She'd forgotten she was supposed to be a dull-wit.

Blast it, it took far more effort to sustain an appearance of stupidity than she'd ever imagined it would. After their drive yesterday she'd flopped across her bed in a near-stupor of witlessness the minute she arrived home. She'd awoken hours later with a stiff neck, still wearing her carriage dress.

Ignorance exhausted her, but there was no help for it. She couldn't change tactics again. Had she said anything intelligent just now? She'd teased Amelia, but surely she hadn't given herself away—

"You're good with her."

Eleanor jerked her attention back to Camden West, who continued to scrutinize her with such intensity she understood how a rodent must feel right before a serpent swallowed it whole.

He offered his arm. "Many people don't know how to speak naturally to children. They talk down to them, or treat them like adults. Have you had much experience with children Amelia's age?"

Eleanor accepted his arm. "No, but I do adore children. They're so funny and clever."

Cleverer than I am. At least, that's how she hoped he'd interpret that comment.

He didn't reply, but a sardonic smile touched the corners of his lips. Eleanor ran a damp palm down the side of her skirt. That smile wasn't a promising sign.

Damn it, she rarely made mistakes or misread people, and it was quite simple, after all—Camden West was a villain. And yet she'd played him wrong from the start. She'd been so certain he'd underestimate her, she'd underestimated *him*. He was far more cunning than any of her other suitors. It was terribly unfair. Why did the one man who wanted to blackmail her into marriage have to be the clever one? If the world were just, he'd have the wit of a boiled potato, and the appeal of one.

No, it wouldn't do. If she wanted to free her foot from Camden West's trap, she'd have to do better than this. She'd have to find another way—

"Ah. These must be the yellow roses I've heard so much about."

Eleanor looked up, surprised to find he'd led her around a tall hedge of boxwood and down one of the more isolated pathways. She glanced behind them, but only a fragment of the house and the crowd on the lawn were visible through the thick wall of roses.

A shiver of foreboding skittered up her spine. If she couldn't see them, then they couldn't see her. What did Camden West mean by bringing her here? She glanced up into his face, but she found nothing there to reassure her. He regarded her with lazy, half-closed eyes, but his sleepy expression was at odds with his glittering emerald gaze.

He stood far too close to her.

"Will you stun me with your knowledge of yellow roses now, Lady Eleanor?" he asked in a bored tone, even as his gaze flicked over her face, noting every change in her expression.

Eleanor moistened her dry lips. "Oh, dear. I wish I could, Mr. West, but I know nothing about roses."

His gaze dropped to her mouth. "Roses, or anything else. That's what you'd have me believe, isn't it, my lady?"

Don't flinch. "I beg your pardon?"

He reached forward and took hold of her chin with long, warm fingers. "I think you know about many things. You're not as feeble-minded as you'd have me believe, or as cold. Right now, for instance, you feel very, very warm."

As if at his command, her chest and neck flushed with heat. Eleanor tried to jerk her chin free, but he held fast, and tilted her face up to his so she couldn't look away. "Oh no, my lady. We're not finished yet."

"Finish it, then. What is it you want?" In her head her voice was cold, her words clipped, but somehow they emerged husky and breathless. Her flush deepened, spread to her cheeks.

He noticed, and a slow, wicked smile tugged at his mouth. "But I can't have what I want, my lady. Not yet. So I'll settle for an explanation instead. Tell me, why are you so kind to my sister?"

Eleanor's knees trembled under her skirts, but even as her body went weak at the look in his hot green eyes, her mind leapt to his challenge. "Why shouldn't I be kind to her? It's the easiest thing in the world to be kind to a child. They aren't liars. It's the adults who are the challenge."

It was far too smart a reply for an addlepated female, but Eleanor didn't care anymore. She hadn't fooled him with her act in any case, and all she cared about at this moment was getting free of his touch.

Before I melt at his feet.

"Some more than others," he agreed with a soft laugh. "But you see, my lady, every time you're kind to Amelia, you make me want you more."

She watched as if in a dream as he lifted his hand and stroked one long finger down her cheek, lingering just at the corner of her mouth. Eleanor's eyes drifted closed. Her bottom lip gave under the slight pressure of that warm finger, and her mouth opened for him.

A harsh, ragged sound tore from his chest. Eleanor opened her eyes. He was staring at her mouth, at the place where his finger caressed her.

When he said he wanted her, did he mean . . .

She jerked her head back in a sudden panic. "You'll never know who you've married. Kind or cold, foolish or clever. How will you be able to tell the difference?"

His fiery green eyes chilled and the cold mask descended over his face again. "Ah, my dear Lady Eleanor. What makes you think it matters either way?"

Chapter Nine

"How can it not matter? Unless . . ."

Her voice trailed off into silence. Cam watched her, waited for the moment when she realized whatever his reasons for choosing her as his bride, they hadn't anything to do with her at all.

It didn't take long. Her features stiffened and her face went so pale he began to fear she might swoon. For the first time since this began, he saw real fear darken her eyes.

"Perhaps you'd better tell me what's truly going on here, Mr. West."

Maybe it was her quiet dignity, or maybe it was the way her eyes had gone so huge in her white face, but Cam felt an odd squeezing sensation in his chest, and Julian's words from the night of the Foster's ball echoed in his head.

*I don't like it. This is b*adly done, Cam.

Perhaps it was. It had begun badly enough, but he'd end it neatly. Quickly.

But to do that, he needed to see Eleanor Sutherland as nothing more than the last act in a play that began eleven years ago, a play with all the wrong players, all the wrong lines. This was a performance, nothing more—a tragedy from the start, both for his mother and Amelia. It was too late for his mother, but he'd sworn to himself he'd put things right for Amelia with this one final act—a final player across the stage.

It was justice, nothing more. Parity. He didn't wish to punish Lady Eleanor—he had no wish to hurt her. He'd be kind to her, and generous. She'd be happy enough. As happy as she'd be in any aristocratic marriage.

He'd told himself this story over and over again, ever since he decided she'd pay the price for another's sins. But what seemed simple enough in theory became another thing altogether when he looked into Eleanor Sutherland's enormous dark eyes.

"Mr. West? Will you answer my question?"

He stared at her, at the stubborn raised chin, the sleek dark hair pulled away from her brow. If anything, her face had grown paler.

Just now, when he'd seen her with Amelia . . .

She'd been kind to his sister. She'd made Amelia laugh, put her at ease with a gentle, warm humor he would have thought a lady like her incapable of. For one moment as he watched them together, he'd felt the cold weight inside him lift, as if a stone had rolled off his chest.

Part of him had welcomed that feeling, had hoped he'd be able to breathe at last—deep warm breaths to thaw the ice that settled around his heart eleven years ago.

He'd almost kissed her.

That part of him, the same part that wanted to breathe, wanted her lips. Craved them. Even now he could feel the soft skin of her cheek against the pad of his finger, the seductive warmth at the corner of her mouth.

But the other part of him, the part he recognized, held back. That part didn't want to know her, that woman he'd gotten a brief glimpse of just now, that warm woman who'd taken pains to make a child feel welcome.

If he knew her, he'd never be able to do this to her.

He could manipulate Hart Sutherland's daughter. He could threaten the *ton* darling and never suffer a pang of conscience. He could force the grand Lady Eleanor Sutherland into marriage with no regrets whatsoever.

But Eleanor? Ellie.

Could he do this to her?

With the Sutherland name behind her, Amelia would have every advantage he could give her. If not true acceptance, then what amounted to the same thing when it came to the ton.

The appearance of acceptance.

But someone who cared for Amelia as he did? Loved her, even? Someone who treated her the way their mother would have done, had she lived? He hadn't even dared to hope for it.

Not until today.

No one but Eleanor Sutherland would do for Amelia, but in a twist worthy of a Shakespearean tragedy, he'd discovered it at the same moment he realized Lady Eleanor deserved better than to be forced into a sham marriage.

If she did deserve better, could he go through with his threats against her?

Cam shook his head. The better question was, could he not?

He wanted her. Not for himself. No, of course not. She wouldn't spare any of her warmth for him when she discovered what he'd done. The lies he'd told. How he'd used her. She'd never forgive him. But for Amelia—

"This isn't a game anymore, Mr. West. I have a right to know what you want from me."

Cam stilled. A right? She had *a* right to know?

A deafening roar filled his ears, and in the next breath the familiar rage flooded through him, sweeping his doubts and qualms and regrets before it.

Ah, there she was. Hart Sutherland's daughter, the grand Lady Eleanor Sutherland, a hard, flashing diamond of the first water. There was the aristocrat never far below the surface, with the same demands and sense of entitlement Cam remembered in her father. So arrogant, the Sutherlands, so certain everyone would accommodate them.

She thought she had a right to know. She hadn't any rights at all. Not with him. Not now, and not after they married. The sooner she made her peace with that, the better.

He stared down at her with what must have been a fearful look, for she shrank back. "You haven't any rights at all, my lady. I've told you what I want. To marry you. I intend to do just that. You may play all the games you wish until then, but I'll have you in the end, or your sister will be ruined."

She raised a hand to her forehead, and Cam saw it shook. Regret and guilt threatened to pull him down again, but he held it back.

"But why?" she whispered. "Why *me*? It is because I've rejected so many suitors? That simply makes me unlucky with suitors, Mr. West. If you imagine it makes me anyone special—"

He grasped her shoulders, desperate to silence her. To stop himself from thinking. "You *are* special. You're a *Sutherland*. That's all that matters."

"All that matters," she repeated, as if she wanted to be sure of his words. "Clever or foolish, warm or cold, rich or poor—none if it matters. *I* don't matter. Is that what you mean, Mr. West?"

Something about the way she asked the question made him hesitate. He looked down at her, at her pale face, the slight tremble of her chin, the pulse leaping in her throat.

If he told her she didn't matter, he'd never be able to take it back. She'd never forget he'd said it, or forgive him for it. He knew it, the same way he knew he must draw another breath, and another after that. But what difference did it make if she despised him? She'd despise him anyway, as soon as she knew the truth.

"Yes. That's what I mean, Lady Eleanor."

She gazed at him for a moment as if she didn't quite believe he'd said it, then her shoulders hunched toward her chest, as if to protect herself from a blow. "I see. Well, I suppose that's it, then."

She didn't argue with him. He didn't hear any anger in her reply. She didn't even raise her voice. But her face just . . . closed.

"Not quite," he said, determined to get every sordid detail out in the open, even as he had to avert his gaze from her ashen face. "We made an agreement. I gave you two weeks of courtship. You agreed to make yourself available to me during that time, but today when I called on you, I found you'd gone out."

"I had a prior engagement, Mr. West, as you saw when you arrived."

Say it. Just say it, and be done with it. "And as *you* saw," he replied, the words bitter in his mouth, "I won't be trifled with. Be faithful to your part of the agreement, Lady Eleanor, or I may be forced to bring my cousin into company with me every time I see you. I think your sister is fond of him, don't you? It would be a pity if that fondness led her into another lapse in judgment."

She went so rigid her body might have cracked under his palms. "Are there any depths to which you won't sink, Mr. West?"

Cam's throat worked, but he couldn't quite swallow down his disgust with himself. "Best not to find out, my lady. Do the honorable thing and keep your word, and you won't have to."

"You *dare* speak to me of honor?"

Her voice was filled with such quiet scorn Cam's cheeks went hot with shame.

*I don't like it. It's b*adly done, Cam.

Too late.

She pushed against his arms. "I wish to return to the house now, Mr. West. Are you quite finished?"

He released her shoulders. "As long as we understand each other, yes."

"I understand you perfectly, sir."

"Very well." He held out his arm to escort her back in the direction they'd come, but she brushed past him without a glance, her back stiff, her head held high.

He let her go.

He'd done nothing wrong. He'd simply made her understand his expectations.

And threatened her. Her, and her sister. He'd told her she didn't matter, that she was a means to an end, and nothing more. He'd made her despise him.

He *had* done something wrong. *Christ.* He'd done *everything* wrong, but he'd done it for the right reasons. For Amelia. Surely that counted for something?

"Lady Eleanor! Have you come from viewing the yellow roses?"

Cam joined Lady Eleanor at the end of the pathway. She was chatting with Lady Archer, who was headed in the opposite direction.

Lady Archer was an older matron popular among the *ton* for nothing better, as far as Cam could tell, than losing at cards, and wearing large, colorful turbans.

"How do you do, Lady Archer? Yes, we've just come from there. The roses are in full bloom and their scent is divine. I'm sure you'll enjoy them."

Cam could tell it cost her an effort to appear carefree, but Lady Archer didn't seem to notice. "My dear." She fixed gleaming eyes on her prey. "How relieved I am to see you looking so well. I've been terribly worried for you."

Lady Eleanor looked taken aback. "Worried?"

"Oh my, yes." Lady Archer twirled her parasol. "For you, and for poor, dear Lady Charlotte."

Lady Eleanor stiffened. "I'm sorry to have caused you any concern, my lady, for as you can see, I'm quite well."

She attempted to sidle around Lady Archer, but the older woman was having none of it. She stepped into Lady Eleanor's way, her mouth curled into a tiny, malicious smile. "You left the Foster's ball so early, my dear, and with no warning. As Lady Hastings said that night, it was as if you'd vanished. You and poor, dear Lady Charlotte. I do hope she's recovered?"

Ah. Even Cam, who was not versed in the myriad ways in which the ladies of the *ton* tortured each other, could see what Lady Archer was about. The *ton* hadn't excused Charlotte Sutherland's behavior the other night. Instead they would bide their time and wait with bated breath to see if the whispers would become a full-blown scandal.

Well, bless Lady Archer and her snide gossip, for she'd just done more to help his cause than Cam could have managed with either word or deed. Try as she might, Eleanor Sutherland could no longer deny to herself the danger of her sister's situation, and Julian's appearance at Charlotte Sutherland's side this morning would feed the flame nicely.

Cam turned to Lady Eleanor to see how she'd receive Lady Archer's veiled threat. Surely she'd show some consciousness of it, some awkwardness—

No. She appeared utterly composed.

She turned a smile upon Lady Archer that was bland and glacial at once. "You're such a dear to be concerned, my lady, but my sister is very well indeed. You can be certain she'll suffer *no* lasting effects at all from that evening."

Cam hid a smirk. Well. That was neatly done.

Lady Archer looked as if she couldn't understand how she'd been so thoroughly disarmed. "Wonderful news, my dear. I couldn't be more delighted to hear it."

"How kind you are, Lady Archer," Eleanor said, with the air of one who meant precisely the opposite.

Lady Archer sniffed. "Yes, well, more than one person at the ball expressed their worry for her, you know. Now," she added, turning to Cam. "Won't you introduce me to your companion?"

"Certainly. This is Mr. Camden West, Lady Archer. He's recently returned to London from India."

Lady Archer looked him up and down, not sure whether or not she need bother with him. His clothing attested to his wealth, but then London was filled with wealthy nobodies far beneath the notice of an aristocrat. He had no choice but to wait while Lady Archer made up her mind whether or not to honor him with her attention.

God, he hated the *ton*. He'd have nothing to do with them at all if it weren't for Amelia.

"Mr. West," she said at last. "What a pleasure it is to meet you. Welcome back to London. Are you related to Mr. Julian West?"

Cam bowed. "Yes, my lady. He's my cousin."

"Indeed?" Lady Archer shot Eleanor a triumphant look. "Well, I suppose you and Lady Eleanor met at the Foster's ball, then, the same night Lady Charlotte met your cousin?"

Eleanor made the tiniest movement then, a mere twitch of her fingers, and yet Cam knew at once she wished him to remain silent.

"Indeed we did." Eleanor gave Lady Archer a smooth smile. "Mr. West and his cousin were kind enough to call our carriage for us when Charlotte took ill."

Lady Archer's lips thinned into what passed for a smile among the *ton*. "Well. What a happy coincidence both Mr. Wests happened to be close at hand just at the exact moment poor, dear Lady Charlotte felt herself failing."

Lady Archer punctuated this jab with a satisfied twitch of her parasol.

Eleanor managed a faintly puzzled expression. "Hardly a coincidence, my lady. Charlotte and Mr. Julian West were dancing together at the time. Weren't they, Mr. West?"

Cam hesitated for the merest fraction of a second—just long enough for Lady Eleanor to feel the power he had over her—then he nodded. "They were. Julian was obliged to escort Lady Charlotte out to the terrace to prevent a swoon, I'm afraid."

Lady Archer's face fell, and she gathered her skirts in her hands, marshalling her forces for a retreat. "Poor, dear Lady Charlotte. But I must be off, my dear, for the roses await. Do give my regards to your mother, and of course, to your dear, dear sister." Lady Archer *tsked* and shook her head, as if Charlotte Sutherland's fall from grace were a foregone conclusion.

"I will, my lady," Eleanor said, in a tone that could freeze water. "I know my mother will be so gratified to hear you asked after Charlotte."

Lady Archer paled a bit at this, for the dowager Countess of Carlisle held a position of distinction among the *ton*, and one did their best not to make an enemy of her.

Cam's lips twisted in a bitter smile. Such was the magical influence of the Sutherlands. That influence was Amelia's due, and he would secure it for her, no matter who he had to manipulate to get it.

"Your sister teeters on the brink of scandal, my lady," he murmured after Lady Archer had flounced off down the path. "She remains safe for the moment, but one word from me . . ."

He fell silent, certain she'd finish the thought in her head.

By the time they reached the main house the lawn was crowded with guests. Ladies strolled the grounds to admire the baskets of flowers, their pale gowns fluttering in the breeze. The gentlemen followed after them and attempted to peek under their parasols, or else they balanced full plates in their laps and picnicked on blankets spread across Lady Abernathy's velvety green lawn.

A group of children shrieked and chased each other, absorbed in game of tag. They ran to and fro across the lawn, some still trailing broken bits of daisy chains. Cam searched for Amelia's fair head among the scattered children, but she wasn't there.

"Where—?" he began, but Lady Eleanor wasn't listening. She'd fixed her gaze on a distant corner of the yard, where Julian and Lady Charlotte sat together on a blanket under a shady tree, surrounded by little girls with piles of daisies in their laps. Amelia was there, her head bent over a daisy chain long enough to wrap twice around her small body. Even from here he could see the smile on her face, hear the giggles and squeals from the circle of little girls as they strung their daisies into endless white and yellow chains.

Cam's breath hitched in his throat. Amelia belonged here, lounging in the grass with a lapful of flowers, the sun warm on her head, not a care in her heart beyond the length of her daisy chain. He could buy her the grand house, the beautiful green lawn, and enough flowers for daisy chains with no end, but he couldn't buy her an afternoon like this one, spent among the children of the *ton*, secure in her place as one of them.

He couldn't buy Amelia acceptance. But he could take it. He could steal it. *An* eye for an eye.

Eleanor Sutherland's freedom for Amelia's. It was a fair trade.

"They haven't moved since we left, my lady." He stepped closer until his body touched hers, his lips a breath away from her ear. "What do you suppose they've talked about, your sister and my cousin?"

She shivered. "Don't."

He angled his head closer to catch a hint of the black current scent of her—so intoxicating, that scent, because he knew the moment he caught it that her lips would taste like that dark, tart fruit.

An answering shudder passed through him. "Such a passionate kiss they shared the other night. Do you think they've thought of nothing else today but that kiss? It must be torture, to sit so close to each other, to remember how it feels when their mouths entwine, and yet not be able to touch."

She shook her head, but didn't speak.

"Yes." His voice was harsh and husky at once. "You deny it, but you know it's true. You know, even now, with all these people watching, he's found a way to touch her. Her hand, her fingers. Both of them drown in that touch."

She didn't move, but Cam saw her dark eyelashes sweep across her cheekbones as her eyes dropped closed. "Stop."

He should stop, but he couldn't, because somehow he wasn't talking about Julian and Charlotte Sutherland anymore. In his mind it was his own mouth, hot and hard against Ellie's, taking her, drowning in her taste.

He brushed a few stray tendrils of hair away from her ear, let his fingertips linger for a heartbeat on her neck, and then his mouth was there, his lips drifting over her cool, white skin, their touch softer than a breath. "But I won't stop. Not until this is over."

She gasped and went still for a moment, but then turned her head aside to escape his caress. "If you have your way, it will never be over."

Another shudder passed through him at her words, but, God help him, instead of the regret and guilt he should feel . . .

It was a shudder of anticipation.

Chapter Ten

Crash!

Ellie leapt backwards as the hat rack toppled onto Madame Devy's spotless display counter. The straw bonnet she'd been pretending to admire slid across the slick surface and fluttered to the floor at her feet.

"My goodness, Eleanor." Charlotte turned from the array of silk ribbons the shop girl had spread across the counter. "Whatever is the matter with you?"

Eleanor gave Madame Devy's disapproving assistant an apologetic smile, retrieved the crumpled bonnet, and shoved it back onto the rack. "Matter? Why, nothing at all."

Nothing at all, except she'd spent the morning peering over her shoulder like a criminal who'd escaped the gibbet, certain any moment Camden West would clamp one of his enormous hands on the back of her neck and drag her away.

She'd ignored their agreement and stolen away from the townhouse before he could call on her.

Again.

"Do you like this color?" Charlotte held a bright blue ribbon up to her face and studied herself in the glass. "To trim my new hat, perhaps? I think the blue is flattering."

"All colors flatter you, Charlotte."

Charlotte dropped the ribbon back onto the counter. "You didn't even look!"

Eleanor didn't hear her. She'd abandoned the hat display for the large window overlooking Bond Street, so she could peek at a tall gentleman in a bottle green coat who'd just passed by.

Not him, thankfully.

Him. Dear God, whatever was she going to do?

Eleanor straightened her spine and turned her back on the window. Find a way out, that's what. After her disturbing conversation with Mr. West yesterday, she was more determined than ever to escape him, no matter what it took.

Playacting hadn't worked, and neither had logic or reason. The time had come to go on the offensive—to storm the stage, as it were. Last night, as she'd lain awake staring at the canopy above her head, she'd begun to assemble her arsenal.

Camden West hadn't told her much yesterday, but she'd listened to what he hadn't said as well as to what he had, and after a sleepless night, she'd come to two conclusions. One, he wanted this marriage far more than she'd first realized, for reasons he didn't intend to share. Two, that he *did* want the marriage so badly would be his undoing.

Eleanor clicked her tongue in mock sympathy. *Poor Mr. West.* He'd forgotten the first rule of gaming. One shouldn't play when one was desperate to win, for their opponent might choose to call their bluff when they least expected it.

This morning, she'd called his.

Risky, perhaps, to disappear again today after yesterday's warning. He wasn't the kind of man one angered on a whim. Then again, it was a calculated risk, and those who were too meek to risk their necks rarely tasted victory.

Wasn't that the second rule of gaming?

Mr. West wouldn't risk his scheme before he'd done his utmost to bring it to the desired conclusion. The *ton* would assume Charlotte was already ruined if she was seen too often in Julian West's company, and Camden West knew that as well as anyone. He was not, to Ellie's great disappointment, a fool. If Charlotte were ruined before he could drag Eleanor to the altar, there was an end to his game. Despite his threats yesterday, she was willing to wager he'd keep his cousin far away from her sister.

"You're not listening to me even *now.*" Charlotte stood with her arms crossed over her chest, glaring at Eleanor.

"I'm not in the mood for ribbons today, I suppose. Shall we go to Mr. Paterson's shop? I ordered a set of the sweetest spinning tops for baby Alec. Perhaps they're ready. It's just down the way. We can walk, and George can follow us with the carriage."

Charlotte brightened at the mention of their nephew. "Yes, all right."

They left the frowning assistant to her ribbons and stepped out onto Bond Street. Eleanor signaled to George to return to the carriage and have the driver follow along behind them.

"Charlotte, I must speak to you about something," Eleanor began as they wound their way through the crowded streets.

"About Camden West, you mean?"

Eleanor's mouth dropped open. "Camden West? Why would you ask that?"

Charlotte shrugged. "He seems to be hanging about an awful lot lately, and he looks at you like a starving man looks at a Christmas pudding."

Heat rushed to Eleanor's face. He does?

No. Of course he doesn't. How foolish. He looked at her, yes, but not with hunger—more the way a swordsman looks at his opponent right before he thrusts at a gap in their armor. "Oh, what nonsense."

"It's not nonsense. I saw it myself."

Eleanor shivered. He'd come up behind her yesterday, his large, warm body so close to hers, and whispered something, something about his cousin and Charlotte, but it wasn't his words she remembered. It was his lips, so near her ear she could feel the heat of his breath. His whisper stirred the hair near her temple, and the brush of his fingers against her neck, then his mouth, so sweet—

Damn him, and damn her for being fool enough to fall into shivering awareness when he touched her. No doubt it was all part of his grand plan to drag her down the aisle. He'd have a far easier time of it if her legs turned to a jelly.

Even if he did truly desire her, what of it? She'd see him sent to the devil before she ever agreed to marry him, and she'd do well to remember that the next time he tried to whisper in her ear or kiss her neck.

"He's courting you, isn't he?" Charlotte asked.

"Not exactly." Eleanor paused. Good God, how to put this? She was hard pressed to make it sound anything but awful. "He's not courting me so much as he's . . ."

Blackmailing me into marriage. The truth hovered on the tip of her tongue. Eleanor tried to push it over the edge, but it hung there, refusing to make the leap into words.

She tried again. "That is, he's—"

"He must intend to court you. If not, his attentions are inappropriate, and he deserves to be thrashed."

Inappropriate? Goodness. Charlotte didn't often lay claim to *that* word. Eleanor glanced uneasily at her, and saw her sister's lips had set into a familiar, stubborn line.

Oh, no.

Eleanor might not like it, but Charlotte was already a player in this little drama. She had to tell her sister *something*, yes, but not so much Charlotte got into a temper. Eleanor could handle Camden West herself, in her own way, from behind the curtain. "Well, he does want to marry me, but his manner of courtship is a trifle . . . unusual."

"Unusual? What does that mean? For goodness sake, Eleanor, will you just say it?"

Eleanor bit her lip. "Well, he might have mentioned—it's a small thing, really—but he might have said something about ruining you if I don't marry him."

Charlotte jerked to a halt in the middle of the street, her mouth falling open. "He what?"

Eleanor winced. "Either I marry him, or he'll expose your lapse in propriety on the night of the Foster's ball to the entire ton."

The people behind them on the walkway made irritated noises as they tried to push past. Eleanor grasped Charlotte's arm and tugged her back into motion. "I'd hoped to dissuade him by now, but it seems he's more determined than I first suspected."

"Dissuade him? A man with no honor, no conscience?" Charlotte's voice rose. "How could you possibly dissuade such a man?"

Eleanor squeezed Charlotte's arm to try and calm her. "Not in the usual way, but I thought he'd reconsider if I pretended to be witless. No man wants to marry a fool."

"A clever idea, but it must not have worked, or else you wouldn't *ever* have told me the truth."

Eleanor heard the accusation in her sister's voice, but she didn't have time for that argument at the moment. "It didn't work, no. It seems . . ."

I don't matter. Is that what you mean, Mr. West?

She cleared the sudden lump of panic from her throat. "It seems he cares nothing at all about me. I can be as dim-witted as I wish, and it won't make any difference. I don't matter at all to him."

Eleanor drew in a deep breath to calm the sudden crash of her heart against her ribs.

All those suitors, all rejected, several of them decent, kind men she'd refused for no other reason than she simply didn't love them. All those suitors, and even the worst among them hadn't erased her as if she didn't exist.

She'd only ever known one man who did. Her father. Hart Sutherland, the handsome aristocrat, the perfect nobleman, every inch the hero, until one looked closely and discovered the villain underneath.

Her father had behaved as if his wife were invisible until, after decades of such treatment, she was. As the years passed, her mother became more and more transparent. Her slippers ceased to make any sound on the marble floors. Her silk skirts didn't rustle, and her voice never rose above a whisper. Her movements were so silent it was as if she weren't there at all.

She became a ghost. Haunting. Haunted.

Her father hadn't been any more interested in his children than he was in his wife, except for Alec, the heir, with whom he'd been brutal. But Eleanor and Charlotte? His daughters hadn't mattered. They didn't exist. They were ghosts.

"But, but . . ." Charlotte was so aghast she could hardly speak. "But if he cares nothing for you, then why does he want to marry you at all?"

Eleanor shook her head. "That's what I don't understand. He won't say, and I can't deter him from this mad scheme unless I know his reasons."

"Not your fortune, then?" Charlotte pressed. "Not social gain?"

"Not money. He's wealthy. He doesn't need my fortune, and he claims it's not my social connections, either, but I do think it has something to do with the Sutherlands. Indeed, he admitted as much."

Charlotte fell silent, her teeth worrying her lower lip. "Julian West. He must know what his cousin is up to, mustn't he?"

Eleanor glanced at her sister from the corner of her eye, opened her mouth to answer, but then closed it again without speaking a word.

Julian West knows. He must.

Camden West knew everything about her. He knew she'd rejected numerous suitors. He knew about Lord Tidmarsh, who'd never even made an offer, and he knew better than to bring his proposals to Alec. He'd watched her for weeks before he made his approach. It was beyond comprehension the incident at the Foster's ball could be a coincidence.

Of course Julian West knew. How could he not?

Yet she looked her sister in the eye, gritted her teeth, and lied. "No, I don't think he does. Camden West as much as admitted to me he simply saw an opportunity and seized it. His cousin doesn't know what he's up to."

"Do you really think so?"

Eleanor's heart lurched in her chest at her sister's hopeful expression, but she pasted a bright smile on her face. It was better this way—better if

Charlotte didn't know. She wouldn't take it quietly if she found out Julian West had intentionally compromised her.

No, it wouldn't do. She couldn't have Charlotte interfering in this. She needed all her wits to deal with Camden West, and she couldn't protect her sister at the same time. It was far better to let Charlotte's little flirtation burn itself out. Julian West was a rake, after all—an innocent like Charlotte wouldn't hold his attention for long. He'd grow bored, and Charlotte would soon forget him. Perhaps she'd come out of the scrape a bit wiser, and ready to look with more favor on a proper gentleman—someone like the Marquess of Hadley, for instance.

Eleanor cleared her throat. "He doesn't behave as if he knows, does he? He's been nothing but a perfect gentleman since the Foster's ball."

"Perhaps you're right. He doesn't act as if he knows."

Eleanor breathed a sigh of relief.

They walked on in silence until they reached Mr. Paterson's shop. Eleanor put her hand on the door to go in, but Charlotte stopped her. "Does mother know about this?"

Eleanor let the door close. "No, and you mustn't tell her."

Charlotte shook her head. "I don't like to keep secrets from mother. If she knew, she might be able to—"

"If she knew," Ellie interrupted, "She'd feel obligated to tell Alec, and how do you suppose he'll react? He'll challenge one of the Wests, and then Robyn will find out, and he'll challenge the other."

"Dear God." Charlotte paled. "You're right. That's just what would happen."

The bell above the door of the shop rang merrily as Eleanor pushed it open and stepped across the threshold. "Mother mustn't find out."

Charlotte didn't follow. "But I don't see that we have any other choice."

The shop bell tinkled a pitiful protest as Eleanor let the door slam closed and stepped back onto the walkway. "Of course we have a choice."

Charlotte considered this. "We'll let Camden West ruin me. He's got you at his mercy, Eleanor, and since this entire disaster is my fault, I will be the one to suffer for it."

Eleanor grabbed Charlotte's hand. "It's *not* your fault. It's Camden West's fault, and don't you forget it. I won't have you suffer for his despicable behavior."

"I went out into the garden alone with Julian West. I let him kiss me—"

"So you deserve to be punished for the rest of your life for one foolish decision? No, Charlotte. I won't hear of it."

She might not understand Charlotte's recklessness. She might not approve of Charlotte's behavior at the Foster's ball, but there'd never been any question she'd defend her, with teeth bared and fingernails curled into claws, if necessary.

Charlotte was her sister, and one didn't turn their back on their sister.

"But you'll agree to be punished yourself? Dear God, I'd rather be ruined than see you married to such a man, Eleanor. I couldn't bear to watch it."

"Oh, don't worry." Eleanor dismissed this with a carelessness she didn't quite feel. "I have no intention of marrying Camden West."

Charlotte stared at her. "I don't see how you'll get around it, unless he ruins me."

"I'll find a way. Have you ever known me to do anything I don't wish to do?"

To Eleanor's surprise, a sudden smile lit Charlotte's face. "I don't think Camden West has any idea what he's gotten himself into. If anyone can find a way out of such a tangle, it's you, Eleanor."

Too right. She'd leave Camden West hanging by his neck from his own rope.

She squeezed her sister's hand. "Thank you. Now, shall we go inside and put Mr. Paterson out of his misery? He's been staring out the window at us since his bell rang, no doubt salivating at the thought of two doting aunts entering his toy shop."

She pulled open the door and entered, much to Mr. Paterson's delight.

"Ah, Lady Eleanor, and Lady Charlotte. Such a pleasure to see you both. Have you come about the spinning tops for the young lord? They're ready. I'll just fetch them for you."

"Thank you, Mr. Paterson."

The beaming shopkeeper scurried off to the back room, leaving Eleanor and Charlotte to wander the shop.

"Oh, look, Eleanor. Aren't these sweet?"

Eleanor walked over to a far corner and found Charlotte standing over a shelf with a display of brightly painted wooden horses. "They are, yes. Our nephew would love this one."

She reached out to stroke a pale blue rocking horse with a long, curling black mane and tail. The horse was fitted with a tiny golden bridle and saddle. The slight pressure of her hand on the horse's nose sent it swaying back and forth.

They watched it rock for a while. Neither of them spoke as the horse slowed and then stopped moving altogether.

"Do you ever think about having children, Eleanor?"

Eleanor froze for a moment, then tapped the horse's nose again to set the toy back in motion.

Their nephew had a special smile for his parents. Every time Delia or Alec came into a room, even if they'd only been gone for a moment, that smile would light up his face. Oh, the child had a similar worshipful smile for her, and for each of the adoring adults who orbited around him, but the smile he gave his parents was different, somehow.

"Yes."

She didn't say anything more, but that one word held a world of longing, and Charlotte heard it. "Forgive me, Eleanor, but all those suitors . . . why didn't you accept one of them? You might have a child of your own by now if you had."

"Yes, I suppose I could." But then she'd have a husband, too—a husband she didn't love, who didn't love her. Wasn't it better, if she could have only a pale imitation of the thing she longed for, to have nothing at all?

She hesitated, but she hated having secrets from Charlotte. "I don't know that I'll ever marry. I may have to content myself with spoiling your children, so see that you have a great many of them, won't you? There's a dear."

Charlotte wasn't fooled by Eleanor's light tone. "Not marry? But how can you say so, when you see how happy our brothers are with Delia and Lily? Marriage has changed them both, and for the better. Why, in Robyn's case I'd even go so far as to say Lily saved him—"

Eleanor laid a hand on Charlotte's arm to quiet her. "They have the best of marriages, yes, but their unions are the exception. Do you think I'd find similar happiness with Mr. Fitzsimmons? Or Lord Tidmarsh?"

"Perhaps not either of them, no, but there are other gentlemen equal to our brothers. London is a big city, after all. You give up too soon, Eleanor."

Was that what she had done? Had she given up?

"If a gentleman happens along and I find myself hopelessly in love with him, I don't say I won't listen to his proposals, but sometimes I think . . ." Eleanor's breath caught painfully in her chest. "I wonder if such a gentleman will ever appear."

"He will, Eleanor." Charlotte squeezed her arm. "He'll be the last gentlemen you'd ever expect, and he'll appear when you least expect it. You just need to be patient."

Eleanor reached out to touch the horse's nose again, but her hand was shaking, and she stuffed it hastily into her pocket before Charlotte could notice. "I suppose, but you can't go on forever, can you? At some point, no matter how much you might wish otherwise . . ." She nodded at the rocking horse, "you come to a stop."

"Ah, but if you do stop," Charlotte said, with a mischievous smile, "All it takes is the right hand to set you in motion again."

Eleanor forced a laugh. "And if the only hand on offer is Lord Ponsonby's, or—"

"Someone like Camden West? I don't wonder you're skeptical of marriage if you believe he's the best London has to offer."

No. Someone like our father.

Hart Sutherland had ignored her. He'd ignored Charlotte. They hadn't mattered at all to him, and yet as bad as that had been, she'd known from quite a young age she and Charlotte had the better end of the bargain.

Alec and Robyn . . . they'd had a special look for *their* father, too, but it hadn't been the look of smiling delight her nephew gave Alec. If baby Alec's look was the sun itself, Alec's and Robyn's look for Hart Sutherland had been the deepest, darkest night.

And Camden West? Despite his reprehensible actions toward her, she didn't sense cruelty in him, but he'd said himself she didn't matter one way or the other to him. Why should she expect her children to matter to him, either? No. The best she could hope for from him was a father who ignored his children, as her own father had done.

It wasn't good enough.

Charlotte lifted the pale blue rocking horse from the display and cradled it in her palm. "I'm going to buy this."

"How nice. Our nephew will love it."

Charlotte shook her head. "I'm sure he would, but it's not for him. It's for you."

"Me?" Eleanor gave a startled laugh. "Whatever for?"

Charlotte tucked the horse against her bodice and marched up to the counter. "To remind you," she tossed back at Eleanor over her shoulder.

"Remind me of what?"

"Not to give up."

Chapter Eleven

"Denny!"

Cam was about to disappear into his study when Amelia came charging from the upper staircase onto the first floor landing.

"What is it, minx? Are you ready to show me your drawings?"

He'd gone into the schoolroom before breakfast this morning, as was his habit, to visit Amelia before she began her lessons. He'd found her huddled over a sheaf of drawing paper, hard at work with her pencil, but she'd sent him away without a peek.

Amelia raced down the remaining stairs and landed with a thump in the entryway. "I finished the drawings, and Miss Norwood says we might color them with pastels after luncheon."

"Did she?" Cam smiled at Miss Norwood, who'd followed her charge down the stairs. The older woman had been Amelia's governess for years, and she'd grown so fond of the child she'd readily agreed to come from Lindenhurst with her when Cam settled in London.

Miss Norwood gave Amelia an indulgent nod. "Oh, yes, indeed. Very fine drawings, Mr. West. I think you'll be pleased at her progress with her pencils."

"I'm sure I will be. Why don't you have a walk, Miss Norwood, or some tea? I'll sit with Amelia for a while."

Amelia grasped Cam's hand and tugged him toward his study. "In here, Denny. This is where you do all your important work."

Cam allowed himself to be dragged to his desk. "Yes, and the study of art is important work. What have you to show me?" He seated himself behind the desk, pushed aside the papers to clear a space for the drawings, and held out his arms.

Aunt Mary scolded him for letting such a big girl as Amelia sit on his lap, and even Miss Norwood looked askance at him, but Cam ignored them. He'd missed his chance to hold his sister on his lap when she was the proper age for it, so he'd do it now.

Amelia climbed up and placed her first drawing in the center of the desk. "See? This is from yesterday, when we were at Lady Abernathy's garden. This is a still life, you know."

Cam grinned at Amelia's lofty tone, but kept his response serious. "Yes. I see. A close drawing of a daisy, I believe, and you've distinguished each petal from the others."

Amelia tilted her head to the side to study the drawing. "I have, haven't I?"

Cam tweaked one of her braids. "Yes. Are the others as nice as this one?"

"I think so, rather." Amelia placed the second drawing on top of the first. "This is another still life, of a whole daisy chain."

Cam lifted the sheet from the desk to study it more closely. She'd painstakingly drawn each separate flower, and even added a fine crosshatch texture to the yellow centers of the blooms. "Remarkable, especially the shading, Amelia."

Amelia grinned with pleasure over his praise, then took the drawing from his hands, lay it back on the desk, and placed the third drawing on top of it. "This is a landscape of Lady Abernathy's garden. I'm afraid I'll use up my green pastel coloring it."

Cam studied the third picture. By God, no other eleven-year-old child had ever drawn so well, he was sure. He'd have to buy her more sophisticated art supplies. "Lady Abernathy does have a great deal of green lawn, but no matter. We'll get you another green pastel. Or a box of green pastels."

"Oh, thank you, Denny. I need a great deal of green for the last two pictures, too, for I've included a lot of trees, even though they're portraits."

Amelia turned over the fourth sheet and Cam gave a shout of laughter. "Is that Uncle Julian?"

She giggled. "Yes, and I didn't make up that expression on his face. He looked just like that, Denny."

The fourth drawing was of Julian, frowning as he forced a daisy onto a bit of string. His brows were drawn together into a look of frustrated concentration as he tried to manipulate the delicate flower with his large hands. The poor bloom looked a bit crushed, as did the three or four forlorn daisies already on the string.

"I brought Uncle Julian's daisy chain home with me yesterday and tried to revive it with a bit of water." Amelia shook her head. "But he'd flattened most of his daisies by the time he got them on the string, and they all died."

"It's a lucky thing you drew them while they were still alive, then. Well," Cam amended with a chuckle, "Mostly alive. For posterity, that is. Daisy chains are not, it seems, one of Uncle Julian's many talents."

Julian himself stuck his head around the study door then. "I believe I heard my name, followed by shouts of laughter. I'm here to defend myself."

"Come see my drawings, Uncle Julian." Amelia beckoned her uncle across the room. "I did one of you."

"And there's no defense for it," Cam said with a smirk.

Julian crossed to the desk, picked up Amelia's drawing, and stared at it for a moment before he comically crossed his eyes. "I don't look like that!"

Amelia giggled. "You did yesterday. Didn't he, Denny?"

"I didn't see him hard at work on his daisy chains, minx, but I'll say this—your other drawings have all been amazingly accurate. Even so, this one of your uncle is my favorite."

Julian dropped into his chair in front of the desk. "A scandalous libel, that's what this is."

"You haven't seen them all yet." Amelia placed the last drawing on top of the one she'd done of Julian.

Cam leaned forward to get a better look, then froze.

Amelia had done a drawing of Eleanor Sutherland.

It was a close-up drawing of the lady, although enough of her upper body was visible to see she was bent forward at the waist, in the way of an adult when they lean down to speak to a child. Her head was cocked just a bit to one side, and her lips were parted in a half-smile. A few strands of her rich, dark hair floated around her face. Amelia had taken a great deal of care with the drawing, and she'd captured Eleanor's lush beauty.

But that wasn't what caught and held Cam's attention. It was the eyes. Did Eleanor Sutherland's eyes really have that soft warmth?

"Don't you like it, Denny?"

Amelia's impatient voice reminded Cam he hadn't said a word yet. "I—I do like it."

"Let me see it." Julian held out his hand and Amelia passed him the drawing. He studied it for a moment, then handed it back across the desk. Not to Amelia. To Cam. "What a fine likeness. I think your brother likes it very much, Amelia. It's his new favorite, I'd wager."

Amelia clapped her hands together. "Oh, it's mine, too! It took me ever so long to get it right, especially her eyes, because they're so dark, but not at all flat like some dark eyes are. What's her first name again?"

Cam cleared his throat. "Eleanor."

"Lady Eleanor Sutherland." Amelia tried the name out. "It's a pretty name."

"For a pretty lady," Julian put in. "Do you think her pretty, Amelia?"

"Oh, yes. Pretty, and so kind. Funny, too. She made a joke about the cakes. Do you think she's pretty, Denny?"

Cam looked at Julian, then back down at the picture of Ellie he held in his hand. "Yes."

Just then Miss Norwood appeared at the door. "It's time for your mathematics lesson, Amelia."

Cam gathered the drawings in one hand and lifted Amelia off his lap. "Off you go, minx. Thank you for sharing these with me." He held out the sheaf of drawings to her.

"Why not leave the one of Lady Eleanor for your brother, Amelia?" Julian asked. "I can tell he admires it."

"All right." Amelia took the other four drawings. "I was going to color them all, but I think Lady Eleanor is perfect just as she is."

"I hate to sound prophetic," Julian drawled as Amelia left, her hand in Miss Norwood's. "But the phrase 'out of the mouths of babes' comes to mind."

Cam took another long look at the drawing, then placed it in the middle of his desk, rose, and turned to stare out the window. "Perfect? Hardly. Lady Eleanor is stubborn, argumentative, and in her worst moments, ice wouldn't melt on her tongue."

"Heavy faults, indeed." Julian stretched his long legs out in front of him. "Why the foolish woman can't simply succumb to your threats and blackmail, I can't imagine."

Cam ignored this. "She's not . . . she's not what I expected. I'll grant you that much."

"No?" Cam didn't turn around, but he heard a faint shuffle of papers, as if Julian had dragged the drawing back toward him across the desk. "What did you expect?"

For reasons he didn't care to probe, Cam had to restrain himself from snatching the drawing away from his cousin. "The usual insipid society belle. Dull. Frivolous. Selfish. Whatever else she may be, Eleanor Sutherland isn't that."

He turned back around in time to see Julian shrug. "You've only known her a few days. Maybe she is all of those things, and you just don't know it yet."

Cam shook his head. "No. She was kind to Amelia at Lady Abernathy's party yesterday. She didn't have to be."

Julian snorted. "That's hardly an accurate measure of her character. Who could be anything but kind to Amelia?"

Cam raised an eyebrow. "Playing devil's advocate again, are you, cousin? I thought you'd be delighted to hear I'm reconsidering my approach to this problem."

Julian straightened from his slouch. "There *is* no problem, except the one you've created, Cam. As I said the other day, it's not too late to change your mind, but at some point soon it will be. Best to end this now, while you still can."

"End it? Christ, Julian. It's your voice that echoes in my head whenever my conscience berates me."

Julian smiled. "I consider that a compliment."

"I'm sure you do. Nevertheless, I have no intention of ending it, especially now I've seen how kind Eleanor Sutherland can be. You heard Amelia just now. She likes the lady."

Julian's smile faded. "Someone should warn Lady Eleanor her kindness isn't about to be rewarded. You sound as if you're saying, Cam, that her goodness somehow justifies your cruelty to her."

Cam gaped at him. *Cruelty?* Surely it wasn't as bad as that?

Clever or foolish, warm or cold, rich or poor. None if it matters. I don't matter.

Her face had shut down when she'd said it, as if someone had yanked closed a curtain in a room filled with light. She'd insisted she wasn't anyone special, and he'd let her believe he thought so, too. He'd let her think the only thing that mattered about her was the name Sutherland.

Wasn't it true, though? Wasn't it the only thing that mattered to him?

God, he didn't know anymore. He knew only that everything about those moments with her had felt wrong. *He'd* felt wrong, as if he wore someone else's skin. Someone he thought he recognized, but didn't.

"Cam?" Julian watched him, a puzzled yet hopeful look on his face.

"I'm on my way over to the Sutherlands now, to call on her. I *will* marry her, but I could perhaps be . . . kinder about it all."

"Kinder about your blackmail? Good of you, cousin."

"Damn it, Julian. Not blackmail, but perhaps some kind of an agreement."

"You expect her to negotiate with you on this?"

"She'll have me either way, so she may as well negotiate. What is a *ton* marriage, if not negotiation? You forget she'd be going through a similar process with whoever she chose to marry."

Julian rolled his eyes. "So you keep telling me. Still, you're moving in the right direction with this. I can at least see a glimpse of the cousin I know, hidden in there somewhere."

Cam plucked his coat off the back of his chair and thrust his arms into it. "What does that mean?"

"That you shouldn't forget who you are." Julian picked up Amelia's drawing of Lady Eleanor. He folded it in half and held it out to Cam. "Here. Take it. Perhaps it will help you remember."

To Cam's surprise, he saw his own hand reach out, take the drawing, and tuck it into his coat pocket.

* * * * *

"Not at home?" Cam stared at Lady Catherine.

"I'm afraid not. She and Charlotte went off to Bond Street to pick up some toy or other for my grandson." Lady Catherine smiled. "I'm afraid they spoil him. But you'll stay and have tea, won't you, Mr. West?"

He'd arrived on the Sutherland's doorstep ten minutes ago, but Eleanor Sutherland wasn't waiting for him in the drawing room. Instead he'd found the dowager countess entertaining two young ladies who'd also come to call—a Miss Darlington and a Miss Thurston. He hadn't met either of them before, but both sat up with interest when he entered the room.

Eleanor Sutherland had slipped through his fingers. Again.

Damnable woman.

She couldn't deny Lady Charlotte was in a precarious position, not after the encounter with Lady Archer yesterday, and yet still she chose to toy with him. Did she believe he wouldn't go through with his threats?

No. Even if she doubted him, she wouldn't be foolish enough to wager her sister's reputation on a guess. Lady Eleanor was many things, but she wasn't a fool. She may well be a mind-reader, though, for no sooner had he made up his mind to be kinder to her than she managed to infuriate him all over again. He could almost believe she did it on purpose, to knock him off balance.

His jaw tightened. He didn't *get* knocked off balance, damn it, and he didn't let his fury get the best of him, but one week in Eleanor Sutherland's company, and he felt like a turtle tipped onto its back, legs flailing madly to right itself.

Worse, he wasn't simply furious. No, there was something else there, as well—something uncomfortable. It felt suspiciously like . . . relief. To find the draperies drawn back and the room alight again. To find the darkness had only been temporary.

He was a bloody fool.

"Mr. West?" Lady Catherine was still waiting for his answer. "Can I tempt you with tea?"

He couldn't refuse, now he was here. "Yes, of course. Thank you."

"How do you do, Mr. West?" cooed Miss Darlington, once Lady Catherine had made the introductions. "Why haven't we met you before?"

Cam took a seat on the settee. "I've just returned to London from an eleven-year stay in India."

"India!" Miss Thurston shrieked, as if they were in a crowded ballroom instead of a quiet drawing room. "How exciting. Whatever were you doing there?"

Cam placed his teacup in the saucer, afraid Miss Thurston's shrill tone night shatter it. "Working for the East India Company."

Silence. Miss Darlington and Miss Thurston visibly deflated.

Jesus. One would think 'work' were a filthy word, and he'd committed an unpardonable *faux pas* by mentioning it in the presence of ladies.

Lady Catherine hastened to cover the awkward silence. "Mr. West just became the newest principal patron of the Society for the Relief of London's Poor & Indigent."

"Indeed?" The young ladies swelled with hope again.

If he *must* work, the least he could do was become staggeringly wealthy, he supposed, to offset the shame of it. The more money one had, the less fussy the *ton* was about how they got it.

He studied the young ladies. They put him in mind of two mosquitos, bursting with a surfeit of blood. They were just the sort of women he'd expected Eleanor Sutherland to be, and it would be far easier if she was, for either one of these two detestable females would accept his suit readily enough.

That Lady Eleanor had turned out to be someone else entirely was either a tremendous stroke of luck, or a disaster. He hadn't yet made up his mind which.

"I beg your pardon, Mr. West." Lady Catherine darted a glance at Cam. "I think you said yesterday you prefer to be a silent patron—"

The sound of voices in the hallway interrupted Lady Catherine's apology, and after a moment, Eleanor and Charlotte Sutherland entered the drawing room.

"Ah, my dears," Lady Catherine said. "Here you are. See who's come to call. Miss Darlington and Miss Thurston, and Mr. West."

Cam stood and bowed to the ladies.

Eleanor Sutherland eyed him, her expression resigned. "Ah. Of course. Mr. West." She dipped into a curtsy. "Miss Darlington, Miss Thurston. Such a pleasure."

Lady Charlotte wasn't as circumspect as her sister. She looked at Cam as if she wished she'd thought to bring a pistol into the drawing room, and she didn't look any better pleased to see Miss Darlington and Miss Thurston.

"Well, Lady Charlotte," Miss Darlington began when they were all seated. "I hear you were taken mysteriously ill at Lady Foster's ball the other night. I trust you are recovered?"

Charlotte gave her a thin smile. "As you can see."

"I confess I'm surprised to see you so looking so well," Miss Thurston said. "Why, it's difficult to believe you were so *very* ill mere days ago."

Lady Eleanor sipped her tea. "Boar's milk."

Miss Thurston gave her a blank look, then glanced at Miss Darlington, who shrugged. "I beg your pardon?"

"Boar's milk. Haven't you heard, Miss Thurston? The latest cure. My sister has been drinking it all week, and as you can see, she's in the pink of health."

"I—boar's milk? Well, I had no idea."

"No. I didn't suppose you had. It does wonders for the complexion, too. You should try it."

Boar's milk? Was there even such a thing as boar's milk? Cam imagined Miss Thurston scouring every apothecary's shop in London for boar's milk, and stifled a laugh.

"Did you hear about Miss Abbott?" asked Miss Darlington, who seemed to think a change of topic was in order.

"I don't believe I know Miss Abbot," Charlotte said.

Miss Thurston tittered. "She's no one special, and not likely to attract the notice of the ton."

"Well, what of her, then?" Lady Eleanor asked, with barely concealed impatience.

"She and her sponsor, Mrs. Bridewell, have appealed to the patronesses of Almack's for a voucher."

Both Miss Thurston and Miss Darlington burst into malicious laugher at this announcement, but none of the three Sutherland ladies seemed to find the information amusing. They sipped their tea, their expressions unreadable.

"Can you imagine?" Miss Thurston continued. "The effrontery of them both, to think Miss Abbott, of all people, should have a voucher."

"Shocking," Lady Eleanor said after a moment.

Did she think it was shocking? Cam studied her, but her face revealed little. He thought he saw a faint look of disgust twist her lips, but he couldn't determine if the look was for Miss Darlington and Miss Thurston, or for Miss Abbott.

It stood to reason it was for Miss Abbott, who'd dared to get so far above herself. Lady Eleanor was clever, even kind, but she was *ton*, too. She might not be quite the despicable snob Miss Thurston and Miss Darlington were, but would she side with the common Miss Abbott?

What were the chances she'd side with Amelia? His sister was bright and funny, but that wouldn't matter to people like Miss Thurston and Miss Darlington, who would always see her as beneath them.

What of Eleanor Sutherland? Something she'd said the other day came back to him then, something about marrying beneath herself . . .

He gripped the handle of his teacup until the fine porcelain threatened to turn to powder between his fingers. If he could judge by the trail of disappointed suitors she left in her wake, every gentleman in London was beneath her—

". . . thank you for your visit," Lady Catherine was saying.

Cam looked up to find Miss Darlington and Miss Thurston taking their leave. He rose to his feet, bowed politely to one loathsome female, then the other, and privately wished them both to the devil.

As soon as the drawing room door closed behind them, Cam bowed to Lady Catherine. "Thank you for the tea. I must take my leave, as well."

"Oh, Mr. West," Lady Catherine said. "I want to invite you for supper tonight, as a thank you for your donation to the Society, and also for being so kind to Eleanor and Charlotte at the Foster's ball. I know this is last minute, but do say you'll come. My sons and their families will dine with us, and I know they'd enjoy meeting you."

Cam tried to hide his surprise. He hadn't expected such gracious attention from Lady Catherine, and he was tempted to accept. Mention of her sons made him hesitate, however. Lord Carlisle and Robert Sutherland were reputed to be protective of their sisters, and Cam didn't want to deal with any rabid watchdogs just yet.

He glanced over at Lady Eleanor, who looked as if she'd like to slap a hand over her mother's mouth to silence her. Did the lady hope he'd decline? Ah, well. He'd have to come, then, watchdog be damned. She couldn't have her own way every time. It wasn't good for her.

He grinned at her, then turned back to Lady Catherine. "I'd be delighted, my lady. Thank you."

"Wonderful." Lady Catherine smiled. "Seven o'clock?"

Cam couldn't resist a triumphant glance at Eleanor. "Of course. Nothing would please me more. Now, I must be off, but may I beg Lady Eleanor's indulgence for one moment on my way out?"

Lady Catherine waved her daughter toward the door. "Yes, go on, Eleanor. We shall see you tonight, Mr. West."

Cam bowed again, then offered Eleanor his arm and led her from the room.

"You see, Lady Eleanor?" he murmured, as soon as they were alone. "No bad deed goes unpunished. You may have avoided me today, but now you'll be cursed with my company for an entire evening."

"Avoided you?" She looked down at the place where her hand rested on his arm. "I'm in your company even now, Mr. West."

Cam tried not think about the warm pressure of her fingers on his coat. "We had an agreement. You will make yourself available to me, or I'll make my cousin available to Lady Charlotte."

"No. You won't."

He stopped in the deserted hallway between the drawing room and the entryway, anger rising at this casual dismissal. "We're not discussing some nonsense about a voucher to Almack's, my lady. I mean what I say."

She glanced toward the entryway, then lowered her voice. "If Charlotte is seen too often in your cousin's company, Mr. West, her fate will be sealed. The *ton* already believes her guilty. They seek only the flimsiest corroboration of it. I'm certain you don't wish to provide them with it. However will you get me down the aisle if you do?"

As quickly as Cam's anger had come upon him it drained away, replaced by a grudging admiration. "Ah. So clever, my lady. But if the worst should happen, and the *ton* does put Lady Charlotte on trial, only Julian and I can ensure she isn't convicted."

"Indispensable, are you?" She spoke defiantly, but she bit her lower lip as if worried.

Cam's gaze darted to her lips and wet warmth filled his mouth, as if he'd tasted something succulent. Sweet.

Black currants.

He took in the flush of color high on her cheekbones, her expressive dark eyes. "Amelia is right about your eyes." He tipped her face up to his with a finger under her chin. "So dark, but not flat. Far from it. Bottomless."

He smiled a little as those lovely widened in astonishment. Whatever she'd expected him to say, it wasn't that. If she knew what he was thinking . . .

Tell her.

"Your mouth makes me think of dark, ripe fruit." He touched one fingertip to her luscious bottom lip and desire shot through him, so fierce it roughened his voice, stole his breath. "Do you taste sweet, my lady?"

He let his fingertips drift over the back of her hand, over the delicate blue veins and the fine bones of her knuckles, her skin so soft under his stroking fingers. She caught her breath as he turned her hand over and traced tiny circles in the center of her palm with the pad of his thumb.

His eyes met hers for a brief moment, then his gaze dropped back to their hands. He stared, mesmerized by the sight of his fingers caressing her. His hand looked too large, too rough, too dark, to touch such fine white skin.

He raised her hand to his mouth and pressed his lips to her palm. "Shall I taste you?"

Not a kiss, only the suggestion of one, the touch so light, so fleeting, over before he could be sure it had begun, but enough, just enough of a taste . . .

"Yes," he whispered. "Sweet."

She gasped when he lowered his head again and the tip of his tongue grazed her palm. He opened his lips to nip at her there, and her gasp turned to a sigh, a moan.

Cam's knees went weak at the sound. Need pounded through him, making his head swim. Madness, to kiss and touch her with her mother and sister just steps away, but he couldn't make it matter. Nothing mattered now but her taste, the sighs and moans he'd wrung from her.

"Ah, Ellie . . ." He dragged the sleeve of her gown away from her wrist and pressed his open mouth to that white, tender flesh. He sealed his lips over her pulse point, felt it surge and flutter against his darting tongue.

He jerked the sleeve higher so he could kiss her arm, devour the delicious skin at the inside of her elbow. In some foggy part of his brain he knew he'd lost control, but he couldn't stop . . .

She gave a soft cry and trembled in his arms.

God, what was he doing? He'd gone mad.

He tore his mouth away from her. He waited for his ragged breathing to calm, then slowly, gently, he eased the sleeve of her gown back down her arm and smoothed it over her wrist.

He met her gaze. Her eyes were half-closed, her mouth soft, open.

"I believe I've shocked you speechless," he murmured. "I didn't think it was possible."

It wasn't what he meant to say, but he didn't know how to tell her it was he who was shocked, he who was speechless.

She didn't answer, but stared at him with wide eyes.

Cam bowed. "Until tonight, my lady."

He left her alone in the hallway, staring after him.

Chapter Twelve

"What's the matter, my lady?" Camden West studied her over the edge of his wineglass. "Don't you care for trifle?"

Eleanor lowered her spoon and placed it next to her untasted dish of trifle. The pudding wasn't the problem. No, the problem sat across the table from her, eating strawberries and cream with every appearance of enjoyment, as if the incident this afternoon had never happened.

The afternoon hadn't gone at all how she'd planned, and she'd begun to despair of the evening, as well. For one, Mr. West should be buried at the other end of the table, far away from her, but her family didn't bother with proper dining etiquette among friends, and this evening they'd paired off and wandered into dinner with their usual disregard for rank.

And she'd ended up across the table from him.

She couldn't imagine what had possessed her mother to invite him, but short of tackling Lady Catherine to the drawing room floor, there'd been no way for Eleanor to stop it.

"You hardly ate any dinner."

Eleanor brought her attention back to her dinner companion, who nodded at her overflowing dish. "I fear for your health, my lady. Even the sweets can't tempt you?"

Hadn't she been tempted enough for one day?

She scowled at him as he scooped up another bite of trifle with his spoon. "I find my appetite has quite deserted me this evening, and I don't care for trifle, in any case."

"Too sweet?" He gave her a diabolical smile. "But that's what makes it so irresistible—the sweet, thick cream with the ripe, red fruit. You should have some. It'll sweeten your temper." He brought a spoonful of strawberries awash in cream to his mouth.

Under cover of the table, Eleanor crushed her napkin between her fingers. He kept using the word *sweet*, and she was certain it wasn't a coincidence.

Do you taste sweet, my lady?

"You'll need all the strength you can muster over the next week or so," he added.

Eleanor frowned. For the battle ahead, she supposed he meant. The battle with *him*. The battle she was, by every measure in which a battle could be judged, losing.

"It's delicious, you know." He closed his lips around the spoon and his eyelids dropped shut as he savored the sweet.

*Don't w*atch his mouth.

It was the fourth time since the soup course she'd had to remind herself not to stare at his lips. Confound the man. Did he have to look as if he experienced sensual delight with every bite? He even made the glazed carrots look enticing.

Eleanor dropped her gaze to her plate and tried not to think about cream and strawberries, sweet and slippery on his tongue. Tried not to think about his tongue at all, or anything else to do with his mouth. How unfair it that was such a detestable man should have such intriguing lips.

*And such a rav*enous appetite.

She poked at a strawberry with the tip of her spoon. It slid off the mountain of cream and landed on her plate with a wet plop. Not that *she* found his lips in any way distracting, of course. No, certainly not. Other ladies might sigh over those full lips. Other ladies might admire those sleepy green eyes, broad shoulders, and that long lock of wavy chestnut hair that fell across his forehead. They might think he was boyishly charming, but she knew better. She knew what a perfidious fiend lurked beneath all that smooth, tawny skin.

Still, in the purely objective sense of the word, Mr. West was handsome. *Damn him.*

Alec touched his napkin to his lips, and placed the cloth next to his plate. "So. West. My sister tells me you're in shipping."

Eleanor looked up from her plate with renewed hope. This was a bit better, at least. Alec could be rather terrifying when he chose, especially if he thought a gentleman might be courting his sister. Perhaps he'd scare Mr. West away. At the very least, it would amuse Eleanor to watch her brother squeeze Camden West until trifle came out of his handsome ears.

Mr. West gave Alec a cool look. "Yes. That's right." He said no more, but fixed an oddly defiant gaze on Alec.

How curious. Did he think Alec would look down on him because he was in trade?

Eleanor shifted uncomfortably in her seat. Camden West, vulnerable? No, she didn't care for that idea. It made him too human. She'd rather imagine his body covered in impenetrable scales or hard plates—then she needn't worry about flinging barbs at him.

Not that she imagined his body at all, of course.

"How did you get into that line?" Alec asked. "Given your success now, you can't have been very old when you started."

Mr. West shrugged. "No. I was just thirteen when a friend of my father's took me on as an apprentice. He ran goods between India and England, and eventually became a shareholder in the East India Company."

Delia, who sat to Alec's right, exclaimed at this. "Thirteen! My goodness. You don't mean to say you went to India at age thirteen?"

Thirteen? Eleanor sat up straighter in her chair, curious despite herself to hear Mr. West's answer. Why, at thirteen he'd have been no more than a boy.

"No, not so young as that, Lady Carlisle, though I was as foolish and headstrong as a thirteen-year-old boy when I did make my first overseas voyage."

"When was that?" Eleanor asked, then wanted to bite her tongue out. Now he'd think she was interested in his answer. Well, she wasn't. Not at all. She focused her gaze on her trifle, just in case some trick of the light made it look as if she were.

He stared at her, as if surprised she'd asked.

He couldn't be more surprised than she was. Why should she care how old he'd been? She didn't want to hear the man's life story, for pity's sake. She wouldn't know him long enough for it to make any difference to her.

"I sailed to India when I was seventeen," he said. "My employer had a large family and didn't care to be away from England for such a long time himself, so he sent me in his stead to secure his interests abroad and expand his shares in the Company."

Eleanor looked around the table to see everyone leaning forward, their trifle forgotten, their attention fixed on Mr. West. She snatched up her spoon and began to dish trifle into her mouth, though each bite tasted like soggy bits of paper. Fine. She'd rather swallow tasteless mush than admit anything about Mr. West's story interested *her.* She refused to allow him to be both handsome and entertaining.

"By God, that's a lot of responsibility for such a young man." There was no mistaking the awe in Robyn's voice, or the look of admiration he gave Mr. West.

Oh, for God's sake. Ellie rolled her eyes at the strawberry balanced on the end of her spoon. "Of course *you* would say so, Robyn, given what you were doing at age seventeen."

There was an astonished silence as every head at the table swung in her direction, and Robyn's wife Lily, who was seated next to her husband, placed her hand over his.

Ellie stared at her lap. What was wrong with her? She never made hurtful comments like that. She could feel her family's curious eyes on her, and her cheeks began to burn with shame. She was about to beg Robyn's pardon when help came from the most unexpected quarter.

"It was a great deal of responsibility, yes, but I had the most tempting inducement to succeed."

Just like that, everyone's attention returned to Mr. West.

Eleanor froze, her gaze on her lap still, afraid to look at him. Had he just . . . helped her? She darted a quick look at him under cover of her eyelashes and found him watching her with the oddest expression on his face, almost . . . gentle?

She lowered her gaze again, confused. Perhaps it wasn't gentleness she saw in his eyes, but pity. He must be quite sure he'd triumph over her if he'd begun to pity her.

Whatever Mr. West's motives were, they succeeded in distracting Robyn. "Indeed? What inducement was that?"

"I'd been in India for six years when my employer offered to sell me a part-share in one of his ships. He wanted me to remain abroad for five more years and help run the business from there so he could remain in England."

"Is it not quite risky, Mr. West, to remain so long in India?" Lady Catherine asked. "What with the dreadful fevers, and cholera?"

"Yes. Risky enough, but like most twenty-three year old gentlemen, I thought myself invincible, and my arrogance paid off. By the time I returned to England, my employer wished to retire. He sold me his three best ships. One of these became the *Amelia*, and she's now the crown jewel of the fleet."

Robyn set his wineglass down with a sharp click. "The *Amelia*? The devil you say."

"Robyn!" Lily glared at her husband, scandalized.

Robyn turned to her. "I beg your pardon, my dear, but surely you've heard of the *Amelia*? That ship's a legend in London. The sailors say she can't be sunk, that she sails with the hand of God on her mast. I hadn't any idea you owned her, West. I'd love to get a look at her sometime."

"I'd be more than happy to take you aboard. I love to show her off."

Eleanor tightened her grip on her spoon. Show her off? Is that why Mr. West wanted *her*, then? To show the *ton* that the finest gentleman among them couldn't bring her to heel, but he could? Despite his denials, perhaps that was the real reason he wanted to force marriage on her. He already had the best ship in London, and now he wanted a famously unattainable woman as his wife.

Another conquest.

Ellie looked at Robyn's eager face, then glanced at Alec, who looked as impressed as Robyn did. *Blast it.* She'd counted on her brothers to despise Camden West, or at least to be suspicious enough of him to hold his feet to the coals. Instead they both looked as if they were about to beg him for a bedtime story.

Tell us more about your ships, Mr. West, do!

What was happening here? Even Charlotte hadn't said a word during his story about India, and Eleanor could swear at one point her sister looked as enthralled as everyone else at the table.

Why did no one see Camden West for the villain he was? Did they not see the man thought to court her? Or, good Lord, was it possible they saw him as a potential match for her, and wished to encourage him?

For pity's sake. Alec had nearly thrown Lord Ponsonby out on his ear when he asked for her hand, and Mr. Fitzsimmons hadn't got the first word of his proposal past his lips before Alec refused him. But now here her brother sat, chatting with Mr. West as if overjoyed at the prospect of welcoming him into the family.

Eleanor narrowed her eyes on Camden West and tried to see him as her brothers might. She supposed his was a commanding presence, in part just because of his height, but also because of the way he carried himself. He had the air of a man confident in his abilities.

Confident. Eleanor felt a scowl tighten her lips. Arrogant was more like it.

Still, her brothers would respond to a man like that, a man who'd turned challenges into remarkable successes. Alec and Robyn weren't like many gentlemen of the *ton*. They'd admire a self-made man like Mr. West, rather than look down on him for being in trade.

Mr. West. *Camden.* She rolled the name around on her tongue. It had a smooth feel to it, rather like sweet, thick cream. She quite liked it, but then smooth could turn bitter in the blink of an eye.

"Your ship, Mr. West. The *Amelia*," Lady Catherine said. "The little girl you brought to Lady Abernathy's garden party yesterday is named Amelia. Did you name your ship for your sister?"

"I did, my lady."

Delia and Lily both sighed at the sweetness of the gesture, and even Charlotte's face softened a bit.

"What a lovely thing to do," Lily said. "I imagine she liked that very much."

Mr. West smiled. "She was . . . quite pleased, yes."

Eleanor stared at him, and a strange feeling blossomed in her belly at his expression. All of his sarcastic grimaces and warning glances hadn't prepared her for the wide, lopsided smile that lit his face now. Two deep dimples flashed at the corners of his lips, like a special reward for those fortunate enough to tease a genuine smile out of him.

He didn't smile much. Perhaps he should do so more often.

What would it be like to wake up next to him every morning? To be the woman who coaxed that smile from him, before his head even lifted from his pillow? She thought of his face this afternoon as he'd kissed her hand, her wrist, his green eyes hidden under heavy lids, his mouth open against her skin, his hoarse whispers . . .

Eleanor twisted her hands in her lap. Foolish, to imagine such a thing. The best she could hope for as his wife was a lifetime of sarcastic grimaces and warning glances.

*You don't matter, E*llie, remember?

Or worse. A lifetime of no glances at all. How long would she be married before her feet didn't make a sound when she crossed the marble floor? How long before she became a ghost?

She reached for her wineglass and found Mr. West staring at her from across the table with that same indecipherable expression she'd noticed earlier. This time she didn't look away, but gazed back at him.

His green eyes warmed as she looked into them. Eleanor caught her breath. So green and soft, like lying back onto a carpet of sun-warmed grass—

"Amelia isn't more than ten years old, is she, Mr. West?"

He tore his gaze from hers, and turned to Lady Catherine. "She's eleven, my lady."

"She can't have been more than an infant when you left for India, then," Charlotte said, "and you've only been back in London for a month. How is it you and she are so close?"

Charlotte's question sounded more like an accusation than a mere inquiry. Now it was her sister's turn to face the puzzled frowns of everyone else at the table.

Mr. West only raised an eyebrow at her, however. "Amelia was only a few weeks old when I left, yes, but I wrote to her every single day while I was gone."

"Every day?" Eleanor's voice sounded too high to her own ears.

"Yes. Every day. My aunt read her my letters, even when Amelia was still an infant. When she was old enough, my aunt made sure she wrote to me every day, as well. We've kept up quite a correspondence, so even with such a distance between us, we've remained close."

Eleanor sighed. A caring brother, then, as well. He'd have her mother in the palm of his hand now too, right along with her brothers.

"Amelia and I are all that's left of my immediate family," he went on. "Our parents are dead. Amelia doesn't remember them, so I've always been more of a parent to her than a brother, especially given the difference in our ages."

Eleanor sucked a breath into suddenly airless lungs.

Not only a caring brother, but a father to that child. Even as young as he'd been, off on his wild adventures, seeking his fortune in India, he'd written to his sister every day, determined to be a part of her life even from that distance, determined she'd know him when he returned.

Devotion such as that, a love so deep as that, was . . . rare.

How could such a hard man be capable of such tender feelings? She'd never have imagined it of him, but then, what did she really know about Camden West? Her eyes met his across the table and her heart began a wild fluttering against her ribs at what she saw in those green depths. She'd seen hints of it before, but never had she seen his eyes burn with it as they did now.

Hunger.

*He looks at you like a starving man looks at a Chr*istmas pudding.

She'd dismissed Charlotte's words, had thought it impossible Camden West looked at her as anything more than a means to some mysterious end.

But this afternoon . . . a simple caress on her hand, nothing more, but the moment he'd touched her, heat had exploded between them, as if a spark had been set to dry tinder.

She saw the same heat in those green depths now, and an answering heat rose inside her. He desired her. Not just as a convenient wife or a mother for his sister, but as a woman. A shiver chased up Eleanor's spine as the spark kindled to life inside her leapt into flame.

His eyes darkened as they swept over her face, lingered on her eyes, her lips. She couldn't tear her gaze away—

Delia's voice broke their stare. "Does your sister still live with her aunt, Mr. West?"

His gaze remained fixed on Eleanor for a heartbeat before he turned to Delia. "No. While I was in India she lived with them at Lindenhurst, my estate in Hertfordshire, but I moved her to my townhouse in Bedford Square when I returned to London."

"Hertfordshire?" Alec asked. "Any good sport to be had there?"

Cam blinked at the change of topic, making Delia laugh. "You'll have to excuse Lord Carlisle, Mr. West. Our own estate in Kent was beset with floods this spring. There was so much water damage we've undertaken some long overdue renovations, and the manor won't be fit for habitation until next spring. Lord Carlisle is quite vexed to lose hunting season at Bellwood."

"He was never so fond of hunting until he found he must miss it," Robyn added with a laugh.

"I haven't been to the estate in some time, but my cousin Julian was there a month or so ago, and he predicted good sport when the season opened." Mr. West hesitated, then, with a glance at Eleanor, "I don't suppose you'd care to spend a few days hunting at Lindenhurst? The estate isn't grand, but it's comfortable, and an easy journey from London—about six miles south of Watford."

Alec rubbed his hands together in anticipation. "Sounds just the thing. Kind of you to offer, West."

"Yes, very kind," Delia said. "Not that you had much choice, after such a broad hint from Lord Carlisle. Are the ladies invited, or is this to be a gentleman's party?"

"Ladies as well, of course." Cam returned his gaze to Eleanor. "What enjoyment is there in a party without ladies?"

Eleanor stared back at him. *A hunting party.* They would be three days at least, and when they returned, her two weeks' grace period would be nearly up. She'd be forced to accept Camden West's proposal, or see Charlotte left to the tender mercies of the ton.

She could refuse to go, but she doubted Mr. West would let her slip though his fingers so easily, and in any case it was plain she couldn't trust her brothers to dismiss her unwanted suitor. If she wanted him gone, she'd have to get rid of him herself.

Very well. She'd go to Lindenhurst, but she'd make quite sure to turn the visit to her advantage. The gentlemen would be off hunting every day. Who knew what she could uncover about Camden West in that time? Lindenhurst must have servants, and servants had secrets.

Eleanor glanced across the table at him. He met her gaze and held it as he wrapped his long fingers around his wineglass and raised it to his lips. Before he took a sip, he tilted it subtly in her direction in a mocking toast.

Eleanor's heated skin cooled to an icy chill. What a fool she was, to believe even for a moment he might desire her. He cared only that he succeeded in forcing her into this sham of a marriage, whatever it took.

I don't matter. Is that what you mean, Mr. West?

The wine burned its way down her throat.

That's what he'd meant, and she wouldn't be foolish enough to forget it again.

Chapter Thirteen

"You don't care for sweets, or from what I could see at dinner, food of any kind, and you don't appear to care for chess, music or conversation. May I ask, my lady, what exactly you do care for?"

For a moment she went still, as if she could evade such a dull-witted predator if she didn't move. When he didn't go away, she laid aside her book with a heavy sigh and looked up at him.

"Perhaps I don't care for anything at all." She glanced toward the other end of the room, where the rest of the party was gathered, then lowered her voice. "You won't wish to be married to such a dull lady, one with no pleasure in food, music or entertainment. A sad prospect, indeed. Don't you agree?"

"Not at all." He came around the edge of the settee and seated himself next to her. He left a respectable space between them, but he lowered his voice and held her eyes as he murmured, "I'm certain I'll find a way to give you pleasure."

Her eyes went darker as her pupils dilated, and a faint flush rose in her cheeks. She knew what he was thinking now, just as she'd known it at dinner.

Cam's mouth went dry as the dainty wash of color spread over her cheekbones and drifted down her throat. Such a delicious pale pink hue, but not what he'd expect for a lady with her lush coloring. He wanted a deeper color, one that matched those black currant lips and dark, silky hair. A heated surge of warm red she felt everywhere, not just on her face and neck.

What would it take to get a true blush out of her?

The room, the music and the snatches of conversation floating toward them faded into insignificance. Nothing else mattered to him but finding out. His gaze drifted over her face, then down to the place where the silk neckline of her gown met her smooth skin. "Such pleasure, my lady, and my privilege and honor to be the one to give it to you."

Her eyes went wide and she lifted a hand to her bosom, as if to shield herself from his gaze. "You take delight in teasing me, Mr. West."

She meant to scold him, but such a low, husky whisper from such plump red lips turned the words into an invitation.

He held her gaze. "I *will* tease you, touch every inch of your skin with my fingers, my lips, but my delight will come when I can take you at last, and it will be your delight, too, I promise you."

Her lips parted on a gasp.

The sound touched his chest, his belly, his cock, as if she'd dragged her palm over his skin. And, God, there it was, the blush he'd known was hidden beneath the girlish pink one.

A woman's blush.

He watched, riveted by that hot, deep surge of red. It flooded her face, throat and bosom then vanished under the neckline of her gown, hidden from his gaze and yet more enticing somehow, because he could imagine the way it would rush across her breasts and her soft belly, her thighs—

"You go too far, sir," she said, but again her voice gave her away, for she couldn't hide her breathlessness.

"Not as far as I'd like to go." *Not nearly as far.* He'd like to slip his hands under her skirts, wrap his fingers around her ankles and ease her flat onto her back on the settee. Then he'd slide his hands up her calves, coax her knees wide, skim his palms higher, to the inside of her thighs, then higher still, until his fingers brushed against her—

"Too far, nonetheless," she hissed, the breathlessness giving way to panic.

She glanced over her shoulder toward the fireplace, but no one else in the room seemed to take any notice of them. Charlotte Sutherland continued to play the pianoforte. Lady Carlisle and Lady Catherine listened and chatted while Lily Sutherland watched her husband and Lord Carlisle play at chess.

"Not as far as I *will* go, once you're mine."

The words hit his ears with the force of a blow, and his desire cooled at once to dismay. *Mine?* Christ, is that how he thought of her now? As *his*? When the bloody hell had that happened?

He'd thought her beautiful the first time he saw her—as he'd told Julian, he wasn't blind. But he'd admired her in much the same way one might admire a lovely piece of sculpture, or a horse with a graceful gait. He'd looked forward to bedding her with the same sort of detached anticipation he felt when he bedded any desirable woman. She was to be his wife, after all, and a man bedded his wife.

For a time. Until he tired of her.

He hadn't expected to *want* her. Hadn't wanted her, either—not more than any full-blooded man would want any beautiful woman.

Not at first. But now . . .

Want her? Christ. It seemed a pale phrase to describe how he felt about her. He *burned* for her. Her taste, her gasps, and that blush . . . he was so hard it felt as if he had a fireplace poker shoved inside his breeches.

His. He thought of her as his. He sure as hell hadn't expected that.

"My brothers, Mr. West." She gestured with her chin toward the other side of the room.

Cam followed her gaze. "They don't appear concerned."

They didn't, much to his surprise. Her brothers weren't what he'd expected, any more than Lady Eleanor was. He'd thought to find two proud, arrogant aristocrats looking down their noses at him from across the dinner table, but instead they were polite and amiable, and their wives no less so. So amiable he'd invited them all to Lindenhurst, for God's sake.

Uncle Reggie was going to have an apoplexy.

"My mother, then." Her throat worked. "For my own sake, as well, I ask you to show me the same courtesy you would show any lady in her home."

It had cost her an effort to say it.

Now it was Cam's turn to flush, and from something far less pleasant than desire. *Jesus.* He'd spoken to her as if she were a common doxy and this were a whorehouse. He ran a distracted hand through his hair and tried to pinpoint the exact moment he'd lost his mind.

He took a deep breath and gathered his wits. "Asked so prettily, I can hardly refuse, but I'll ask for a favor in return."

Her lips tightened. "I believe I'll withhold my consent until I know what the favor is."

Cam couldn't prevent a smile at that. "Nothing so terrible. I want you to call me Camden, and permit me to use your given name, Ellie."

Odd, how natural the name felt on his lips. He'd never called her by her first name before, but at some point he must have begun to think of her as Ellie.

Her full lips turned down at the corners. "That's two favors, Mr. West."

Cam stared at her mouth. Dear God, was that a pout? The fireplace poker in his breeches seemed to think so. He couldn't resist a pout at the moment, not if he were going to act the gentleman and treat her like the lady she was. A gentleman did not suck a lady's pouting lower lip into his mouth and tease it with his tongue.

He tore his gaze away and cleared the hoarseness from his throat. "Is that a refusal, Eleanor?"

"I doubt it would make any difference if it were, for you'll have your way whether I agree or not." She plucked at a fold of her gown, worrying it between her fingers. "I see what you're doing."

Good. At least one of them did. "Is that so?"

She kept her eyes on the crushed bit of silk. "You think to work on me by small degrees. One moment I've agreed to use your given name, and the next we're joined in marriage. It won't work, you know."

Cam laughed. "If it were so easy, we'd be enjoying wedded bliss even now."

"*Bliss?* That's a bit much, even for you." She glowered at the fold of silk between her fingers.

He reached across the settee and snatched the cloth away, determined to make her look at him. "Come, Eleanor. You just said it won't work, so you've no reason to deny me the favor. If you do, I'll be forced to conclude you think it *will* work, and you're afraid of me."

She frowned. "*Afraid?* What nonsense."

Cam said nothing, but waited for her answer and tried not to notice even her frowns were seductive. More so because she seemed not to know they were, but thrust out her lower lip as if she hadn't any idea she was slowly driving him mad.

"Very well, Mr. West—that is, Camden."

He stilled at the sound of his name on her lips, aware of a strange leap in his lower belly.

"In celebration of this new intimacy between us," she continued, her voice heavy with sarcasm, "Allow me to pay you a compliment. How clever you are to invite my family to your estate to hunt. It will be far more difficult for me to avoid you when I'm a guest in your house, as I'm sure you're aware."

It had crossed his mind.

But only after he'd extended the invitation. "Now, Eleanor." He paused to savor the taste of her name in his mouth. "That was mere luck, not design on my part. You were there. You know I couldn't avoid the invitation."

"Well, Mr. West—"

"Camden. Or Cam, if you prefer."

She drew in a long, patient breath. "Well, Camden, you were quick to take advantage of the opportunity."

He shrugged. "Of course I was. But if you're worried about my having, ah . . . unfettered access to you, you can always remain at home."

Another faint blush rose in her cheeks at the innuendo. "Leave you alone with my family for days on end? I think not. My brothers seem far more eager than I am to accommodate you. I can't account for it at all, in fact. Another rare stroke of luck for you?"

He gave her an angelic smile. "The virtuous are favored with luck."

"*Virtuous?* You can't be serious—"

She began to sputter with indignation, but stopped when she noticed his wide grin. "Virtuous now, are you?" An unwilling smile touched the corners of her lips.

He leaned back against the settee. "Yes, and virtue should be rewarded. Don't you agree?"

"No. Virtue is supposed to be its own reward."

"Not this time. So I'll beg another favor of you, Eleanor."

She gave him an incredulous look. "You've used up all your favors, Mr. West."

"Camden. This favor benefits us both."

She shook her head. "Impossible. We're on opposing sides."

"At the moment, yes, but can't we play together for the duration of the hunting party at Lindenhurst?"

She eyed him as if she were waiting for some trick—for him to pull a card from his sleeve or a hidden rabbit from his coat. "What, a truce? How does that benefit me?"

"Well, it would make things much pleasanter between us, for one."

She jerked up in her seat, her eyes wary. "I don't *want* things to be pleasant between us." She plucked at her skirts again, avoiding his eyes. "It will only make this harder."

Cam stared at her, unable to say a word as realization dawned on him. *I'm making* a mess of this.

She'd told him the day after the Foster's ball that gossips always exaggerated. He should have listened to her, but instead he'd listened to the gossip, to every whisper and rumor about Lady Eleanor Sutherland, the haughty, proud *ton* darling, the tease, so cold, so arrogant she'd already rejected five suitors.

Nothing had been good enough for Hart Sutherland, either. It stood to reason any child of his must be formed from the same clay her father had been.

Except she wasn't.

He never imagined she'd have such fight in her, such spirit, or such intelligence. He never expected to be fascinated by her. To want her, to want to unravel her, to turn her inside out, to see her from every angle. He never expected he'd want to know her.

He never expected her at all.

He'd taken the wrong approach with her from the start. Even during those brief weeks he'd courted her, he hadn't taken the time to get to know her. He'd danced with her at a few balls and exchanged pleasantries with her, but he hadn't *seen* her—not the truth of her.

Lady Eleanor Sutherland was not a woman to be bullied into marriage. But she might be courted into it. Coaxed. Persuaded.

Seduced.

He never expected to want her, and he damn sure never expected *her* to want him.

But she did.

She'd gasped this afternoon when he kissed her palm, sighed when he took her wrist with his mouth. And tonight, that breathlessness in her voice, her blush—it wasn't only from embarrassment. He knew the look of a woman flushed with desire.

Julian was right—he hadn't thought this through properly. Force wouldn't work with Eleanor, but where it failed, finesse would succeed. The flower didn't force the bee to sip the sweet nectar. It lured it. Tempted it, until the bee couldn't resist a taste. God, he couldn't conceive of a more erotic challenge than to entice a woman like her, to arouse her to such heights she'd take him inside her. Just the thought of it set his blood on fire.

Once he'd taken her body, her hand would follow as a matter of course.

"You'll have to come up with a better reason than that if you wish to persuade me into a truce, Mr. Wes—that is, Camden."

Persuade her? Yes, he'd persuade her, to all manner of wicked things, but he couldn't seduce a woman whose hands clenched into fists every time she saw him. He'd backed her into a corner with his threats, and now he had to find a way to entice her back out of it, or she'd fly at him with claws bared every time he approached.

"How shall I persuade you? What do you want?"

"I want to know why you want to marry me. Surely it would be much easier to choose a woman who *wants* to marry you, so I assume you have some reason to want me, in particular. I want to know what it is."

It was a shrewd question. She knew there was no hope of dissuading him from his scheme unless she understood the reasons for it. She had no hope of dissuading him at all, of course, but she couldn't know that.

But Cam hesitated. He didn't intend to hide the truth from her forever. Sooner or later, he'd have to tell her. Sooner or later, yes, but he'd hoped for later, after they were married. She'd hate him for it, but by then it would be too late. Too late for both of them, for she'd never forgive him, and he . . .

He'd have to live with the knowledge that he'd earned her hatred.

Something pierced his chest at the thought, something bitter and sharp, like regret. He swatted it aside. He had no use for regret. It was a paltry thing when weighed against justice.

Parity. The Sutherlands owed Amelia a decent life. He would see to it they paid. "A truce for the duration of the hunting party. I'll reveal my reasons to you at its conclusion."

She leaned toward him. "I have your word on this?"

He didn't give his word lightly. When he gave it, he kept it. "You have my word."

She leaned back against the settee and released the breath she'd been holding. "Then we have a truce. For the moment, that is."

A moment was all he'd need. "I believe I'll take my leave before you change your mind." He rose from the settee. "Will you see me out?"

She remained seated. "One more point first, if you please. Your cousin will not accompany us to Lindenhurst."

It wasn't a question.

Cam hesitated, then inclined his head in agreement. It was for the best, anyway. Julian was far too interested in Lady Charlotte already.

Eleanor rose from the settee and followed him to the other side of the room.

Lord Carlisle looked up from the chessboard as they approached. "Off already, West?"

Cam nodded. "Yes, my lord. I've a few details to see to if we're to hunt this week."

Robert Sutherland glanced up from the chess board. "Good man."

To Cam's surprise, Lord Carlisle rose and extended his hand. "Kind of you to invite us to your estate. I'm looking forward to it."

Cam shook the proffered hand, then turned to bow to the ladies. "I thank you for your invitation this evening, Lady Sutherland."

She smiled. "My pleasure, Mr. West."

Lady Carlisle and Lily Sutherland smiled and offered cordial goodbyes, but Lady Charlotte, who'd ended her recital in a discordant crash of notes, only glanced from him to her sister, her brow furrowed, then turned away.

Eleanor followed him out of the drawing-room, but she came to a stop fewer than five paces from the door. "Good night."

He raised an eyebrow. "You don't intend to see me out?"

Did she think he'd taste her again, as he had this afternoon? Did she think he'd take her ripe red mouth with his, her lips sweet and tart at once, a fruit so succulent one taste made the juice run down his chin?

She sidled back toward the drawing-room. "I thought I had. Rylands is waiting in the entryway. He'll see to you."

She thought to foist him off on Rylands, did she? He caught her hand and drew her toward him, away from the door. "Must I define the word truce for you, Eleanor?" He eased her back against the wall.

Dear God, her scent.

"I know what a truce is, and it doesn't include . . . this."

He held her between the wall and his body and leaned closer, until his mouth nearly touched hers. "What do you mean by *this*, Eleanor? Do you think I intend to kiss you? Shall I take your lips with mine, to seal our truce?"

She shook her head, but she didn't speak.

God, he wanted to kiss her, burned for the feel of her lips soft and open against his, her every gasp and sigh caught in his mouth.

Cam stilled her with gentle fingers on her chin and stared down at her. Her eyes had dropped closed and her long lashes fluttered against her flushed cheeks. She drew a deep breath and her lips parted on a long, unsteady sigh.

All he needed was a single moment, and here it was. *Now.* He tilted her head up to his and leaned down.

She trembled against him, her fingers shook in his hand, and her breath caught in her throat in a sigh, or a sob, or something partway between the two.

Cam's fingers tightened on her chin for a moment, then his hand fell away.

He couldn't do it. Even as he cursed himself as every kind of fool, he couldn't do it.

He wanted to take her lips with his more than he wanted to draw his next breath, but not like this—not with her family on the other side of the door. Not while she trembled in his arms. To take her this way felt wrong, as if he were cheating mere minutes after he'd agreed to a truce.

Yet he couldn't quite bring himself to release her, so he leaned forward and brushed his lips, soft as a breath, against her forehead.

"Good night, Eleanor."

Chapter Fourteen

"You're quiet this afternoon, Eleanor. One would think you'd have quite a lot to say today, but you've been quiet since we left London this morning."

Eleanor opened one eye and contemplated her sister's grim expression. Charlotte sat across from her in the carriage, watching her with narrowed eyes, the corners of her mouth turned down.

She knew why Charlotte was upset, of course, but they couldn't discuss Camden West now, since Delia and Lily had joined them in the carriage for the ride to Lindenhurst.

She closed the eye to avoid her sister's stare. "Are you asking why I'm quiet, Charlotte? Or accusing me of something? It sounds like the latter."

"You may call it an observation."

"You can hardly blame her, Charlotte," Delia said.

Delia had graciously offered to take a rear-facing seat, but now she twisted around and craned her neck to catch a glimpse of the gentlemen, who rode just ahead of the carriage. The day was fine and they'd left the hood down, so they had an unimpeded view of the three mounted riders.

An unimpeded view of Camden West, graceful and commanding in the saddle, his dark blue coat pulled tight across his wide shoulders, his gray breeches straining to contain his muscular thighs.

Not that she cared about his thighs, of course. She was a lady, after all, and ladies didn't ogle a gentleman's thighs.

But what kind of gentleman wore such tight breeches?

Lily giggled. "Delia's right, Charlotte. That man is handsome enough to render any woman speechless."

Eleanor opened one eye to peek at Camden, then closed it again at once. No—not safe yet. She'd been unable to take her eyes off him all morning, and until she could, she'd keep them closed. Why, oh why did he have to appear to such advantage on horseback? Was it too much to ask he be slump-shouldered and awkward in the saddle?

Delia turned back around in her seat. "So pleasant, too, and that story he told about his travels in India? He's rather fascinating. Both Alec and I thought so."

Ellie grunted in reply. So much for Alec's protective instincts.

"His devotion to his sister is what struck me," Lily said. "It's singular, don't you think, for such a young man, especially given the disparity in their ages? It's lovely to watch them together."

She gave Ellie a playful nudge in the ribs.

Eleanor reluctantly opened her eyes. Amelia had opted to ride with the gentlemen rather than remain in the carriage, and now she trotted alongside her brother, chatting and laughing with him, the jaunty little feather in her riding cap waving in the breeze. They were utterly at ease with each other, even though he'd been absent for most of Amelia's eleven short years of life.

Then again, one could be physically present in a child's life, and still be absent in every way that mattered. Ellie knew that better than most, and as she watched Amelia prance along on her mare, she couldn't prevent a burst of admiration for Camden West. She almost envied the little girl. Whatever else might be true of him, he'd brave the flames of hell for his sister.

*He'd force a lady into marriage fo*r her, as well.

Amelia West was somehow connected to this mad scheme of her brother's. Eleanor knew it. She could feel it, just as surely she could feel the breeze against her face. But how? She was missing a vital piece of this puzzle, and nothing less than a hope of getting it could have induced her to agree to a truce with the man. One didn't make a deal with the devil, no matter how handsome and persuasive he was.

Especially then. After all, he wouldn't be the devil if he weren't both.

Shall I take your lips with mine?

Eleanor shivered at the memory of those whispered words, the feel of his warm lips against her forehead. He'd wanted her mouth. She'd felt the thrum of desire in his powerful body, so close to her own. Her heart had slammed against her ribs as his mouth descended, but a moment before his lips met hers, he'd hesitated. One heartbeat. Another. Then a soft touch, his lips against her forehead, so chaste, and almost . . . tender.

A villain with a conscience. It should have reassured her, but somehow, it made it worse.

She'd been . . . disappointed. Eleanor's face heated, but she couldn't deny she'd thought of nothing since then but how it would feel to have his lips pressed against her own. He'd taste sweet, like strawberries drowned in rich cream—

"Of course," Lily went on, oblivious to the drift of Ellie's thoughts. "Robyn could talk of nothing but the ship. The *Amelia*. He'll tease mercilessly, I'm sure, until Mr. West takes him to see it."

"Robyn's just as useless as Alec, then." Charlotte had remained ominously silent while Delia and Lily effused over Camden, but she never could hold her tongue for long.

Lily's face darkened, as it always did when anyone dared to cast aspersions on Robyn. "What in the world does that mean, Charlotte?"

Oh, no. For the third time that morning, Ellie wished her mother had decided to accompany the party to Lindenhurst. She'd put a quick stop to this discussion. Unfortunately, she'd opted to remain in London with her grandson instead.

Ellie gave Charlotte a warning nudge with her toe, but Charlotte ignored her. "Why, they may as well strip Ellie down to her corset and stockings and deliver her to Mr. West's bedchamber, for they certainly made no attempt to chase him away."

Delia's and Lily's identical blue eyes went wide with shock.

"Charlotte!" Eleanor cried, even as she knew it was too late. "For pity's sake, will you hush?"

Delia ignored Charlotte, however, and instead leaned forward and fixed her eyes on Ellie. "He is courting you, then? Alec and I thought so."

Ellie stared at Delia, taken aback by the look of satisfaction on her face.

She hadn't a chance to say anything, however, for that same look sent Charlotte headlong into a temper. "For pity's sake, Delia—of course he's courting her, if *that's* what you wish to call it. One needn't be a mind reader to see that. What I fail to understand is why neither you nor Alec did a thing to discourage him."

Both Delia and Lily looked at Charlotte as if she'd lost her mind.

"Why would she wish to discourage him?" Oddly, Lily directed this question to Charlotte rather than Ellie. "Unless this is about his being in trade—"

Charlotte waved an impatient hand in the air. "No, no. I don't care about that. None of the family does. You know that, Lily. No, I—I simply don't like the man, that's all."

Lily opened her mouth to argue, but Delia interrupted her. "That's all very well, Charlotte, but I rather think Ellie's opinion is the one that matters, and she seems quite taken with Mr. West."

Eleanor's mouth dropped open. Taken with him?

"Yes," Lily put in, before Ellie could gather her wits. "I thought so, and I know Robyn did, too."

"Alec, as well," Delia added, addressing Ellie. "Why do you think he didn't try to discourage Mr. West? He perceived an interest on your part, and believed he acted according to your wishes."

Ellie opened her mouth, but no words emerged. She hadn't said or done a thing to make her family think she encouraged him.

Had she?

Dear God, could she have encouraged him without realizing it? "Whatever made you think I wished for his suit? What did I do?"

Delia and Lily looked at each other, then back at Ellie.

"It's the way you look at him, I suppose," Delia said. "There's something in it that reminds me of how Alec looks at me."

"Yes, and you looked at him a good deal, you know," Lily put in. She sounded a trifle defensive. "And when he spoke of his sister, your face went . . . softer than I've ever seen it."

No. No, it hadn't. Surely it hadn't.

Had it?

"It's your head that's gone soft, Lily," Charlotte snapped. "I grant you he's a devoted brother. No one could hear that story about his sister and remain unaffected by it, Ellie included, but it doesn't means she wishes to be tied to the man for life."

Still, as she spoke, Charlotte gave her sister an appraising look, and Ellie could see doubt begin to take root. God help her, after the almost-kiss last night, and Delia's and Lily's observations this morning, she'd begun to doubt herself.

Lily turned in her seat to observe the gentleman in question. Ellie's gaze followed hers, and her mouth fell open. Drat the man! How had he contrived to look more virile than usual the very minute they turned their gazes upon him? Even from here she could see his powerful thighs, hard and tight against the saddle as he raced Amelia to a line of trees and back again.

"Tied to Mr. West?" Lily turned and met Ellie's eyes. She raised a brow. "I can think of far worse fates."

Charlotte didn't look amused, but Delia choked back a laugh. "Do you mean to say, Ellie, you don't encourage him?"

Yes. No. Damn—that is, drat it, what did she mean? She hardly knew anymore.

Wait. Of course she knew. "I don't encourage it, no. I have no wish to marry Camden—that is, Mr. West."

Anna Bradley

She gave Charlotte a nervous glance, hoping her sister hadn't heard Camden's first name slip out. It seemed to roll quite readily off her tongue.

Charlotte stared back at her, lips tight.

She'd heard.

Delia glanced behind her to the trio of gentleman, then turned back to Eleanor. "Well, it's too late to do anything about it now."

Eleanor slumped back against her seat. It was a devil of a time for her sisters to finally catch on. They must be in Hertfordshire by now.

Silence descended on the carriage for a while, until Charlotte interrupted it. "Are you quite sure, Eleanor?"

Eleanor jumped. "Quite sure of what?"

"That you don't mean to encourage Mr. West?"

"I think you'd suit." Lily gazed hopefully at Eleanor.

Eleanor looked from one expectant face to the other. No matter what she said, she'd disappoint someone, and they'd never cease plaguing her. "I—I don't—"

"Stop the carriage, driver. Would any of you ladies care to ride the rest of the way? West says we'll be there in another half hour."

The four ladies looked up in surprise to find Alec had brought his horse up alongside the carriage. They'd been so distracted by their squabble, none of them had noticed him.

Ellie began to rise from her seat before the carriage even came to a complete stop. "I'll ride." It was either ride or throw herself from the moving carriage.

The driver pulled to a halt and she stepped down. Alec handed her his horse's reins and took her place next to Charlotte.

Eleanor mounted and rode away from her tormentors as if the hounds of hell were chasing her. She'd managed to put about ten paces between herself and the carriage before Camden drew his horse up next to hers. "I didn't dare hope for your company this morning, Lady Eleanor. If this is a result of our truce, I'm sorry I didn't suggest it earlier."

Eleanor sighed. From the proverbial pan straight into the fire.

Still . . . she glanced back at the carriage. She could see by the look on Charlotte's face her sister's temper hadn't improved. She swung back around on the saddle to face Cam. "I congratulate you, sir. You're the less objectionable of two offensive options."

To her surprise, he grinned. "Those aren't truce-worthy sentiments. You'll have to do better than that, or I'll be forced to wave a white flag in the air every time you insult me, to remind you of our agreement."

Ellie felt a smile threaten. How ridiculous! He was a very devil, but a devil with a playful side. Irresistible. "Nonsense. You don't have a white flag."

He shrugged. "No, but I do have a white cravat, and I won't hesitate to use it. Try and explain *that* to your sisters."

Eleanor cocked her head to the side, considering. "All right, then. You are *much* less objectionable than my other offensive option."

"I'll make do with that."

Amelia, who never seemed to be far from her brother, drew her horse up next to Cam's. "Will you ride the rest of the way, Lady Eleanor?"

Eleanor couldn't help but smile at the child's eager expression. "Certainly, if you like, though in exchange you must tell me all about Lindenhurst, Amelia. Do you ride often while you're there? I see you're an accomplished horsewoman, so I imagine you must."

Amelia glowed at the praise. "Oh, yes. I've had Penelope since I was five." She reached down to run a gentle hand over the mare's neck. "She's a gift from Denny."

"How lovely she is," Eleanor said, with a sidelong glance at Cam.

"There are ever so many pretty paths and places to ride near the house," Amelia went on. "Will you let me show you while we're there?"

"I'd consider it a great favor if you would. You must know the grounds better than anyone. Do you miss your home, now you live in London?"

Amelia shrugged with the blithe unconcern of a child who finds a home everywhere she goes. "Not too much. I ride in London every day, in one park or another, and besides, Gunter's is in London."

"Amelia has a weakness for lemon ices." Cam grinned at his sister.

Eleanor arched an eyebrow at him. "The whole of London has a weakness for lemon ices."

"Do you?" Amelia asked.

"Oh, yes. Lemon ices, marzipan and sugared almonds in particular. All sweets, really."

"Except trifle." Cam's words were innocent, but his voice . . .

Eleanor darted a look at him and caught her breath. Oh, my, but he looked—*wicked*. She meant to turn away, but she found herself gazing at his mouth instead.

Strawberries, warm from his tongue, his lips sweet with cream.

"Do you like sweets after all, my lady?" He held her gaze. "Ah, I knew you must have pleasure in something."

Eleanor flushed and forced herself to look away.

"London has the best sweets." Amelia spoke with the air of one who has settled the matter. "I like living there. Sometimes I do miss Lindenhurst, but my home is wherever Denny is, you know, and Denny doesn't like it there."

Eleanor jerked her attention back to Amelia, startled by this information. "He doesn't?"

"Amelia—" Cam began at the same time.

Amelia ignored his warning in favor of Eleanor's question. "No, not at all. We haven't been back once since he returned from India."

"Indeed?" How interesting. At last, here was some information on the elusive Camden West. Even better, it was information he didn't want her to have.

God bless them, siblings with loose tongues.

"Why, how surprising—" Ellie began, prepared to get as much information as she could, politeness be damned, when she was interrupted by a shout from Robyn.

"Ellie!"

He'd ridden some distance ahead of the rest of the party, but now Ellie looked up to find him charging toward them. He pulled his horse to a sharp stop next to Cam's. "Ellie, you know where we are, don't you?"

"We're in Hertfordshire, Robyn," Ellie said, with exaggerated patience.

Robyn rolled his eyes at her. "Yes, I realize we're in Hertfordshire, but do you know whose estate is less than two miles east of here?"

Dread pooled in Eleanor's belly as she realized what Robyn meant. *Oh, no.* No. He couldn't be so dense as to bring up Durham now, right in front of Camden West.

"Robyn—"

"The Marquess of Durham!"

Blast him, he *was* dense enough.

Devil take them, siblings with loose tongues.

Cam shifted his mount a little closer to Robyn's, an intrigued look on his face. "Yes, that's right. His estate lies not three miles from Lindenhurst. Are you acquainted with him?"

"Not really," Ellie said. She shot a warning look at Robyn.

But he either didn't notice it, or chose to ignore it. "Of course we know him. We'd be family even now if Ellie hadn't sent him on his way."

If she could only manage to remove her riding boot, she could throw it at her brother's head.

Cam turned his gaze upon Ellie, and a mocking smile spread over his face. "Is that so? I've heard rumors about Lady Eleanor's numerous suitors, but I hadn't heard the Marquess of Durham was among them."

Robyn shrugged. "Oh, not many people know about it. It was before her first season. Shall we go tour the estate? I've heard it's impressive, though of course we never had a chance to find out. Too bad, too. Durham's a good fellow."

Ellie didn't say a word, but the heat of her glare must have at last penetrated Robyn's thick skull, for he finally seemed to catch on. "Oh, well, perhaps not. That is . . . Amelia! Do you fancy a race?"

Amelia, who'd grown bored and begun to squirm in her saddle, perked up at this. "May I, Denny?"

Cam looked as though he couldn't get rid of the two of them fast enough. "By all means."

The two trotted away, for all the world as if they'd not left mayhem and destruction in their wake.

Eleanor flicked the reins, set Alec's horse to a walk, and waited.

Cam brought his horse into step beside hers. "Six."

"I beg your pardon?" Eleanor asked, though she knew very well what he referred to.

"Six suitors. Not five, and one of them the Marquess of Durham. Respectable family, wealthy, intelligent, and not yet in his dotage. Handsome, too, if the ladies can be trusted. I can't think of a single objection to him."

Eleanor's fingers tightened on the reins. She'd heard this all before. "No one can."

"*You* did."

She had, yes, but she didn't intend to explain the nature of that objection to Camden West. He'd think she was mad, just as everyone else had. Mad, or selfish, or intolerably arrogant.

And maybe she was. Maybe, after all, she had no right to believe she could have more than anyone else did, and yet it had always seemed such a simple thing to her, to want love—to expect it, even. To wait for it.

But now . . . tears burned the back of Eleanor's eyes. It seemed love wasn't so simple, after all.

When she didn't reply, his mouth twisted with a strange, bitter smile. "Your father must have indulged you just as your brother does, if he allowed you to refuse such an advantageous offer."

Her father. *Indulgent.* For a single moment she was tempted to tell him all about her father, just to see the shocked look on his face.

"Why do you avoid Lindenhurst?" she asked instead. "It's your home, isn't it?"

He hesitated. "A trade, Eleanor? My secret for yours?"

Another deal with the devil? It was becoming a habit, and yet she hadn't much choice. She could try and get the information from Amelia later, but she didn't like the idea of involving the child in this mess.

The devil it was, then. "Oh, very well."

"Lindenhurst was my home until I was thirteen, then things changed, and it wasn't anymore."

It wasn't anymore?

"Julian's father, my Uncle Reginald . . . he took over the estate, and my mother and I removed to a cottage on the property. We lived there for four years, until my mother died. Then I went off to India."

Dear God. Surely he didn't mean to say his uncle had snatched the estate right out from under him and his mother? Eleanor swallowed around the lump in her throat. "Your uncle and aunt still live there?"

"Yes. My uncle and my Aunt Mary took Amelia in when I left. She was raised at Lindenhurst. It's her home, but it's not mine, and hasn't been for a long time."

"That was . . . kind of them."

"My aunt has been good to Amelia."

He didn't say a word about his uncle's goodness.

"I see Aunt Mary occasionally in London," he went on. "I've seen my Uncle only once since I returned from India, when I asked him to remove from my London townhouse. He wasn't pleased, to say the least."

Eleanor frowned. "But it's *your* townhouse."

"Yes."

She half-turned in the saddle, but she could only see his profile. "Lindenhurst is your estate. It belongs to you, doesn't it?"

He inclined his head. "Yes."

Eleanor's mind raced, trying to make sense of the peculiar tale, but he'd hidden more of the story than he'd revealed. Then a thought occurred to her. "What did your uncle say when you told him about the hunting party?"

He gave a short laugh. "He didn't care for the idea, but there's little he can do. As you said, it's my estate."

She hesitated, not sure if she should ask the question that hovered on her lips. "Why don't you order them to remove from Lindenhurst, as well?"

He turned then, so she could see his entire face. His green eyes had gone flat and cold. "Because I owe them."

"Owe them?" Eleanor repeated, shivering despite herself at the look in his eyes.

"Yes. They've raised Amelia since birth. I pay my debts, my lady. I collect them, too."

Eleanor stared at him. What would it be like, to owe such a man a debt? Her entire body went cold at the thought. Did he believe her indebted to him? Was that why—

"A trade, Eleanor, remember? Why did your father allow you to refuse the Marquess of Durham?"

She didn't want to tell him, didn't want this strange, tempting man inside her head, where he could see her secrets. But it was too late. She paid her debts, too.

She took a deep breath and raised her gaze to his. She thought his green eyes flared with a brief heat before he murmured, "Why, Ellie?"

She raised her chin. "He didn't allow it. He never found out about Durham's suit at all."

Chapter Fifteen

Cam stared at her, sure he'd hadn't heard her right. "Your father never knew about Durham's offer," he repeated, his voice flat.

Impossible. The late Lord Carlisle had cared for nothing more than his own consequence. He'd have made it his business to know about his daughter's prospects, and he would never have permitted her to toss away the chance to become a marchioness.

A cold, bitter anger seized him. She was lying. She was her father's daughter, after all. He'd been a liar, too.

She flinched at his obvious skepticism, but said nothing. Her dark eyes narrowed, moved over his face. Whatever she saw there made her stiffen in the saddle.

Damn her. She looked at him as if . . . as if he'd disappointed her.

Cam clenched his fists until his fingers threatened to snap into pieces. She had no right to look at him like that, to make him feel as if he'd wounded her somehow. He didn't owe Eleanor Sutherland anything. Quite the opposite.

His voice sliced through the silence between them. "Do you expect me to believe that?"

She didn't answer for a moment, then she shook her head. "I don't expect anything of you."

Another lie. "Ah, but I expect something from you, my lady. The truth. Shall we begin again? How is it you did not become the Marchioness of Durham?"

She wheeled her horse around, as if prepared to flee. "I told you already. I can't help it if you don't like my answer."

He didn't like it because it was a lie. "Such an accomplished actress, and yet this is an unconvincing performance. You'll have to do better, because I don't believe you."

Her face hardened. "Pity, but whether you take or leave my answer hasn't anything to do with me. Do as you wish."

Cam squeezed the reins until the worn leather between his fingers creaked a protest. "I choose to leave it, and it has everything to do with—"

Before he could spit out the rest of his furious reply, he'd choked on the dust kicked up by her horse. He leapt after her in a second flurry of pounding hooves, devouring the space between them. She hadn't gotten far before he caught up to her, grabbed her horse's reins and forced her to an abrupt halt.

She kept her seat with ease, but she turned on him in a breathless rage nonetheless. "Have you lost your wits? What do you think you're doing? You nearly unseated me!"

He tossed the reins back to her, but seized her wrist so she couldn't bolt again. "We're not done talking."

She tried to tug her arm free. "I am."

He held her fast. Her wrist felt small, the bones fragile between his fingers, but fragility was an illusion when it came to Eleanor Sutherland. "Is this how you honor your promises? We have a truce."

She jerked her chin up. "I've honored the truce. You asked your question, and I answered it. We're done."

He urged his horse closer so he could study her face. "I'm not."

"What's the point in proceeding? I'll only lie to you again, won't I?"

He eased his grip on her wrist. "Then tell me the truth, Eleanor."

"Lie. Truth. What's the difference? People believe what they wish to believe. It's easier for you to believe me a liar, just as it's easier and more entertaining for the *ton* to call me Lady Frost behind my back. You don't want the truth any more than they do."

Cam hesitated. If he didn't find out her story now, he'd never get another chance, truce or not. He could at least hear her out. She'd done as much for him. "You must admit it's difficult to believe your father would allow you to refuse Durham, Eleanor."

"I told you. He never found out about it."

"How could he not?" His earlier anger surfaced again, but he made an effort to keep his voice calm. "Durham would have had to ask for your hand—"

"He did ask for my hand." She tugged at her wrist, and this time he let her go. "He asked Alec."

"Why," Cam asked, disbelief ringing in every word, "would he ask your brother for your hand, instead of your father? The earl?"

She looked him in the eye. "Because I made certain he would. It wasn't as difficult to arrange as you might think. For the better part of a year before my father died, he was . . . oh, shall we call it ill? Durham brought his suit directly to Alec, with no questions asked."

Durham had asked her brother for her hand, and bypassed the earl entirely? *What bloody rubbish.* From what Cam knew of him, Durham was an honorable man. He'd never have agreed to such a scheme, unless—

My father? He never found out.

He froze, staring at her, her words echoing in his head until they began to take on a new meaning. She hadn't said her father didn't care about Durham's suit, or even that he hadn't known about it. She'd said *he never found out.*

It could only mean one thing. She and her brother had hidden the offer from her father. They'd orchestrated the proposal. Planned it, no doubt secretly, and then they'd seen to it Durham appealed to Alec for her hand, rather than to Lord Carlisle.

Ellie hadn't wanted to marry Durham, and she knew her father would make her, regardless of her wishes. She knew he'd force her into a marriage she didn't want.

Just as you'll force her. . .

Cam pushed the thought away before he was obliged to examine it. "What do you mean, he was ill?"

She gave a hollow laugh. "I mean what the *ton* always means when they use the word "ill" with no explanation."

"Enlighten me." Cam's voice was tight.

Her face went hard. "Very well. He spent the last year of his life in a dark study, the draperies drawn, awash in drink and refusing to admit his creditors. It was a simple enough matter to hide Durham's proposal from him."

Jesus. Cam stared at her, shocked into silence as the fairy tale of the perfect, aristocratic family crumbled into dust. He'd told himself that tale over and over again. In his version, there'd been no happy ending for his mother. For Amelia. For *him.* Only for them, the Sutherlands, and he'd envied them bitterly for it—hated them, even. In his head, their lives had been filled with fine horses, the most extravagant balls, and a grand, wealthy father, beaming over them all with pride. With love.

It was nothing more than an illusion, then, spun to life inside the head of a lonely, angry young boy. Even when he'd grown into an adult who'd known better than to believe in fairy tales, he'd never questioned it.

Until now. Now a different picture emerged, a far uglier one.

How had he not seen it before? He knew better than anyone that Hart Sutherland was the kind of man who withheld everything he could—held it tightly, in clenched fists. Why wouldn't he do the same to his own family?

Had he imagined their lives to be perfect so he'd be justified in his hatred for them? He'd never met them, had never even seen the Sutherlands until he returned from India. He'd fed his illusion on speculation, not fact. On fiction, not truths. Ellie accused him of believing whatever was easiest, and here was proof of it.

"If you don't believe me," she muttered, "ask Alec. Before you do, though, perhaps you should ask yourself what reason I have to lie."

Christ. She'd told him the truth. Her story was too ugly to be a lie, yet as ugly as it was, he wanted the whole of it. "You said something about creditors?"

Had there been no money, then? No fine horses, and no fancy balls?

She lifted her chin, but her face was white. "One after another, each more irate than the last. Had my father chosen a less convenient time to die, we'd have lost everything. But die he did."

Thank God. The words hung between them, unspoken. Cam didn't know if they were his words, or hers. "Your brother inherited the title, and put things to rights."

"Yes, and so Lady Ice was born, for I would have been compelled to accept whoever offered for me if it hadn't been for Alec."

Whoever offered? No matter how inferior they were, and regardless of their character. The thought made him grit his teeth. "The other five suitors, Ellie. Why did you reject them?"

She sighed, the sound so weary Cam's own shoulders sagged. "I refused Mr. Fitzsimmons because of his mistresses. He had three of them—at least, three that I knew of. Perhaps he had more. And I saw no reason why my dowry should go toward settling Lord Ponsonby's gaming debts. Twenty thousand pounds lost at hazard seemed sufficient enough reason to refuse him."

*Thank God for A*lec Sutherland.

For such a woman to be wasted on *whomever offered*—it seemed nothing short of criminal, and yet aristocratic ladies like Ellie were sold to the highest bidder every day, all across England. It was the way of things, and the aristocracy never blinked at it.

And he was no better.

No, he was worse, because he didn't even intend to buy her. He intended to steal her. Intended to, and would still, no matter that his chest went tight at the thought, for he hadn't any choice. Or, rather, he did, but the choice was no choice at all, for he'd always choose Amelia over any of the Sutherlands.

So he would steal her, and he'd steal *from* her too, just as Julian warned him he would.

"But what of Durham? He's as unobjectionable as they come. Plenty of young ladies would be thrilled to have him."

"Oh my yes, and all of them willing to tell me so, and take me to task for my cruel dismissal."

"Your brother said no one knew about his suit—"

"Not at first, but word got out. It always does."

Yes, it did. He knew that well enough. Word would get out about Amelia, too, but by then she'd be a Sutherland, or as good as one.

"Why, then?" Cam wasn't sure why he persisted in his questions. He didn't want to know, didn't want to think about her reasons or her hopes or her dreams, but somehow it was of crucial importance he know it all—that he understand the extent of his crime.

She kicked her horse into a fast walk, as if she could escape the place and the conversation at once. "I begin to think I don't . . . that is, I don't wish to marry. I don't believe it will make me happy."

But she would marry, and soon, despite her wishes. She may have escaped Durham, but she wouldn't escape him. He followed her. "So cynical. Why should you not be happily married?"

She slanted him a skeptical look. "Are you such a strong believer in marriage, then, Camden? Do you believe in love at first sight, as well? Oh, but wait . . . that must be why you wish to marry me. Love."

There could have been innuendo in her words, but there wasn't. She wasn't flirting with him. Just the opposite. She thought the very idea absurd, and he . . .

He'd have preferred flirtation. Anything even, to such bitter sarcasm.

But she was right. He put as much faith in true love as he did in mermaids and dragons—they were fairy tales. Illusions, nothing more, but for some inexplicable reason, he didn't like to hear his own cynicism echoed by her. She was too young, too lovely to be so jaded.

The thought was so ironic it left a taste of metal in Cam's mouth.

You deserve to choke on it.

"You've no reason to think people can't be happy in marriage, Eleanor. Your brothers appear to be satisfied with their spouses. With two such examples before you, you must have some faith in the institution."

"Satisfied?" She looked at him the way a schoolmaster looks at a student right before he canes him for stupidity. "They are much more than that. My brothers are deeply in love with their wives, and their wives are mad for them. But they are the exception, not the rule. You couldn't have chosen poorer examples to make your point."

Cam remained silent. He couldn't argue with her. Mermaids, dragons and Lady Eleanor Sutherland's brothers. He wouldn't have believed such love existed if he hadn't seen it with his own eyes.

"My sisters-in-law are fortunate in their marriages, but most ladies are forced to settle for far less. Dangerously less, in the worst case."

She shouldn't have to settle for less. *But she would.* If she didn't, Amelia would have to, and Amelia already had less. Much less.

Didn't she?

Amelia had him. She had Julian, and Aunt Mary. It was true she'd never known that sweetest, purest love—the love a parent had for their child—but she'd never lost it, either.

It had never been Amelia's to lose.

But dangerously less—what did Ellie know about that? Cam shifted uneasily on the saddle as he pictured Hart Sutherland, with his cold eyes and thin, cruel mouth. He pictured Lady Catherine, gentle and sweet-tempered, and his stomach roiled with nausea.

Whatever had happened between his mother and Hart Sutherland, Amelia hadn't had to watch it. But however bad it had been between Lady Catherine and Hart Sutherland, Ellie had seen it all. It seemed incredible to him Amelia could ever have been more fortunate than Lady Eleanor Sutherland, but maybe this *was* a fairy tale, after all.

Or maybe the most poignant ironies were the stuff of truth, not fairy tales.

But what difference did it make? Hart Sutherland stole something from his mother and Amelia, and Cam would have it back, one way or another. "You won't have to worry about the worst case when we're married."

She laughed, but the sound was cold—not a laugh at all. "Oh, no, of course not. I've no reason at all to worry, given our delightful courtship."

Cam flinched. *A fair hit.* She had no reason to trust him, and any number of reasons not to, but then she hadn't looked at this from every angle yet. "You're so determined to escape me, you haven't even considered the advantages of the arrangement."

She raised an eyebrow. "Yes. I can't think how I could have overlooked them. Pray explain them to me."

"You'd have far more freedom than most women enjoy in marriage. You could do whatever you wish."

"I do whatever I wish *now*. I may legally be my brother's responsibility, but Alec doesn't limit my freedom."

Cam couldn't argue that point. Lord Carlisle gave his sisters an unusual degree of latitude. "You wouldn't be mocked as a spinster."

She tossed her head. "Do you suppose a lady who's refused a marquess cares for the opinion of the *ton*? They mock me even now. I'm Lady Frost, remember? Why, I have my own special section in the betting book at White's—wager after wager, all concerning my affections and marriage prospects."

Cam's jaw clenched. He'd put a stop to that at once. He'd not have every sotted nobleman in London wagering on his wife.

"You should make a wager yourself," she added. "Just think, if you can bring me to heel, you stand to gain a fortune."

Cam stiffened, but he ignored her comment. "If you truly want freedom, you should marry. A married woman has, ah, certain opportunities forbidden to maidens."

Her cheeks flushed. "What, you mean to take lovers?"

That was what he meant. He imagined another man kissing her, touching her, his fingers trailing across that fine, pale skin . . .

Then he imagined himself breaking the man's fingers. One by one.

In time his fierce possessiveness would fade, though. Of course it would. Once he'd had his fill of her. "Yes." He had to force the words through gritted teeth. "Have you ever had a lover, Eleanor?"

She stared at him, shocked. "No. Of course not."

"Ah." He drew closer to her and lowered his voice. "You don't need to be in love to experience the pleasures of the flesh, and those pleasures can be . . . tremendously gratifying."

She stared at him as if transfixed, then cleared her throat. "Those pleasures . . . ah, I—that is, I imagine you'd wish to avail yourself of them?"

Cam's groin went tight. "Immediately, often, and for as long as we both agree to indulge. You'll be my wife, after all, and there is the matter of consummation."

She seemed to consider that. "And once we agree we don't care to indulge anymore? In each other, that is. You will take a mistress, and I will take a lover?"

"Yes." He managed to choke the word out past the fury clawing at his throat.

She nodded, and hope took flight in Cam's chest. He'd have her no matter what, but he'd rather have her willing.

"You haven't mentioned anything about the consequences of these pleasures," she said. "What of that matter?"

"What, you mean children?" Cam paused, aware he was in dangerous territory. He'd given some thought to children, of course, but he hadn't come to any decision. "I haven't a title to pass on, and I have Amelia."

Her face paled. "Ah. So you don't want them?"

"I didn't say that. I only meant I don't require them—"

Her voice came like the crack of a whip. "And if I should *require them*, Camden? Or, heaven forbid, if they should appear, regardless of your requirements? That does tend to happen when two people engage in pleasure, *immediate*ly, and often."

"We can negotiate for children, Eleanor. If you truly wish for them, you'll have them."

"*Negotiate*. How generous of you, and yet what I truly wish is for my children to have the care and attention of a loving father. You can't offer me that."

He opened his mouth to contradict her. To argue. To lie. But the words wouldn't come, and they lapsed into a tense silence.

Julian had tried to warn him. Cam hadn't listened. Hadn't cared.

*Eleanor Sutherland's freedo*m for Amelia's.

Parity. It had seemed a fair trade at the time.

But that was before *Ellie*—before the reality of her. The truth of her, and not the illusion he'd created. That was before he understood just how much he'd be taking from her.

Cam tried to push the thought away, but something inside him kicked up in protest—his conscience, perhaps.

Or his heart.

He became so lost in his thoughts he scarcely noticed in which direction they rode, but at last a shout from Amelia roused him.

"Denny! There's the cottage." Amelia pointed at the small stone gamekeeper's cottage standing on the edge of the estate. "We're here."

Here. Lindenhurst. He hadn't been back for more than ten years, but as Cam stared at the cottage, every moment of the time he'd spent in that cramped place rushed back at him as if no time had passed at all.

He shivered, remembering. The walls, always damp to the touch, even in the summer, and the floors, always freezing under his feet. Four long years he'd lived there, and in that time he'd never been warm. Not once.

Amelia had been born in that cottage. His mother had died there.

All at once he wasn't a man anymore, but a fatherless nine-year old boy.

"Cam?" Eleanor drew her horse alongside his. "Cam?"

He turned to look at her, but he didn't see her. He saw his Uncle Reggie, four years after his father had died, telling his mother she was a disgrace to her dead husband's name. He saw his Aunt Mary, tears on her cheeks, her hand over her mouth, holding in her sobs as his uncle told Sarah West they couldn't live in the manor house anymore—that she and Cam would have to go and live in the cottage now.

He saw Hart Sutherland leaving his mother's tiny bedchamber in the cottage, fastening his falls as he went.

He'd been thirteen when Hart Sutherland seduced his mother. Thirteen years old.

He'd been seventeen when she died. He saw her lying in a bed, the white sheets soaked with blood, clasping Amelia to her breast.

He shouldn't have come here.

"Cam? Are you all right?" Eleanor reached toward him, hesitated, and then placed her hand on his arm.

He looked down at her pale fingers against his coat, then turned to her—tried to see her. Tried to feel the warmth of her hand upon him. Tried to feel her. Her.

He couldn't. He could only see Uncle Reggie. Hart Sutherland. They'd taken from him. Stolen. From him and Amelia. From his mother. Now it was his turn to take.

An eye for an eye.

Lady Eleanor's future for Amelia's. It was a fair trade.

Cam pulled his arm away.

"Denny, look!" Amelia trotted up the long drive that led to the estate, then turned and waved gaily to Cam. "We're here at last!"

Chapter Sixteen

Ghosts flitted among the tall yew trees lining the main drive up to the manor house.

Amelia waved back at Cam and Eleanor one more time before she wheeled her horse around and pranced toward the house, Robyn behind her. The carriage was some distance away, but it passed onto the drive in front of them and followed the circular path that led to the front entrance, and still Cam didn't stir from his place at the end of the drive.

No one else seemed to notice the ghosts.

Eleanor glanced toward the house and got a vague impression of a three-story manor with neat rows of windows before she turned her attention back to Cam, who continued to sit motionless atop his horse.

Only Cam could see them.

She could hear Amelia's excited shouts even from this distance, but they were muted, and she couldn't hear what the child said. She shaded her eyes and looked toward the house again. The commotion on the drive had attracted the attention of someone inside—a woman had emerged from the doorway, kneeled down on the wide stone steps and opened her arms.

Amelia flew into them.

Mary West.

Eleanor looked back at Cam, then rubbed her fingers against the middle of her chest to ease the ache there. This was wrong. Wrong, that he should be left at the end of the drive to stare up at his home as if he didn't recognize it. As if he were unsure of his welcome.

She didn't know why her chest ached, or what she was waiting for. She should ride up the drive and join her family. Leave him here to face his ghosts alone. She didn't owe him any consideration, and judging by the way he'd just snatched his arm away from her, he didn't want any.

But she didn't move. "Cam?"

He turned toward, but his face was blank, as if he'd forgotten she was there.

"Shall we go up?" Eleanor nodded toward the house. "The others are waiting."

He glanced up the drive. His face was pale and set, but her words jarred him from whatever trance he'd been in, and he nudged his horse forward. "Yes. Yes, of course."

The horses' hooves made a muffled crunch against the gravel drive as they rode slowly toward the manor house, the air so still, so silent, the sound seemed deafening.

"There you are," Charlotte called when they neared the entrance. "I thought you'd never come up. I hope you didn't ride for too long, Eleanor."

Eleanor shook her head, but didn't answer. She watched as Cam dismounted and walked toward the woman who stood in the drive, waiting to receive him.

"Aunt Mary." He kissed her on the cheek.

She smiled and laid a palm against his face, but her expression was melancholy as she gazed up at him. "Camden. Welcome home."

Some of the color seeped back into his face at her words, and the tight ache in Eleanor's chest began to ease.

But her relief was short-lived.

"Back here now, are you? I'd have thought you'd have plenty to occupy you at your fancy townhouse in London."

Eleanor turned to find a tall, grey-haired man standing just outside the door, his lip curled with distaste as he glared at Cam. There may have been a strong resemblance between the two men at one time, but the older man's handsomeness had long ago succumbed to age and bad temper. His jaw sagged with years of dissatisfaction, but above his hard mouth and reddened nose his watery green eyes were still shrewd. Shrewd, and ruthless.

Reginald West.

Mary West's spine went stiff and she seemed to shrink down until she was absorbed into the gravel at their feet. Her hand dropped away from Cam's face and she darted a guilty look behind her. "Reginald—"

"Where's Julian?" the man snapped, as if his wife hadn't spoken.

Cam bowed stiffly. "Good afternoon, Uncle Reggie. Julian had business in town. He wasn't able to accompany us."

Reginald West grunted. "Business. You didn't invite him, more likely. Want to keep it all to yourself, don't you?"

Cam said nothing in reply to that, but turned toward his guests. Robyn had dismounted and now stood by his horse, his face puzzled. Only Ellie was near enough to hear the exchange between Cam and his uncle, but the air around them all buzzed with tension, as if a violent storm were about to crash down on their heads.

The ladies fell silent. Everyone seemed frozen in their places—all but the horses, who shifted their feet nervously. After a moment, Alec reached up to assist the ladies down from the carriage.

The movement loosened Cam's tongue. "These are my friends from town. Lord and Lady Carlisle, Mrs. Lily and Mr. Robert Sutherland, Lady Eleanor and Lady Charlotte Sutherland. My aunt and uncle, Mary and Reginald West."

"Sutherland." No one heard Aunt Mary's faint exclamation except Eleanor, who was close to Cam, still mounted on Alec's horse. She turned just in time to see the woman's face drain of color.

Eleanor's hands went icy cold. *What* in the world—

"Sutherland." Reginald West turned narrowed eyes on Cam. "What are you about, boy?"

Cam closed in on his uncle. He kept his voice low, but Eleanor heard him, and shivered at the menace in his tone. "I'm not a boy anymore, uncle. You'd do well to remember that. Just a bit of hunting," he added aloud, stepping back. "Has there been any good sport?"

Reginald West had lost some of his bluster at Cam's warning. "I—I've no idea. I haven't been out."

Cam turned toward his guests. "Some luncheon, I think, and then hunting this afternoon? Ladies, we apologize for abandoning you so soon, but perhaps Amelia will show you the gardens later." He held out his hand to his sister.

Amelia took it with an artless smile. "The rhododendrons are in bloom now, aren't they, Aunt Mary? Purple ones. There are purple ones in London, too, but they're not as nice as these. Will you come see them after luncheon, Lady Eleanor?"

Eleanor dismounted and handed her reins to a groom. "Yes, of course. A walk in the garden after luncheon sounds just the thing."

She soon discovered a walk in the garden *instead* of luncheon would have been even better. Despite Amelia's sunny presence, it was a tense affair. Reginald West sat at the head of the table, ate a good deal, drank more, and spoke only to Alec. He seemed somewhat appeased to have an earl at his table, but Alec, who was forced to endure the man's officious attention, looked less so.

Eleanor picked at her food and sneaked looks at Aunt Mary, who ate little and didn't say a word, but darted nervous glances between her husband and Cam, cowering whenever she caught her husband's eye.

"This is the strangest luncheon I've ever had," whispered Charlotte, so softly the words were more like breaths of air. "I can't choke down a bite."

Eleanor didn't show any sign she'd heard her sister, but whispered back, her lips hardly moving. "Pity. The squab is excellent."

Charlotte let a faint snort escape her at this, but only Eleanor noticed it.

They'd done this often as children. Their father had insisted on utter silence at table, but Ellie and Charlotte, who were always seated at the furthest remove from him, had flouted this command at every meal.

Quietly.

For a moment Ellie could almost imagine they were back at Bellwood, each with one eye on their father and the other on their plates, carrying on near-silent conversations without discernably moving their lips. They fell back into it now as a matter of course, as if by mutual consent. They often had moments like this, pockets of time when they seemed to fall into each's other's minds.

Perhaps it was like this for all sisters.

Charlotte lifted her fork and let it hover in front of her mouth. "I don't mean the food, and you know it very well, Eleanor. What in the world are we doing *here*? Hunting party, indeed."

Eleanor raised her napkin and patted daintily at her mouth. "Oh, but we are hunting."

Charlotte took a sip of her wine. "Are we, indeed?"

Eleanor stuffed a bite of squab into her cheek with her tongue, and under the guise of chewing said, "Camden West knows far too much about me, and I know nothing about him. I need information, and I will have it by the time we leave."

"Ah. And here I thought you'd given up. I spent the entire ride here choosing your trousseau in my head. Everything was black. Black night rails, even."

"I can't imagine why you think I'd give up. Have you ever known me to before?"

Charlotte made a subtle movement with her shoulders Ellie interpreted as a shrug. "No, but you seem rather cozy with Mr. West."

Eleanor stabbed at her squab with her fork. First she was taken with him, and now she'd cozied up to him, as well? Everyone around her had gone mad. "Cozy like a snake, right before it strikes."

She glanced from under her lashes at Cam, who was seated several seats away from her, on the other side of the table. He looked as though he'd been bitten already, and the poison had reached his heart.

Eleanor did her best to ignore the way her own heart squeezed in response to the pained look on his face, but her appetite vanished. She laid her fork beside her plate and tried not to think about what it must have been like for him to grow up with Reginald West's frigid eyes upon him.

"Where do you plan to get all this information you need?"

Charlotte's words were almost inaudible, but they jolted Eleanor from her reverie.

She couldn't afford to sympathize with Cam, or worse, imagine how he must have been as a boy, with tousled chestnut hair and sad green eyes—

Charlotte nudged her with a foot under the table. "Eleanor? How will you get the information?"

"The servants, and possibly also from that quarter." She nodded subtly toward Mary West.

Charlotte flicked her eyes in Mrs. West's direction without moving her head. "Yes. That might do. Shall I see what I can find out, as well?"

"No. I don't want to attract Cam's attention. He'll notice if we both start questioning the servants. Just keep Delia and Lily occupied while I slip away this afternoon."

"He is rather inconveniently clever," Charlotte muttered. "Observant, as well, for even now he looks as if he suspects us of something."

Eleanor darted a quick look at him. She and Charlotte had perfected their skills with years of practice, and yet here was Camden West, about to catch them out at it. He looked like a green-eyed cat about to slam a paw down on the tail of a fleeing mouse.

Eleanor picked up her fork, choked down her squab, and didn't raise her eyes again until luncheon was over. As soon as Mrs. West rose from the table the gentlemen disappeared, eager to get to their sport while there was still plenty of daylight. All but Reginald West, who disappeared into his study, much to Eleanor's relief.

Perhaps he'd stay there for the rest of their visit.

"If you ladies would like to see the gardens, Amelia will be happy to take you." Mary West stroked Amelia's hair back from her face. "I'll make sure your rooms are ready for you so you can rest when you've returned from your stroll."

Amelia led the ladies out to the gardens, beaming with pride when they all exclaimed at the delightful riot of colors spread before them. Like the manor house, the gardens were not grand, but so charming, especially the rhododendrons, which bloomed in a wild profusion of every hue of purple imaginable, from the richest plum to the palest lilac.

"They're set against the green shrubs to show off their color, Lady Eleanor," Amelia told her. "All different shades of purple. My Aunt Mary says my mother had a flair for color, and that's why the gardens are so pretty."

"Did your mother design the gardens, Amelia?" Eleanor asked, surprised.

"Yes. I didn't ever know her, you know," Amelia said, drifting into a new topic the way children tend to do. "She died when I was born. Her name was Sarah."

Eleanor's throat closed. She took Amelia's hand. "I'm sorry you didn't ever know her."

Amelia gazed up at her, and a shadow of a frown passed across her innocent face. "You look sad, Lady Eleanor, but I wish you wouldn't be, for there's no need. I have Denny, you know, and Uncle Julian and Aunt Mary."

She didn't mention her uncle Reginald. Both Cam and his sister had a habit of pretending the man didn't exist.

"You have a beautiful garden, as well," Lily said. "If you ever feel lonely for your mother, you can come here to remember her."

"I can't think of a lovelier memorial to her," Charlotte added. "Now, didn't I see a bridge when we came up the drive? It looked as if there were some wildflowers growing there. Will you show us?"

Amelia, overjoyed to find that such fine ladies appreciated her home, agreed at once. "Yes, if you're not too tired for a walk. It's not far."

Eleanor slipped her hand out of Amelia's. "You all go on. I think I will retire to my room for a short rest. I might have ridden too far today after all, Charlotte." She gave her sister a meaningful look.

Charlotte caught on at once. "Oh . . . ah, yes, you do look fatigued, Eleanor. You go rest, and we'll find you a bit later."

"All right." Amelia looked disappointed to lose her favorite, but she brightened when Charlotte took her hand. "What sorts of wildflowers grow in Hertfordshire, then?"

"Oh, all kinds. Poppies, and butterfly bush . . ." Amelia's voice grew faint as she and the other ladies drifted in the direction of the bridge.

Eleanor watched them go, then hurried back to the house. She found Mary West at the bottom of the main staircase, talking to one of the maids.

Mrs. West turned to Eleanor with a wan smile. "Your room is ready, Lady Eleanor. Winnie will show you up."

The maid curtsied.

Eleanor held out her hand to Mrs. West. "You're very kind. I do hope we've not inconvenienced you too much with our visit."

Mary West looked surprised, but after a brief hesitation she took Eleanor's hand. "This is Camden's home. He's welcome to bring whomever he wishes, whenever he wishes."

Not everyone welcomes him.

Eleanor blinked, surprised to find the words on the tip of her tongue. Did she think to champion Camden West now?

What foolishness.

She bit the words back, wondering at her vehemence. Mary West didn't deserve her ire, and she didn't want to alienate Cam's aunt when the woman could prove to be an invaluable source of information.

Still . . . she'd try her luck with Winnie first. The maid was less likely than Mrs. West to tell Cam Eleanor was asking questions.

She turned a dazzling smile on Winnie. "I'm ready."

Winnie led her upstairs and showed her to a comfortable bedchamber on the third floor that overlooked the gardens. "Here you are, my lady. Shall I open the window? There's often a nice breeze in the afternoon."

Eleanor untied the ribbons under her chin and laid her bonnet on the bed. "By all means. Have you been at Lindenhurst long, Winnie?"

Winnie tugged on the window, which opened with a protesting creak. "Oh yes, my lady. Since I was a wee young thing."

Ah. *Perfect.* "Indeed. So you must have been here when Amelia was born."

Winnie smiled. "Aye. I was at that, and such a sweet little babe she was. Hardly ever cried, that one."

"Amelia came to live here when Mr. West went to India, didn't she?"

Winnie retrieved Eleanor's bonnet from the bed and began to brush the dust off it. "That's right. Mr. Reginald didn't like it, but Mrs. Mary insisted. Put her foot down, she did. Never seen her do the like before, but she was right to do it."

"Yes, of course she was. Anyone would have done the same, I'm sure." Eleanor let just a thread of doubt enter her voice.

A dark look passed over Winnie's broad face. "Not anyone."

Eleanor gave a little laugh. "Surely no one at Lindenhurst would refuse a home to a newborn infant, and Amelia their own family, too."

She waited.

There was a brief pause, then Winnie said, "There's those that could, depend upon that, my lady."

"Why Winnie, you say that as if you have someone in mind." Eleanor slid her gloves off her fingers, looking down at her hands to hide her expression. "But who? Who could be so cruel?"

Winnie frowned. "I don't like to say, but I'll tell you this, my lady. It's not right, closing the door on your own kin." The last was said with a dark frown and a rather forceful blow to Eleanor's bonnet.

"I should say not." She waited, but Winnie didn't elaborate.

A little nudge, perhaps.

"I think you said before Mr. Reginald West didn't like it when Amelia came to Lindenhurst. Surely you don't mean to say *he* would turn his back on his family?"

Winnie's frown grew fiercer. "I don't see why not. He done it before."

Eleanor's heart began to pound. "Before? When was that?"

Winnie wrinkled her brow as she thought back through the years. "Way back, before Amelia was born, and Mr. Camden not yet thirteen when Mr. Reginald done it. An awful business, it was."

"Yes. I imagine it was."

"Shameful. Poor Mr. Camden still a child, and innocent." Winnie tutted disapprovingly. "Then poor Mr. Julian, so heartbroken over his cousin. Like brothers, they were. Still are, come to that."

Eleanor held her breath and kept quiet. So it was true. Reginald West had tossed Cam and his mother out of their home, because of . . . some dreadful business in which Cam had been innocent. But what? She focused all her energy on Winnie to will her into revealing it.

Winnie's frown faded a little as she thought about Cam and his cousin. "Rascals, of course, the both of them, as boys are. Into everything, but they had good hearts, for all that. Well, of course we hardly ever saw Mr. Julian after Mr. Camden left, always off with his cousin as he was."

Camden West, a good heart? A damaged heart, perhaps, but then she'd have a damaged heart herself if she'd been tossed out of her home by her own uncle.

Winnie thrust out her chin. "A fit punishment for Mr. Reginald, for no matter what else one might say of him, he always loved Mr. Julian more than anything—too much, maybe, and Mr. Julian hardly even able look at his father after Mr. Reginald told Mr. Camden and his mother to leave."

Lindenhurst was my home until I was thirteen, and then things changed, and it wasn't anymore.

Eleanor's knees began to shake and an odd, hollow feeling lodged in her chest. He'd been so young—a boy. Just a boy, and his own uncle, a man who should have protected him, had instead snatched his childhood home out from underneath him. "But why would they agree to leave? Mr. West couldn't throw them out of their own house. Could he?"

Foolish question. He could. He had.

Winnie sighed. "Mr. Camden was only a boy, and Mrs. Sarah . . . well, maybe she believed she deserved it, poor lady."

"Deserved it?" Eleanor cried. *No one deserved that.* "Dear God. How could she have deserved it?"

She bit her tongue as soon as she heard the urgency in her voice, but it was too late.

Her cry alerted Winnie, and the maid remembered her duty at last. She flushed and didn't answer the question, saying instead, "Would you listen to me go on? You looked peaked, my lady."

"Yes," Eleanor murmured. "I am rather tired."

Winnie gathered up the bonnet. "I'll just take this down for a good brushing then, shall I? Please rest, my lady. Someone will come up with tea for you in a few hours."

Winnie crept guiltily from the room and closed the door behind her.

Eleanor sat on the bed, her hands clenched in her lap.

This is why you came here. To get his secrets.

"Not this," she whispered to the empty room. "Not this secret."

She tried to shut her mind to the truth, tried to shy away from it even as her brain calculated numbers. Ages. Years.

Reginald West couldn't have taken Lindenhurst from Cam and his mother unless Cam's father hadn't been here to prevent it.

He hadn't been here, then. He'd left, or he'd died . . . *before A*melia was born.

Years before.

One hot tear slid down her cheek, but Eleanor swiped it angrily away and refused to allow the others to fall.

*For pity's sake. Don't cry. You just got exactly w*hat you wanted.

Chapter Seventeen

Cam flung himself onto an overstuffed leather sofa and dropped one heavy boot on top of the low table in front of him. This is *not* how he'd imagined his evening would unfold.

And he *had* imagined it—at length. He'd indulged in one heated seduction scenario after another, each with the same outcome, but not once had he imagined he'd spend his evening playing a game of hide and seek with Eleanor Sutherland.

Where the devil was she? She hadn't been at cards in the drawing room with the rest of the party, and she hadn't been in her bedchamber. She'd been at dinner, for God's sake. How could a flesh and blood woman vanish in the brief half hour the gentlemen had been at their port?

Flesh. Pale at first, then flushed with desire, her skin smooth, silky. Just a glimpse of the tender white flesh at the inside of her arm drove him mad. He could spend hours on just her wrist, worshipping it with his mouth, tasting her pulse as it fluttered wildly under his tongue . . .

Damn it. Not again. He dropped his foot to the floor and shifted against the sofa to ease the uncomfortable tightness in his breeches. How many times a day could a man ignore an erection before it began to affect his health?

Surely he'd reached his limit.

He peered into the dark corners of the library, but he could discern only shadows, and none of them were shaped like the maddening female who'd managed to slip his grasp this evening.

He'd know that shape, for he'd spent all day thinking about it. *Her.* He'd been so distracted it was a wonder he hadn't stumbled into a covey and been shot by one of his future brothers-in-law. Had either of them known what Cam was planning to do to their sister, they'd have shot him on purpose. Through the eyes.

*Or be*tween the legs.

First he'd envisioned a bedchamber seduction—her bedchamber, then his. Commonplace, perhaps, a seduction in a bedchamber, but private too, which was important, as there were sure to be . . . noises.

That fantasy had given way to another more imaginative one that involved a slippery frolic in the bath, and yet another where he took her atop the wide mahogany desk in his uncle's study. Still clothed. Him, not her. She'd been unclothed in that one. In all of them.

Gloriously so. Not just her wrists, either. All of her.

Cam made a disgusted noise in his throat and slammed his boot back onto the table.

Christ. Hide and seek.

Not that the idea didn't titillate. It did. Though in his current state, anything would. Still, one sought with an expectation of finding, and as it was, his grand seduction was still missing one essential element.

Eleanor.

Should he check behind the draperies? Damn it, where in the bloody hell—

"I suppose I can conclude from that ferocious frown you're not yet betrothed."

Cam leapt to his feet and whirled around. Julian stood there, a wide grin on his face. One of the glass doors leading from the library onto a secluded stone terrace stood partway open.

"It's a good thing I didn't come here to bludgeon you, Cam, or you'd be dead by now. Distracted, are you? Dare I ask by what?"

Cam scowled. "Jesus. May I ask why you're creeping about Lindenhurst in the dark, Julian?"

"Well, it hardly makes sense to creep about in the *light.* Defeats the purpose of creeping entirely, if you ask me."

Cam crossed his arms over his chest. "I didn't ask you. You're not supposed to be here at all, as you know. I promised Ellie you wouldn't be."

Julian's grin widened. "Ellie now, is it? Well, you've made some progress, then."

Not as much as he should have, and it was damned irritating. "What the devil are you doing here, Jules?"

"But I'm *not* here, dear cousin. Not to anyone who might object to my presence, that is."

Cam raised an eyebrow at him. "You assume *I* don't object."

Julian crossed the room and flopped into the seat Cam had just vacated. "You never have before, though you look as though you'd object to anything at the moment, out of sheer spleen. Is Lady Eleanor proving to be more stubborn than you'd anticipated?"

Cam ran a distracted hand through his hair. "She's proving to be more *everything* than I anticipated."

"Ah." Julian didn't look surprised. "She won't burst through the doors and catch me here, will she? I'm sure you'd hate to go back on a promise to her."

"I don't know." Cam slumped into a chair across from his cousin. "I can't find her."

Julian gazed at him for a moment, then burst into laughter. "You've lost her? My, she is a wily one. Did you check behind the draperies? That's where you always used to hide when we were boys."

He'd been about to, but Julian didn't need to know that. "For God's sake Jules, do you really think Lady Eleanor Sutherland would hide behind the draperies?"

"I don't see why not. It's a perfectly good hiding place." Julian crossed one long leg over his knee. "Come now, Cam. There are only so many places she could be."

Cam sighed. "I know, and I've checked every one of them, from the nursery to the billiards room, including her bedchamber."

Julian's smiled faded. "I hope you don't mean you entered her bedchamber without her consent."

Cam slanted him a sardonic look. "I'm blackmailing her into a sham marriage, Julian. Do you suppose I'd draw the line at entering her bedchamber uninvited?"

"I don't pretend to know where you'd draw the line anymore, Cam." Julian hesitated. "Perhaps she's with her sister? I hope to God you didn't enter Lady Charlotte's bedchamber, as well."

"Why is that? Would it bother you if I had?" Cam stared at his cousin until Julian looked away. "Are you here to bed Lady Charlotte? Because if you've got some foolish idea of declaring yourself to her—"

Julian jerked to his feet. "*Bed her*? What a romantic notion, and such a charming way of putting it. Christ Cam, I don't recognize you anymore."

Cam felt a prickle of conscience, but he remained silent, and after a long moment, Julian sighed. "I'm not here for Lady Charlotte. I'm here for you."

Cam had a feeling he knew what was coming. He also knew it would do no good. "I think I'd prefer the bludgeoning."

"This scheme to marry Eleanor Sutherland is going to end badly, Cam. You may think it's the best way to protect Amelia now, but don't you see? She'll grow to love Lady Eleanor, and she won't thank you for what you've done when she'd old enough to understand you betrayed an innocent lady. You risk your relationship with Amelia if you persist in this scheme."

"I'd never hurt Amelia, Jules. You know that."

"Not intentionally, no, but hurt her you will. And what of Lady Eleanor? You'll hurt her, and in a way she can't forgive. Christ, Cam—you'll hurt yourself. Don't you see?"

I don't matter. Is that what you mean, Mr. West?

Cam's hands clenched into fists whenever he thought of how Eleanor had looked that day—of the way her face had closed. He'd told her she didn't matter, and he'd hurt her in a way he still didn't fully understand.

But he shoved the regret away, far back into the darkest part of his heart where all the other ghosts lived. He'd make it up to her. He would. He'd be more careful in the future. He wouldn't hurt her again, and besides, that had been before he fell—

He caught himself. Before he what?

"No one will get hurt, Julian. I swear I'll be good to her. I'll take care of her."

But Julian shook his head. "It won't matter. It won't make up for what you'll take from her. You're making a mistake. I was wrong not to tell you so from the moment you mentioned this madness. Let it go, Cam."

No. He couldn't let it go. He couldn't let *her* go. "I—I can't. I want her, Julian."

That brought Julian up short. He sat back down and leaned toward Cam, his arms resting on his knees. "Want her? You mean, you desire her? She's beautiful, certainly."

Yes, she was beautiful, but he'd known that all along, from the first moment he'd seen her. He'd wanted her then, yes, but now . . . he thought of her dark eyes, and the way she hid them behind those long, thick lashes. The way she hid her truths from him.

He wanted to *know* her. Her secrets, the ones that mattered and the ones that didn't. He wanted to know what she'd looked like as child, and whether or not her laugh matched her smile—her real laugh, not the sarcastic one. He wanted to know if her hair reached her waist when it was unbound, how it would feel gathered in his palms, twisted in his hands, how it would feel spread across his chest.

*I want t*o lay her bare.

"You've known many beautiful women," Julian said, when Cam didn't speak. "Known them, had them, and quickly grown tired of them."

Cam shifted in his chair. "It's more than that. More than just her beauty."

"What, then?"

He didn't know how to explain it. It had to do her devotion to her sister, and the way she continued to defy him when any other woman would have given in long ago. It was her fierce spirit, and her belief in herself. It was all of those things, and yet more than that, too. He was drawn to the spark in her—wanted to warm his hands in it, touch it, even if it burned him. "Her passion, I think. That's part of it, anyway."

Julian's face paled. "Her passion. Cam, tell me you haven't—"

Cam smiled a little at his cousin's stern expression. "No. I haven't. We haven't, that is." Not from lack of trying on his part, but he didn't mention that to Julian. "Not that kind of passion."

Julian ran a hand down his face, hesitated, then, "If you care for her, Cam, then you have no choice but to let her go."

"No." Cam shook his head. "Even if I wanted to, it's gone too far for that."

And I don't want to. I don't even think I can.

For a long time after that neither of them spoke, but sat quietly in the dark library.

After a while Julian cleared his throat. "I can't support you in this business with Lady Eleanor. I know I said I would back up your story about Lady Charlotte if it came to that, but I can't do it. I won't stand in your way, but I won't help you, either."

"You won't have to. It won't come to that."

"What if it does? It would leave me with only two choices, and I can't live with either of them. Betray the cousin who's a brother to me, or betray the woman . . ." Julian didn't finish the sentence, but took a deep breath and said, "I can't be party to such a dishonorable scheme."

Cam flinched.

Julian met his eyes. "I cannot ruin Charlotte Sutherland. Not even for Amelia. Not even for you. I can't do it, Cam."

Something tore into Cam's chest then—something that was both pain and pride. Pride in Julian, in the man he was. A wry smile touched his mouth, despite the heaviness in his chest. "How is it, Julian, that you never turned into an utter villain? Your father spoiled and indulged you, and it should have ruined you, yet you remain the best of men. You make me wish I were a better man."

"You *are* a better man. Damn it, Cam, why don't you believe that?"

Cam shook his head. He wasn't a good man, but even when they'd been boys, Julian had been too partial to see it. He'd always been on Cam's side, no matter what.

Now it was his turn to be on Julian's side. "Never mind about Charlotte Sutherland. I release you from your promise. You'd have been of little use to me anyway. You're hopeless at blackmail, you know."

Julian only laughed, but the lines of tension around his mouth relaxed. "Quite."

"Go on then, go back to London, and do whatever it is you *are* good at—seducing actresses, and being charming."

Julian hesitated, then, "I'm thinking of leaving London, Cam."

"Leaving?" Cam stared at him, hoping he hadn't heard right.

"I've got a chance at a place in the 10th Royal Hussars. I've asked my father to purchase the commission, but he's refused—something about not wanting his only son to die in battle, or some such nonsense."

A cold, hard stone settled in Cam's stomach. "You want me to purchase it for you."

"I haven't decided whether or not to take the place, but if it comes to the point, yes."

Cam shot to his feet. "For once Uncle Reggie and I are in agreement. I don't want you to die in battle any more than he does."

"What would you have me do, then? Join the church? Or gad about London year after year, drinking, whoring and gambling away yours and my father's fortunes?"

"You don't have to do any of those things. There are other options. You could come and work with me. I've asked you dozens of times."

"No, Cam. What kind of man drags around on his cousin's coattails all his life?"

"Not that, then. You don't have to do anything you don't want to do."

"Yes, I know. That's the problem. I can do anything, or nothing at all." Julian shook his head. "I can't live that way."

So you'd rather become cannon fodder?

Cam opened his mouth to say it, but closed it again without a word. He'd gone off on his own adventure to India, and it had changed him—made him a man. Didn't Julian deserve the same chance? As long as he remained here, his father would be forever watching over his shoulder. He sighed. "The commission is yours if you decide you want it."

"I knew you'd see reason." Julian grinned.

"Reason?" Cam snorted. "I'm much more likely to see your father's fist in my eye."

"I doubt it. You're far too tall now for him to reach your eye."

Julian crossed the room and opened the glass door, then turned back to Cam. "Do you remember when we were boys and we used to play hide and seek? You didn't have much imagination as a child, you know—always hiding behind the draperies."

Cam smiled a little at the memory. "But different draperies each time, cuz. It worked well enough. As I recall, it used to take you ages to find me."

"That was because we could never agree on who should hide, and who should seek. We both wanted to hide, every time."

An unexpected wave of sadness washed over Cam. "With no one to seek, there was an end to the game, I suppose."

Julian gave him a puzzled look. "But it wasn't the end at all. We still played the game, and we had a grand time, too. Don't you remember?"

It was true. They had. How had he forgotten? "I do. I remember."

"Ah. I thought you must."

Julian stepped outside, into the darkness, and eased the door closed behind him. He filled his lungs with the cool night air, then let his breath escape in a long sigh. For the first time since this business with Lady Charlotte began, he could breathe again.

It was done.

Done, yes. For him, but not for Cam.

Julian glanced back at the dark window of the library. He'd done all he could do. Now he could only hope Cam would come to the right decision on his own, before it was too late. Too late to fill his lungs with the cool air—too late to draw his own deep, cleansing breath.

He looked up to see the sky had gone the deep midnight blue of all early summer skies. When he and Cam were boys, they'd spend the summer nights lying on their backs in the grass, dew seeping into their shirts as they watched the stars swim to the surface, one by one, winking in the deep blue ocean above them. He'd always loved that about Lindenhurst. From here it seemed as though you could see every star in the universe.

It had grown quite late, so he took care his boots didn't ring against the stone terrace as he made his way toward the back of the house where he'd left his horse. He wouldn't reach London before midnight, and it was dark, despite the stars—

He stopped. Froze for a moment. Turned.

Every night afterward, for months, years, he'd think about this moment and wonder what had made him turn. Had he sensed her before he saw her? Or did he catch her scent? Every night afterward, for months, for years, he'd remind himself it didn't matter why he'd turned. It mattered only he *had*, and he'd seen her.

Nothing was ever the same again, after that.

She'd never given him permission to call her by her first name, and yet that's the name that rose to his lips, as if it had always been there, waiting for him to speak it.

"Charlotte."

She turned, and he caught a glimpse of her just for a moment, bathed in starlight, her hair a dark cloud against her white neck. For months afterward, for years, he'd wonder why she hadn't looked surprised to see him standing there.

Had she been waiting for him? She couldn't have known—

"I knew you'd come."

Julian's breath stopped in his lungs. She'd thought of him? Had she wanted him to come?

"Did you hope I would?"

She laughed softly, and to Julian it was as if the sound was born of the night itself, and yet still hers, all the same.

"You already know I did."

Something in his chest leapt toward her then. His heart, he thought it was, but it didn't matter, really. Whatever it was, it was a part of him, and he'd never get it back from her. Didn't want it back.

"You already know," she said again, the laugh still in her voice.

He did know. He'd known since the first moment he saw her. No. Before that. He couldn't remember a time now when he hadn't known.

He hadn't come here tonight for Cam.

He'd come for her.

He should leave. Leave her here, untouched, alone in the starlight. But he wouldn't reach London before midnight, and it was dark, despite the stars . . .

This is what he told himself as he held out his hand to her.

Chapter Eighteen

"Don't say, Mrs. Mullins, they hid the kittens in the kitchens? Why would they bring them here?"

Eleanor leaned toward the cook across the scrubbed surface of the scarred wooden table, a grin on her lips. She'd come down to the kitchens for less than honorable reasons, but at some point during her conversation with Mrs. Mullins, she'd begun to enjoy herself.

Mrs. Mullins's kind blue eyes twinkled with merriment. "Dear me, who knows what goes through young boys' heads? I suppose they thought it would be warm in here, what with all the cooking. It took me days to figure out where all the cream had got to."

Eleanor curled her fingers around her cup of warm milk. "They sound terribly naughty, both of them."

"Oh my yes, they were. Good boys though, and they've grown into fine men too, though I don't have to tell you so, being as you're betrothed to Mr. Camden."

Eleanor squirmed against the wooden bench. She didn't like to lie, but really, it was just a tiny little one, and Mrs. Mullins wouldn't talk to her about Cam if she knew the truth.

Though what the truth was at this point, Eleanor couldn't say. It had started simply enough, but everything had become so confused, she was certain of only one thing. She had to *know*. Cam's whole story, not just fragments of it.

"Did Cam come see you today, Mrs. Mullins? I hope he wouldn't forget the friend who sneaked him sweets and saved his kittens."

"Oh, he wouldn't forget me, my lady. He came after the gentlemen got back from their sport, and dear me, such a handsome man he's grown into. Even when he was just a lad I knew he'd be handsome. I'd have recognized him anywhere, with those green eyes, though I haven't seen him these eleven years."

"Yes, he told me he hadn't been back to Lindenhurst since his return from India." Eleanor kept her voice casual, but her heart began to hammer in her chest. "He didn't say why. He doesn't speak much of his childhood."

Mrs. Mullins twirled her mug between work-roughened hands. "Bad memories, I daresay."

"How old . . ." Eleanor took another breath, and plunged ahead. "How old was Cam when his father died?"

Mrs. Mullins shook her head, her expression grim. "Nine."

Nine years old. Eleanor should have been able to release her breath then, for she'd guessed correctly. Cam's father hadn't left. He'd died.

But the breath wouldn't come. "How?" She choked out.

"Fever. It was that quick." Mrs. Mullins tapped the table once with her finger. "He didn't recognize his wife and son at the last."

A green-eyed, tousled headed boy, nine years old, rescuing kittens and pilfering sweets one day, and the next . . .

She released the breath on a shudder. The next, his father was dead.

"After that, well, Sarah West was never right again."

"No. She wouldn't be."

Had Sarah West been more fortunate than Ellie's mother, or less so? She'd known love. She'd had that much, at least, but oh, so briefly, and at the end she'd been left with nothing, because once you gave your heart, you never got it back.

Eleanor took a sip of her warm milk, but the lump in her throat remained. "Reginald West moved his family to Lindenhurst after Cam's father's death?"

Mrs. Mullins nodded. "There's no telling what might have become of Mr. Camden if his cousin hadn't come to live here."

Eleanor tried to smile. "To save kittens, and steal sweets?"

"Oh, much more than that. He saved Mr. Camden, too." Memories drifted over Mrs. Mullins' face. "I've never known a boy with a more affectionate heart than Julian West. Pure gold, his heart, just like his mother's."

It was a wonder a man like Reginald West hadn't tarnished her heart—hers, and his son's. That he hadn't crushed their every decent impulse. Ellie had seen it happen before, seen a man squeeze until the people around him became unrecognizable . . .

"Some here don't think of it as so," Mrs. Mullins said, "but I've always thought it was a blessing they came, despite what happened afterwards."

Eleanor gripped her mug, her knuckles white.

Amelia. She'd happened afterwards.

She didn't dare ask Mrs. Mullins if Sarah West had remarried. She wasn't sure she wanted to know the answer. "You mean Cam and his mother being forced to leave Lindenhurst?"

Mrs. Mullins' lips went tight. "They removed to the gamekeeper's cottage, at Mr. West's insistence. Those of us who'd known the first Mr. West were heartbroken over it. No matter what Sarah West had done, Lindenhurst was her home, and she was a widow with a young child."

Cam's mother had done something, then . . .

Something. Eleanor could hardly be at a loss to imagine what. The secret she'd been chasing, the secret she'd been so eager to discover—it wasn't Cam's secret at all.

It was Amelia's.

She wrapped her fingers around her mug to stop their trembling. "Cam and his mother lived with the Wests at first? For nearly four years, until . . ."

Until Reginald West had learned of Sarah West's disgrace.

Mrs. Mullins leaned toward her across the table. "Yes, and things might still have been well, but for—"

"Lady Eleanor," a low voice drawled from the door. "I find you at last."

Eleanor whirled around, half-rising from her seat. Cam leaned against the doorframe, his arms crossed over his chest. He'd shed his coat, and the white cambric of his shirt stretched tight over his powerful shoulders.

Dear God. He looked . . . huge. Huge, and furious.

He eased away from the door and sauntered into the room. "I've been all over the house, searching for you. Odd, but I hadn't thought to look in the kitchens."

His green eyes glittered with anger as they settled on her face.

Mrs. Mullins rose from her place at the table. "Why, good evening, Mr. Camden. What brings you to the kitchens?"

"Good evening to you, Mrs. Mullins. Amelia asked for some warm milk. I wanted the walk, so I came down to fetch it for her. Would you mind bringing it up to her for me? Lady Eleanor and I have a matter to discuss before she disappears again."

"Of course." Mrs. Mullins bustled over to the stove and poured the rest of the warm milk into a mug.

Eleanor jumped to her feet, the bench behind her nearly toppling over backwards. "I'll come with you, Mrs. Mullins. I'd like to say goodnight to Amelia."

She wasn't usually such a coward, but Camden West had a menacing look about him at the moment, and better a coward than a fool. She began to edge around the wide wooden table, but before she took two steps, Cam moved in front of her, trapping her between the bench and his body. "It's all right, Mrs. Mullins." He never took his eyes off Eleanor. "Go on ahead. A word, Lady Eleanor?"

Eleanor watched in despair as Mrs. Mullins disappeared through the kitchen door, mug in hand.

"Alone at last," Cam murmured. "Now, my lady, suppose you tell me what you're up to?"

Eleanor had to crane her neck to see his face. Had he become larger since the last time she saw him? The backs of her knees hit the bench. No, he wasn't larger. She'd just never stood this close to him before—close enough to feel his heat wrap around her body.

Far too close.

She should have scrambled over the table and leapt for the door while she had the chance. "Up to? Why, nothing at all. I fancied a warm drink and came down to fetch one. Surely there's nothing so terrible in that?"

"No, warm milk is innocent enough, but you could have rung for it from your bedchamber. Instead you crept down here to corner Mrs. Mullins in the kitchens."

"Corner her? What nonsense. Why should I—"

"I searched the house for you. Everywhere but the kitchens."

Eleanor dropped her eyes to avoid his gaze, but raised them again at once when she found herself staring at the open neck of his shirt, at a bare patch of sun-kissed skin.

Don't think about his skin. "I was in my bedchamber, reading."

He raised a knowing eyebrow, and slowly shook his head.

She stared at him for a moment, then gasped, outraged. "You entered my bedchamber, without my consent, as if you—"

"Own the house? Yes, just like that."

Eleanor huffed out a breath. "I must have been in Charlotte's bedchamber when you came, then."

"Ah, Eleanor." He touched his fingertips to her chin. "You blush when you tell a lie. Did you know that?"

She knew. She just hadn't realized *he* did. "I—I'm not lying."

"Of course you are. I can see it on your face, just here." He drew one finger across her cheekbone. "But it's worth listening to your lies to see that blush."

Dear God. How could one finger wreak such havoc with her breathing? She fought not to close her eyes as his finger dipped down to trace her jaw and the line of her neck.

He leaned closer, his breath warm against her ear. "The blush begins at your cheeks, but I can't see where it ends." He trailed his fingers down her neck to trace her collarbone. "Is it here? Or lower?"

She tried to turn her head away, but he cupped her cheek in his hand to still her.

Don't look at him.

She closed her eyes so she couldn't see the heat in his—so he couldn't see it mirrored in her own.

"No, Eleanor." He sank his long, warm fingers into the mass of hair at the back of her neck. Hairpins pinged onto the wooden table and skittered to the floor, and a long lock came loose and brushed against her neck. "Don't hide from me."

She forced a laugh even as her knees went weak at his touch. "Why should I wish to hide? I'm not afraid of you."

His smile mocked her. "Ah, but you're afraid of yourself. Your cleverness won't help you this time, Eleanor. Cleverness is no match for desire."

Eleanor stared at him, at the tousled hair falling across his forehead, the green eyes gleaming under lids gone heavy. At his mouth, his lips. Heat seared her, scorched every part of her body, and yet the lie sprang easily to her lips. "I don't desire you."

His mouth lifted at the corners. "Liar."

So soft, that one word. Not the accusation it should have been, but tender, and it was that which undid her. She closed her eyes again. He was too close. She had to do something to shut him out.

But he wouldn't allow it. "No. Look at me. See me."

She grasped his bare forearms with both her hands to push him away, but her fingers curled into his skin. Held on. "Do you suppose I don't see you? I have from the very start."

His fingers sank deeper into her hair. "What do you see, Eleanor? You asked me once if I was a gentleman or a scoundrel, and I told you—"

"Both. You said you were both." She closed her eyes, remembering. She'd thought his answer absurd at the time, because one was either the villain or the hero. Never both at once.

Except it wasn't that simple, and she should have known better even then, because she'd learned long ago the truth was never simple. That line between hero and villain, good and bad, devil and angel was blurred, indistinct. Maybe it had always been that way, and she'd refused to see it.

He stroked a finger down her cheek. "We see what we want to see, Eleanor. It's easier that way. You taught me that."

She opened her eyes. "What do you want from me, Cam?"

He laughed, the sound harsh, as if it were torn from his chest. "I want so much from you, I don't even know where to begin."

She scraped her nails over the flesh of his forearms. To hurt him? Or because she wanted to *feel* him, his skin under her fingertips? "Yes, you do. You searched for me, and now you've found me. End this. Tell me, then let me go. What do you want?"

He shuddered at her touch. "You."

Her breath hitched in her throat. Oh, God, it would so easy to give herself to him. To give in. To let herself drown in him and forget everything else. Everything she'd learned about him, and about Amelia. Not to have to think about how she could use it against them.

Or if I can bear to.

He stroked his thumb across her lower lip. "I want your mouth."

Were his hands shaking?

She let her fingernails sink deeper into his flesh, because she did want to hurt him, and to keep him near her at the same time. "Then take it. That's what you do, Cam—you take. It's all you know how to do, so do it now."

Heat flared in his eyes at her words. "Because that's what a villain would do, isn't it, Eleanor? So much easier that way." He shook his head, his eyes never leaving hers. "But I won't make this easier for you. Ask me to kiss you."

Oh, it was wicked, and he was the devil, after all. She could feel the fires of hell licking at her heels, the flames green, like his eyes. To withstand the lure of his kiss was hard enough, because she wanted it so badly. *Wanted him.* She wanted his lips on hers, and never in her life had she been afraid to take what she wanted.

But to ask for it . . .

She looked at his mouth, his lips, and without her consent, her own lips parted.

He drew a ragged breath. "Ask me, Eleanor."

She couldn't give in to him, because if she did, if she did . . .

A kiss. One kiss. A small surrender only, but a surrender still, and surely one would lead to another. "You'll take everything from me, Cam." She searched his face. "You'll take everything, and I'll have nothing left."

"No." His hoarse voice scraped against her nerve endings, but his fingers were gentle as they stroked her collarbone. "I give you my word. Ask me."

Her breathing quickened to match his, and her tongue darted out to wet her lips. "Kiss me."

His eyes went dark, but he didn't move. "Say my name."

No denials then, and no half measures. Stripped bare.

She lifted her chin. "Kiss me, Cam. I want your mouth." She reached up to trail her finger across the seam of his lips. "You're a hard man, but your lips feel soft. Are they? I want to taste you—"

A strangled moan tore from his throat. "Stop it."

His warm palms slid down the sides of her neck to grasp her shoulders, and for a moment she thought he'd push her away. But he pulled her closer, so close she could see the wild beat of his pulse at the base of his throat, and she wanted to taste him there.

She didn't mean to touch him, didn't want to, but her hands moved to his chest. His muscles leapt to meet her touch and his heart throbbed under her palm, but it wasn't enough. Touching him—it wasn't enough. "A kiss, Cam. This isn't a kiss."

He brushed his lips over hers, so soft, once, again, then lingered there, firm and warm before he drew back to murmur, "Is this what you want?"

Yes. God, yes.

He coaxed her with light touches of his lips and tiny kisses against the corners of her mouth. His kiss was gentle. Gentle, even as she felt the anger and desire leap inside him, felt the muscles in his body draw tight, felt him strain to bank his passion as it clamored for release.

Screamed for it.

This man, who'd never been taught to give, only to take . . .

*He kiss*ed her gently.

Panic rose in Eleanor's throat. *No.* She didn't want this—his gentleness, his tenderness. She didn't want him to give anything to her. She couldn't fight him if he did.

She wrapped her arms around his neck, tugged hard at the tousled chestnut waves at the back of his head, and parted her lips for him.

He groaned when he felt her mouth open under his. "God, *yes.* Give me your mouth."

She nipped hard at his bottom lip. "I'm not giving, Cam. I'm *taking.* I'd think a man like you would know the difference."

His breath was short, harsh. "Take more."

She fisted a handful of his shirt and dragged it aside, and then her lips were on his jaw, his chin, his neck, her tongue against the pulse point that had fascinated her earlier. He made a choked sound, and she felt the vibration of it against her mouth as she licked him there.

His taste.

His skin was so hot it seared her tongue, his taste earthy, clean—a faint trace of salt and shaving soap. He tasted like a man.

"More. Take more." He was panting now, shaking with need and the effort to restrain himself.

She worked the neck of his shirt open and spread the material wide with impatient fingers—*oh God*, his chest was a wall of muscle, the skin smooth, except for the dusting of hair there, not like the tawny hair on his head, but darker, crisp, thicker.

Eleanor swallowed. She wanted to run her hands over his chest, his shoulders, his belly, touch the smooth, warm skin stretched like velvet over his hard muscles. She wanted to touch his nipples, taste him there. Would they rise to meet her fingers, her mouth?

Did she dare?

She darted a glance at his face. He watched her, his pupils huge under his half-closed lids. "Take more," he whispered.

She brushed a thumb across one of his nipples, felt him shudder at her touch.

"*More.*"

She opened her mouth over the center of his chest and kissed him there once, before trailing her tongue over the dark flesh of his nipple.

"*Ellie . . .*" He surged to life, his hands rough over her back as he dragged her against his body with a harsh groan, his mouth taking hers, ravenous now—his tongue hot, insistent, his control shattered. "Is this what you want?" he demanded against her mouth. "To tease me until I lose control?"

She couldn't answer. He stole her breath. Her will.

"Do you want me to beg, Eleanor? Would that satisfy you?" He wrapped his hands around her waist and for one dizzying moment the floor dropped out from under her feet. Then she felt a hard wooden surface beneath her and she knew he'd lifted her, set her before him on the table. He slipped his hands under her skirts and closed them around her ankles. "Because I'd sink to my knees even now, just for another taste of you."

He dragged his tongue across her lower lip and slid his palms up her calves until he reached the inside of her knees. Warm fingers dipped under her garters to tease against her bare flesh, then he pressed her knees apart and moved between them so he was *there*, the neck of his shirt open, his body hard, primed from the teasing touches of her hands and mouth.

She'd wanted this—wanted *him*, and she wanted him still.

"You drive me mad. You're all I can think about." He caught her earlobe between his teeth and bit down, then pressed his hot mouth behind her ear, against her neck. Eleanor's head fell back as he nipped and teased the sensitive flesh. He wedged his body tighter into the space between her legs, his breath shuddering through him. "Do you think I won't take you? Because you're right, my lady. I do know how to take. God help me, it's all I know."

Eleanor moaned as he dragged his hands down her legs and out from under her skirts. Relief or protest, that moan? Oh, she didn't know, and Cam, ruthless in his desire, gave her no time to think before his hands gripped her waist. He stroked her there, then teased his fingers higher, so slowly she wanted to scream, did scream, silently, when at last he cupped the firm curves of her breasts in his palms. He found her nipples and his clever fingers slid over the silk of her gown, his fingertips relentless against the straining peaks.

"How else shall I take you?" He pressed his lips to her neck, then the base of her throat. "With my mouth?" He slipped two fingers into the neckline of her bodice, dragged it lower, and opened his mouth over the top of her breast. "Here," he whispered. His hot breath fanned over the damp spot he'd made on her skin.

Dear God. As if in a dream, Eleanor felt her ankles lock together behind his hips.

His laugh was soft, dark—triumphant. He traced his tongue along the narrow band of lace at her bodice, then pressed his lips to the top of her other breast. "Here."

She plunged her fingers into his hair, held him tight against her as she arched into his mouth. He groaned and slid lower to scrape his teeth over the tip of her breast before he sucked her nipple into his mouth, wetting the silk. "Here. This is what you want, isn't it, Ellie? You want me to take you here."

Eleanor couldn't speak, only writhe against his mouth as his tongue flicked against the hard peak. When she thought she'd go mad from the caress, he raised his head. His palms rested against her neck for a moment, then he took her face in his hands and turned it up to his. "Ah, my lady, I'm a villain, after all, because I'll take you any way I can get you."

His eyes dropped to her lips right before he took them again with a pained groan. He kissed her and kissed her, his tongue plundering the depths of her mouth until she could do nothing but kiss him back, her body aching with a desire she'd never believed possible.

"Which are you doing now, Eleanor," he gasped, when he released her lips at last. "Giving, or taking?" He let his forehead rest against hers. "Do you even know?"

God, she was such a fool. Giving, taking—what difference did it make? Could she even do one without the other? She didn't know—she knew only she shouldn't be doing either. Not with him. He was far too dangerous, because if she let him touch her again, she'd give him everything.

Not just her body. Everything.

She stared at him, dark eyes into green, her skin on fire, still panting from his kisses and the wicked touch of his hands. "Let me go, Cam."

She placed her palms flat against his chest and forced herself to push him away.

"No. Ellie, I—"

"Yes." She grabbed his wrists and pulled his hands away from her face. "Will you go back on your word?"

He didn't move or answer, just stood there and looked down at her fingers, wrapped around his wrists. His labored, shallow breaths seemed loud in the otherwise silent room.

Eleanor released him and held her own breath, and after what seemed an eternity, he stepped back, away from her.

Without a word she slid down from the table. She'd taken a few steps toward the door when his voice stopped her.

"I told you I'd let you go. I never go back on my word, my lady."

No. He never did. She froze for a moment, her back to him, his words echoing in her head until she couldn't deny the truth any longer.

He wasn't a villain, and he wasn't a hero.

He was both.

Chapter Nineteen

Eleanor leaned her forehead against the window and dragged her fingertips over the cool glass. The sky over the garden had been pale pink when she'd first looked out, but the sun had long since crested, and now it shone with a determined brightness, turning the rhododendrons below into a mass of blazing purple.

It would be a warm day today. It was warm even now, but Eleanor wrapped her arms around herself to contain a shiver, and turned away from the window.

I never go back on my word, my lady.

Of all the things Cam had whispered in her ear last night, it was this, oddly, that echoed in her mind. She'd dreamed of those words, and of green eyes gone dark with desire, of warm hands sliding up her calves to her knees, his long fingers skimming under her stockings, opening her to him . . .

In her dream, she gave him everything—her body, and her heart. In her dream, she'd offered her heart even as she'd known she'd never get it back.

But it hadn't mattered. It didn't, in dreams.

I never go back on my word.

His words troubled her because they were true, and they shouldn't be. The sort of man who'd force a woman into marriage, a man of his word? Ludicrous. A villain with a hero's scruples? Laughable.

But it was true. He'd honored every truce, kept every promise. Now it only remained to be seen if he'd have his way in the end. *Have her.* He'd sworn he would, and he hadn't broken a promise yet.

And she . . . she hadn't any promises to break, because she hadn't made any, aside from the one she'd made to herself. To marry only for love.

Nothing had changed. Cam wanted her, but desire wasn't love. It was a dream only, an illusion that faded into nothing without love to feed it. The only true thing was the promise she'd made to herself.

Eleanor crossed over to the window with halting steps, and gazed down at the profusion of purple flowers below. She saw Amelia as she'd been yesterday, her fair hair haloed by the sun, her face alight with excitement and pride as she dashed from flower to flower, and Ellie's fingers curled into the windowsill.

See how they're all different shades of purple, Lady Eleanor?

There was a faint knock at the door, and she froze, turned, a hand to her mouth. Surely the hunting party had left by now? Even if they hadn't, surely he wouldn't—

He would. He had. Last night. He'd entered her bedchamber. She hadn't been here, but if she had been, and they'd been alone . . .

"Eleanor?" Charlotte called. "Are you awake? Open the door."

Eleanor heaved a sigh of . . . relief? Yes, of course it was relief, and hurried across the room.

"You weren't at breakfast." Charlotte closed the door behind her. "I was worried. Did you ring for a tray? Goodness, Eleanor, you're not even dressed yet."

"No. I didn't sleep well." Eleanor dropped onto the bed and slipped under the coverlet, shivering. Her whole body felt cold.

Charlotte perched on the edge of the bed. "I'm sorry."

Eleanor studied her sister, who despite her pink cheeks, had shadows under her eyes. "You look as if you didn't sleep much yourself, Charlotte, though I must say you look well in spite of it." She tilted her head to the side. "You're glowing, rather."

Charlotte flushed an even deeper pink. "Am I? Well, I, ah—I believe I got too much sun yesterday, that's all. Shall I ring for tea?" She leapt off the bed, made a great show of ringing the bell, and then busied herself with rearranging the items on Eleanor's dressing table.

"I suppose," Eleanor replied, without enthusiasm. The nerves in her belly whined in protest at the thought of eating. "Have the gentlemen left for their sport yet?"

"Yes. Mrs. Mullins sent them off with a large hamper, so I doubt we'll be troubled by them until much later this afternoon."

Cam was away for the entire day then, which left the way clear for Eleanor to finish what she'd begun with Mrs. Mullins last night. When he returned this evening, he'd find his marriage plans had gone up in flames.

Her heart shuddered in protest at the thought, but this madness between them had to end. She'd never trust Cam—not now, after the way they'd begun, and she couldn't love a man she couldn't trust. Absurd, then, the sinking feeling in her stomach. She should be pleased. She *was* pleased, only there was this pain in her chest—

Charlotte studied her, her expression shrewd. "You look ill. You've found out something, haven't you?"

Eleanor hesitated. "I have, yes."

"Well?" Charlotte made a beckoning motion with her fingers. "What is it?"

Eleanor bit her lip. If she told Charlotte what she knew about Amelia's birth, there would be an end to this. She may find she couldn't bring herself to use the information, but Charlotte might not have the same scruples.

That was what she wanted, wasn't it? To free herself from Camden West, and never look back? Yes, yes—of course it was. And yet . . .

Part of this drama had yet to unfold. She still didn't know why Cam insisted on marrying only *her*. The Sutherlands were known to be a tight-knit family, and they'd never turn their backs on Amelia because she'd been born on the wrong side of the blanket. Certainly it was to Amelia's advantage for Cam to make this marriage, but there was more to it than that. There had to be.

"Eleanor?"

Tell Charlotte what you know, and end this.

"I can't say just yet," Eleanor said, disgusted with herself even as the words left her mouth. "It's only servants' gossip at this point, and we need more than that."

Charlotte wrinkled her brow. "More? Well, where do you plan to get it?"

Eleanor plucked at the covers. "Mary West. I need to get her away from her husband if I want the truth, though."

"Yes. He looks like the sort of man who'd lie on principle, doesn't he? How the father could be so different from his—ah, that is, it shouldn't be too difficult to get her alone. I think she avoids her husband. I know I would, in her place."

Eleanor looked at Charlotte's flushed face and frowned. "Are you quite all right, Charlotte? You look strange."

"Very well, indeed. Now, this information you have. Is it the sort that will put an end to Camden West's scheme for good?"

Eleanor drew in a deep breath. "Yes, but I warn you, Charlotte. It's ugly. So ugly, I'm not sure I can bear to . . ."

But she had to, didn't she? Cam hadn't left her any other choice. He may be a man of his word, but he was also a man who'd used threats and coercion to manipulate her.

Everything he's done, he's done for Amelia.

Eleanor wrapped her arms around her knees. It didn't matter. It didn't change anything—

You'd do the same in his place.

She would. She was.

"I didn't suppose it would be pretty, Eleanor." Charlotte's voice softened when she looked into Eleanor's face. "Oh, dear. That bad? Well, perhaps you won't be forced to use it, after all."

"Not use it?" Eleanor stared at her sister. "I don't know what you mean. I don't see any way around it."

Her only hope was Cam would see reason, and the threat against Amelia would be enough to silence him about Charlotte's lapse with Julian West. She prayed he wouldn't force her to make the secret about Amelia's birth public, for if he did, well . . .

Then she'd see how far she was willing to go to hold onto her chance for love. Perhaps, after all, she was the villain.

Charlotte shrugged, but she didn't quite meet Eleanor's eyes. "Oh, one never knows. Something could happen, something unexpected that will change the situation entirely."

Eleanor couldn't imagine what. They'd been rather short on miracles up to this point, and she didn't expect one now. "I wouldn't plan on it, Charlotte."

But Charlotte didn't appear to hear her. She'd turned away to study her reflection in the glass, a dreamy expression on her face. "You'll speak to Mary West today?"

"Yes, if you'll keep her husband away."

"I will. Perhaps we can return to town early, if all goes according to plan." Charlotte's cheeks flooded with pink again, and she smiled at her reflection. "I find myself quite anxious to be back in London."

* * * * *

Eleanor was anxious as well. To be in London, or anywhere but Lindenhurst, doing anything but what she was doing, which was sneaking about after Mary West like a thief intent on pilfering a pocket.

She'd dressed and made it downstairs in time for luncheon. As Charlotte predicted, the gentleman were absent, including Reginald West, who'd left to settle some business in Watford. After luncheon Amelia and the other ladies had gone off to sketch some local ruins.

"Are you sure you won't come with us, Lady Eleanor?" Amelia asked before they left. "Lady Charlotte said you like to sketch. I wanted to ask your advice on my drawings."

Eleanor winced at the hopeful note in the girl's voice, but she shook her head. "I'm sorry, Amelia. I've the headache, and I don't want to make it worse by being in the sun all day. But I'd like to see your progress, and I can see the ruins, after all, if you'll come to my room this evening and show me your sketches."

Amelia had brightened at that prospect, but her sweet smile had only made Eleanor feel worse, and she struggled to smile in return.

Now she was struggling again, this time to make her feet follow Mary West, who'd disappeared into the kitchen garden a few moments ago. "Good afternoon, Mrs. West," she called as she ducked through the door leading from the stillroom to the walled garden behind it.

Mary West was leaning over a tall rosemary bush, a pair of shears in her hand, and a basket at her feet. "Why, Lady Eleanor. What are you doing out here? I thought you had the headache."

Eleanor forced a smile. "I rested a bit this afternoon, and I feel much better now. I thought perhaps some fresh air—oh, how pretty it is."

She glanced around the garden, wondering if Sarah West had designed it. Neat gravel paths lined a series of well-tended garden beds. In the corner, Eleanor saw a row of trellises, all of them loaded with peas, and in the opposite corner a handful of espaliered apple trees, so tall they reached the top of the wall and were hanging over the other side, heavy with unripe fruit.

"What have you there?" She crossed over to Mrs. West and gestured at the basket. "Rosemary?"

"Yes. Mrs. Mullins says we're to have lamb tonight, and Camden is partial to fresh rosemary with his lamb."

Eleanor's heart twisted in her chest as she looked down at the heaping pile of rosemary in Mary West's basket. Such a little thing, and yet it was plain to see the woman cared for Cam as much as she did for Amelia.

Did he know that? Had he ever known it?

Mrs. West looked down at the shears in her hand, then back up at Eleanor with a self-conscious smile. "I could ask Mrs. Mullins to do this, of course, but she's so busy, and I like to muck about in the gardens when I get the chance."

How often was that? Not very, Eleanor guessed. Reginald West seemed like the kind of man who'd care little if his wife had her pleasures. "It smells lovely out here. May I help you?"

Another smile. "All right." She handed Eleanor the basket. "I'll cut if you'll carry the basket. We can get some dill as well, for the bread."

Eleanor took the basket from Mrs. West's outstretched hand. "Another of Cam's favorites?"

"Yes." Mrs. West set to work on the rosemary, clipping where the herb's woody stalks had grown too long. "Camden seems quite . . . fond of you."

Eleanor nearly dropped the basket. *Fond?* Cam felt something for her, but Eleanor didn't imagine it was fondness. Frustration, yes. Irritation, certainly.

Desire. Her stomach fluttered at the thought.

She took care to keep her voice light. "Indeed? What makes you say so?"

Mrs. West kept her eyes on her work. "He doesn't come to Lindenhurst anymore. He's certainly never brought friends here."

"Oh, well, I'm afraid my brothers teased him into making the invitation. They're keen to hunt, you see."

Mrs. West gave her a sidelong glance. "I don't think he did it for your brothers, Lady Eleanor."

"Perhaps not." She paused, then, "His memories of Lindenhurst are not, I gather . . ."

Say it, you coward.

". . . all pleasant ones?"

Mary West's hand never faltered over the rosemary, but Eleanor felt the woman stiffen beside her. "He told you about his father, then? About . . . what happened?"

I found out. "Yes," Eleanor lied, biting the inside of her cheek until she tasted blood on her tongue. "Cam's father died when he was a child—nine, I think he said."

Clip, clip, clip. Rosemary fell into Eleanor's basket, but for a time Mrs. West didn't speak. At last she darted a glance at Eleanor. "He must be fond of you, indeed, if he told you that story."

Eleanor pressed her lips together, afraid if she opened her mouth the truth would tumble out.

Mrs. West sighed. "James West doted on them, you know, both Camden and Sarah. Camden was devastated when he died, and Sarah, well, she fell apart, and she never could pull herself back together again."

Eleanor plucked a few blades of rosemary from a stalk, rolled them between her fingers, and inhaled the sharp lemon scent. She remained quiet, hoping the silence would further loosen her companion's tongue.

It did. "I don't like to think about what my husband did to Sarah and Camden, Lady Eleanor. It devastated me at the time, and I regret it even now, all these years later. Sarah was like a sister to me, and Camden is as dear to me as my own son. But James's death broke Sarah. Changed her. Otherwise she would never have—"

Mary West broke off and turned to look at Eleanor. Her face was ashen, and etched with deep lines of pain.

Eleanor's throat worked, but somehow she managed to keep her voice steady. "She never would have what, Mrs. West?"

"She never would have taken up with such a man. He pursued her relentlessly—wouldn't leave her alone until at last she gave in, almost from exhaustion, I think. Either that, or she was so grief-stricken over James she just didn't care what happened to her anymore."

"What did he . . ." Ellie stopped, cleared her throat. "What did he do to her?"

Mrs. West looked down at her hands, still clutching the shears. "He used her—ruined her. Three years she stayed with him, so many years, and they turned out to be the last years of her life. But for all that, I don't believe he ever cared for her. I'm sorry, Lady Eleanor, so sorry to say it, but he abandoned her the moment he found out she was with child."

Ellie stared at her, puzzled. Why should Mrs. West apologize to her? Did she think Ellie was offended by Amelia's birth? She would never hold an innocent child responsible for her father's sins. Just thinking about such a man caused Ellie's throat to burn with bile. Despicable, to seduce a woman broken by grief, then to leave her and his own child to suffer. What kind of man—

"Reginald found out, of course," Mary went on. "One can't hide a thing like that for long, and Sarah was careless. He turned her out of the house, though he hadn't any right to. Lindenhurst belongs to Camden."

Eleanor went still, the blades of rosemary still clutched between her fingers. It was all true then, what Winnie and Mrs. Mullins had said. Amelia had been born on the wrong side of the blanket. Sarah was her mother, Cam was her half-brother, and her father . . .

Grief and fury gathered in Eleanor's throat, choking her. *That lovely child.* Perhaps one could excuse Sarah West, but the father . . .

God only knew who he was. It hardly mattered. Amelia would carry the stain of illegitimacy all her life, even if by some miracle her father chose to acknowledge her, which was doubtful. If he intended to, he'd have done so long before now.

"I think Sarah knew she wouldn't survive the birth," Mrs. West said. "The pregnancy was a difficult one, but oh, she wanted Amelia. So badly. Loved her, and taught Camden to love her too, despite his hatred for Amelia's father. Perhaps she thought the child would save her, but . . ."

Mary West's eyes filled with tears. Without thinking, Eleanor reached for her, took her hand. "But?"

"There were complications. Bleeding. Sarah died within an hour of Amelia's birth."

Eleanor released Mrs. West's hand, her arm falling slack at her side. "What of Cam?"

"Camden was filled with grief, with rage." Mary swiped the back of her hand under her eye. "I wanted to help him. I wanted to bring him home to the manor house, but Reginald wouldn't hear of it. He's never liked Camden, you see—perhaps because Julian is so devoted to him. I suppose my husband is jealous of that. Camden left for India soon afterwards."

Dear God. Cam. What had Mrs. Mullins said? That all might still have been well after his father died, and perhaps it would have been, if it hadn't been for a man who'd cared for nothing but his own pleasure. He'd shamed and ruined Cam's mother, and Reginald West, the one person left who had the power to protect them, had tossed them both aside. Abandoned them. Stolen from them.

Cam's world had fallen apart.

Rage. Yes, it would have consumed him then—it did still, even now. She'd seen it, in the shadows of his green eyes. Rage. Bitterness.

The ghosts only he could see.

And Amelia, left motherless in her first hour of life, and burdened with her father's sin. Cam was determined to give her everything that had been taken from them. It must have been terribly difficult for him to leave Amelia with the Wests for eleven long years, but he'd done it, because he knew it was best for a young child to have a home. Security. A mother, in Mary West.

He'd been young when he'd left for India, but he'd behaved like a man, risking everything to amass a fortune, to make an easier path for Amelia.

To clear it of the rocks others had thrown in her way.

Everything he did, he did for Amelia. Eleanor had known it, deep down in the dark part of her heart where she hid things from herself. She hadn't wanted to admit it, but she'd known his mad marriage scheme was as much about giving as taking.

Take from her, give to Amelia.

She wanted to hate him, but even as she gasped with anger and pain at the injustice of it, even as she vowed to thwart him still, his courage, the force of his will, and the depth of his love for his sister—it stole her breath away.

Mary turned pleading eyes on Eleanor. "I couldn't help Cam, but I got a second chance with Amelia, and I tried to do what was right by her. I tried to do what Sarah would have wanted."

Eleanor touched a gentle hand to Mary West's shoulder. "Amelia's lovely, Mrs. West. Truly. I'm sure her mother would have thought so, too."

Mrs. West managed a watery smile. "You're kind, Lady Eleanor. I didn't expect you to be so kind."

Shame clutched Eleanor by the throat. *Kind.* No. She wasn't kind.

Even now she stood at the edge of Amelia's path, a rock held in her hand.

Chapter Twenty

The lamb was roasted to perfection and liberally sprinkled with fresh rosemary, the bread was hot and fragrant with dill, the peas glistened with new butter, and the wine was excellent.

But no one was eating.

Aunt Mary sat, hands folded, her eyes on her plate. Charlotte Sutherland studied the dish of new potatoes the footman had just served. Eleanor, her face troubled, seemed to be speaking to Charlotte out of the corner of her mouth. Robyn Sutherland, who'd applied himself to his meal with gusto just moments before, had abandoned his plate in favor of his wineglass. The rest of the party was silent, not sure where to look next.

Cam forked another succulent piece of lamb into his mouth. It was a waste of an excellent meal, if you asked him. He took a sip of his wine and returned the cold stare aimed at him from the other end of the table.

Uncle Reggie, the author of all this distress, his heavy face flushed with drink, glowered back at him. "Well? What have you got to say for yourself, sir?"

"The lamb is delicious."

Uncle Reggie's face went a deeper shade of red. He sputtered, so furious the incoherent sounds refused to form themselves into words, never mind a sentence.

Cam sampled his peas. This could be it, at last—Uncle Reggie's apoplexy.

His uncle drained his wineglass for the third time since the peas had been served. "It pleases you to make jokes, I see. I wonder if you'll be so pleased when Boney sends your cousin back to England without his legs. That is, if he returns at all!"

Ah. That's what the fuss was about. Uncle Reggie knew Cam had agreed to purchase the commission for Julian. He couldn't fathom how his uncle had discovered it so quickly, unless Julian had sent word from London.

If he had sent word, it might mean he'd decided to accept the commission. Cam's heart froze at the thought, but he kept his face expressionless. He wouldn't give his uncle the satisfaction of seeing his concern. "I have more faith in Julian than you do, I see. He'll return, and in one piece."

Uncle Reggie slammed his fist down next to his plate. His fork skittered to the floor and a footman leapt forward to retrieve it. "Just how would you know that?"

Because any other outcome is unthinkable. So Cam wouldn't think it.

"He'll come back because you deem it so?" Uncle Reggie gave a bitter laugh. "If the great Camden West with his spectacular fortune says it's so, then it must be so."

Cam looked down the table at his uncle with a mixture of disgust, frustration and a vague sense of pity. If Reggie could have kept Julian forever at Lindenhurst, wrapped in cotton wool, he'd have done it. He'd always doted on his son to such an extreme degree it was more mania than anything else.

It was a kind of love, Cam supposed. But a poor kind.

Spittle flew from his uncle's mouth, and he was so sotted he was nearly face down in his plate. Watching him now, Cam understood more clearly than ever why Julian had to leave London. "Julian is an adult, and in full possession of his faculties. He's made his choice. There's naught for us to do now but trust it's the right one."

"You don't want him to come back," Uncle Reggie spat. "You see this as your chance to get rid of him, and you've taken it. You've always been jealous of him."

Aunt Mary looked up, her face white. "Reginald! For pity's sake."

Enough. Cam placed his wineglass next to his plate. "Have a care, uncle." He spoke in low tones that nevertheless carried to the other end of the table. "There is a limit to my tolerance."

He was left to speculate whether or not his uncle would have been wise enough to heed this warning, for at that moment Eleanor half-rose from her seat and dropped her napkin on the table. "I beg you will excuse us. My sister—"

Lady Carlisle rose as well. "Charlotte?"

Cam took in Lady Charlotte's pallor and motioned to one of the footmen. "Arthur, Lady Charlotte is ill. Escort her to her room, then send Winnie to attend her."

Charlotte waved the footman off with a shaky hand. "It's nothing. Just a sudden headache."

"Nonsense." Eleanor took Charlotte's arm. "You look as if you're about to swoon. Come along."

The footman caught Charlotte's other arm and he and Eleanor hurried from the dining room, supporting Charlotte between them. Lady Carlisle and Lily Sutherland followed behind them.

The room fell silent. Uncle Reggie had slipped into a sudden doze, exhausted by his fury and the better part of a bottle of wine. Aunt Mary touched a tentative hand to his arm, but Reggie only snorted and slumped further down in his chair.

Cam sighed, then gestured to the second footman. "George, attend my uncle, if you would."

George darted forward, grasped Uncle Reggie under his arms, hauled him up from his chair, and dragged him from the room. Aunt Mary followed, her face red with shame.

"By gad," Robyn murmured. "That was neatly done."

"Handy thing to have about," Lord Carlisle said. "An unusually large footman, I mean."

Cam gave a humorless laugh. "I don't wish to shock you, gentlemen, but that was not the first time George has been called upon to perform that service. Shall we have some port? I believe dinner is over."

They sat in the dining room for another half hour, then his guests wandered off to pursue of game of chess in the drawing room, leaving Cam alone.

He rose, grabbed the bottle of port and made his way to the library. There was no point in sitting around like some besotted tragic hero. Eleanor wouldn't come back downstairs tonight.

He sat in the dark and drank his port, running his finger over the top edge of his wineglass, thinking of how passionate she'd been with him in the kitchen last night. Her sighs and moans, the way she'd pressed herself against him—dear God, she'd driven him mad.

Did she know how much he wanted her? Had she understood he'd been one kiss away from snatching her into his arms and stealing away with her to his bedchamber? He'd dreamed about her, about laying her across his bed, pulling every pin from her hair, sliding those stockings from her long, long legs, and . . .

Damn it. This was becoming a habit, sitting alone in a dark library with a hard cock, drowning in fantasies about Eleanor.

One kiss away—so close, and yet not close enough, and one couldn't seduce in half-measures. Either he'd had her, or he hadn't. Either she was a virgin, or she wasn't.

The party would return to London the day after tomorrow, and Ellie had no more reason to marry him now than she had when they'd arrived at Lindenhurst.

He was almost out of time.

He had one more night to make her his, but even if the opportunity arose, he wasn't sure he could take her. He wanted her desperately, but if she asked for his promise again, he'd give it to her, and once he did, he'd keep it.

Cam downed the rest of his port in one swallow, then filled the glass again. Her sister's indisposition gave her the perfect excuse to remain upstairs. If he hadn't seen Charlotte's near-swoon for himself, he might believe it was all a ploy so Ellie could avoid seeing him tonight.

Sweet, sweet Ellie, with her black currant lips and her hot, seeking tongue . . .

"May I come in?"

For a moment he thought he'd conjured her straight out of his fantasies and through the library door. He waited for her to come to him, sink onto his lap, brush his hair back with a cool hand and lower her lips to his.

Instead she stood at the open door, her expression growing puzzled. "Cam?"

Not a fantasy, then. She was really here. He leapt to his feet, amazed by his good fortune. "I—yes, of course."

He hadn't lit a lamp, and he didn't make any move to light one now. In the feeble light from the hallway he thought he saw a faint flush rise to her cheeks, but she didn't object to the dimness. Just as well. By some divine stroke of luck he had her here alone, and whatever might happen, he didn't intend to lose this opportunity. "How does your sister do? She looked ill when she left the dining room."

Eleanor frowned. "I don't think she is ill after all, merely agitated, though she refuses to say why. She also refused every offer of assistance. In fact, she chased us all out of her room, even me." She perched on the edge of the leather sofa, her hands folded in her lap. "It's just as well, as I wish to speak to you."

And I wish to make love to you, on that sofa, with your arms around me and your fingernails in my back.

"Perhaps we can both get what we wish for this evening, my lady."

"I wish you would stop calling me that."

Cam raised an eyebrow, surprised. "What? My lady? But that's what you are, isn't it?"

She clenched her hands together until her knuckles turned white. "It's not the title. It's the way you say it."

"Oh? How is that, my lady?"

But he knew. He said it like a caress. Like a secret, whispered in her ear.

"Like you . . . like—I'm not *your* lady. I'm not your anything."

"Ah." He sat down next to her and reached for her, but slowly, the way one might reach out to stroke a wild animal. "But you will be."

Eleanor leapt off the sofa, away from him. "No. I won't." She paced over to the fireplace. "That's what I came to tell you. This is over, Cam."

*The devil it was. It had*n't even begun.

"If it's over, why do you run away from me every time I try to touch you?"

She lifted her chin. "You don't need to touch me every time I get near you."

Yes, I do.

"Run, then," he murmured, an unmistakable challenge in his voice. "It won't do you any good. There's no place in the world so far away I won't follow you—"

Cam stopped, stunned into silence.

Jesus. It was true. He'd follow her to the ends of the earth if he had to. Not because of Amelia, or to satisfy some twisted sense of justice, or because she was Hart Sutherland's daughter.

*Because s*he was Eleanor.

Eleanor, with that maddening blush, stubborn chin, and those dark eyes—eyes that turned so soft when she looked at Amelia.

Would her eyes ever soften for him like that? If they never did, it would be no more than he deserved. He'd told himself he didn't care if she despised him. He'd told her it made no difference if she were foolish or clever, mad or sane.

He'd told her she didn't matter.

It was a lie.

She was all that mattered.

He rose from the sofa and moved toward her. "Eleanor, listen to me—"

"No." She held out a hand to keep him away. "I spoke with your aunt this afternoon, while you were out hunting, and she told me everything."

Halfway across the room to her, Cam froze. "Everything."

"Don't blame her. I—I said I already knew. Mrs. Mullins told me about your father. Your aunt assumed I knew the rest, and I didn't correct her. I warned you, Cam." She gave him a defiant look, but her lower lip trembled.

Cam stared at her and noticed for the first time the hectic flush across her cheekbones, the way her fingers clutched at the folds of her gown. "Yes, I suppose you did."

Was that why he'd brought her here? In some deep part of his mind, where he tried to keep the scales of justice balanced, maybe he'd wanted her to fight him.

It was one way to justify seducing her.

He knew she wouldn't pass up the chance to unearth his secrets, and what better place to do so than Lindenhurst? He'd suspected as much when he discovered her in the kitchen with Mrs. Mullins last night, but he hadn't cared—hadn't even tried to stop her. Not really. He'd been so desperate to taste her, to touch her, he couldn't think of anything else.

*Now she k*new everything.

Or she thought she did. But how much did she know? She might know what had happened to his father, but did she know about Amelia's father? "Tell me what you know, Eleanor. I give you my word I won't lie to you."

She straightened her shoulders and folded her hands in front of her again, stiffly, like a headmistress about to deliver a lecture to a room full of naughty boys. "Your father died when you were nine."

Despite her dignified pose, her breath caught a little here, and Cam felt a hollow echo of it in his chest. Was she sorry for him? For the boy he'd been, perhaps, but not for the man he was. Not for him.

"A fever. Mrs. Mullins said it was quick."

Quick, yes. Wasn't it supposed to hurt less if it was quick?

It hadn't. His father's death had nearly killed his mother, and his nine-year-old world had cracked open and splintered into thousands of tiny shards. He'd been buried in the debris. There'd been so much of it when he emerged at last, much later, he didn't recognize himself anymore.

Had Mrs. Mullins told her that?

Eleanor began to rush over the words now. Poison was like that. Once you'd swallowed it, you became desperate to purge yourself. "Your uncle and aunt and cousin came to live with you then, and Julian became like a brother to you. Mrs. Mullins said all might still have been well, despite your uncle's cruelty, but—"

She stopped, and Cam saw she was shaking. She didn't want to say it—didn't want to know this story. Knowing it hurt her.

But not as much as it hurt him.

He laughed a little, but the sound was bitter. "But what, Ellie? You've come this far, and now I'll have the whole of it. You'll want to get such an ugly story out, you see, otherwise it will fester and burn inside your heart until it leaves a gaping wound."

Her composure fled then, and she brought her hands up to cover her face.

He did cross to her then, to grasp her wrists and force her hands back down. "Look at me. What did my Aunt Mary tell you? Something about my mother, I think?"

She shook her head, her dark eyes huge in her white face.

"You said you wanted the truth, Eleanor. What did my aunt tell you about my mother?"

"She said—she said . . . your mother was shamed. Ruined. Your uncle found out about it and forced you and your mother from your home."

Cam dropped her hands. "My mother's downfall was a great stroke of luck for my uncle. He'd been trying to find a way to steal Lindenhurst for three years by then, and this—well, you can imagine how delighted he was to find a reason to be rid of us at last."

Her face flushed with anger. "Why did you let him, Cam? Lindenhurst belongs to you. He had no right. Even your aunt said he had no right."

Cam ran a hand down his face. God, he was tired. Tired of this tragedy. Tired of himself. "I was a boy. Just a boy, and still grieving."

Her hand went to her mouth, but he heard the sound just the same—a soft sob.

Pity. She pitied him.

His jaw went hard. No one pitied him. Not anymore. "I'm not a boy any longer. No one takes anything from me now. I'm the one who takes. When I want something, I take it, and I want you, Ellie. So much." Despite his harsh tone, his voice broke a little on the last words.

"No, you don't," she whispered. "You want something, but you don't want me."

But he did want her. More than he'd ever wanted anything. He held out his hand to her. "Yes, Eleanor. I do."

For one moment her face softened, and his heart surged in his chest. If she'd only believe him—

But then her eyes went flat, and she backed away from until she came up against the fireplace and could go no further.

He followed her. "Don't run away now. You haven't told me the best part yet."

"The—the best part?"

His lips twisted in a mockery of a smile. "Come now, Eleanor. Clever as you are, you must have drawn your own conclusions. My mother was disgraced to such a degree my uncle was able to snatch Lindenhurst out from under our feet, and my father died years before Amelia was born. You've said this much. Why not unburden yourself completely?"

She must have seen he'd allow her no quarter, for she lifted her chin and said, "You and Amelia don't share a father. She's your half-sister, and she's illegitimate."

He cupped her cheek gently in his palm, but his face felt stiff and hard. "That's right, Ellie. Amelia was born on the wrong side of the blanket. She's a by-blow, a bas—"

"Don't!" She put her hands over her ears and shook her head. "Stop it, Cam."

His hand dropped to his side. "Do you think it's any less true of if I don't say it aloud? How naïve you are. You may cover your ears all you like, but it doesn't change anything."

She lowered her hands, her face defeated.

He moved closer to her—close enough to touch her again, but he didn't. He kept his arms at his sides. "Tell me, Eleanor. Earlier, when you came in, you said "this is over," or something equally dramatic. What did you mean?"

She pressed her hands flat against the fireplace in back of her, as if she wished she could push it out of the way and escape him. "Just what I said. It's over. You have information on my sister I would prefer didn't become public, and—"

"And now you have information on my sister, too. Is that it?"

"I should think it would be obvious."

His hands closed around her upper arms. "But I want to hear you say it just the same, and don't think to look away from me when you do. When you threaten someone, you look them in the eyes."

Eleanor Sutherland was no coward. She did look into his eyes, just as he'd bade her. "If you ruin Charlotte, I'll ruin Amelia."

He shouldn't have looked into her eyes.

He should have known better, because as blinded with fury as he was, he could see the wretchedness in those dark depths, the shadows underneath that spoke of her sleeplessness. Her misery.

She didn't want to do this, not to Amelia, and perhaps not even to him. Would she go through with her threats? She'd told him she wouldn't give up, and he believed she wouldn't.

Even when she should. Even when holding on would devastate her.

She took a deep breath. "I will not marry you, Cam. You will release me at once from your demand. If you do not, as surely as you will ruin my sister, I will ruin yours."

Cam went still. He'd known she was going to say it. He'd expected to feel rage when she did. Rage and bitterness and yes, hate—the same hate he'd felt for Hart Sutherland. But Eleanor wasn't her father, and even now, when she had such hateful words in her mouth, he could never hate her.

God, it was so simple. Had it always been this simple? He could never deceive her. He could never manipulate her, or coldly seduce her. He could never hurt her.

He loved her. He could only ever love her.

But with that love came an aching sadness. So far down, that ache. Deeper, even, than his heart.

This is how badly she wants to be free of me.

Cam looked down at her, into those dark, pained eyes. She didn't know. She thought she knew everything, but she didn't know it all.

Your mother was shamed. Ruined.

She'd never once mentioned Hart Sutherland.

Chapter Twenty-one

"You don't want to do this, Ellie."

Eleanor watched him. Waited. The silence stretched between them until her nerves screamed with it, and still he said nothing more, but continued to gaze down at her, his green eyes shadowed with . . .

Pity? No, not that. She might have understood pity, but pity would not make her breath catch in her throat and her heart thrash painfully in her chest. Pity would not make her mouth fall open in astonishment.

Only one thing could, and it was the last thing she'd expected.

Hurt. She'd hurt him.

Before she could think to stop it, before she even realized she felt it, it was upon her. It swelled in her throat, burned the back of her eyes. Her hands shook with it, her chin trembled with it—an answering hurt, wrenched from a place so deep inside her she staggered when it was jerked free.

When had it happened? When had his pain become her own?

He reached to steady her, his hands gentle on her shoulders. "Eleanor, please. You don't want to do this."

This was his response? She'd braced herself for fury, accusations, threats, and denials. She'd answered each of them in her head. She knew just how she'd respond—how she'd meet his fury with her own.

But this? One sentence, his voice soft, his hands on her shoulders to steady her, and his eyes—such a dark green now, and clouded with pain. A forest shrouded in fog.

No. She hadn't prepared herself for this. Couldn't have, even if she'd tried.

She pressed her hands harder against the fireplace behind her, and harder still, until the cold from the stone under her palms stole up her arm and didn't stop, didn't stop until it crept into every part of her body.

Into her heart.

And with it, a helpless fury. At him, yes, for making this so hard. For daring to be hurt.

But mostly at herself, because hurting him shouldn't be the hardest thing she'd ever done.

*You don't w*ant to do this.

No, she didn't want to do this, but she had no choice. He'd *made* her do it. Forced her to do it, and now he was making her heart twist with misery inside her chest.

She tugged her shoulders free. "What I want doesn't matter. What matters is Amelia. Do you wish to see her secret exposed for all the *ton* to gossip over?"

"I don't wish it." His voice was quiet. He reached out, brushed a lock of her hair behind her ear with careful fingers. "But neither do you."

She flinched away from the soft touch. "I told you. It doesn't matter what I wish. You know what will happen once the *ton* hears the truth. They'll never accept her. The gentleman will speculate about her, and the ladies—they'll be worse. They'll sneer at her, whisper about her, and titter over her from behind their fans."

Threaten me. Rage at me.

But he wouldn't. Instead he moved closer. His warm fingers stroked her cheek. "And when they do it will break your heart, Ellie, as surely as it will break hers."

Her heart. Oh, God, he was troubled about *her* heart, after she'd threatened Amelia?

The dark room pressed in on her as panic welled in her chest. She couldn't bear it—his hurt, or his tenderness. "She'll blame you for it. She'll hate you for it. If I were in her place, I'd hate you, too."

*Bla*me me. Hate me.

But even as she lashed out at him, tried to slice at him with her jagged words, he touched her, soothed her, his hands gentle on her face, in her hair, against her neck. His green eyes were still dark with hurt, but as they searched her face, she saw something else there, something that silenced her protests, froze her in his grasp.

Longing.

"Do you hate me even now, Eleanor?" His voice was husky, and so quiet it seemed to come from the darkness itself. "Is there no hope for us?"

Before she could answer, he bent his head and touched his lips to hers.

Eleanor trembled at the restrained passion in his kiss. He held his desire ruthlessly in check, his lips tender on hers, the kiss a confession, and a question.

Is there no hope for us?

A wish, and a plea.

His hands moved to cradle her face. He stroked his thumbs across her cheekbones and pressed his lips harder against hers, but soft still, so sweet, his touch, as if he sought to give back to her some of what he'd taken.

She couldn't let him—couldn't take what he'd give her. She'd found a way to escape him at last, but his kiss would imprison her again, and this time it would be far worse.

This time, she'd want to stay.

"No, Cam." She turned her head aside and pushed against his chest.

He raised his head, stared down at her. Half his face was lost in the shadows, his breath shallow and quick. Just when she thought he'd take her lips again, he set her away from him. For a moment he seemed to struggle with himself, then, "Go to bed, Eleanor."

She didn't move. She couldn't. She could only stare up at him, a cold ache in her chest.

He ran a weary hand through his hair. "Please. Now. If you stay here, I'll kiss you again, and this time I won't be able to stop."

And I won't be able to make you.

Somehow she managed to grasp her skirts and turn away from him. She fled up the stairs, and within minutes she was in her bedchamber, her back flat against the closed door.

Dear God. What had just happened?

She pressed a shaking hand to her forehead and tried to think, but the thoughts were jumbled in her head. Had he freed her, or did he still think to force her into marriage? Oh, she didn't know, because his words were tangled up with the memory of his mouth on hers, so soft and sweet—not a claim, and not a demand. A plea, yes, but something more than that, too, something infinitely more precious . . .

A gift.

She touched her fingers to her lips. *Why?* What had he—

The door vibrated against her back. Eleanor jumped away from it, then whirled around to stare at it. Someone had knocked. Had Cam followed her? If he had, how would she ever be able to escape him a second time, when every inch of her heated skin clamored for his touch? She wouldn't answer the door—

"Lady Eleanor? I've brought my sketches, as I promised."

Amelia.

Eleanor's body sagged with relief. Of course. She'd invited Amelia to her room this evening so she could see her sketches of the ruins. Had that only been this afternoon? It seemed impossible her entire world could have tilted off its axis in a matter of a few hours.

She opened the door and Amelia stood there, clad in her night dress, her fair hair in two plaits down her back. Her face was eager, and she had a sketchbook tucked under her arm.

Despite her agitation, Eleanor made herself take a deep breath. She forced a smile to her lips. "Amelia. Come in. You've finished your dinner?"

"Yes, ages ago. Miss Norwood and I ate early, in the nursery, though I do think it would have been so much nicer if I were permitted to have my dinner downstairs, as I do with Denny when we're in London."

Ellie thought of the dismal dinner they'd had this evening, of all the dismal dinners she'd had as a child, trapped at a grim, silent table with her father, and she shook her head. "Oh, I don't know. Dinner in the nursery sounds quite cozy." She walked over to stir the fire, then took a seat on the bed. "You're fond of Miss Norwood, aren't you?"

"Oh, yes. We've been looking at the drawings I did this afternoon. I only made two, but Miss Norwood says they're both good enough to show you."

Some of the tension drained from Eleanor's body, and she patted the space next to her. "Well, I'm glad we have Miss Norwood's approval, for I'd very much like to see them both."

Amelia came over to the bed, sat down and opened the sketchbook flat across her lap. She flipped through a few of the pages and laid the two sketches of the ruins side by side on the bed.

Eleanor scooted forward to look, and her eyes widened. The sketches were the work of a child, yes, but a talented child, the pencil strokes confident, the lines true. "Oh, how wonderful, Amelia. My goodness. You did both of these in one afternoon?"

"Yes." Amelia gave her a shy smile. "Do you like them?"

"I do." Eleanor traced a finger over some of the pencil lines. "This looks a bit like the remains of a moat. Are these castle ruins?"

"Yes. Denny says it was built way back when the Normans came to conquer England. There was a moat, and these stones here were the castle keep. I used to think it looked like just a pile of old rocks, but once Denny explained it to me, I could see how it used to be a castle, long ago."

A lump formed in Eleanor's throat. She couldn't think of Cam just now. "Did the ladies enjoy the ruins? I can't imagine their sketches are any nicer than yours."

"Oh, they are, though," Amelia said, without rancor. "Especially Lady Charlotte's. She's very good with her pencils, isn't she? But she says you're better than she is."

Eleanor smiled. "It's kind of her to say so, but I'm not sure it's true. I do love to study art, but I've never been devoted to my pencil. Charlotte though, well, even as a child she loved to sketch, and her passion shows in her drawings. That is what true art does, really—expresses emotion."

Amelia seemed to consider that. "Like this, you mean?" She turned over a few of the pages a pulled a loose paper from her book.

Eleanor bent over it to get a closer look, then laughed at the picture of Julian West, struggling to string a limp daisy onto a thread. "Yes, just like that. Has your uncle seen this drawing?"

Amelia gave her a sly smile. "He has. He said it didn't look like him, but then Denny said it did, and Uncle Julian said it was something, something like a lib-lib—"

"A libel?"

"Yes. A scandalous libel, he said, whatever that means."

"What did your brother say to that?" Eleanor asked, unable to resist.

"He said the picture was his favorite." Amelia cocked her head to the side. "But that was before he saw the picture I drew of you."

Eleanor stilled. "You drew a picture of me?"

"Yes, and then Uncle Julian said that one was Denny's favorite." Amelia frowned. "It must have been, because he took it, and he never gave it back to me."

Eleanor stared at Amelia, unable to speak. It meant nothing, of course. Less than nothing. She couldn't quite make herself believe it, however, and warmth surged into her cheeks.

Amelia gave her a curious look. "Are you all right, Lady Eleanor? You look warm."

"Yes, yes. Quite all right." Eleanor cleared her throat. "I think it's time you called me Ellie, don't you? We're friends, after all."

Amelia clapped her hands together. "I should like that more than anything. I don't have many friends, you see."

Ellie gazed at Amelia's bright face, and a sharp arrow of pain pierced her chest. No, she wouldn't have many friends, would she, surrounded as she was by adults? Ellie's own childhood hadn't been easy, but she'd had Charlotte and her brothers, and she'd never been lonely.

Amelia, though—she was so young, and so much had already been taken from her.

You'll take more.

Eleanor's chest burned with shame.

"I always wished for a sister," Amelia said, her tone wistful. "A younger one, so I could show her things, and share things with her, the way Denny does with me."

Eleanor placed her hand over Amelia's small one. "That's the best part of having a sister—sharing things."

It was, and yet she couldn't recall the last time she'd shared anything with Charlotte. It had been weeks. Perhaps she shouldn't have lied to her sister about Julian West. If she'd been honest from the start . . .

No. There was no sense in regret, especially not now. She turned her attention back to Amelia. "What kinds of things would you show her?"

Amelia considered it. "All sorts of things, like the garden here at Lindenhurst, and how to ride a horse, and I'd take her for a lemon ice at Gunter's."

"Those are just the kinds of things a little sister would enjoy, I think. A friend would enjoy them, too, so perhaps we should go to Gunter's together for lemon ices when we return to London."

Foolish of her, to promise such a thing to the child, when not half an hour ago she'd threatened to expose Amelia's secrets to the *ton*. Cam may never let her see Amelia again after they left Lindenhurst.

But it was difficult to care how foolish it was when the promise made such a smile bloom on Amelia's face. "Truly? Just you and me?"

No matter what else might happen, Eleanor vowed to herself she would have lemon ices with Amelia at Gunter's. "Just you and me."

Amelia bounced up and down on the bed. "I wish we could go back to London now!"

"When you wake up tomorrow morning, it's only one more day until we do."

To Eleanor's surprise, Amelia frowned. "I suppose you'll send me to bed now."

"Do you? I'm not sure why."

"Because grownups always talk about going to sleep right before they send you to bed."

Eleanor chuckled. "I daresay they do, but I won't send you to bed if you don't wish to go. Aren't you tired, though?"

"Just a little." Amelia ran her hand back and forth across the coverlet. "I'll go soon, but before I do, won't you tell me a bit about what you and Lady Charlotte used to do when you were little girls? Then I'll know what to do if I ever have a younger sister."

Eleanor hesitated. "Goodness, we did so much, I hardly know where to start."

Amelia knew, however. "Start with how you used to brush each other's hair."

That startled a laugh from Eleanor. "Brush each other's hair? Where did you get the notion that sisters brush each other's hair?"

"From the Mowbray sisters," Amelia said, as if everyone in their right mind should know perfectly well who the Mowbray sisters were.

Eleanor raised an eyebrow. "And who would they be?"

Amelia giggled. "Oh, they're Lord and Lady Mowbray's grandchildren. The Mowbray's estate borders Lindenhurst, you see. Their grandchildren come twice a year to visit, and Lady Mowbray brings them here to play with me. Aunt Mary says she does it to get them off her hands, for they're quite naughty, you know."

"Are they, indeed?"

"Oh, yes. There are three of them, and they're forever squabbling over one thing or another. But Adele Mowbray told me they brush each other's hair every night. They used to kick up such a fuss over having their tangles brushed out, one evening their maid threw the brush across the room and refused to do it ever again."

Eleanor choked back a laugh. "I can't say I blame her."

"Me, either. So now they do each other's. I asked Adele if it was wretched, but she said no. She said it was quite nice, and the only time all three of them can be together without fighting."

"They sound awful."

"Oh, they are. But you see, sisters do brush each other's hair." Amelia eyed Eleanor's coiled hair with interest. "I had it from Adele Mowbray herself, and she'd know."

Eleanor, who had by now deduced the purpose of this conversation, reached over to tweak one of Amelia's plaits. "But your hair is already brushed and bound."

"Yours isn't."

Eleanor hid a grin. "Hmmm. So it isn't. Amelia?"

"Yes?"

"Would you like to brush my hair?"

Amelia leapt off the bed. "Yes, please. How did you know?"

Eleanor rose from the bed and grabbed her brush from the dressing-table. "Oh, a lucky guess. Mind the pins. There are about a thousand of them, and you'll have to get them all out or else they'll become tangled in my hair while I sleep."

Amelia dragged the pillows from the bed and plopped them onto the floor in front of the fire. "I will. Will you sit here?"

Eleanor settled onto the rug, pulled her knees up and hugged them with her arms.

Amelia began to pluck the pins from her hair, one by one. "You were about to tell me about when you and Lady Charlotte were girls."

"That's right. I was. Let me see." Eleanor tapped her fingers against her legs. "We learned to ride together. There's a lovely wood on the grounds at Bellwood, our home in Kent, and we used to ride there and pick bluebells."

Pluck. "Did your papa teach you to ride?"

Hardly. "No, our brother Alec taught us—me and Charlotte, and our other brother, Robyn."

Amelia dropped a handful of hairpins on the floor next to Eleanor. "Uncle Julian taught me. Uncles and older brothers are quite as nice as younger sisters, I think."

"They are, rather."

They both fell silent for moment to consider the merits of uncles and older brothers, then Eleanor said, "I hate to say it, but Charlotte was a naughty child, just like the Mowbray sisters. She was always the first to dirty her frock, or race Robyn on her horse, or climb to the top of the oak tree so she could peer into the governess's window on the third floor."

Amelia paused her rhythmic strokes to consider this. "She does sound naughty."

"Oh, she was. Once she even climbed the tree at night and scratched at Miss Lettings' window until the poor old thing heard her at last, then nearly had an apoplexy to find Charlotte's face leering at her through the glass."

Amelia dropped another handful of pins on top of the mound on the floor. "There, that's all of them, I think. Was Miss Lettings your governess?"

Eleanor breathed a sigh of relief as the last cursed hairpin slid free and her hair tumbled down her back. "Yes. One of many, I'm afraid. She left soon after that, which was, of course, what Charlotte wanted all along."

"Oh, my. I suppose Charlotte was punished?"

Ellie's smile faded. "That time she was." By their father, who'd been livid to find he was to be put to the inconvenience of securing another governess for his daughters.

"But not every time?"

"Not as often as you'd think. Certainly not as often as she deserved."

Amelia gathered a thick lock of hair in her fingers to work through a knot. "Why not?"

Ellie didn't answer at once, but closed her eyes and let Amelia pull the knots from her hair.

*Because I m*ade sure of it.

She was still making sure of it, even now. "She didn't often get caught. I was usually the only witness to her crimes, and I never told."

Amelia's small fingers plucked at the knot until she'd worked through it, then she picked up the brush again. "I suppose you were naughty yourself, and didn't want her to tell on you."

Eleanor turned her head to the side so Amelia could brush the hair by her ear. She'd been as naughty as Charlotte, but in a different way. Even as a child, she'd been careful to pull the strings from behind the curtain. "I was as bad as Charlotte was, but that's not the reason I didn't tell."

"Why, then?"

Eleanor clasped Amelia's wrist and drew the child around to stand in front of her. "Because sisters protect each other, Amelia."

"But what if your sister did something terrible, and you were very angry with her?"

Eleanor shook her head. "Sisters do not turn their backs on each other, no matter what."

Amelia ran a finger across the bristles of the brush. She remained quiet for a long moment, then, "Do you think . . . do you think that might be true of a friend, too?"

Eleanor looked into Amelia's dark, uncertain eyes, and the knots that had tied themselves in her chest began to come loose. She could never hurt this child—could never betray her, no matter what happened with Cam.

She rose to her knees and pulled Amelia into an embrace. "I do. I do think so."

Amelia's body relaxed against her, and her arms went around Eleanor's neck. "You'll always be my friend, won't you, even if you don't marry Denny?"

Eleanor froze in the child's arm. *Dear God.* Had Cam told Amelia they'd marry?

She eased Amelia away from her. "Where did you get the idea I might marry your brother?"

Amelia flushed guiltily. "I heard Denny and Uncle Julian talking about it. Denny said he would marry you, but Uncle Julian said you didn't want to. I can't think why you wouldn't, though, because Denny is the handsomest man in the world. Don't you think him handsome?"

"I—I do think him handsome, but—"

"He's so funny and smart too, and very nice. I do wish you'd change your mind and marry him, after all."

Eleanor didn't know whether to laugh or sob. "There's more to it than that, Amelia."

"Oh, I know. You must love him too, but why shouldn't you love Denny?"

Eleanor took Amelia's hands in hers. "I don't know how to answer that, but I'm certain about this much. When I do marry, it will be for love, and for no other reason."

Amelia's brow furrowed. "Of course it will be. What other reason is there?"

What other reason, indeed? "Ladies marry for many other reasons, Amelia, but they shouldn't, and for me, there will never be another reason."

This didn't satisfy Amelia. "But then why—"

Eleanor was saved from answering the next question by a knock at the door. She squeezed Amelia's hands one last time, then rose to open it.

Miss Norwood was standing in the hallway. "Oh, my lady. Good evening. I do hope Amelia hasn't been bothering you all this time. She was to make a quick visit only, but she's been gone this age."

Eleanor smiled. "She's no bother at all, Miss Norwood. Quite the opposite. Amelia?"

Amelia didn't look pleased to be dragged away in the middle of such an interesting conversation. "Oh, all right. I'm coming."

"You should be in bed, miss," the governess scolded.

"Yes, Miss Norwood." Before Miss Norwood could lead her away, however, Amelia grasped Eleanor around the waist and hugged her hard. "Good night, Ellie."

Eleanor hugged her back. "Good night, Amelia." She gave one of Amelia's plaits a gentle tug.

After she'd closed the door behind Amelia and Miss Norwood, Eleanor wandered over to the bed, not quite sure what to do with herself. She began to straighten the coverlet and noticed Amelia had left her sketches on the bed. Eleanor picked them up and was about to put them aside when there was another knock on the door.

She crossed the room and opened it. "Amelia, you forgot—"

Her voice trailed off into silence.

Cam stood there, one long arm braced against the doorframe above his head. "Eleanor. May I come in?"

Chapter Twenty-two

He held his breath as Eleanor hesitated in the doorway, one emotion chasing another across her face. Indecision. Suspicion. Doubt.

Please. God, please. He'd go to his knees and beg her if he had to. "I'll leave the moment you ask me to."

Her fingers twitched on the knob, and after what seemed an eternity, she stepped aside. "I can't refuse, can I? It's your house, and as you keep reminding me, you may go wherever you please."

Cam winced. It seemed a shoddy ploy now, one of many he'd used over the past few weeks, and yet he crossed the threshold into her room just the same. This time, the ends justified the means. This time, he'd come to tell her the truth.

"What do you want, Cam?"

Everything. I want everything from you, but I'll take anything you'll give me.

He couldn't say it. Not yet. Instead he stood motionless in the middle of the room, his back to her as he tried to compose his face—tried to think of what he *could* say. "I just want to talk to you."

She drew a long, slow breath. "There's nothing more to talk about. I've said everything I wish to say."

He turned to face her, because when he told her the truth, he'd look her in the eyes. "But I haven't—"

The words died on his lips.

Masses of dark hair tumbled about her shoulders and over her breasts in lush waves that hung to her waist. In every one of his heated fantasies he'd buried his face in her hair, and now he ached to run his hands through that dark silk. He'd pictured her thus, her hair unbound and wild, spread across his pillow, tickling his chest. Dragging across his stomach. But his imagination hadn't done her justice.

His fingers flexed, but he kept his arms at his sides.

A wave of pink washed over her face as he continued to stare at her without speaking. "Cam?"

"I—your hair." He waved a hand stupidly at her. "It's loose. I've never seen it loose before."

She raised a self-conscious hand to her hair, then brushed past him. She hurried to the fireplace and grabbed a handful of hairpins from the floor.

"Don't." Cam's voice was hoarse.

She turned, the pins cradled in her palm. "I think you'd better go, Cam."

He stepped toward her. "Please. Not yet."

She closed her fingers around the hairpins until he knew they must be stabbing the tender flesh of her palms. "You said you'd go the moment I asked you to—"

"I will, but please, not before I've talked to you." He held out his hands in front of him. "Please. I won't touch you, Eleanor."

Unless you ask me to.

An absurd hope. She'd never ask. Even now her eyes had narrowed with suspicion.

"Very well. Talk."

Cam rubbed the back of his neck. Christ, there was so much he had to tell her, and so much of it ugly and painful, he didn't know where to begin.

*Beg*in at the end.

He dropped his hand and straightened. "I overheard you with Amelia, just now. She must not have closed the door all the way when she came into your room."

Eleanor's face paled. "You—you found the door ajar, and rather than knock, you stood in the hallway and listened to a private conversation?"

Pointless, to deny such a small sin, when he'd done far worse. "Yes."

Her face went from white to red, then back to white, and her chest heaved with anger. "How much—what did you hear?"

I heard enough. "You told Amelia about Charlotte, about when you were children, and about how you—"

He stopped, the words caught in his throat. Eleanor loved Charlotte with the same fierce devotion he did Amelia, and he'd used that love against her. He'd taken something fine and pure and twisted it in his hands until it became vicious, unrecognizable.

But that would still be true, whether he forced the words past his lips or not. All he could do now was make amends. He drew a ragged breath. "How much you love her, and how you'd never turn your back on her."

For a moment her face softened, but then she jerked her chin up. "See how clever you are, Cam? You chose just the right threat."

He was halfway across the room to her before he realized he'd moved. "No more threats, Eleanor."

She backed away from him. "I don't believe you. What else did you hear?"

What he'd heard then . . . his chest ached with the memory of Eleanor's voice, so warm it was more a touch than a sound, like a hand against his cheek, or arms sliding around his neck. Her soft inflection when she'd spoken to Amelia—God, he'd never forget it. Something had leapt to life within him then, had made his blood surge through his body with such wild abandon he'd had to brace himself against the wall to keep from staggering.

He'd promised not to touch her, but no force in the world could have kept him from moving closer to her then. "Amelia asked if friends could care as much about each other as sisters did, and you said . . . you said they could."

He took another step toward her. Another, until he was close enough to touch her. He moved slowly to give her time to retreat again, but she remained still, watching him.

He wrapped his hand around her fingertips. "I went to find Miss Norwood after that, and I didn't hear any more. But I didn't need to. By then, I knew."

Her dark eyes held his, as if mesmerized. "You . . . knew?"

He lifted her hand to his mouth, let his lips brush against her knuckles and the back of her wrist, over the pale, tender skin he'd longed to taste again. "I knew you'd never hurt Amelia, Eleanor. You care too much for her."

Her hand jerked at the warm press of his lips, and the hairpins slipped from her palm to scatter across the floor.

"It's true, isn't it?" He pressed his mouth to her open palm. "Tell me."

God, he hadn't meant to touch her. He'd come here to tell her the truth, and he had to do it *now*, before he couldn't remember anymore what was true and what was a lie. Before he could think of nothing but the satin of her skin beneath his lips.

Just one more taste. She gasped as he kissed the tips of each of her fingers, one by one, then drew them into the warmth of his mouth. Her eyes dropped closed, but still she didn't speak.

"You could never hurt her, could you? You need to say it, Eleanor."

Say it for yourself, not for me.

He already knew the truth. He knew she'd never hurt Amelia, despite her threats, but he wasn't sure *she* knew it. If she didn't say it now, if she didn't admit it to herself and to him, then she'd always wonder if she were capable of such cruelty.

No. He didn't want that for her—couldn't bear it. He raised her hand to his face, pressed her palm against his cheek. "Open your eyes, Ellie. Please, love. Look at me." He took her face between his hands and let his fingers tangle in the thick locks of hair at her temples. "You have to say it."

She opened her eyes. "I could never hurt her." Her voice was low, pleading. "I couldn't hurt Amelia any more than I could hurt Charlotte, or Alec or Robyn."

He leaned toward her, pressed his mouth to her forehead. "I know it. I know you can't."

She pulled back to look into his face, her eyes stricken. "What if I had done it? Oh, God, that sweet child. What if I had gone through with it, and ruined her?"

"Hush." He kissed her forehead again. "You didn't hurt Amelia, Ellie. I don't believe you ever would have, but in the end it wouldn't have made any difference if you had told her secret."

She shook her head. "How could it not?"

He sighed. "My Uncle Reggie knows the truth. He's threatened before to make the circumstances of Amelia's birth public, and now he's furious with me for buying Julian's commission. It's only a matter of time before he exposes her."

Her brow furrowed. "But then why did you . . ."

All at once she stopped speaking and gazed up at him, her dark eyes softer than he'd ever seen them. She'd never looked at him that way before, and it made his breath catch.

Tell her now.

He might never see that look in her eyes again once she knew the truth, but he couldn't begin anew with her with all the lies still between them. He opened his mouth to tell her everything, but before he could say a word her face went white, and she began to tremble.

"Eleanor?" His fingers touched her chin and titled her head back, so he could see her face. "What is it?"

She looked up at him with panicked dark eyes. "I can't hurt Amelia, but I can't let you hurt Charlotte. I don't know what to do. You'll take everything from me, Cam, but sometimes I don't *want* to fight you anymore."

Pain tore into him—pain, or pleasure so sharp it felt like pain. It thundered through his chest, sweeping before it that hard, dark coldness that had lived at the center of him for as long as he could remember, that kernel of fury and despair, hidden under layers of lacerated skin, so deeply embedded he thought it could never tear free.

And then his mouth was on her temples, her eyelids, her cheeks. He buried his face in her hair and between kisses he murmured to her—he didn't know what he said, just disjointed words and promises—that he'd never hurt her, that he'd be good to her, so good. He wanted her, so much, more than he'd ever wanted anything.

He brushed his mouth over hers, and when her lips parted for him he took her harder, greedy for the taste of her, his fingers tightening in her hair. Her tongue crept out to touch his and Cam groaned, lost to the desire pounding through him. Again and again he kissed her, his mouth hot against hers, until her body softened and she pressed her warm palms against his chest with a sigh.

He burned where she touched him. His mouth, his body. He'd wanted her forever, it seemed, just as she was now, her scent teasing his nostrils and fistfuls of her silky hair spilling over his palms.

Lose yourself in her. There would be time for truth later, time for explanations and apologies.

For regrets?

Cam tore his mouth from hers to gaze down at her. Her dark eyes were squeezed closed, her lashes fanned out against the smooth, pale skin of her cheeks. "If you want me to go, Eleanor," he murmured, his lips against her ear, "tell me so now."

But she didn't tell him to go. She flattened her hands against his chest and her fingers curled into his waistcoat. "Why, Cam? If you knew my threat against Amelia to be an empty one, why did you make me admit I'd never hurt her?"

He touched his mouth to hers again, but he let himself linger for a moment only, then he pulled away before he could kiss her again, before he couldn't stop. "So you'd know you never could have. So you'd know it was the truth."

"But . . . why should it matter to you if I know it?"

He cupped her face in his hands. "That threat would have haunted you, Eleanor. I couldn't let that happen."

She searched his face, her eyes alight with that same astonished wonder he'd seen earlier. "But why should you care if it haunts me? I threatened to ruin your sister. Perhaps I deserve to be haunted."

"You don't deserve it." His green eyes were fierce. "I *should* care. I do care."

She released him, and Cam's heart plummeted in his chest as he waited for her to push him away.

He'd go. He'd do whatever she asked of him.

She touched the top button of his waistcoat. Opened it.

"Eleanor?" He watched as her slim, white fingers moved to the second button of his waistcoat, then the third.

He gazed down at her in disbelief. Her mouth was soft, open. She rose to the tips of her toes, and titled her head back. An invitation.

"Ellie? Do you want this?"

She drew his waistcoat over his shoulders and let it fall to the floor.

He pulled her closer, held her tighter, felt her tremble as her breasts were crushed against his chest. "Do you want . . . me?"

Her eyes never left his as she reached down and loosened the top button of his breeches.

Cam tried to catch his breath as she tugged his shirt free and slipped her hand underneath to touch his bare stomach. He threw his head back to give her access to him, groaning his pleasure as she kissed his throat, his neck, her lips drifting over his collarbones before they came to rest in the center of his chest, over his heart.

He panted as her kisses drifted over his skin, but he fought against the fog of desire, struggling to remember . . . something. Ah, God, he couldn't think—not when her mouth was on him, and her hands, her soft hands stroking his stomach, his muscles jerking, leaping to meet her touch, his breath coming fast now, harsh in his chest, and her hand drifting lower . . .

Yes. God, yes.

He closed his eyes. It didn't matter. Whatever he'd wanted to know, whatever he'd wanted to say, it didn't matter. All that mattered was this, her hands and her mouth on him. All that mattered was she wanted him . . .

Wanted him. Cam opened his eyes. She hadn't said she wanted him. She hadn't said a word. Even as she ran her eager hands over his body, even as she made him ache for her, she remained silent.

He gasped when she slipped a finger inside the top of his breeches. His hands shot out to grasp her waist and pull her hard against him. He pressed his palm into the arch of her lower back, his hips tight against hers so she could feel how hard he was for her. He nudged against her once, then again, subtle but insistent. "Do you feel me, Eleanor? That's how much I want you. Tell me what you want, sweetheart. Tell me what to do."

He gathered handfuls of her long hair, twisting it around his hands and tangling his fingers in the dark silk of it, as he'd dreamed of doing. He held her to his chest, waited. Life had taught him to take, not give, but this

. . . he couldn't take this from her. She had to give herself to him—all of herself, willingly, with no reservations.

She looked into his eyes. "I want you. Stay with me."

She took his face between her palms and opened her lips over his on a sigh that weakened his knees. He slipped inside to stroke deep into her mouth, to coax her tongue to meet his. Her caress was hesitant, then bolder, her tongue seeking his. He groaned into her dark, sweet mouth, his kiss harder now, more demanding. He wrapped an arm around her back and swept her up, cradling her high against his chest. "Hold onto me."

She twined her arms around him, and he shivered with desire when she brushed her hand over the back of his neck and threaded her fingers in his hair. He carried her across the room, lay her on the bed and gazed down at her for a moment without a word.

She was his, and he wanted to give her everything.

He brushed the backs of his fingers against her cheek, then gathered up a lock of her hair and let the long strands drift through his fingers. "Beautiful."

Her face was cast in shadows, but he could feel her eyes on him, on his face and body, touching every part of him. He let his hand fall away, then held her gaze as he pulled his shirt over his head and let it fall to the floor.

The bed sank under his weight as he stretched out next to her, took her hand and pressed it against the center of his chest. She twined her fingers with his, so their clasped hands lay over his heart.

Chapter Twenty-three

Eleanor watched the firelight caress the hard planes of his face, softening them and burnishing his skin to a dark gold.

Such a simple thing, to take his hand, to ease him down beside her and let the warmth of his body envelop her skin. She closed her eyes and let her breath rush through her lungs in a sigh, then opened them again as strong fingers cupped her jaw.

His whisper was soft and dark against her ear. "Kiss me."

Eleanor hesitated, then brushed her mouth over his firm lower lip, her first stroke shy, tentative. He made a small, strangled sound in his throat and caught her hand to press it harder against his chest. Encouraged, she kissed him again, but she lingered this time to savor his taste. Port, was it? A fine one, rich and spicy against her tongue.

Dear God. He's delicious.

She stroked the tip of her tongue across the seam of his lips, then opened her mouth over his to taste him deeply. His chest vibrated with a groan, and he closed his hands around her upper arms to drag her closer. "*Yes.* Give me your mouth."

Eleanor pressed her mouth to his with a gasp, thrilled at the rough command in his voice, his possessive touch. He'd been careful with her up until now, hesitant, as if he were afraid she'd flee at any moment, but with each brush of her mouth against his he grew wilder, his body tensing with unleashed desire.

She licked into his mouth again and again, desperate for more of his taste, but after a dozen dizzying kisses he drew away from her, laughing softly at her whimper of protest, and slid his hands over her back, searching for the row of tiny buttons on her gown. He tugged on them until he'd loosened her tight bodice, then slipped his fingers underneath the thin muslin of her shift. "So soft." He stroked the bare skin of her neck. "I want to see all of you." He traced a finger over the swells of her breasts, right above neckline of her gown. "Show me."

Eleanor froze. He wanted her to . . . bare herself to him? She let her gaze wander over his naked chest. Her breath caught at his masculine beauty, the raw power of his body, the layered muscles, hard and sleek under his tawny skin. Would he get pleasure from her body, as she did from his? He was perfection, but she was pale, fine-boned. Perhaps he'd think her too small, or—

"Don't hide from me, Ellie. Show me."

Eleanor shivered. His voice was gentle still, but she knew at once he'd accept no excuses, no evasions. If she wanted him, she'd have to offer every part of herself to him. Willingly. Eagerly. He'd allow nothing less.

She gazed at him, the square jaw, the strong curve of his chin, the high, proud cheekbones—a stern face, yes, but soft now, with his chestnut hair falling over his brow and his eyes, so hot, green flames, yet still soft, for all that. Even when she'd threatened to expose Amelia's secrets, his eyes had been soft when they touched her face.

You don't want to do this, Eleanor.

Even as she'd railed at him, tried to hurt him, threatened the sister he loved so dearly, he'd been worried for her.

*You could never hu*rt her. Say it.

Eleanor looked into the dark forest of eyes. He'd made her say it. To admit it, to him and to herself, because he wanted to tear her free from something so ugly. How had he known, even before she had, she could never hurt Amelia? He'd *seen* her, even before she'd seen herself, and he'd trusted her, even when she hadn't trusted herself.

*I should c*are. I do care.

What would it be like, to have such a man care for her? Love her? Even as she'd struggled with him, even as she'd fought him, hated him, she'd been stunned by the depth of his love for Amelia. How would it feel, to have that kind of love for herself?

Is there no hope for us?

Was there? She didn't know. Perhaps she'd never be able to trust him after the way they'd begun, and yet . . .

Wasn't that what hope was? A dream that defied logic. A waking dream . . .

He watched her with shadowed green eyes. Waited. If she wanted him, she'd have to give. Herself, with no reservations. Somewhere deep inside her she'd known this moment would come, except it wasn't as she imagined it would be. She thought she'd feel as though she'd lost something to him, but instead it felt like she'd been given a gift the moment his hand closed around hers.

Eleanor slipped a finger under the narrow band of ribbon and tugged her sleeve down, baring her shoulder.

Cam watched her, his eyes burning. "The other one." He drifted one finger down her neck and under the sagging neckline of her gown to stroke the warm valley between her breasts. "All of you."

She grasped her other sleeve, her gaze holding his as she eased it down, the fabric dragging over her skin as she freed herself from the heavy silk, until nothing held the bodice up now except her hand fisted in the neckline.

Cam's breath was short, harsh. "Show me."

She let the material slip from her fingers, and the gown fell to her waist. Underneath she wore only a sheer white shift, and he could see . . . she closed her eyes as heat rushed into her cheeks. He could see the outline of her breasts, and, *dear God*, her nipples, hard against the fine fabric, seeking his touch—

Eleanor shivered as his warm palms cupped her breasts.

"Open your eyes."

She stole a glance at him from under her lashes. He continued to caress her, but his eyes were riveted to hers. "Look at me when I touch you." He brushed the pads of his thumbs over her nipples, once, more a breath than a touch.

Eleanor gasped and threw her head back, but he shifted closer to her and tangled a hand in the hair at the back of her neck to bring her gaze back to his. "No. Watch me."

A strangled moan tore from her throat as he stroked her nipples again. She quivered in his arms, overwhelmed by the feel of his rough fingertips against the straining peaks.

His laugh was soft, dark. "Do you want me to touch you, Ellie?"

"*Yes.* I want you to touch me. Please, Cam."

He groaned and trailed his hands from her breasts up the front of her neck in one smooth stroke. "Do you want more?" He plucked at the fabric of her shift, toying with the bow there.

Eleanor released a shaky breath. "Yes."

He slid his fingers under the loose fabric and slipped it off her shoulders. "I do, too. So much more. I want everything from you."

Cool air rushed over her breasts as he drew the shift down, baring her. She lifted her chin a fraction, fighting the urge to close her eyes again as his gaze dropped to her breasts. His mouth went slack and a hot flush of color swept across his cheekbones, and a surge of triumph washed over her, dizzying her.

"Eleanor." All hints of teasing fell away as he fought to catch his breath, his cool composure shattered. Dear God, the way he looked at her . . . his gaze was hot, hungry. Eleanor's pulse throbbed, sending a wild surge of blood to the warm, secret places of her body.

"Come here." He crooked one long finger, beckoning to her, but he made no move to touch her. He simply waited, his green eyes glittering with desire.

She didn't think to question him, or to disobey his command, but crawled across the bed to him. With one quick move he wrapped his arm around her waist, tugged her onto his lap, and buried his face in the hollow between her neck and shoulder. "God, your scent." His low grown vibrated against her skin. "I've dreamed of this, of tasting you."

In the next breath his mouth seemed to be everywhere at once, on her lips, the sensitive skin behind her ear, her neck, her throat. She wrapped her fingers in his chestnut hair and rose to her knees, urging him to take more, but he pulled away, took her chin between his fingers, and forced her gaze to his.

"I'm going to kiss you here." He traced his finger around one swollen nipple. "Don't close your eyes, and don't look away. Watch, Eleanor—watch me when I put my mouth on you."

Eleanor cried out as he caught a hard, pink nipple between his teeth and bit down gently. "Oh. Cam, I—I . . ."

"Shhh. Let me taste you." His mouth closed over her nipple, his lips and tongue hot and rough, devouring her. He drew hard on the swollen bud, then—oh, God, he was *licking* her with the tip of his tongue, darting over her nipple again and again, like a cat licking cream from a dish.

He pulled away at last when she began to tremble in his arms. She moaned a protest and reached for him, but he grasped her wrists in his hands and held them over her head, then eased her back flat against the bed. "Are you going to be mine?" His breath was hot against her ear, his words urgent.

His? Yes. For now, for this moment, she was his. Once this moment had passed . . . oh, she didn't know, but it didn't matter whether or not she knew the answer, or if she spoke the truth or a lie. All that mattered was this moment, and she would have promised him anything. "Yes."

"Say it." He lowered his head and dragged his tongue across her nipple again. "Tell me you're mine."

Eleanor sank her fingers into his hair and pulled him tighter against her breasts. "I'm yours, Cam."

He froze for a moment, then drew in a deep, shuddering breath and buried his face in her neck. "Again. Say it again. You're mine."

The fierce possessiveness in his voice made her tremble, but even as her heart gave an anxious throb in her chest, she could deny him nothing. "Yes. Yours, Cam."

He opened his mouth against her neck and sucked her tender flesh between his lips until her back bowed from the delicious torment, then his fingers went slack around her wrists. "Take off your gown."

She looked up into his wicked green eyes. He'd make her yield in every way to him, and then he'd take . . .

He bit down on her earlobe when she hesitated, a tiny punishment. "Take off your gown and your shift."

She shivered at the demand in his voice, but even as dark thoughts danced around the edges of her mind, she caught the mass of silk fabric bunched at her waist, her eyes on his. She raised her hips from the bed and slid her gown slowly, oh so slowly down her body, over her belly, her thighs—

Cam bit out a groan and grasped the silk in his fist. He stripped the gown from her body with one tug, then drew her shift over her head and tossed them both to the floor.

Eleanor trembled, bare before him, and waited for him to say something. Anything. But he remained silent as he took in every inch of her, his gaze heating her skin everywhere it touched.

Dear God, why didn't he speak? When she couldn't take his silence any longer she began to rise, to reach for the coverlet.

"No." Cam said, his voice a low rasp. He placed his palm between her breasts and eased her gently back down against the pillows. "No. Let me look at you. Ellie." His voice trailed off, and his throat worked. "I knew you'd be . . . but I never imagined, could not have imagined you . . ."

Warmth swelled in her chest, pressed against her rib cage, and pooled in her belly. She'd been called lovely before, beautiful even. Her past suitors, smooth-tongued and glib, had written odes to her lips, expounded on the fineness of her skin and compared her hair to a gleaming waterfall.

But none of them had ever touched her heart. Cam, with his broken words, his awkward lapses into silence—he made her heart soar.

He made her want to give him everything.

She reached for him, let her hand rest against his cheek for a moment, and then traced a fingertip around his lips before skimming her palm over his neck and throat.

He closed his eyes as she pressed her hand over his heart. "Yes. Touch me."

Eleanor lifted his hand to her lips and kissed it, her tongue lingering at the center of his palm as her gaze wandered over him, at his skin tinted gold from the firelight. She'd never dreamed a man's body could be so beautiful.

She slid a hand over his shoulders, then trailed her fingers over his chest until they came to rest on his taut belly. "I was wrong. You don't pad your coats, after all."

He blinked, surprised. "No. Did you suppose I did?"

"I thought you must." Her lips quirked. "The shoulders and the chest." She rose up and pressed her lips to his chest, and he shuddered with pleasure when she dragged her fingernails gently over his nipples. "But this . . ." She bit her lip as her gaze roamed over his powerful shoulders and arms, his muscular thighs. "This is all you." She slid her fingernails over his hard belly, relishing the feel of his flesh sliding under her palm. "And your skin is so smooth. Like warm silk."

He groaned low in his throat, moving restlessly on the bed as she teased her hands over him. "Eleanor?"

She raised her gaze to his. His green eyes were darker than she'd ever seen them, his eyelids heavy. "Yes?"

He took her hand and dragged it across his belly until the tips of her fingers met the top of his breeches. "I don't pad my breeches, either." He moved her hand lower still, his breath leaving his lungs in a heated rush as her fingers curled instinctively around him. "This is all me, too."

Her eyes never left his as she twisted open the buttons on his falls and slipped her hand inside to brush against the hard flesh there. "Oh," she murmured, surprised. This part of him felt so *alive*. It twitched in her palm, as if it sought her touch. She held him, her hand still. Cam didn't speak, but a strangled cry escaped him and he arched into her touch when she stroked her hand once over his hot skin.

Eleanor tightened her fingers around him then, thrilled at his low moan and the way his hard flesh throbbed against her hand. Dear God, she wanted touch him like this forever, to watch his face and listen to the low, broken sounds coming from deep in his chest as his powerful body shook. She wanted to see him lost in pleasure, helpless against it.

She watched, fascinated as his back arched and his hips moved in rhythm with each of her strokes, but after a moment he reached down and grabbed her hand to still it. "Enough."

He pulled away from her and rolled off the bed, and Eleanor nearly leapt off after him. "Cam? Where are you—"

The words died in her throat. He stripped off his breeches and smalls with one deft tug. Eleanor swallowed, hardly knowing where to look first. He was magnificent—smooth bronze skin poured over muscle, his body lean, hard, graceful, every line in perfect symmetry, as if a sculptor had carved him.

He joined her on the bed again and she reached for his shaft where it jutted proudly from his hips, eager to resume her exploration, but Cam caught her hand with a strained laugh. "No."

Eleanor made a half-hearted attempt to get free. "But I want—"

He moved to lay over her, the dark hair on his legs tickling her thighs. "You want to drive me mad." He raised her arms over her head and this time he held them there with a hand around her wrists. "But it's my turn now." He nudged her legs apart with his knee and slipped his hand between her open thighs to cup her there.

Eleanor gasped at the intimacy of it. Heat rushed over her and she trembled at the caress. "Cam, I—"

"Shhhh." His tongue brushed against her ear as his fingers danced over her, teasing at her damp flesh, stroking her between her legs. "I want to taste you." His soft hair dragged across her heated skin as he moved lower to press open-mouthed kisses between her breasts, then lower still, his tongue licking a path down her stomach to her belly-button.

He released her wrists and his hands slid down her sides to her hips, then his palms were between her thighs, easing them open, wider, then wider still . . .

A strangled cry left Eleanor's lips as his fingers moved delicately between her legs, his thumbs opening her gently. He lowered his head and . . .

Taste her? Surely he didn't mean . . . surely he wouldn't—

"Wanted you like this forever. Dreamed of tasting you," he groaned, right before his hot tongue snaked out to touch her, *there*, where his fingers had been, and dear God, it felt like . . . oh, she didn't know! She'd never felt anything like it before. She knew only it was wicked, what he was doing, wicked and exquisite, and she couldn't make herself stop him, couldn't think—

He did it again, his soft tongue tracing lazy, maddening circles over her swollen flesh, making her gasp. Her hands fisted in his hair to . . . drag him away? Drag him closer?

"Does it feel good?" His whisper was low and urgent, his breath hot against her damp flesh. "Tell me."

Eleanor made an incoherent sound in answer—a gasp or a moan, she didn't know which, only that she'd never made that sound before in her life.

He pressed his tongue harder against her, his mouth relentless, devouring her, flicking again and again over that tiny knot of flesh hidden in her folds until she could no longer keep her hips still, and writhed against the bed.

Cam's breath hissed from his lungs when she arched under his hands. "*Yes*, Ellie, yes—Give me everything."

He murmured to her between teasing strokes of his tongue, his voice low and wicked, and his fingers were everywhere, one spread low over her belly to hold her still, the other thrusting slowly into her wet heat, his tongue hot and slick, working her until her back bowed with each stroke.

Just when she thought she couldn't take another moment of his delicious torment, he slid a second finger inside her. "Ah, yes—so sweet and wet, Ellie." His strokes were more insistent now, faster, his breath ragged. "Come for me."

She didn't understand his words, but it didn't matter—it was enough to hear his voice wash over her, move through her heart as the knot he'd tied inside her body drew tighter and tighter until it unraveled in hot waves of pleasure. Eleanor cried out, her fingers pulling Cam's hair as he stroked her through a bliss more intense than any she'd ever known. He didn't stop until her body went limp against the pillows, then he released her thighs and moved to lie beside her. His mouth took hers, stealing each sigh from her lips until she calmed at last, then he brushed her tangled hair away from her face.

"So beautiful." His voice was soft, filled with wonder, but strained, breathless, and his shaft leapt against her belly. She shifted against him, squirming lower on the bed so his hard length nudged between her thighs.

Cam moaned, his big body shaking as she urged him to lie on top of her. "Tell me you want me." He held still, his hips tight against hers. "Tell me you'll give yourself to me."

Oh, she did—she wanted him, against all reason, whether she should or not.

"Tell me." He moved his hips in a gentle thrust.

She gazed up at his stark, beautiful face, into his intense green eyes, dark with longing, and all thoughts of resistance melted away. "I want you. Don't stop, Cam."

He released a long breath, and his lips met hers, the kiss so tender Eleanor had to pull away. His face softened as he looked down at her. He caressed the insides of her thighs, then pushed them apart gently to open her to him. He settled between her legs, his lean hips opening her wider. "Don't be afraid."

Eleanor only nodded, for how could she tell him it wasn't the physical pain she feared, but the pain to her heart?

A ragged groan tore from his throat as he braced himself over her. The tip of his cock nudged against her entrance, then he thrust into her in one quick, powerful stoke. Once he was buried deep inside her, he went still. "Ellie?" He turned her face to his with a gentle hand on her cheek. "I don't want to hurt you."

She'd gone stiff beneath him, stunned at the sudden, sharp pain, but she could already feel her body closing around him, accepting him, tugging his hard flesh deeper inside her. She slid her arms around him and sank her fingers into the arch of his back. "You feel so . . . big. So hard."

Some of the tension eased from him, and he laughed softly. "You feel—*ah*, Eleanor. You feel beautiful, so hot and sweet. I can't get enough of you."

Encouraged by his words and the feel of her body easing around him, she moved, just the tiniest circling of her hips, but Cam gasped and threw his head back as if he'd never before felt such astonishing pleasure. "Yes. God, yes."

He began to move inside her then, his movements slow, careful. His body coaxed hers until each stroke took on an urgent necessity. "Cam," she gasped, sinking her fingernails into his sweat-slick back. "Cam."

He thrust deep into her with a powerful surge of his hips. "Do you need more?"

Eleanor closed her eyes and cried out at the exquisite sensation of him filling her. "Yes. Yes."

She thrust her hips upward in a desperate attempt to repeat the sensation, but Cam held her to the bed with his hands, and with a dark laugh resumed his slow, measured strokes. "Not yet."

He held back ruthlessly, keeping her just on the edge of release until, maddened, she broke free from his grasp and pulled him hard against her with her legs around his waist. She locked her ankles around his taut hips and pressed her mouth to his neck to suck and bite at him, his skin salt and musk under her tongue.

Cam gave a fierce, guttural cry and surged against her, all restraint at an end as he worked to give her what she needed. He twisted a fist in her hair to draw her head back so he could see her face. He thrust into her again, then again, hard and fast and deep. "*Eleanor*. Come with me."

Eleanor arched against him, panting, her eyes locked with his. "Oh, oh . . ."

"*Now*." He slid a shaking hand between her open thighs to stroke her and she cried out, her legs tightening around him as she exploded beneath him.

"Yes, Eleanor. *So good . . .* " Cam's hips thrust furiously as he drove into her, until at last he cried out with savage triumph, shuddering over her, his back bowing as he came to his own release.

His arms collapsed beneath him and he sagged against her, his body spent. For long moments they lay there and he held her, the only sound their mingled breathing.

Eleanor reached up to stroke his damp hair, dazed. He was . . . dear God, he was magnificent. She'd never dreamt she could feel such pleasure, and he'd been so tender, so careful of her. Her heart crashed against her ribs now, just thinking of it. To experience such pleasure in his arms, it made her . . .

Vulnerable.

He eased to his side, gathered her against him and buried his face in her hair. He murmured to her, his voice hoarse—he told her she was beautiful, exquisite, that she'd given him such pleasure—but his words washed over her, soundless, drowned as each desperate beat of her heart echoed in her ears.

She'd given him everything.

When she didn't reply he pulled back to look down at her, an anxious frown creasing his brow. "Eleanor. Are you all right? Oh, God, I didn't hurt you?"

She shook her head, too numb to speak. No, he hadn't hurt her.

But he would.

Panic began to well in her chest. She could become a slave to it. To the pleasure, yes, but also to *him*, his fingers under her chin as he tipped her face up to his, his green eyes, dark with passion, his whispered words in her ears, so sweet she'd never be able to deny him anything.

Oh, dear God. What had she done?

He'd take everything from her now, until there was nothing left, until she was so empty inside she no longer recognized herself. She'd become a ghost, haunted and silent, her feet soundless against the marble floors.

The villain, or the hero, but never both at once.

He wrapped an arm around her neck and urged her head down to his bare chest. He toyed with her hair for long moments, then heaved a deep, satisfied sigh. "I knew it was a good idea to bring you to Lindenhurst."

Eleanor's breath froze in her lungs. "What did you say?"

Cam twined a long lock of her hair around his finger. "Just that I'm glad we came here."

She shouldn't be here. Not with him. Not like this.

"Why? Because you managed to lure me into your bed?" Eleanor heard the fear in her own voice, cold and brittle, like glass shattering.

"This is your bed, sweet." His voice was teasing. "But yes, since you ask, I would have gone much farther than Lindenhurst to have you."

She tensed. "How much farther, Cam? Far enough to orchestrate a seduction? To ruin me? It's a good plan if you want to trap a lady into marriage."

Silence. A pause, then Cam's body went rigid beneath her. "Don't, Ellie. Please."

She had to close her eyes against the quiet agony in his voice. Oh, God, she didn't want to do this, but the panic pressed in on her from all sides, and the coverlet was too tight over her, too hot, smothering her, and she had to get away, *now*, because if she didn't, she'd sink down into him and never rise again, and he'd own her . . .

She kicked at the covers twisted around her legs and struggled out of his arms. His body was too warm, too seductive, his heartbeat too loud in her ears—

Cam caught at her waist to stop her but she jerked away and scrambled off the bed. Her gown lay in a discarded heap on the floor. She struggled into it, then turned back to face him. Her heart twisted in her chest when she saw he'd gone as white as the bedsheet still bunched around his waist. "Do you deny it?"

"Don't do this."

The pleading note in his voice stabbed at her, and she had to force herself not to cover her ears. "Do you deny it?"

He seemed to fight with himself for a moment, then, "It might have begun that way, yes, but now—"

"It won't work."

His expression changed then, his mouth hardening. "What do you mean, it won't work?"

She laughed, the sound high-pitched, unnatural. "Just what I said. It won't work."

He rose from the bed and crossed the room to retrieve his breeches. Eleanor averted her eyes from his naked body. She didn't want to see him, to see how beautiful he was. It made her weak.

"Explain." He stood in front of her, his arms crossed over that massive chest, every line of his body rigid.

Eleanor lifted her chin. "I don't care if I'm ruined. It doesn't matter. It changes nothing. I won't marry you."

Chapter Twenty-four

"You might not care if you're ruined, but I do. And you're wrong, Eleanor. It does matter, and it does change everything."

Cam dragged his shirt over his head. His body had gone cold, numb. What had happened? She'd given herself to him. She'd let him hold her, her head nestled into his chest, and now this? She was wild-eyed, frantic.

"Sit down." His heart thrashed and bled into his chest, but he forced himself to stay calm.

Her eyes widened in astonishment. "I've just told you I will never marry you, Cam. This is where the conversation ends, not where it begins." She edged around him and crossed the room to open the door.

Cam's lips moved, stretched into a humorless smile. "No, Eleanor. It isn't. We've just begun."

She paused, her hand on the knob.

He gestured toward the settee. "Earlier this evening, in the library, you said you knew everything. You don't. I thought you might wish to know it, but I'd prefer it if you sit. It's not the sort of story you should hear while standing."

She opened the door, gestured for him to leave. "I know enough."

Cam didn't move. "You said my mother *was ruined*, as if it were a thing that could happen by accident, like falling off a horse, or getting caught in foul weather. It isn't."

"What does that mean?" Her voice was strained but patient, as if she were calming a hysterical child.

But Cam wasn't a child. He hadn't been a child since he was nine years old, and far from being hysterical, he'd never felt more detached. It was damned odd, since he hadn't told this story before in his life, to anyone.

Even Julian only knew bits and pieces of it. "It means it wasn't an accident. Someone ruined her. I thought you might like to know who it was."

Her shoulders went stiff, and an odd expression flitted across her face. "Why should I care to know? It can't make any difference to me."

Cam didn't answer, but held out his hand to her. "Come away from the door, Eleanor."

She hesitated, but then she closed the door and stepped back into the room. He gestured toward the settee again, and she sat.

He remained standing. "You don't have the whole of Amelia's story. Not even close. You know she's illegitimate, but you didn't say a word about her father."

"I assumed he was some aristocrat or other. Your aunt didn't say so, but who else—"

"Who else but an aristocrat would ruin a grieving widow and then abandon her as soon as he put a child in her belly? Who else, indeed? You're quite right. He was an aristocrat who cared for nothing but his own gratification."

He paused, confused at the cold, hard edge in his voice. This wasn't how he'd meant to tell her, but here was the old ugliness, sucking all the air out of the room.

"Surely you don't claim an unfamiliarity with self-gratification, Cam?"

Cam caught his breath as pain shot through him, followed by a cold fury. Was that what she thought? That he'd made love to her only to gratify his lust? Damn it, he wasn't at all like Hart Sutherland. "You went to great lengths to get Amelia's sordid tale, Eleanor, but you abandoned the chase before you had the choicest bit of gossip. However will you become a competent blackmailer if you give up so easily?"

Eleanor flinched, and shame rose in Cam's chest at the bitter sarcasm in his voice. He didn't want to hurt her, but the despair he'd felt as a child was lodged in his throat, and he had to get it out before it choked him.

"My mother was beautiful," he went on, struggling to stay calm. "Amelia looks like her. She has similar features, and the same fair coloring."

Eleanor twisted her hands in her lap. "Angelic."

*Angel*ic, and cursed.

The harsh reply rose to Cam's lips, but he bit it back. "Yes. Her beauty was out of the common way, and she attracted attention. Even after my father died and she was broken by grief, she was still lovely. Haunted but lovely, maybe even more so than she'd been before, for a certain kind of man, anyway. The kind that preys on vulnerability."

"Yes, I think I know the kind of man you mean," she said, not looking at him.

Does she imagine I am such a man?

Cam's hands tightened into fists. "My mother was on a ride one afternoon when she was unfortunate enough to catch the attention of the aristocrat in question. He'd been to Aylesbury and was headed back down to London by way of Watford. He saw her out on her horse."

"And her fate was sealed, because she happened to be in the wrong place, and to stumble across the wrong man."

Cam dug his fingernails into his clenched palms as another wave of pain and anger swept over him. "Fate is cruel—is that what you mean to say? Crueler to some than others, I think."

She didn't answer.

"My father had been dead nearly four years by this time, but my mother's sorrow hadn't faded. She never would have taken up with such a man if she hadn't been so lonely, so wretched. The moment she did, of course, my uncle discovered it, and he wasted no time in tossing us out."

"Did she . . . do you suppose she loved him? The aristocrat?"

He shook his head. She hadn't loved him, but in the end it didn't matter, because Hart Sutherland had broken her nonetheless, as surely as Ellie would break him if he let her walk away. "No. She couldn't love anyone else, not after my father. One doesn't ever get over a love like that, do they?"

She jerked her gaze from her lap to his face. "No. No, they don't."

Neither of them spoke for a moment, then Cam broke the silence. "However she may have felt about him, you can be sure he never loved her. He kept her for three years, right up until she told him she carried his child. He was furious. He accused her of trying to squeeze money of out him for her brat, though she'd never asked him for a shilling, and he'd certainly never been generous with her."

Eleanor released a long, shaky breath. "What . . . what did he do? What happened?"

"Come now, Eleanor." His laugh was short, bitter. "You know what happened. He left her, without warning, and without a word. Amelia was born seven months later. My mother held her for a little while, but then she started to bleed. She died within the hour."

His mother, pale and lifeless, the white sheets soaked with her blood . . .

The old misery clawed at him. He gulped in air to loosen the fist clenched inside his chest, but it only squeezed harder. Why should Ellie be spared? No one else had been. His mother. Amelia. Himself.

"This is the child you thought to toss to the *ton*, Ellie, an innocent to ravenous wolves. A child without a mother, whose father abandoned her while she was yet in the womb."

She choked back a sob, and the small sound cleaved Cam's heart in two. Pain poured into his chest from the wound, but he grabbed the raw edges of his flesh with both hands and held them together, determined to finish this before he bled to death.

"Do you think the *ton* will find her angelic, Eleanor? Or will they simply see a bastard when they look at her?"

Tears rushed to Eleanor's eyes. "I never wanted to hurt Amelia. I didn't have a choice."

Her tears slashed at his open wound, but when his mouth opened, more hurtful words poured out. "Choice is a luxury. Amelia never had one. I was kind to you, Eleanor, when I made you admit you could never hurt her. I kept you from doing something unworthy of you."

"Unworthy of me," she said dully. "Not of you, though."

He snorted. "Lady Charlotte is hardly a defenseless, illegitimate orphan, is she? She's had every advantage of money and birth, just as you have."

Her dark eyes flashed. "So we deserve it? Is that what you're saying?"

"Yes," he shot back. "Not because of your advantages, but for another reason altogether."

"I find myself weary of your reasons, Cam. I don't want to hear any more."

But she would hear it, whether she wanted to or not.

Cam stalked over to the settee and loomed over her, his legs thrown wide, his body rigid. "Oh, you'll hear it, my lady, and right through to the finish."

In some dim part of his mind he knew he'd lost control, but the realization came too late, and from too great a distance. The weight had crushed him for so long he'd had to heave it off his chest with a mighty shove, and now it tore free with a vengeance, gained momentum, and flattened everything in its path.

Eleanor looked up at him, her eyes stained with tears. "We've had some advantages. I don't deny it. But we've had difficulties too. Do you suppose we haven't? It may shock you to hear it, but aristocrats aren't exempt from pain, any more than anyone is. We've overcome obstacles you know nothing about."

Oh, but he did know, and it was time she did, as well. "What, you mean your father? Yes, he was rather a challenging obstacle, wasn't he?"

She stared at him, open-mouthed. "He—what do you know about my father?"

"Quite a lot, as it happens. Perhaps as much as you do."

Her face went so white he knelt down in front of her and took hold of her upper arms. He looked down at his hands, clutching at her, and watched his fingers tighten as if they weren't a part of his body at all.

"No, you don't," she whispered. "You can't know anything about him."

A deep, frozen calm crept over him. He saw his hands fall away from her, heard his own voice, polite and distant, as if he asked if she took sugar in her tea, or observed the weather was unseasonably warm. "But I do, my lady. I knew him. He was the type of man who preyed on other's vulnerabilities, wasn't he? The type of man concerned only with his own gratification."

Ellie shot to her feet, but she had to grope for the arm of the settee to steady herself. "Stop it!"

But he couldn't stop. The words began to pour from him now, blood from a deep, open wound. "The kind of man who'd ruin a woman broken by grief—a widow. The kind of man who'd abandon her without a second glance when he found she carried his child. The kind of man who'd leave that child without ever seeing her, without ever offering a penny of support for her, and without ever acknowledging her."

She was gasping for breath now. "No. You're lying. I know you're lying."

She tried to break away, but he grasped her shoulders and turned her back to face him. A sense of unreality swept over him as he looked into her dark eyes.

Hart Sutherland's eyes.

"No Ellie, you know just the opposite. You know it's true. You have only to look at Amelia's eyes to see it. She looks very much like my mother, yes—the fair hair, the pale skin. But my mother had green eyes, and Amelia's are dark, almost black. Have you ever noticed that, Ellie? Her eyes look like yours, don't they? You must have your father's eyes too, just as Amelia does."

"He wasn't a good man." She was pleading now. "I know that. I don't pretend he was, but that—what you accuse him of, it's—"

"Unforgiveable. Worse than unforgiveable. It's the kind of sin that demands restitution. Don't you agree, Ellie? An eye for an eye."

She'd begun to claw at his hands to get free, but as soon as she absorbed those words, she went still. "All this time, you said it had nothing to do with me. That I didn't matter. All that mattered was I was a Sutherland."

But she did matter. She was all that mattered.

A tide of bitter regret threatened to drown Cam, and he had to fight the urge let his head fall into his hands. Why had he been so vicious? He'd meant to be kind, to tell her gently . . . yet the truth itself was vicious. How could he deliver such a violent blow with a gentle fist?

Blow. Fist. Christ, what had he done?

She sagged against him and he lowered her gently to the sofa, cursing himself.

"It started that way, but it's not true anymore. Please listen to me. I don't want to punish you, Ellie. Perhaps I did at one time, but not anymore."

I only want you.

She stared at him, dazed, her eyes vacant and glassy, and the silence stretched between them until he could bear it no longer. "I swore to myself when Amelia was born I'd do everything in my power to right the wrong done to her. The support of the Sutherland family won't smooth her way entirely, but it's the best hope she has for the future she deserves."

She didn't reply to that. She simply stared at her lap, as if she hadn't heard him, or couldn't make sense of his words.

"It was either you or Charlotte," he said, forcing the rest out, determined to finish this, whatever it took. "I chose you, because of the two of you I thought you were more likely to recognize your obligation to Amelia."

Her head came up at this. "My obligation? I'm obliged to marry you because of my father's sin? My God, Cam—if he could do such a thing to your mother, to Amelia, then he had fewer moral compunctions than even I suspected. What if everyone he wronged demands restitution of me? Are you willing to loan out your *wife* to them all, so I can right my father's wrongs? It's only fair, after all. An eye for an eye, isn't that right?"

An eye for an eye. How ugly it sounded. How brutally unfair it seemed, when she said it. Yet it was justice, wasn't it? Parity?

He grasped her cold hands in his. "I meant your obligation to Amelia. She's your sister, as much as Charlotte is—your family, as well as mine. Will you turn your back on her, now you know the truth?"

But he hardly knew what the truth was anymore, because this wasn't about Charlotte or Amelia or the Sutherlands now. It wasn't about threats, or truces, or secrets, or justice.

It was about Eleanor. Him, and Eleanor.

He ached to press her hand to his face and whisper promises in her ear, to soothe away the hurt he'd caused. Promises he'd keep. That he'd take care of her. That he'd be good to her. That she'd never regret becoming his wife.

That he loved her.

But it was no use. She wouldn't listen to him. Making love to her had stunned him, devastated him, but she saw it as just another ploy to manipulate her. She'd think the same of his declaration of love, and why shouldn't she? His mouth still burned from his threats. It was a mockery to speak of love with such bitter lips.

It started as a tragedy, so why shouldn't it end as one?

"We would have supported her, you know," she whispered, her voice filled with such sorrow he had to close his eyes against it. "The Sutherlands, I mean. We'd have done it without the threats, without coercion. Happily. We'd have welcomed her with open arms. Charlotte, Alec, Robyn—all of us, even my mother, who . . ." She caught her breath on a sob. "Who had every reason to hope she'd never again be asked to forgive another of my father's cruelties toward her."

Her words hit him like a blow across the face. No one who'd known Hart Sutherland had escaped without scars. No one, no matter their rank, or their legitimacy.

"We could still. It's—it's not too late." She stumbled over the words. "If you would but trust my family, there's no need for us to marry."

"*No*, Eleanor." The words leapt from his mouth before he realized he'd formed a conscious thought. Maybe the Sutherlands would welcome Amelia. Maybe they would stand by her and ease her way into society. He could believe it of them. They were kind, decent. Like Eleanor, they were not what he'd expected.

But it didn't matter. She'd said it wasn't too late, but it was.

For him, it was.

Did she believe she could give him everything, shatter so sweetly in his arms, and he'd let her walk away from him? Even now she might carry his child in her belly. Did she think he'd allow his own child to suffer Amelia's fate? Did she think he'd let history repeat itself?

He took her hand between both of his, his grip fierce. "No."

Fall at her feet, take her hands, beg her . . .

She didn't argue with him. She didn't even try to withdraw her hand, but it rested like a dead thing between his, cold and lifeless. She wasn't fighting him anymore. The thought should have given him hope, but it didn't.

He released her hand, and it dropped to her side. "You believe Amelia shouldn't be punished for an accident of birth. She bears no fault in it, so she shouldn't suffer for it. Is that right, Cam?"

Had the room grown cold? He felt chilled to his very soul. "Yes."

"But you think it fitting I should?"

He opened numb lips to answer her, but there was no answer to that, and his throat closed before he could utter a word.

She didn't seem to expect an answer. She went to the door, opened it, and stood there, head bowed, waiting.

Take her in your arms. Beg her pardon, and tell her, tell her . . .

But he didn't. He didn't say a word, because there was nothing he could say she would believe. For a long moment he gazed at her, his heart cold and hollow in his chest. Then he walked across the room and out the door.

Eleanor closed it behind him, and she didn't move for a long time afterwards. When she began to shiver from the cold she changed into her dressing gown and wrapper and sat on the edge of the settee, careful not to think of anything.

The fire died away sometime during the night, but she didn't go to her bed. She couldn't, not after she'd been there with Cam.

She folded her hands mechanically in her lap and sat, back straight, and didn't think of anything. She didn't make plans. She didn't try to find a way out—a way to jerk the strings into place. She sat and let emotions wash over her. Memories. Her father, with his cold, dark eyes. Charlotte, as she'd been as a child, with her muddy pinafores and wild black curls. Amelia, asking if Eleanor would always be her friend. Cam, speaking to her of obligations.

And at last, just Cam. She squeezed her eyes shut, but she could see him still, his green eyes tender as he made love to her, his hands cupping her face, his voice, whispering she was beautiful.

She was still there when Charlotte found her, hours later. "Eleanor? What are you—dear God, you're like ice. What's happened?"

Eleanor turned to Charlotte, surprised to see her there. "Happened? Oh." She pulled her wrapper tighter around her throat. "I'm going to marry Camden West."

Chapter Twenty-five

She could almost believe nothing had changed.

Eleanor stood to one side of the ballroom, her gloved fingers wrapped around a glass of lemonade, a stiff smile pasted on her face as she watched the dancers whirl from one side of the floor to the other.

It looked the same. The same colorful silk gowns and blinding white cravats. The same throats and wrists adorned with the same flashing jewels. The same gilt mirrors reflecting the same couples, shuffling through the same figures of the same dances.

It might have been any ball, at any time, in any townhouse in London. It might have been Lady Foster's ball, six weeks ago.

Except it wasn't.

The smooth, glittering surface appeared undisturbed, but underneath it the currents ebbed and flowed, surged and retreated. Eleanor struggled to remain upright as the sand shifted beneath her feet. Her jaw ached, and her palms were damp inside her tight gloves.

Charlotte was dancing with the Marquess of Hadley again. There was nothing so unusual in that, perhaps. Hadley had never made a secret of his admiration for Charlotte, and he often asked her to dance. Charlotte, ever gracious, often accepted him, but while she clearly liked the Marquess, she'd never shown any marked partiality for him.

Until now. Since their return from Lindenhurst four weeks ago, Hadley's suit had met with an unusual degree of success. He gazed down at Charlotte tonight, besotted as ever, his handsome face alight as if he couldn't imagine being anywhere else, with any other lady in his arms. Whether Charlotte had accepted his suit or not, Eleanor hadn't the faintest idea. Charlotte hadn't confided in her.

Charlotte hadn't spoken more than a dozen words to her since their return.

Eleanor gazed listlessly at the dancing couples. Cam was a head taller than most of the gentlemen, and she found him easily—there, at the other side of the room. She'd pled fatigue and begged to be excused from this dance, so Cam had escorted Lily to the floor. He led her effortlessly through the steps now, his face frozen into the same polite mask he'd worn since Eleanor accepted his proposal the evening before they'd left Lindenhurst.

For a man who'd gone to such lengths to secure his bride, he'd been subdued to find he'd won her at last. He'd said nothing at first, but had stood with his head bowed. He hadn't looked at her, and he'd been silent for so long Eleanor had wondered if he even wanted her anymore. But then he'd kissed her hands, and murmured something appropriate about the honor she did him, which had struck her as ludicrous, given their circumstances.

He'd asked Alec for her hand the next day, and her brother had given his enthusiastic blessing.

And then . . . nothing.

They hadn't spoken of it since. Eleanor had dutifully informed her mother of her impending nuptials, and since then Cam, his mask firmly in place, had been an ideal suitor. He called on her every day. He took her driving. He escorted her to routs, balls and musical evenings. They'd been to Gunter's for lemon ices with Amelia on three separate occasions.

He hadn't missed a step. His mask had never slipped. Not once.

She expected every day for him to insist they call the banns, but here it was, weeks later, and he hadn't mentioned it. He hadn't told Amelia about their betrothal, either—if he had, Eleanor was certain Amelia would have asked her about it.

Perhaps he'd at last come to his senses, and changed his mind. Absurd, of course, that this possibility should leave her with such a strange, empty feeling in her chest. It wasn't as if this were a love match.

"My dear." Lady Catherine laid a hand on Eleanor's arm. "You look exhausted. Too much excitement, I daresay. Shall I have our carriage called? Charlotte may come home with Robyn and Lily later, if she chooses—oh, wait. Here's Charlotte now."

Eleanor looked up to see Charlotte and Hadley winding their way through the crowd, with Lily and Cam behind them. Charlotte's face was flushed, and she was laughing at something Hadley was saying. She'd never looked lovelier, and yet . . . behind the laughing mouth, the lines of her neck were taut, her jaw hard, her fingers twisted in her silk skirts.

A chill shot up Eleanor's spine.

"My goodness, it's warm," Charlotte said as she joined them. "Eleanor, come out to the terrace with me, won't you? I need a breath of air."

"I'd be delighted to escort you, Lady Charlotte." Hadley offered his arm.

Charlotte tapped him playfully with her fan. "No, indeed, for I need you to fetch me some lemonade. Perhaps Mr. West can accompany you?" Charlotte glanced at Cam. "My sister looks parched as well, and I'm sure her drink has grown warm."

Cam bowed to Eleanor, his face distant. "Of course. Shall we, Hadley?"

As soon as the gentlemen were out of earshot, Charlotte grasped Eleanor's arm and tugged her through the French doors behind them and out onto the terrace. "We'll be back directly, mother," she called, and Lady Catherine waved them on.

"For pity's sake, Charlotte." Eleanor rubbed at the red marks Charlotte's fingers had left on the bare skin above her glove. "Whatever is the matter with you?"

Charlotte drifted to the edge of the terrace to stare out into the dark garden beyond, but she looked at it as if she didn't see it. She saw another garden, under a different moon, on another night, six weeks ago. Eleanor couldn't have said how she knew this, but she did.

After a moment Charlotte murmured, "Perhaps I did lure him, after all."

Eleanor joined her at the terrace railing. "Lured who?"

Charlotte didn't answer, but continued to gaze into the garden, her face unreadable. After a long moment she turned to face Eleanor. "I want to know why you've agreed to marry Camden West."

Eleanor's shoulders went rigid at the unexpected question. "I can't think why you'd ask me that, Charlotte, when you know very well why. Because of Amelia, and the scandal with Julian West. Because I haven't any other choice."

"No." Charlotte shook her head. "You tell yourself those are the reasons, but they aren't. I want to know the real reason."

Eleanor tried to laugh, but the sound she made was brittle, false. "The real reason? That sounds quite dramatic, but I'm afraid it's far less mysterious than you think. The reasons I've given are sufficient to explain my actions."

"Sufficient, yes, but not the truth, for all that."

The truth. Eleanor's fingers curled into her palms. How strange, that Charlotte would think she even knew what the truth was anymore. "I don't know what you mean."

Charlotte raised an eyebrow. "Don't you? Very well, Eleanor. Let's start with this, then. Tell me, what did mother say when you told her about Amelia being our father's child?"

Ellie and Alec had told their mother about Amelia's parentage as soon as they'd returned from Lindenhurst. Like the rest of the family, Lady Catherine was shocked by her late husband's cruelty, and anxious to do whatever she could for Amelia. "Just what we imagined she'd say—Amelia is a lovely child, and she's proud to call her a Sutherland."

"So are we all," Charlotte said. "We'll do everything we can for her. The family will take care of Amelia. There's never been a question of that. You don't need to accept Camden West on Amelia's account then, do you? It's not as if we'd turn our backs on her if you didn't marry him."

"But there's still the question of what's owed to her—"

"You aren't the one who owes that debt, Eleanor, no matter what Camden West might say, and I think you're well aware of that."

Eleanor's mouth went tight. "There's the other matter still."

"Ah, yes. The other matter." Charlotte leaned against the railing, her eyes on the garden again. "I doubt there will be any gossip, but if there is, it will die a quick death."

"Indeed? I wish I could be as sanguine as you are."

"Oh, you can be. Hadley has made me an offer, and I've accepted him."

Eleanor drew in a long breath. She'd known it, even before Charlotte said it, in the same way she knew each time her sister looked into the garden, she saw Julian West.

Six weeks ago Eleanor would have been thrilled at this news, but now her heart sank. "Charlotte, are you . . . do you love him?"

Charlotte hesitated, then, "He's a good man, a steady man, and I've no doubt he loves me."

Eleanor squeezed her eyes closed. It wasn't what she'd asked, yet it was an answer all the same.

"So you see," Charlotte went on, "you no longer need to marry Camden West to save my reputation."

Eleanor gripped the railing to steady herself. *Of course.* Charlotte's marriage—to a Marquess, no less—would silence any wagging tongues, no matter what Cam or Julian West might say. The *ton* wouldn't dare insult the new Marchioness of Hadley, and after all, no one cared if Charlotte were ruined. They only cared if she were a scandal.

Charlotte's voice came to her as if from a distance. "There's no reason you can't walk into the ballroom this minute and jilt Camden West. He hasn't any power over you now. I expect you'll want to do so right away, won't you?"

Eleanor's heart rushed into her throat. It was true. She could walk away from Cam tonight, this very moment, if she chose. She could forget him—

forget the way his eyes turned as soft as spring leaves when he looked at her, forget the warm pressure of his mouth against the pulse at her wrist, the sound of her name on his lips.

Something shifted inside her then, shook loose, fell away. She turned to Charlotte, stricken.

"Shall we try again?" Charlotte asked. "Why have you accepted Camden West?"

Eleanor stared out into the dark garden. She tried to speak, but the words wouldn't come. If she said it aloud, it would be real, and then, then . . .

But Charlotte read the truth in her face. "Marry him or don't, Eleanor, but don't lie to yourself."

Eleanor had the oddest urge to cover her face with her hands, but it was too late. Her polite mask dissolved, exposing the raw skin beneath.

Charlotte touched her hand. "Not long ago you told me you would never marry without love. I believed you then, and I believe you still."

Eleanor looked down at Charlotte's hand, but it was Cam's hand she saw, touching hers.

She'd taken his hand. That night at Lindenhurst, she'd taken his hand in hers and urged him to lie next to her, and it had been the simplest thing in the world. Then she'd panicked, and she'd been hateful to him. He'd been so tender, and she'd thrown it all back in his face, and now maybe he would never believe she cared for him, no matter what she said.

Behind them the first few notes of the waltz drifted through the French doors. "We've been gone too long." Eleanor took Charlotte's arm and turned back toward the ballroom. "Mother will wonder where—"

"Why did you tell me Julian West wasn't involved in his cousin's plan to trap you into marriage?" Charlotte pulled her arm from Eleanor's grasp. "That day we went shopping, the day I bought you the rocking horse, you denied it, but all along you knew he was, didn't you?"

Eleanor looked down at her hands to avoid her sister's eyes. "I knew. That is, I suspected."

"But instead of confiding in me, you misled me, to keep me out of it. You said Julian didn't act as if he knew, and then you said he seemed taken with me."

"He *did* seem taken with you."

"Taken. Yes, you have no idea how right you are. The moment you suggested it, I seized on it, because I wanted it to be true. You've always been clever at that, Eleanor—at telling people what they want to hear."

Eleanor stiffened. *Clever.* It sounded like an accusation. "I beg your pardon. I thought it better you didn't know. I wasn't sure what you'd do if you did, and I knew I could manage it—"

"On your own?" Charlotte's laugh was short, hollow. "Yes, you always think so. You didn't trust me, Eleanor. I suppose you think I can't be trusted with anything more important than rocking horses."

"But I do trust you, Charlotte!"

But Charlotte plunged ahead, as if she hadn't heard. "As it happens, you couldn't manage it on your own, after all. You're as good as wed to Camden West, and I—I . . . dear God, what a fool I've been."

The cold shiver Eleanor felt earlier shot down her spine again. "What do you mean, you've been a fool? I know you rather liked Julian West, but—"

"Liked him? Oh, Eleanor. It's far worse than that. I thought I loved him, and he's ruined me."

Eleanor's breath stopped. She gulped at the cool night air to will her lungs back into motion.

*Ruined. No. It couldn't be. When? There ha*dn't been time—

Her hand flew to her mouth. *Oh, dear God.* Lindenhurst. Julian West had come to Lindenhurst. It would have been the easiest thing in the world for him to find Charlotte, seduce her, then creep out the next morning, before anyone was the wiser.

Charlotte watched with a grim smile as Eleanor reached the obvious conclusion. "I see you've worked out for yourself how it happened. While you were busy uncovering Camden West's secrets, I was, well . . . revealing mine to his cousin."

Eleanor clawed at the railing. The stone scraped her fingers raw, but she didn't feel it. *This was her fault.* Why hadn't she told Charlotte the truth? She should never have lied, but she'd been so sure she could manage Cam, so sure she could take care of everything herself, and—

Oh, no. She froze as realization dawned.

It wasn't true. It couldn't be true.

But it was. It was the only explanation for Charlotte's sudden change of heart about Hadley. She'd accepted him, a man she liked and admired but didn't love, because of her disastrous affair with Julian West.

Eleanor groped blindly for Charlotte as a wave of nausea hit her.

Charlotte squeezed her hand. "As soon as you told me about Amelia, I realized my mistake. I knew it wasn't possible Julian could be ignorant of the circumstances of her birth, and even less so that the seduction at the Foster's ball was a coincidence."

Eleanor's eyes filled with tears. She'd been so intent on jerking the strings from behind the curtain, she'd forgotten who was on the other end, and now Charlotte would pay the price for it. "I'm sorry, Charlotte—so terribly sorry." She wanted to say so much more, but her throat closed, and she fell silent.

Charlotte's face softened. "I don't blame you for it. I went into the garden with him. I let him seduce me. Nothing you did afterward could change that."

Eleanor looked down at Charlotte's hand, still wrapped around hers. "You *should* blame me, Charlotte. I never should have—"

"You're my sister, Eleanor. I would forgive you anything." Charlotte smiled, but she looked as if her heart would break. "Let's not ever mention it again. It's done."

Eleanor nodded. She didn't trust herself to speak. They stood for some time, gazing silently out at the garden, but at last Eleanor roused herself. "Do you suppose he cares for you? Julian West, I mean."

Charlotte shrugged, but her chin was trembling. "He says he does."

"But you don't believe him?"

"It doesn't matter whether I believe him or not. I can never trust him now."

Eleanor paused. She had to ask. She had to know. "Yet you love him still, don't you?"

Charlotte's face crumpled. "I thought I loved him, but I believed he was someone else."

Someone else.

A gentleman or a scoundrel, a hero or a villain . . . or both at once?

Julian West had made a mistake—one mistake. A grievous one, yes, but that one mistake wasn't who he was. It wasn't *all* he was, any more than Cam's mistakes were all he was.

Blackmail, threats, revenge—yes, Cam was guilty of it all. Fury, bitterness, and the ghosts only he could see. He'd let them into his heart, and they'd torn it open. But for all that, he was a man of his word, and somehow, despite everything, his heart could still hold love so deep, so abiding, it took her breath away. Amelia, Mary and Julian West—one had only to look at Cam to see he'd move heaven and earth for any of them.

A hero, or a villain. Cam was both, and so were they all. "It's not too late, Charlotte—"

"It *is* too late. For me, it is. I trusted Julian West. I shouldn't have, and I won't make that mistake again. But you, Eleanor—it's not too late for you."

"But—"

"How can you think I'd marry him now? I've refused to even see him."

Eleanor thought of what Mrs. Mullins had said about Julian West, about never having known a boy with a more affectionate heart than his.

Pure gold, his heart.

Her heart began to bleed then, bleed for Julian West. Perhaps he didn't deserve her pity. Perhaps, after all, one mistake could condemn a man to a lifetime of regrets. What had Cam said about fate? It was crueler to some than others.

But it shouldn't be, and it didn't have to be. Not this time. "You can't marry Hadley, Charlotte, not if you're still in love with—"

"No." Charlotte snatched her hand away. "Don't say his name to me. After tonight, we won't speak of him again. I'm to be married to a kind, decent man who loves me, and I will grow to love him back. I'm sure of it."

Perhaps she would, or perhaps . . .

One never gets over a love like that, do they?

A tiny corner of Eleanor's heart—the part that whispered Julian West was the one love her sister could never recover from—withered in her chest.

"He said . . ." Charlotte drew in a deep breath, but her voice still shook. "When I accepted Hadley, he sank to his knees and told me I'd made him the happiest of men. I *will* grow to love him, Eleanor. How could I not?"

Warmth rushed through Eleanor, warmth for Hadley, who looked at her sister as he had tonight, as if she were a gift, and he was the most fortunate gentleman in the world. Perhaps it would all work out for the best.

Pure gold, his heart.

Eleanor cleared the lump from her throat and struggled to lighten her tone. "I suppose mother is ecstatic? I expect to be put to work right away on the wedding."

Charlotte shook her head. "No, there will be no grand wedding. Alec granted his permission this morning, and Hadley obtained a special license this afternoon. We're to be wed tomorrow morning, then we'll leave at once for Hadley's seat in Hampshire."

Eleanor stared at her. "What? So soon? Why?"

"Hadley's mother is ill, and she wishes to see her son married right away. Of course I couldn't object, and I have my own reasons to wish to be married quickly."

Eleanor's gaze dropped to Charlotte's belly. *Of course.* She moved her hand unconsciously to her own belly then, astonished she'd only just thought of it. But Cam—he'd have thought of it. He'd never allow his child to bear the stigma of illegitimacy.

She pressed her hand tighter against her belly. Was that why he insisted on the marriage still? Perhaps it wasn't about her at all anymore.

"I'll send a letter to Jul—to *him*," Charlotte said, her voice strained. "Tomorrow, once Hadley and I are wed. If he ever cared for me, he'll honor my wish that he never contact me again."

Eleanor didn't reply to that, because there wasn't anything she could say.

"Eleanor, do you . . ." Charlotte's voice trailed off for a moment, then, "do you think less of me? Because of what happened with . . . because of what I did?"

Eleanor took Charlotte's hand, her grip fierce. "No. Never."

Someday, someday soon, after she'd spoken with Cam, she'd tell Charlotte the truth about those nights at Lindenhurst, but for now . . .

"You're my sister, Charlotte. I could never be anything but proud of you. I told a dear friend of mine recently that no matter what, sisters stand by each other. And so we do."

Charlotte let out a shaky breath and squeezed Eleanor's hand. "And so we do."

Chapter Twenty-six

Cam came to a halt at the bottom of the dark staircase. He wanted to fall into his bed and put an end to this evening—to this day, to these past weeks—but the staircase unfolded before him in an endless procession of steps, the upper landing so impossibly high, so far away, so obscured by shadows it seemed insurmountable. A mountain, not a staircase.

He'd left the ball early. It wasn't much past midnight now, but it felt later. Darker. Quieter.

He worked his fingers into the tight knot at his throat and clawed at the fabric until his cravat hung limp around his neck.

There. The cravat was a start. Now, the stairs. One at a time.

Step. She'd worn a deep wine-colored gown tonight. The color flattered her creamy skin and dark hair and eyes. Hadn't she worn a similar color, the first night he'd seen her? Yes. He'd thought at the time the color echoed her scent, that faint hint of black currants.

Step. Lovely. Always she was lovely, yet tonight she hadn't looked the same to him. Other gentlemen watched her, admired her. Cam saw the way their eyes followed her, and he wondered why none of them noticed something was missing.

The spark, the flash in her dark eyes.

Step. He'd noticed, as he should. He was the one who'd stolen it from her.

More steps, more sharp clicks as the bottom of his shoes hit the cold marble. Endless, these stairs.

One step at a time.

She'd left the ball early, claiming fatigue, but her sudden departure had more to do with whatever her sister had said to her out on the terrace. Two dances elapsed before they returned, and when they did, Eleanor's face was pale and her eyes red, as if she'd been crying.

Step. He hadn't objected to leaving early. No doubt she was fatigued. God knew he was. It exhausted him to pretend, to play this never-ending game of charades.

Cam reached the second floor landing at last. He drew a deep breath and turned right, toward Amelia's bedchamber. He opened the door and waited for his eyes to adjust to the dark.

"Denny? I'm awake."

He'd known she would be, but Amelia expected the usual mild scold, so he indulged her. "You should have been asleep long ago, minx."

Amelia sat upright, propped against a mound of pillows. "I wasn't tired."

"You will be tomorrow." Cam sat down on the edge of the bed. "You can't stay up until all hours and wait for me to return when I go out in the evenings."

Amelia fiddled with one of her pillows. "I know. I promise this is the last time. Since I *am* awake, though, won't you tell me about your evening?"

"I've heard that promise before."

Amelia turned appealing dark eyes on him. "Please?"

He gave her his best stern look. "Very well, then. But this is the last time." They both knew it wouldn't be, but he always said so, and Amelia always nodded in agreement. "All right, then. What do you want to know?"

"What did Lady Eleanor, that is, Ellie—what did Ellie wear tonight?"

He'd known Amelia would ask questions about Eleanor. He'd tried to brace himself for it, but it hurt to talk of her. To think of her. "A wine-colored silk gown. Short lace sleeves and a square neck, with a scalloped lace edging."

Amelia nodded with approval. She insisted upon hearing every detail of the gowns. "Color of the lace?"

"Black," he answered promptly. Amelia had trained him well.

"On the skirt, as well? Did she have a sash?"

"Not a sash, really, but there was some black ribbon or cording, I believe, on the waist and sleeves. The skirt did have lace, yes, in a narrow pattern down the front and along the hem."

"Jewels?"

"A ruby necklace, and hair combs, rubies and diamonds."

"She wore her hair up, then. Simple or fancy?"

Cam drew a deep breath. Her heavy dark hair had been gathered into a loose knot at the back of her head, and the long white nape of her neck had driven him mad all evening. "A simple chignon, with tendrils trailing over her shoulders."

Amelia sighed with delight. "Oh, my. Did she look beautiful?"

"Yes." She'd looked beautiful, that quiet, wan Ellie. That Ellie who wasn't Ellie at all.

"Did you dance every dance with her?"

"We danced three times."

"Does she dance well? She must."

"Yes. So graceful. I've never seen another lady to equal her." Such exquisite agony, to hold Eleanor in his arms with all the empty, silent space between them.

Amelia gave another girlish sigh. "I can't wait until I'm old enough to go to balls and dance with all the handsome gentlemen. You were the handsomest gentleman in the room, weren't you?"

There was only one acceptable answer to this question as far as Amelia was concerned, so Cam gave it. "Yes, of course. The tallest, too."

He waited while she mulled this over. She'd ask about gowns, then about the music and the supper—

"When will you and Ellie get married?"

Cam's heart lurched at the unexpected question. He hadn't yet told Amelia about the betrothal. He'd meant to, ever since the last evening at Lindenhurst when Eleanor accepted his suit, but now it was weeks later, and he still hadn't said a word. He hadn't had the first of the banns called yet, either.

He was waiting for something. Hoping for it. Yearning for it, but as each day slipped into night it drifted further and further away, and trying to hold onto it was like clutching at the sun to keep it from sinking below the horizon.

That night at Lindenhurst, the night they'd made love, Eleanor had given him everything. She'd placed her body and her pleasure in his hands, yes, but she'd given him her trust, too. He'd felt it in every sigh, every gasp, every kiss, and it had devastated him. Humbled him. It was the sweetest pleasure he'd ever known.

Then, in the next breath, it was gone. She'd taken it back again. She'd given him that precious gift, then she'd taken it away, and left him broken from its loss.

So he waited. He counted each breath, each beat of his battered heart, and waited for her to give it back again. He held off on calling the banns, held off on telling Amelia, because he kept hoping . . .

But every day the sun set, despite his best efforts to stop it, and it had yet to rise again.

"Denny?" Amelia watched him, puzzled. "When do you think you and Ellie will marry?"

"I—why do you think we intend to marry at all?" His voice wasn't quite steady.

"Because Lady Charlotte told me you would, in the carriage on the way back to London from Lindenhurst." She gave him a strange look. "Why wouldn't you marry? You love Ellie, don't you?"

He thought of her, of how she'd looked tonight, her jewels sparkling in her dark hair, so beautiful she made his heart ache. But her beauty, her name, her father's name—it wasn't enough. It all meant nothing if she lost that spark, that flash in her eyes that made her who she was.

He wanted *her*. All of her. Anything less was unbearable. "Yes. I love her. My best hope for you is someday you'll find someone you love as much as I love her."

Someone who loves you in return.

Amelia smiled then, as if she'd heard his thoughts. "She loves you, too, Denny. She must, otherwise she'd never have agreed to marry you."

Cam shook his head. "People marry without love all the time, Amelia."

"Not Eleanor. She never would, no matter what. She told me so."

Cam stilled. "She told you . . . what, exactly?"

"She told me ladies marry for all kinds of different reasons, but she never would. She said she wouldn't marry for any reason other than love."

Cam stared at her, his breath frozen in his lungs. *Love.* He almost laughed; it was so simple.

Three seasons. Six suitors. Six offers. Fine gentlemen, some of them. Advantageous offers. Any other lady would have accepted, any other lady would have been thrilled . . .

Any other lady, but not Ellie.

Six refusals.

She'd never told him why, and he, in his arrogance, imagined he already knew her reasons. Vanity, at first, and then later, after he knew her better . . . a wish for freedom? Yes, that was part of it. She'd told him that much, but it wasn't her only reason.

Love. He should have known, should have seen it, but it had been easier for him to remain blind, to pretend she lost nothing by marrying him. To tell himself he'd be good to her, kind to her. To tell himself he wasn't stealing from her.

The night they'd made love at Lindenhurst, for the most fleeting of moments, she'd given everything. *To him.* And he'd taken it, as if he had a right to it. Afterwards, she'd been afraid. Vulnerable. He should have held her in his arms until her panic faded away. He should have fallen to his knees in front of her in gratitude.

He should have told her he loved her.

Instead, he'd raged at her. He been brutal, and afterwards, when she was pale and trembling from the shock, he'd spoken to her of obligations.

He'd wanted to hurt her that night, to punish her for taking the gift of herself away. Never once had it occurred to him he didn't deserve her gift. Never once had he thought he wasn't worthy of it.

Not once, until now, had he understood such a gift wasn't something he could take.

He could take her freedom. He could take her body. He could take her name and use it, use her, both for Amelia and for himself. He could take her future away, and tell her she owed it to him. Tell himself she owed it to him, too.

An eye for an eye.

But he couldn't take her love. He couldn't force it from her, or steal it from her. She had to choose to give it to him. She had to reach down into her heart, past the panic and the fear, and offer it to him willingly.

Her love was the only thing that mattered. It had always been the only thing that mattered. The best he could do, the most he could do, was try and deserve it.

"Denny? Why do you look like that? You're scaring me."

Cam jerked his attention back to Amelia. He took her hand. "I'm sorry to scare you, minx. I need to explain something to you, and it may be difficult for you to understand. I'm not going to marry Ellie, despite what Lady Charlotte said. Ellie . . . she doesn't love me."

Amelia stared at him for a moment, then she shook her head. "Yes, she does. She said—"

"I know what she said, sweetheart, but when she said she'd only marry for love she didn't mean she wants to marry me."

"But that doesn't make any sense, Denny. Why shouldn't she want to marry you? I know she loves you."

Cam smiled a little. To Amelia, there could be no question of any lady resisting him. "I know this won't make much sense to you, but the truth is, I didn't give her a chance to say no to me. I haven't been fair to her."

Amelia considered that. "You mean, you cheated? Like when someone cheats at a game?"

It seemed as good an explanation as any. "Yes. Something like that."

"Beg her pardon, then. She'll forgive you."

"Perhaps she would, but forgiveness isn't love, Amelia. Even if she forgives me, I don't think she can—" Cam stopped, swallowed. "I don't think she can love me. Not after I cheated at the game."

Amelia gripped his hand hard. "Won't you even try? You said you loved her, Denny. Surely that matters more than some silly game?"

He wished it were that simple. "If I try she might give in, but if she did, it would be because she loves *you*, Amelia, not me. That might be good enough if I loved her less, but I love her so much I want her to have everything. She wants to marry a gentleman she loves—she told you so herself. Do you understand?"

Amelia didn't answer for a long time, but at last she nodded.

"I thought you would. Now here, I want you to have this." Cam reached into an inside pocket of his coat and pulled out a piece of paper. It was nearly worn through at the creases, as if it had been folded and unfolded many times.

Amelia took the sheet and unfolded it. "This is the drawing I did of Eleanor, from that day in Lady Abernathy's garden. Have you carried it in your pocket all this time?"

"Yes. But now it's time I give it back to you."

Amelia looked down at the limp paper in her hands, then back up at Cam. "But . . . you said it was your favorite."

Cam took the paper from Amelia. "It is." He gazed at it for a long time, traced his finger over the eyes, the curve of the chin. "But it doesn't belong to me." He held it out to her.

She hesitated, but at last she took it. "Perhaps I'll give it to Ellie. She might like to have it. You don't mind if I bring it to her, do you, Denny?"

"No. I don't mind." He leaned forward to look into her eyes. "Whatever happens between Eleanor and me hasn't anything to do with you, Amelia. You know that, don't you? You'll still see the Sutherlands, as often as you like. Eleanor cares a great deal for you. She'll always be your friend, just as she promised she would be."

But she wouldn't be his. Never his.

Amelia nodded. "I know."

Cam rose from the bed, aching with weariness in his body and his heart. Tonight he'd try to sleep, but tomorrow he'd do what he should have done weeks ago. Tomorrow, he'd call on Eleanor, and he'd release her from their engagement.

He drew the covers up under Amelia's chin. "Now go to sleep."

"All right. Good night, Denny."

"Good night, minx."

Amelia lay awake for a long time after Denny closed the door behind him, thinking. Finally, she kicked off the covers, rose, and lit the lamp Miss Norwood always left on the table by the window. She picked up the drawing of Eleanor that lay on the coverlet, smoothed it out, careful not to tear it at the creases, and brought it close to the light.

Yes, she'd drawn the eyes just right. It had been a challenge to capture the dark, velvet softness there, but she'd done it. She could draw Ellie's eyes from memory now, too. She only had to imagine how they went soft when Ellie looked at Denny, and she knew just how to draw them.

She shook her head. *No, it wouldn't do, would it?*

Amelia gazed at the picture for a while longer, then she folded it again, and slipped it under her pillow. She blew out the lamp, swung her legs up onto her bed and burrowed into the nest of blankets, rubbing her cold feet against each other to warm them.

No matter what Denny said, it simply wouldn't do.

Chapter Twenty-seven

"I want the commission, Cam."

Cam had been shuffling papers from one side of his desk to the other for hours, unable to put his mind to anything except the talk he'd have with Eleanor later this morning, but now he looked up to find Julian standing in front of his desk. "The commission?"

Julian's face was pale and set, his spine rigid. "The place with the 10th Royal Hussars. I want it."

Cam fell back against his chair. He hadn't seen much of Julian since they'd returned from Lindenhurst. His cousin was in and out of the townhouse at odd hours, and when he was at home, he was quiet and distracted. Cam had convinced himself Julian had forgotten all about the commission in favor of a new mistress or some other diversion.

Not so. *Jesus*. He felt like a chunk of marble under the sculptor's chisel. Small pieces of him were being chipped away, leaving nothing but dust and crushed rock at his feet.

First Eleanor, now Julian.

"Cam?" Julian's voice was tense. "You told me the commission was mine if I wanted it."

Cam drew a deep breath. He'd promised it, and he wouldn't go back on his word. "I did, and it's yours. I'll make the arrangements. When will you go?"

"Now. I leave within the hour."

"Now? That soon?" Cam dragged a hand down his face. "But Amelia isn't here. She and Miss Norwood left an hour ago to sketch while the morning light held. You won't leave without saying goodbye to her?"

"Damn it." Julian's expression turned bleak. "I have to, Cam. If I don't leave right away, I won't have time to get to Lindenhurst and see my parents before I join my regiment."

Cam studied his cousin for a moment in silence. *No.* That wasn't the reason. Something was wrong. Julian looked as if he hadn't slept in days. Dark circles ringed his eyes, at least three days' worth of stubble shadowed his jaw, and he held himself stiffly, as if he were in pain. "Is there some other reason you need to leave right away?"

Julian's face went hard. "I need to get out of London."

Cam hadn't noticed it at first, but now he could see Julian held a scrap of paper in his hand, paper he was slowly crushing in his fist. "Julian, what's—"

"I'll miss you, cousin. You'll have to be your own conscience now. See you don't become too wicked while I'm gone."

Cam rose, came around the side of the desk and held out his hand to Julian. "I'll do my best." There was more to say, so much more, but he looked into Julian's dull eyes, and he knew his cousin wouldn't hear him. "You'll do your best, too?"

Do your best not to get killed. The words hung in the air between them, unspoken.

Julian grasped his hand. "Always. You'll tell Amelia I said goodbye? I'll write to her every day, just as you did when you were in India. Tell her I'll buy her all the lemon ices she can eat when I return, all right?"

If you return.

Cam couldn't say it. He could hardly even think it, so he said the only thing he could say. "I'll tell her. Julian?"

Julian was nearly out the door, but he turned back. "Yes?"

Cam swallowed. "See you don't . . . disappoint Amelia."

"Disappoint a lady?" For the first time since he'd entered the study, Julian's mouth turned up at the corners. Not a smile, but a bitter, angry twist of his lips. "I never do, cuz. I never do."

* * * * *

Eleanor sat on the settee in the drawing room. A book lay open in her lap, but she wasn't reading. It was too quiet to read. She couldn't recall her home ever being this quiet before. This still. This empty.

An hour ago the front door had closed with a muted thud behind the new Marchioness of Hadley and her adoring spouse. Charlotte and her husband were on their way to Hampshire, and they didn't intend to return to London until next spring.

It was done.

It had been a rather lovely wedding ceremony—quiet and subdued, yes, but lovely still, in great part because of Hadley, who'd been aglow with happiness to have secured Charlotte at last. One couldn't see the joy on his face without being moved by it.

Charlotte had been pale but steady, and she'd smiled at Hadley as she spoke her vows. If she felt any regret over giving up Julian West, it hadn't shown on her face. She'd made her choice, and, for better or worse, she'd made her peace with it.

Now if only Eleanor could do the same. Hadley would cherish her sister, so perhaps it was all for the best, this marriage. And yet . . .

"I beg your pardon, Lady Eleanor. You have a visitor."

Eleanor looked up, surprised. She hadn't heard Rylands come into the room. A nervous flutter tickled her stomach. When she hadn't been thinking of Charlotte as she lay awake last night, she'd been staring at the canopy above her, eyes wide open, thinking of Cam, the feel of his fingers under her chin as he tilted her face up to his, the way his green eyes darkened with desire right before he took her lips.

Is there no hope for us?

Today, at last, she had an answer for him. "Very well. Thank you, Rylands."

The butler bowed and returned to the entryway.

Eleanor rose from her seat, the book still clutched in her hands, her eyes fixed on the door. Goodness, her knees felt shaky—

"Ellie! How do you do? I've waited this age to see you."

Eleanor blinked. It wasn't Cam after all, but Amelia. She nearly sagged with disappointment, but she did her best to hide it. "Good afternoon, Amelia. I hope you'll come see me whenever you wish, and not wait for formal calling hours. We're friends, aren't we?"

"I told Miss Norwood as much, but she insisted we wait, and now I have only a little time to talk to you before Denny gets here."

Another surge of disappointment. Cam wasn't with his sister, then. "You came with Miss Norwood?"

"Yes. She's off to have tea in the kitchens. I want to speak with you *alone.*" Amelia swelled with importance. "It's a delicate matter, you see."

Despite her low spirits, Eleanor suppressed a smile. Charlotte was gone, but Amelia was here, and as long as she was, Eleanor wouldn't feel too lonely. "Well, it sounds as if we'd better sit down."

Amelia gave her a grave nod. "Yes. I think that would be best."

Eleanor gestured Amelia to the settee and they sat, side by side. Eleanor waited, but now Amelia had her attention, she seemed unsure where to begin. "Well, you see, it's just this . . ."

Eleanor touched Amelia's hand. "Yes? You can tell me anything. You know that, Amelia."

"I know." Amelia fidgeted with one of the blue silk pillows on the settee, but after a moment she met Eleanor's gaze, and whatever she saw there seemed to encourage her. "It just won't do. There. I've said it."

Not all of it, Eleanor hoped, for this sounded like the end of the story, not the beginning. "What won't do?"

"Why, you and Denny. Lady Charlotte said you were to marry, but Denny told me last night you won't, so I've come to tell you it just won't do."

For one awful moment Eleanor felt dizzy, as if the settee underneath her had tipped over, but then she realized it was her heart plummeting from her chest to her stomach that made her head swim.

Not marry. Cam had said they wouldn't marry. He'd changed his mind, then. That's why he hadn't called the banns or told Amelia about their betrothal. He didn't want her.

Ice spread from her heart to every part of her, until she was so brittle, a touch would crack her, shatter her into a thousand frozen pieces.

This is what it feels like to lose him.

A hysterical laugh threatened. How fitting, that fate should snatch him away at the very moment she realized she loved him. He'd said fate was cruel, and it was true. Cruel and mocking.

Eleanor took a deep breath and forced herself to address Amelia calmly. "He told you that last night?"

Amelia was watching her with an intent expression far too wise for her tender years. She looked, rather suddenly, just like her brother. She fumbled in the pocket of her dress, pulled out a folded piece of paper, and held it out to Eleanor. "Yes. He gave me this."

Eleanor took the paper, unfolded it, and smoothed it out on her knee. She gazed at it for a moment, then looked up at Amelia. "It's a drawing of me. Is it one of yours?"

"Yes. I drew it the day after we made daisy chains in Lady Abernathy's garden. I showed it to Denny when I finished. He asked if he could have it, and he's kept it since that day. Until last night, that is, when he gave it back to me."

"He . . . he kept it?"

"Yes. He's had it all this time, folded up in his pocket."

Tears blurred Eleanor's eyes. Lady Abernathy's garden party was weeks ago. That was the day he'd told her she didn't matter, that he cared only that she was a Sutherland, yet the very next day he'd slipped this drawing into his pocket, and he'd carried it with him everywhere ever since. All those weeks, he'd held it next to his heart.

"I won't tell all of Denny's secrets," Amelia said, once again sounding far more mature than her years. "I hope he'll tell you most of it himself, but just in case he doesn't tell you everything, I did think you should know . . ."

Eleanor had been staring at the drawing, but her head jerked up at this. "Yes?"

"He said he cheated at the game, whatever that means. I suppose it's rather bad, though, isn't it? He said you could never love him, because of the way he'd cheated."

"But I cheated, too." Eleanor choked the words out through cold lips.

She'd lied to herself, just as Charlotte said she had. For weeks she'd told herself she didn't want to marry Cam because she could never love him, but the truth was, she was afraid of him. Afraid to love him. She hadn't wanted to give him her trust or her love, because she thought she'd lose herself if she did, just as her mother had when she'd married Hart Sutherland.

She hadn't understood then love wasn't losing yourself.

It was finding yourself.

And Cam . . . oh, he was far from perfect, but then so was she, and together they were more perfect than they could ever be apart.

"I told him you'd forgive him for cheating," Amelia said, "but he said forgiveness isn't the same thing as love. But you love him too, Ellie. I know you do, because I can see it in your eyes when you look at him. Anyway, why shouldn't you love him? Denny's the best man ever, and the handsomest, and the tallest, too."

Eleanor smiled a little at Amelia's vehemence. Young as she was, Amelia knew quite a lot about being a fiercely loyal sister. "Yes, he is. All of those things."

Amelia beamed. "I knew you thought so, too. He's coming here this afternoon to say goodbye to you, so I made an excuse and scurried on ahead to get to you first, because, well . . . it won't do."

"No." Eleanor swiped a hand under her eye. "No. It won't do."

"I want you to have that." Amelia nodded at the drawing still spread open on Eleanor's knee. "Denny said it didn't belong to him, but it really does, doesn't it? It's yours now, so you can do whatever you like with it, but I thought you might want to give it back to him."

Eleanor opened her arms to Amelia, who scooted across the settee and dove into them. "What a grand idea." She kissed the top of Amelia's blonde head. "Yes. I think that will do."

* * * * *

Cam dragged himself up the stairs of the Mayfair townhouse and waited for Rylands to answer his knock. He'd known this moment would arrive—for weeks, perhaps, he'd known, and now it had, he was desperate to get it over with, in the same way a man who'd been shot was desperate to have the surgeon remove the ball.

It hurt less if it was done quickly, or so he'd been told. Painful or not, it would be fatal. Extracting a ball from a beating heart generally was.

"Good afternoon, Mr. West." Rylands opened the door to admit him, and held out his hands for Cam's hat and coat. "Lady Eleanor is in the drawing room."

She was alone, standing by the window looking out into the garden, but she turned when he entered.

"Good afternoon, my lady. I—" He froze partway across the room, and his words died on his lips. She looked different. Something in her face, or perhaps in her eyes. A spark, or—

No. She didn't look different. She looked like herself again, like the Eleanor he remembered. The Eleanor he'd fallen in love with.

Cam drank in the sight of her even as pain sliced his heart to ribbons. Did she know, somehow, he'd come to release her from their engagement? He couldn't see how she could, but it didn't matter. The spark was back in her beautiful dark eyes, and he'd do whatever he must to keep it there.

*Ex*tract the ball.

"I came here to—"

"Charlotte was married this morning," she interrupted in a rush. "To the Marquess of Hadley."

Cam stared at her. "Married?" Jesus, that was sudden. For some reason Julian's pale, rigid face flashed through his mind. *No, surely not. Surely that wasn't why*—

"Yes." Eleanor laughed, but she looked nervous. "We've kept it rather quiet, but I thought you should know."

*That he sh*ould know? Why—

Realization slammed through him with the force of a blow. Lady Charlotte was married, which meant her reputation was now secure. His threats against her had been rendered meaningless, and Eleanor wanted to make sure he understood that.

No wonder, then, the spark was back in her eyes. She was free of him at last. If his heart hadn't been reduced to a bleeding pulp, he might have laughed to find she'd gained her freedom mere hours before he gave it to her willingly.

"I offer my congratulations, and my heartfelt wishes for Lady Charlotte's happiness." His voice sounded stiff, awkward, but he drew a deep breath and pressed on, desperate to get it done. "I came this morning to release you from our engagement. I—I was wrong to do such a . . . I regret, deeply, that I . . . I beg your pardon for my dishonorable actions, Lady Eleanor."

He owed her more than that, so much more than such a brief, stammering apology, and yet it was the best he could do. He couldn't look at her, at the spark in her eyes that made his chest ache, but at the same time he could hardly tear his eyes away from her. It took all his control to make his formal bow and turn away.

"Wait."

Cam didn't turn, but closed his eyes at her quiet command. He couldn't look at her again, not now—

"Cam. Please."

Please. That was all it took, one soft word, and he could deny her nothing. He braced himself, but his heart wrenched horribly in his chest when he faced her again.

"I have something here. It belongs to you." She reached for his hand and slipped a piece of paper into his palm.

Cam stared down at it. The drawing. Amelia's drawing of Eleanor. Amelia must have been here, must have given it to her. He shook his head. "This doesn't belong to me." His voice was a hoarse rasp. "It belongs to you."

She reached out and wrapped both her hands around his to close his fingers over the drawing. "It did, but now I'm giving it to you."

He didn't speak—he couldn't. He could only gaze at her, his fingers going tight around the paper as if he'd never let it go.

She looked a little uncertain now, but her eyes were soft. "I told you about Charlotte only so you understand I've no other reason to say what I'm about to say, aside from it being the truth. I don't wish to be released from our engagement, Cam. I want to marry you."

"You want . . ." Cam forced back the joy that surged wildly inside him at her words, certain he'd misunderstood her. "No, Ellie, you don't."

She took a step closer to him. Another. He looked down in disbelief as she took his hands in hers and smiled up at him. "Have you ever known me to do what I don't wish to do, Cam?"

Cam's eyes slid closed again. Oh, God, he wanted to believe her so badly, but it was impossible she could want him. "What I did, all the things I said . . ."

She pressed her hand against his cheek. "What you did, what you said—it's not all you are." She raised one of his hands to her lips and pressed a kiss to his palm. "The man you truly are—a man of his word, who loves with such a rare, deep love—I'm in love with that man. With you. I don't want to be released from our engagement. I only ever wanted to marry for love, and I love you, Cam."

Cam heard a deep groan and realized it came from him, that she'd torn it straight from his heart. Then he was holding her, and she lay her head against his chest, as if his arms were the only place she ever wanted to be. "Eleanor. God, Eleanor, I love you so much. I wanted to tell you, but I didn't think you'd believe me, not after all I'd done—"

She wrapped her arms around his neck and pressed a kiss on his chin. "I do believe you, and that's all that matters. Whatever may have happened before this moment, well, perhaps it's best forgotten. No one cares about the start of the play, Cam. They only care about the wedding at the end."

Cam touched his fingers to her chin to raise her face to his. "This isn't the end, sweet—it's just the beginning."

"A comedy, a farce, or a drama?" She smiled up at him. "What's it to be, do you suppose?"

"All of those things, likely, but not a tragedy. I never could abide a tragedy."

She laughed, delighted, and he couldn't help but kiss her then, his mouth hot and hungry against hers. She opened her lips to him and he surged inside with a groan. He kissed her until both of them were gasping for breath, and he was in danger of ravishing her on the dainty blue settee, with Rylands mere feet away.

He tore his mouth from hers, but he held her close and buried his face in her hair. "I don't deserve you, but I'll try to. I'll try and be a better man—"

Eleanor laid her fingers against his mouth to hush him. "A truce?"

He smiled, his lips opening under her fingers. "It's worked so far, hasn't it?" He kissed her fingertips. "What are your terms?"

"You don't try to be anything but who you are, the best of who you are, and I promise I'll do the same. And I'll kiss you again, right here and now."

Cam gazed down at her, at the spark in her dark eyes that lit a fire inside him. "Ah, my lady." He gathered her against him, and his arms and heart had never felt so full. "How can I refuse?"

Notes

On page 317, Eleanor refers to hope as a "waking dream." The original quote, "Hope is a waking dream," is attributed to Aristotle, by Diogenes Laertius.

Please turn the page for an exciting sneak peek of Anna Bradley's next historical romance

LADY CHARLOTTE'S FIRST LOVE

coming soon!

Chapter One

London, July 1816

A scandalous wager, a marchioness in disguise and a notorious London brothel. Julian couldn't deny it had all the makings of an excellent farce.

Off stage, it was rather less amusing.

Bloody hell. One would think a marchioness who gambled with her reputation would choose an anonymous brothel in a quiet part of the city for her whorehouse romp. Instead, the Marchioness of Hadley had chosen this one.

Devil take her.

He peered into the dimly lit parlor. Despite the muted light and the haze of acrid smoke, he could see the place was crowded with fashionably dressed gentlemen. A man might tend to ignore everything else when he cupped a plump breast or a shapely thigh in his hand, but if one of these drunken dandies happened to recognize him, he'd have a glorious headline in the scandal sheets tomorrow:

Triumphant Hero Returns to London, Frolics with a Whore

A dark-haired doxy sidled up to him and gave his arm a flirtatious tap. "In or out, guv. Wot will it be?"

Julian raised an eyebrow. "In *or* out? Must I settle for one or the other?"

The doxy blinked at him, then broke into a hoarse cackle. "Aw right then, luv, how's this? In or out, or *in and out*." She punctuated the feeble jest with a rude hand gesture.

Julian's lips quirked. Ah, there it was. A quick-witted whore. It was something new, anyway.

Encouraged, the doxy rose to her tiptoes, put her mouth to his ear and whispered in what she no doubt imagined to be a seductive voice, "It's wot ye came fer, innit?"

It stood to reason. If a man wanted ale, he went to an alehouse. If he wanted to shoe his horse, he went to a blacksmith. If he wanted a woman and one wasn't readily available, he went to a whore. It was a simple enough matter.

Except it wasn't. Not this time. "No. I came for a marchioness."

The doxy flashed a gap-toothed grin. "'Course ye did. Dinnit I tell ye, guv? I'm a duchess, I am."

Julian rolled his eyes. No doubt this duchess was much like every other—more trouble than she was worth—but he couldn't hover in the entryway all night waiting to snatch a wayward marchioness. He needed a prop, and a doxy in the hand was worth two anywhere else.

Well. Not quite *anywhere* else, but he wouldn't be here long enough to maneuver her into a more satisfying location. Damn it, it was just like his cousin Cam to send him off to a whorehouse in pursuit of a marchioness instead of a whore.

But it could be hours before Lady Hadley deigned to appear, and in the meantime . . .

He let the dark-haired doxy drag him across the threshold into a shadowy corner of the parlor. The gentlemen around him lounged on sumptuous red velvet divans, glasses of port or whiskey in their hands, many of them with women in various stages of undress perched on their laps. The low, continuous buzz of conversation was occasionally punctuated by a high-pitched squeal or giggle.

"There now," his doxy cooed, "not so hard, was it, luv? Don't you worry, though," she added with a smirk. "It will be once the duchess gets ahold of it."

Julian felt an embarrassingly quick surge of interest in his lower extremities. He hadn't had a woman in . . . well. He couldn't quite recall how long it had been, but long enough so even the doxy duchess held a certain appeal. Every other part of him might rebel at the thought, but his body demanded a woman. The need was like a flea crawling under his skin, and the more he tried to ignore it, the more pressing it became.

He'd have to mount something other than his horse, and soon, so he may as well scratch the itch here and now. It insisted on being scratched, and it would have its way whether he willed it or not. If he tried to return to his old life with such a burden of lust in his loins, there was no telling how he'd be tempted to satisfy it.

The doxy ran her hands up the front of his chest, unbuttoning his waistcoat as she went. "That's it. Just relax, now, luv."

The burden in question began to swell insistently against his falls, much to the doxy's approval. Her eyes widened with appreciation. "Coo. Yer a duke right e'nuf, eh, guv? Naught but a duchess will do fer that bit—but wot's this, now?" She dove for his waistcoat pocket, her fingers as deft as any thief's, and held up a round, flat object.

Julian grabbed her wrist, hard—much harder than he'd intended to—and held on until her hand fell open. "Don't touch that." He snatched it away from her.

She gave him an indignant look. "I wasna going ter take it, guv."

He stared down at her thin fingers, dumbfounded, a wave of confused shame washing over him. *Jesus.* He hadn't meant to grab her like that. She'd only reached into his pocket, but he'd reacted as if she'd put a blade to his throat.

"Well, what it is, then?" the whore demanded. "The crown jewels? Must be, fer you to take on so."

He opened his palm to reveal a pocket watch in a plain, gilded case. He hesitated for a moment, then flicked it open and turned the watch in her direction. "It belonged to a friend of mine, and it's . . . well, I don't like anyone to touch it."

Her nose wrinkled with disdain. "Wot, that's all? Wrong time too, innit?"

Julian snapped the case closed. "Yes. It doesn't tell time anymore. The winding key is gone. Lost for good." The watch was useless now, but he didn't have it to keep the time. Ridiculous, to believe time *could* be kept. A man couldn't keep it any more than he could catch the sun and balance it on the horizon. He might keep a coach and four, hounds, a mistress—but he didn't keep time.

It kept him.

The whore made a disgusted noise, released her grip on his waistcoat and turned away from him to screech into the parlor. "Mrs. Lacey! I got's a jumpy one here fer ye." She gave Julian one last offended look, stuck her nose in the air, and flounced away.

Well. Maybe she was a duchess, after all.

A female shape detached itself from a knot of people in the parlor and materialized out of the gloom. A woman, tall, with generous white breasts spilling from the top of a tight bodice sank into a low curtsey in front of him. It was the kind of curtsey that invited a gentleman to ogle her bosom, and Julian obliged.

"Good evening, sir. I'm Mrs. Lacey."

Red. Her hair, her lips, her scarlet-colored gown—everything about her was red except her eyes, which were a watery green. She was attractive in that hard, painted way the better-looking prostitutes were attractive.

She assessed him with a practiced eye, and then held out her hand, a small smile on her full lips. "You're a pretty one, aren't you? What's your name, luv?"

"Does it matter?" She might recognize his name. He'd been mentioned in the papers more than once since his regiment returned to England.

She chuckled. "Not in the least. You may call me Evie. What shall I call you?"

He shrugged. "Call me whatever you want."

She gave him a curious look. "I don't want anything, luv. Gentlemen come to me to get what they want. So. What do you want?"

One marchioness. Was it possible she'd already come and gone, and he'd missed her? "I'm looking for a woman."

The red lips curled upwards. "Are you now? Imagine that."

"No, that is, not a woman, but—"

"Sorry, luv." Mrs. Lacey shook her head. "This isn't that kind of house. Try Fleet Street."

For God's sake. He was going to strangle Cam. "A lady, Mrs. Lacey. I'm looking for a lady."

"A lady?" Her brow furrowed as if she couldn't imagine why he'd want such a troublesome thing. "This isn't Almack's, luv. The gentlemen here don't have much use for ladies. They come for a tumble, not a quadrille. So, do you want a tumble, or not?"

The knot in Julian's lower belly tightened, and hope creaked to life inside him. Mrs. Lacey looked as if she knew a great deal about fleshly desires. He'd promised Cam, but there was no sign of Lady Hadley yet, and well, this was a brothel.

"Such a fine, strapping young buck you are." Mrs. Lacey's green gaze lingered for a moment on his shoulders and chest, then moved lower, and lower still. "It's not healthy, luv, for such a vigorous gentleman to deny his urges."

Urges. Yes. He did have those. "No, not at all healthy."

Mrs. Lacey's eyes gleamed in the muted light. "That's right. Now come with me, luv, and we'll find you just the right lady to satisfy those urges. What do you fancy?"

Anything in skirts. "Blonde, with blue eyes." It was as good a choice as any.

"Ah. That's easily done." Mrs. Lacey glanced around the room, then crooked a finger at a young woman who stood by the fireplace, chatting up a scrawny lad with a lopsided cravat. "Mary. Come here, my dear girl."

Mary abandoned her young man without a backward glance, and hurried across the room to Mrs. Lacey's side. "Yes, mum?"

Mrs. Lacey urged the girl forward into better light so Julian could get a look at her. "This gentleman would like a companion for the evening. Do you suppose you could entertain him?"

Mary's eyes went wide when she got a close look at Julian. "Oh yes, indeed, mum." She gave Mrs. Lacey a sidelong glance that made the older woman chuckle, and added, "Thank you, mum."

Julian studied the girl. She was young, but not too young, with fair-skin, light yellow hair and dainty lips, faintly pink. Everything about her was pale and indistinct, like the sun hidden under layers of haze and London smog, pretty in its way, with a wan kind of beauty.

She wasn't perfect, but she was here, and that was good enough for him. He nodded once at Mrs. Lacey. "She'll do."

Mrs. Lacey smiled. "Then I wish you an enjoyable evening."

Julian watched her go, her lush, wide hips swaying, then turned back to Mary, his eyebrows raised expectantly.

"Fancy a drink before we go up?" Mary jerked her head toward a group of gentlemen who staggered about the center of the parlor, groping at females and guffawing loudly. Julian watched with distaste as one man stumbled to his knees and grasped at a whore's skirts to try and drag himself back up. "Sometimes the gentlemen likes a drink or two first. To relax, I s'pose."

Julian shook his head. There was only one thing that would relax him, and it wasn't drink. "No, I don't care for—"

His words were drowned out by a sudden explosion of catcalls and whistles behind him. Gentlemen who were still lucid enough to stand lurched to their feet and crowded into the front of the room, craning their necks to see what fresh new mayhem was on offer. Whatever they saw caused the low din of conversation to rise until it reached a fever pitch of male voices raised in shouts of approval.

Julian growled with frustration as sweaty bodies surged against him. He took Mary's arm and tried to disappear up the stairs, but men pressed against him from all sides and blocked his path to the second floor. *Jesus.* He'd anticipated sweaty body parts pressed together, but his fantasies hadn't included foul male odors and coarse body hair.

After a great deal of scuffling and good-natured shoving the crowd parted, and four ladies in masques emerged from the chaos of eager male bodies and swept into the room.

"Come here, love, I've got something special for you!" One of the gentlemen made a clumsy grab for the lady closest to him—a tall, slender blonde with a jeweled black masque obscuring the upper part of her face. She dodged him, stepping neatly out of the way of his groping hand.

The crowd roared with laughter. "Looks like she doesn't want what you've got, Dudley!" shouted one delighted onlooker.

"Can't say I blame her," yelled another. "All the doxies in London know what you've got, my lord, and there's nothing special about it!"

The crowd erupted with laughter again. The four ladies took no notice of the heaving herd of rogues on either side of them, but made their way down the center of the room as if they were on a promenade through Hyde Park with the pink of the *ton*, not in a west end whorehouse with shrieking men ogling them from all sides.

They were rather too much like the pink of the ton, in fact.

Julian watched with narrowed eyes as the ladies made their way through the crowd to a corner of the room and settled gracefully onto two divans near the fire. A footman leapt forward to attend them, and one of the ladies—another blonde, this one petite and curvy—spoke to him. He rushed off at once to do her bidding, leaving the four ladies alone.

There was a brief silence—a breathless pause, the room frozen in a ludicrous tableau as everyone waited to see what they'd do.

The petite blonde waved a casual hand at the lady across from her, this one a redhead, her fair skin an unearthly white in the dim light. The entire room seemed to hold its breath as the redhead reached into the reticule in her lap. She took out a lacquered case, slid it open and drew out—

"Cor," Mary breathed at his side.

Four cheroots.

She offered one to each of her three companions. The other ladies accepted and held the thin, brown cheroots between gloved fingers as they turned to their fourth companion.

And she . . . Julian went still, every muscle in his body drawing tight. Mary giggled nervously at his side, but he ignored her, his gaze fixed on the fourth lady.

She wore tight, elbow-length black gloves, and carried a tiny bag on a string around her wrist. She dipped her long, satin-covered fingers into the bag, took out a small bundle, smoothed the wrappings aside, and withdrew a bit of cloth. Every eye in the room was on her as she rose, crossed to the fireplace and knelt down to touch the cloth to the fire. It caught at once, and more than one man in the crowd drew in a quick, sharp breath, as if the sight of that tiny flame had snapped them from a collective trance.

The lady held the lit cloth to one end of her cheroot and sucked gently on the other end until the tip glowed red in the dim room, then she tossed the cloth into the fire, resumed her seat and handed her lit cheroot to the petite blonde next to her. One by one, each lady passed their cheroot to the next, until all four tips burned like identical red eyes.

"The way's clear now, guv."

Julian started, then turned to Mary in surprise. "What?"

She jerked her head in the direction of the stairs. "Don't ye want to go up?"

"Not yet." Julian let his gaze wander back to the fourth lady. "I think I'd like a drink, after all."

Mary shrugged. "All right, then."

He led her to a dark corner of the room, to another red velvet divan where they were cast in shadows, but which still afforded a clear view of the four ladies, who now sat, as prim as a quartet of governesses, sipping at the whiskey the footman had delivered and occasionally touching their cheroots to their lips. No one approached them despite the earlier burst of excitement at their arrival, for by this time it was obvious they weren't here for the gentlemen's amusement.

Why precisely they *were* here—well, that was anyone's guess. They weren't whores. They were ladies—*ton*, if one could judge by their fine gowns and jeweled masques.

Julian's lips stretched into a mocking smile. Four bored aristocratic ladies out on a whorehouse adventure. It wasn't unheard of—more than one titled lady had set out to test the *ton*'s limits for scandal—and yet a clandestine visit to a west end whorehouse was more than enough to leave a lady's reputation in tatters. Nothing but four silk masques stood between these four and social ruin.

Quite a risk for a bit of fun.

Julian leaned back against the divan, let a healthy swallow of whiskey burn a trail of fire down his throat, and studied the fourth lady. Her masque covered the entire upper part of her face, just as the other ladies' did, and yet . . .

A masque couldn't cover everything.

She had dark hair, coiled into a mass of heavy curls at the base of her long, slender neck, red lips, an elegant body, too slim, but still curved where a man wanted curves. No wan, indistinct beauty here, but a lush, glorious explosion of warmth and color, like a blazing sun in a pure blue sky.

The kind of sun it hurt to look at.

Masque or no masque, it made no difference. He'd have recognized her anywhere.

*Charlo*tte Sutherland.

No, not Sutherland. Not anymore. She was the Marchioness of Hadley now.

Now what would make a Marchioness abandon her grand country estate for a Covent Garden whorehouse? Wilted roses in the flower gardens, perhaps, or lazy servants? Whatever it might be, it hadn't anything to do with him. She looked perfectly content to stay where she was. Despite his promise to Cam, Julian decided he'd leave her here, teetering on the edge of scandal.

He tipped the rest of his whiskey into his mouth and turned to Mary. "I'm ready. Shall we go upstairs?"

She rose to her feet. "Whatever you say, guv."

He was halfway to the stairs when it happened.

Charlotte laughed. Soft, a titter more than a laugh. No one else in the noisy room noticed it. Well, no one would, would they? No one, that is, who hadn't heard that laugh before, low and suggestive, her red lips pressed to his ear. Her laugh pulled him back at once, back into the dimly lit room, away from Mary and the sweet release her body promised.

As little as a year ago he'd dreamed of that laugh, dreams of such exquisite yearning he couldn't tell whether they were dreams at all, or nightmares. Odd, how much could change in a year. Dreams faded. A man traded one nightmare for another. Brides became widows, and widows became whores.

What the devil was she doing here? She should be tucked away in Hampshire like a proper little widow, mourning her late husband, not in some whorehouse in the west end, drinking whiskey and blithely courting ruin with every draw on her cheroot. Courting ruin and laughing about it, as if her family's reputation were of no consequence. As if Cam and Ellie weren't at this very moment torturing themselves with visions of her disgrace.

Julian dropped his empty glass onto the table with a dull thud. Very well, he'd escort the marchioness out of here just as he'd promised he would, but he'd be damned if he'd be a gentleman about it. After all, a marchioness who entered a whorehouse shouldn't expect to be treated like a lady.

"Here. Take this." He took Mary's wrist, turned her hand up, then reached into his pocket, grabbed a fistful of coins, and dropped them into her open palm. "I won't need your company tonight, after all, but I do need a room. Which one is yours?"

Mary gaped at the pile of coins in her palm for a moment, then her hand snapped closed. "Top of the stairs, last room on the left."

"Stay out of it for a time, until you see me leave the house. Can you do that for me, Mary?"

She gave him a curious look, but she knew better than to ask questions. "Whatever you say, guv."

"Good girl."

Julian walked back across the parlor and resumed his seat on the divan. He signaled to the footman for another glass of whiskey, and settled in to watch, and wait.

Chapter Two

Red velvet divans, flocked silk paper on the walls, a fine Axminster carpet in shades of red, black and gold on the floor—if it weren't for the cheroot and the whiskey, she might have been in Lady Sutton's drawing-room.

The cheroot, the whiskey, and the half-naked whores, that is.

Charlotte blew a thin stream of smoke through her lips and tried to imagine the expression on Lady Sutton's face if she found out her drawing-room resembled the inside of a whorehouse. A laugh bubbled up in her throat, trapped the smoke in her lungs, and sent her into a coughing fit that had her gasping and wiping her eyes.

Wretched things, cheroots.

"My goodness, Charlotte." Lady Annabel gave her a disapproving look and drew expertly on her own cheroot. "Do be quiet. You'll attract attention."

Lady Elizabeth snickered. "It's a bit late for that, Annabel. We gave up being inconspicuous when we strolled into a whorehouse."

"Don't inhale the smoke, Charlotte. Like this." Aurelie Leblanc, the Comtesse de Lisle, touched the thin cheroot to her lips for a moment, then lowered it again without drawing on it. "See? No coughing."

Lady Annabel frowned. "That's cheating, Aurelie. The wager is—"

"Cheating?" Lady Elizabeth snorted. "What nonsense. The wager is we light the cheroots and stay in the brothel long enough for them to burn to the end. We never said we'd smoke the awful things."

"That's splitting hairs, Lissie." Lady Annabel took another draw on her cheroot to emphasize her point. "It's the spirit of the thing that matters, and I never cheat on a wager."

Lady Elizabeth gave her an arch look. "Honor among thieves, Annabel?"

"No. Honor among wicked widows." Lady Annabel adopted a virtuous tone. "After all, my dears, if we don't have our reputations, we don't have anything at all."

A moment of stunned silence greeted this statement, then all four ladies laughed appreciatively.

"A bit late for that as well, I'm afraid." Lady Elizabeth downed the rest of her whiskey in one swallow, then indicated their surroundings with a wave of her empty glass. "Have you forgotten where we are?"

Lady Annabel shrugged. "We're wearing masques. If no one recognizes us, it's just as if we weren't here at all."

Aurelie giggled. "A convenient sort of morality, is it not?"

"My dear." Lady Annabel smiled through a thin curl of smoke. "Is there any other kind?"

Charlotte studied her cheroot. It looked as long as it had when she'd first lit it, the blasted thing. "As far as the spirit of the wager is concerned, Annabel, I think our honor is safe, regardless of whether or not we smoke the cheroots. Lord Devon wagered we wouldn't enter the whorehouse. The cheroots and whiskey are incidental."

Aurelie downed her whiskey, and stubbed out her cheroot in the empty glass. "*Certainment.* We've won the wager already, and here's the proof." She held up the cheroot for their inspection, then threw the remains of it into her reticule. "Just as well, too, because that dreadful cheroot is staining my glove."

Lady Annabel continued to smoke her cheroot with every appearance of enjoyment. "Lord Devon is terribly wicked, is he not? Imagine his challenging us to enter a whorehouse! We should cut his acquaintance, my dears."

"He's no wickeder than we are." Charlotte had no intention of cutting Lord Devon. Wicked or not, he'd proved most diverting at a time when she badly needed the distraction. "In any case, I confess I've always wanted to see the inside of a brothel."

Lady Elizabeth nodded. "Oh, I have, as well. I thought it would be different, though—more exciting, somehow."

Charlotte glanced around the room. "More exciting than bare-bosomed ladies being pawed at by sotted gentlemen? Yes, there's nothing so unusual in that, I'm afraid." One could see the same thing in many aristocratic ballrooms in London, though the *ton* did their best to hide their sins under a thin veneer of respectability. Failing that, they hid in secluded alcoves and behind the shrubbery in dimly lit gardens.

"No. It looks rather like Lord Harrow's ball last week." Lady Elizabeth sounded disappointed. "Even the same people are here. Look, there's Lord Dudley. Oh dear. I'm sorry for that poor woman he's groping, for I suppose she has to have him, doesn't she?"

Aurelie observed the couple for a moment. "Not to worry, *ma petite*. He doesn't look as if he's in any condition to, ah . . . perform."

Lady Annabel snorted. "No, he doesn't. With any luck he'll lose consciousness. I hope she fleeces his pockets if he does."

Charlotte said nothing, but reached up to make sure her masque was securely tied. She hadn't noticed Lord Dudley before. She scanned the room again to see who else she'd overlooked. For pity's sake, half the *ton* was here. The male half. She knew, of course, that aristocratic gentlemen spent more time with whores and their mistresses than they did their own wives, but good heavens—weren't there other bordellos in London?

If any of these gentlemen were sober enough to focus, they'd recognize her easily, even with her masque on. Charlotte chewed on her lower lip. No, it wouldn't do at all for Ellie and Cam to discover this latest escapade. She never should have promised her sister she'd give up her mad frolics, for she'd known even as the words left her mouth it was a promise she couldn't keep.

Wretched things, promises.

She'd take care to avoid them in future. It was one thing to be a scandal, but quite another to be a scandal *and* a liar. She rose to her feet. "This was amusing enough for a time, but it grows dull. Shall we go find Devon?"

Annabel took a final draw on her cheroot. "Dear me, Charlotte. Bored in a bordello? How jaded you are."

Charlotte shrugged. "Perhaps it's more amusing for the prostitutes."

"Perhaps," said Lady Elizabeth. "But I draw the line at finding out. Besides, I believe the cheroot has made Aurelie ill." She held out a hand to help the Comtesse rise from the divan.

Lady Annabel jumped to her feet. "Oh, dear. She looks quite green. We'd better hurry."

Every eye in the room turned in their direction as they made their way to the door, but this time the men's scrutiny felt more ominous. No one said a word to her, and no one approached, but Charlotte's flesh prickled in warning. The sooner they rejoined Devon, the better—

Oh, hell and damnation. She still had the blasted cheroot clutched between her fingers. It had burned to the end at last, and now it threatened to singe her glove. She hurried back to the fireplace and tossed it into the flames. If some leering scoundrel got a peek under her masque because of that dratted cheroot, she was going to have Annabel's head—

"Leaving so soon, sweet?" A strong, muscular arm snaked around the middle of her body and jerked her to an abrupt halt. "But we haven't yet been introduced."

For a moment Charlotte froze with shock—only a moment, but that was all it took for her friends to vanish into the crowd. "Unhand me, sir," she ordered in the haughtiest, most marchioness-like tone she could muster.

"Unhand you? Oh, no. I don't think so." The voice was low, and so close she felt his breath tickle her ear. "What fun would that be?"

He spoke pleasantly enough, but underneath the amusement was a thread of ice that made Charlotte squirm in his grasp. "Release me this instant. How dare you?"

He jerked her back against a chest as hard and unyielding as a stone wall. "How dare I claim a whore in a whorehouse? I assure you, sweetheart, it takes no daring at all."

Charlotte could tell by the width of his chest and the hard muscles bulging in his forearm it would do no good to struggle, so she went still and tried to collect her wits. No doubt her friends thought she was right behind them. They'd return for her when they realized she wasn't, and—

"Not much of a challenge, I admit, to bed a whore," he went on, "but sometimes a man wants his pleasures to come easy." He ran a caressing hand over her hip and around the curve of her bottom, then pulled her tighter against him. "And you, sweetheart, are easy."

Charlotte's eyes widened. *Oh, no.* His chest wasn't the only hard thing pressed against her back. He was becoming . . . engorged. He'd soon lose all use of his mental faculties, and she'd never be able to reason him out of this madness. She took a deep breath and forced herself to speak calmly. "Sir, you can't possibly think to—"

"Take you right here in the parlor, with every drunken scoundrel in London gaping at us? Tempting thought, but I'm a gentleman, sweetheart. I have a room upstairs."

Upstairs? Oh, for pity's sake. Where were her friends? Why hadn't they come back for her yet? If they returned and couldn't find her . . .

Charlotte gave an experimental kick and managed to land a blow to his shin. She heard a pained grunt behind her, but instead of loosening his grip he hitched her higher against his chest, so only the tips of her slippers touched the floor.

"Come now, sweet," he crooned into her ear. "I promise I'll take good care of you."

Charlotte was rather alarmed by this point, but somehow his low rasp penetrated the fog of panic in her brain. *His voice.* For one wild moment she thought she recognized it, had heard it before, whispering in her ear, promising . . . *something.* She stilled, trying to place it, but the memory danced just outside her grasp.

"That's better," he murmured. "You don't really want to give all these fine gentlemen a show, do you?"

Fine gentlemen. Of course. She was in a whorehouse, wasn't she?

She was in a whorehouse, her friends had abandoned her, and this large, amorous gentleman—who thought, quite reasonably, that she was a whore—was about to drag her upstairs. The other fine gentlemen in question—all of whom also believed her to be a whore—ogled her with ill-concealed excitement. A number of them had staggered to their feet and edged closer to get a better look at the struggle, so she and her tormentor were now surrounded by a circle of drooling scoundrels.

Any of whom could decide at any moment to tear off her masque.

She let her body go limp against her captor's hard chest. Her best alternative by far was to let him take her upstairs, and then try to reason with him in private. If that didn't work, she could always bash him over the head with the washbasin. Whorehouses did have washbasins, didn't they? One would think they'd need them—

"Wise choice, love." The arm wrapped around the middle of her body eased a fraction when she made no move to flee. "You won't regret it."

You will. Best not to say so aloud, though. She'd need the element of surprise to escape unscathed this time. She permitted him to maneuver her across the room toward the stairwell, and up the stairs in front of him, his hand heavy against her lower back. Once they reached the second floor he hurried her down the hallway to the last door on the left, and thrust her through it.

The door thudded closed behind him, and she heard the unmistakable scrape of the key as it turned in the lock.

Charlotte scurried away from him before he could grab her, toss her onto the bed and . . . well, do whatever gentlemen did with whores, which was, she guessed, not the same thing they did with their wives. She wasn't certain, having never been mistaken for a whore before, but she had a vague notion gentlemen tended to skip the preliminaries where prostitutes were concerned, and she'd rather not reason with him while flat on her back.

"I haven't got all night, love." His boots rang on the wooden floor, and she felt the heat of his body close behind her, though he didn't touch her. "Take off your clothing and lay down on the bed."

Charlotte took a quick survey of the room. *Ah.* There, on a table by the far side of the bed—a washbasin, old and chipped, to be sure, but if she couldn't make him see reason, it would do the job. She took a stealthy step toward it, drew a steadying breath into her lungs and turned to face him. "I'm afraid, sir, you've made a rather unfortunate mistake—"

She got no further. The words lodged in her throat, and her sentence ended on a choked gasp. Every limb in her body went numb with shock, and for one horrible moment she was paralyzed, unable to think or do anything other than stare up at him.

Oh God, she'd dreaded this moment—dreaded it and longed for it since his regiment returned to England. Now the moment was here. He was here. *Julian.*

"It's you who's made the mistake, sweetheart, not me."

His voice. She *had* heard it before, soft in her ear, his whispered promises—*he loved her, his heart was hers, always*—and, oh, she'd believed him, she'd treasured his every word, and trusted him with the absolute trust of first love. It made her chest ache even now, more than a year later, to think of such a love.

Maybe he had loved her. Maybe he'd meant to keep his promises, but it hadn't made any difference then, and it made even less difference now.

"Do you like what you see?"

She jerked her gaze from his face and shoved the memories back into their secret places in the darkest corners of her mind. Such a question needed no answer. It was like asking if she preferred a sky obscured by thick, black clouds where once there'd been nothing but stars.

His face, that handsome face, once so dear to her. He was handsome still—more so, even, now that life had filled in the hollows of youth and etched faint lines of experience into the corners of his eyes. He had the same dark waves falling in a silky drift across his forehead, and the same wide mouth with the full, sensuous bottom lip. She'd spent hours tracing his lips with the tips of her fingers.

But his eyes . . . they were wrong. They were still dark and liquid with a slight upward tilt at the corners, and a long, thick fringe of sooty lashes, but there was no joy in them. No kindness. They were suspicious. Watchful.

At one time she'd thought his eyes the very essence of him. Perhaps they still were.

Her silence didn't seem to matter to him.

"I'm afraid it makes no difference whether you like it or not." He eased his coat over his shoulders and tossed it onto a bench at the end of the bed.

"It matters only that I like what I see, and I do, sweet. I like it very much, and I've paid to see all of it, so remove your clothing."

His tone was bland now, nearly inflectionless. If she hadn't known every nuance of his voice, hadn't heard it echo in her dreams, she might have missed the subtle note of challenge. But she heard it, and as soon as she did, she knew.

Her masque hadn't fooled him. He knew who she was. He'd known from the first moment he saw her. She was sure of it. How could he not? He'd brought her up here on purpose then, so he could . . .

What? Teach her a lesson. Put her in her place.

Her breath caught on a strange, grim little laugh. Did he really believe there was a lesson she hadn't yet learned? Did he truly think she hadn't been shoved into her place, again and again and with such brutal force it had taken every shred of strength she could muster to crawl out of it?

"Remove your clothing."

Charlotte crossed her arms over her chest. "Why are you doing this?"

"Doing what, sweet? Getting what I paid for?"

If he felt any remorse—or any emotion at all—it didn't show in his face. He was utterly composed, in perfect control of himself. Bored, even, like a lazy cat who held a mouse's tail under his paw, and was biding his time until he slashed a claw through its belly.

Bored, yes, but not so bored he was ready to end his game. Very well. She'd end it for him.

Charlotte reached behind her head to untie the silken cords of her masque, but Julian grabbed her wrists to stop her. "*No.* I said remove your clothing, not your masque. I'm not interested in your face. Leave the masque on."

*Oh, yes. He kn*ew who she was.

Charlotte stared up into his hard, dark eyes. He thought she wouldn't do it—he didn't even *want* her to do it. He wanted her to admit she'd been a fool to risk her reputation by entering a whorehouse, to crumple at his feet and beg his forgiveness so he could refuse to give it to her.

But she was done begging for forgiveness. His, or anyone else's.

So instead she did the one thing she could think to do under the circumstances. She curled her lips in a slow, seductive smile, and turned around to present him with her back. "Aw right guv, if ye say so. It's yer coin, right enough. Help wif my buttons, won't ye, luv?"

Oh, how she wanted to see his face then, to read his expression as she gave him just what he asked for.

But not what he wanted.

He made a faint sound, an angry, strangled word, or a harshly exhaled breath. "Do you think I won't?"

He would, or he wouldn't. It didn't matter which. Either way he'd lose, because this wasn't what he wanted. "Aw, come on, luv. Why should I think that? Ye've got a right lusty look about ye, ye do, and ye did say you liked what ye seen. Or mayhap," she added, her voice as smooth as silk, "Ye don't like it as well as ye thought ye did, eh?"

She felt his hands against the back of her neck, his fingers twisting the top button of her gown. "Or maybe I like it even better."

Cool air touched her skin through the flimsy material of her shift as he worked her buttons one by one until her gown was open all the way down to the small of her back. He settled his hands against her waist, his fingers stroking over the soft flesh there before he eased her hips back against the front of his falls.

A tremor passed through her, but otherwise she didn't move. He was calling her bluff? Surely he wouldn't—

"What's the matter, *luv?*" He grazed his teeth over the sensitive skin under her ear. "You haven't changed your mind, I hope? It's a bit late for that. Once a man's desires are roused, there's only one way to satisfy him. I would think you'd know that, being a prostitute."

Anger stiffened her spine, and her resolve. "A woman don't get ter change 'er mind no matter what, prostitute or not. I'd a thought ye'd know *that*, being a man."

A low chuckle was his only answer, but he gripped her shoulders, his palms hot, heavy. She braced herself to resist him, to dive across the room for the washbasin, but his touch turned gentle as he slipped his fingers under the edge of her shift to stroke her bare shoulders. She sucked back a gasp as he moved closer, so close his warm breath drifted over her skin. Her eyes fell closed, but just when she thought he'd put his mouth on her, he grasped her shoulders and spun her around to face him.

Charlotte caught her breath.

His perfect impassivity was gone. His eyes were no longer cold, his face no longer composed. His cheekbones were flushed with color, and his breath came fast and hard. "Unbutton my waistcoat."

"No need fer that, luv." Her voice wasn't quite steady. "If ye'll just strip off yer breeches—"

He made a harsh sound in his throat, and caught her wrists to press her hands against his chest. She could feel the thud of his heart through the silk of his waistcoat. "Do it. Unbutton my waistcoat."

He held her wrists until she worked the buttons loose, then he dragged her hands up his chest and pressed them tight against his neck. He stared down at her, his dark eyes burning. "Take off my cravat."

The command was low and hoarse, almost inaudible, but his voice throbbed with an intensity that brooked no argument. His words echoed inside her, and this time Charlotte didn't think to resist him, but untied the knot, unwound the long piece of linen and drew it away from his neck.

He took the cravat in shaking hands, and let it slip through his fingers and flutter to the floor. "Put your arms around my neck."

She stared at the smooth olive-tinted skin left bare by the loose neck of his shirt, and a sense of unreality swept over her, as if time had somehow shifted, reversed, and they weren't here at all, in a whorehouse, with long months of bitterness and unanswered questions between them, and suddenly she wished it were so, longed for it with an ache so deep she staggered under it.

She closed her eyes and slid her arms around his neck, but even as she sifted the soft waves of his hair through her fingers, she knew it was hopeless. No matter how brief, how fleeting that sweet, perfect first love might be, one only ever got a single chance at it.

She'd had her chance, and she'd lost it. She'd never get another.

ABOUT THE AUTHOR

Once upon a time, on a dark and stormy night, **Anna Bradley** sat with quill in hand to write a book about two people who meet, fall in love and live happily ever after.

OK, so that's not quite true. It wasn't a dark and stormy night, and there was no quill; only a computer. But Anna did sit down, her fingers at the keys, her head full of stories about love and happily-ever-afters.

And so a writer was born.

Anna is from Maine, and attended college on the east coast. Being a practical girl, Anna chose to major in English literature at Wheaton College, then went on to get a Master's degree at the University of Maine in, yes, you guessed it—English literature.

Anna's wily, career-savvy choice of major paid off. She landed a job with Chawton House Library, a rare books library featuring works by British women writers from the 1600s through the Regency period. This job required that she read books, and write about books, and buy rare books from cool places like Sotheby's. At night, after the library closed, Anna sometimes fondled the smooth leather covers of these books and dreamed of becoming a writer.

Anna's reading, writing and fondling led to an enduring passion for stories about love, life, and romance. Anna writes sassy, steamy Regency historical romance, often with garters, cleavage-baring gowns and riding crops. History is sexier than you think, Gentle Reader.

Anna lives near Portland, OR, where people are delightful and weird and love to read. She teaches writing and lives with her husband, two children, a variety of spoiled pets, and shelves full of books. Readers can visit her website at www.annabradley.net

CPSIA information can be obtained
at www.ICGtesting.com
Printed in the USA
LVOW10s0846240917
549870LV00001B/158/P